Debbie Macomber

Christmas in Seattle

featuring
Christmas Letters and *The Perfect Christmas*

MIRA

All the characters in this book have no existence outside the imagination of the author, and have no relation whatsoever to anyone bearing the same name or names. They are not even distantly inspired by any individual known or unknown to the author, and all the incidents are pure invention.

Published in Great Britain 2009
MIRA Books, Eton House, 18-24 Paradise Road,
Richmond, Surrey, TW9 1SR

CHRISTMAS IN SEATTLE © Harlequin Books S.A. 2009

The publisher acknowledges the copyright holder of the individual works as follows:

Christmas Letters © Debbie Macomber 2006
The Perfect Christmas © Debbie Macomber 2009

ISBN 978 0 7783 0395 4

60-1109

Printed in Great Britain
by Clays Ltd, St Ives plc

Dear Friends,

From the very first year Wayne and I were married, I've written a Christmas letter. The response to those early family letters encouraged me to try my hand at writing, so in some ways my Christmas letters are responsible for one of the stories you're holding now. My heroine in *Christmas Letters,* Katherine O'Connor, known to all as K.O., experiences a revelation of her own. It's because of a Christmas letter she's writing that she first meets our hero, Wynn Jeffries. Is it coincidence or is it…fate?

I've always enjoyed writing romantic comedies, especially those with a Christmas theme. And what could be funnier than a "perfect" Christmas? I'm sure you know why I smile every time I think about it. Because a perfect Christmas (at least in my experience) simply doesn't exist. My heroine Cassie in *The Perfect Christmas*, like me, gazes at those lovely family-photo Christmas cards with a sense of awe – everything l ooks so…well, perfect. This is what Cassie wants, and she's determined to make it happen. And so the fun begins…

I've always believed there's a special connection be-tween the writer and the reader, a connection revealed through the characters and the story. If I cry, I know you will, too. If I laugh, so will you. Well, I want to tell you that I laughed my way through this book. Every story should be this much fun to write!

In case you're interested in what Christmas in the Macomber household is like, let me give you an idea. I put up a Christmas tree for every family – five in total – so the grandkids know which tree belongs to them. I've lost count of the number of Nativity sets I have all over the house. Some are large and ornate, others small and fragile. A few have missing pieces, but we've always managed to find the baby Jesus. Then there's the entertaining. I host several Christmas teas, pot-lucks and a progressive dinner, plus I arrange cooking-with-Grandma sessions for the grandkids. In other words, it's pretty chaotic around our house in December. Wayne and the dog have been known to hide in the basement for a good part of the month.

Yet, despite the chaos (and having to haul husband and dog back upstairs), that's about as perfect as Christmas gets for me. I surround myself with family and friends. You can be sure there'll be plenty of home-baked goodies and a glass of egg-nog for all.

If you're looking for a few hours of escape from the Christmas craziness this year, then sit down by the tree or the fireplace and lose yourself in *Christmas in Seattle*. (Let me know if K.O.'s or Cassie's Christmas – or mine – is anything like yours. You can reach me at www.debbiemacomber.com or PO Box 1458, Port Orchard, WA 98366, USA.)

Merry Christmas!

Debbie Macomber

Christmas Letters

To Katherine Orr
Better known as
K.O.
for her encouragement and support
through the years

Prologue

Zelda O'Connor Davidson
76 Orchard Avenue
Seattle, Washington
Christmas, 2006

Dear Family and Friends:

Merry Christmas, everyone!

Let me warn you—this Christmas letter won't be as clever as last year's. My sister, Katherine (whom you may know better as K.O.), wrote that one for me but, ironically, she hasn't got time to do this year's. Ironic because it's due to the popularity of that particular letter that she's managed to start a little business on the side—writing Christmas letters for other people!

(She offered to write mine, of course, but I know that between her work doing medical transcriptions, her job search and her Christmas letters, it would be a real stretch to find the time.)

So, here goes. The twins, Zoe and Zara, have recently turned five. They're looking forward to starting kindergarten next September. It's hard to believe our little girls are almost old enough for school! Still, they keep themselves (and us!) busy. So do our assorted pets—especially the dogs, two Yorkies named Zero and Zorro.

I'm still a stay-at-home mom and Zach's still working as a software programmer. This year's big news, which I want to share with all of you, has to do with a wonderful book I read. It changed my family's life. It's called *The Free Child* and it's by Dr. Wynn Jeffries. My sister scoffs at this, but Dr. Jeffries believes that children can be trusted to set their own boundaries. He also believes that, as parents, we shouldn't impose fantasies on them—fantasies like Santa Claus. Kids are capable of accepting reality, he says, and I agree! (See page 146 of *The Free Child*.)

So, this Christmas will be a different kind of experience for us, one that focuses on family, not fantasy.

Zach and the girls join me in wishing all of you a wonderful Christmas. And remember, a free child is a happy child (see page 16).

Love and kisses,
Zelda, Zach, Zoe and Zara
(and a wag of the tail from Zero & Zorro)

Chapter 1

It *was* him. Katherine O'Connor, better known as K.O., was almost positive. She squinted just to be sure. He looked identical to the man on the dust jacket of that ridiculous book, the one her sister treated like a child-rearing bible. Of course, people didn't really look like their publicity photos. And she hadn't realized the high and mighty Dr. Wynn Jeffries was from the Seattle area. Furthermore, she couldn't imagine what he was doing on Blossom Street.

She'd never even met him, but she distrusted him profoundly and disliked him just as much. It was because of Dr. Jeffries that she'd been banned from a local bookstore. She'd had a small difference of opinion with the manager on the subject of Wynn's book. Apparently the bookseller was a personal friend of his, because she'd leaped to Dr. Jeffries's defense and had ordered K.O. out of the store. She'd even suggested K.O. take her future book-purchasing business elsewhere, which seemed unnecessarily extreme.

"K.O.," Bill Mulcahy muttered, distracting her. They sat across from each other at the French Café, filled to capacity during the midmorning rush. People lined up for coffee, and another line formed at the bakery counter. "Did you get all that?" he asked.

"Sure," K.O. said, returning her attention to him. "Sorry—I thought I saw someone I knew." Oh, the things she was willing to do for some extra holiday cash. One witty Christmas letter written on her sister's behalf, and all of a sudden K.O. was the most sought-after woman at her brother-in-law's office. They all wanted her to write their Christmas letters. She'd been shocked to discover how much they'd willingly plunk down for it, too. Bill Mulcahy was the third person she'd met with this week, and his letter was the most difficult so far. Leno or Letterman would've had a hard time finding anything amusing about this man's life.

"I don't know what you're going to write," Bill continued. "It's been an exceptionally bad year. As I explained earlier, my son is in a detention home, my daughter's living with her no-good boyfriend and over

Thanksgiving she announced she's pregnant. Naturally, marriage is out of the question."

"That *is* a bit of a challenge," K.O. agreed. She widened her eyes and stared again at the man who waited in the long line at the cash register. It *was* him; she was convinced of it now. The not-so-good doctor was—to put it in appropriately seasonal terms—a fruitcake. He was a child psychologist who'd written a book called *The Free Child* that was the current child-rearing rage.

To be fair, K.O. was single and not a mother. The only child-rearing experience she'd had was with her identical twin nieces, Zoe and Zara, whom she adored. Until recently, anyway. Overnight the five-year-olds had become miniature monsters and all because her sister had followed the "Free Child" rules as set out by Dr. Jeffries.

"My wife," Bill said, "is on the verge of a breakdown."

K.O. pitied the poor woman—and her husband.

"We've written Christmas letters for years and while life wasn't always as perfect as we—well, as we implied…" He let the rest fade away.

"You painted the picture of a model family."

"Yes." Bill cleared his throat and offered her a weak smile. "Patti, that's my wife, chose to present a, shall we say, rosier depiction of reality." He exhaled in a rush. "We never included family pictures and if you met my son, you'd know why. Anyone looking at Mason would know in a minute that this kid isn't a member of the National

Honor Society." He released his breath again and shook his head sadly. "Mason's into body piercing," Bill added. "He pierced his eyebrows, his nose, his lips, his tongue, his nipples—"

K.O. stopped him before he went any lower. "I get it."

"You probably don't, but that's lucky for you. Oh, and he dyed his hair green."

"Green?"

"He wears it spiked, too, and he…he does this thing with paint." Bill dropped his voice.

K.O. was sure she'd misunderstood. "I beg your pardon?"

"Mason doesn't call it paint. It's some form of cosmetic he smears across his face. I never imagined that my son would be rummaging through his mother's makeup drawer one day."

"I suppose that is a bit disconcerting," K.O. murmured.

"I forget the actual significance of the black smudges under his eyes and across his cheeks," Bill said. "To me it looks like he's some teenage commando."

Yes, this letter would indeed be a challenge. "Have you thought about skipping your Christmas letter this year?" K.O. asked hopefully.

"Yeah, I'd like to, but as I said, Patti's emotional health is rather fragile. She claims people are already asking about our annual letter. She's afraid that if we don't send it the same as we do every year, everyone will figure out that we're pitiful parents." His shoulders drooped. "In other words, we've failed our children."

"I don't think you've necessarily *failed*," K.O. assured him. "Most teenagers go through a rebellious stage."

"Did you?"

"Oh, sure."

"Did you pierce anything?"

"Well, I had my ears pierced...."

"That's not the same thing." He peered at her earrings, visible through her straight blond hair, which she wore loosely tied back. "And you only have one in each ear—not eight or ten like my son." He seemed satisfied that he'd proved his point. "Then you'll write our Christmas letter and smooth over the rough edges of our year?"

K.O. was less and less confident that she could pull this off. "I don't know if I'm your person," she said hesitantly. How could she possibly come up with a positive version of such a disastrous year? Besides, this side job was supposed to be fun, not real work. It'd begun as a favor to her sister and all of a sudden she was launching a career. At some stage she'd need to call a halt—maybe sooner than she'd expected.

Her client shifted in his seat. "I'll pay you double what you normally charge."

K.O. sat up straight. Double. He said he'd pay double? "Would four days be enough time?" she asked. Okay, so she could be bought. She pulled out her Day-Timer, checked her schedule and they set a date for their next meeting.

"I'll give you half now and half when you're finished."

That seemed fair. Not one to be overly prideful, she held out her hand as he peeled off three fifty-dollar bills. Her fingers closed around the cash.

"I'll see you Friday then," Bill said, and reaching for his briefcase, he left the French Café carrying his latte in its takeout cup.

Looking out the windows with their Christmas garland, she saw that it had begun to snow again. This was the coldest December on record. Seattle's normally mild climate had dipped to below-freezing temperatures for ten days in a row. So much for global warming. There was precious little evidence of it in Seattle.

K.O. glanced at the coffee line. Wynn Jeffries had made his way to the front and picked up his hot drink. After adding cream and sugar—lots of both, she observed—he was getting ready to leave. K.O. didn't want to be obvious about watching him, so she took a couple of extra minutes to collect her things, then followed him out the door.

Even if she introduced herself, she had no idea what to say. Mostly she wanted to tell him his so-called Free Child movement—no boundaries for kids—was outright lunacy. How could he, in good conscience, mislead parents in this ridiculous fashion? Not that she had strong feelings on the subject or anything. Okay, so maybe she'd gone a little overboard at the bookstore that day, but she couldn't help it. The manager had been touting the benefits of Dr. Jeffries's book to yet another unsuspecting mom. K.O. felt it was her duty to let the poor woman know what might happen if she actually followed Dr. Jeffries's advice. The bookseller had strenuously disagreed and from then on, the situation had gotten out of hand.

Not wanting him to think she was stalking him, which she supposed she was, K.O. maintained a careful distance. If his office was in Seattle, it might even be in this neighborhood. After the renovations on Blossom Street a few years ago, a couple of buildings had been converted to office space. If she could discreetly discover where he practiced, she might go and talk to him sometime. She hadn't read his book but had leafed through it, and she knew he was a practicing child psychologist. She wanted to argue about his beliefs and his precepts, tell him about the appalling difference in her nieces' behavior since the day Zelda had adopted his advice.

She'd rather he didn't see her, so she dashed inconspicuously across the street to A Good Yarn, and darted into the doorway, where she pretended to be interested in a large Christmas stocking that hung in the display window. From the reflection in the window, she saw Dr. Jeffries walking briskly down the opposite sidewalk.

As soon as it was safe, she dashed from the yarn store

to Susannah's Garden, the flower shop next door, and nearly fell over a huge potted poinsettia, all the while keeping her eyes on Dr. Jeffries. He proved one thing, she mused. Appearances were deceiving. He looked so...so normal. Who would've guessed that beneath that distinguished, sophisticated and—yes—handsome exterior lay such a fiend? Perhaps *fiend* was too strong a word. Yet she considered Wynn Jeffries's thinking to be nothing short of diabolical, if Zoe and Zara were anything to judge by.

No way!

K.O. stopped dead in her tracks. She watched as Wynn Jeffries paused outside her condo building, her very own building, entered the code and strolled inside.

Without checking for traffic, K.O. crossed the street again. A horn honked and brakes squealed, but she barely noticed. She was dumbfounded.

Speechless.

There had to be some mistake. Perhaps he was making a house call. No, that wasn't right. What doctor made house calls in this day and age? What psychologist made house calls *ever*? Besides, he didn't exactly look like the compassionate type. K.O. bit her lip and wondered when she'd become so cynical. It'd happened around the same time her sister read Dr. Jeffries's book, she decided.

The door had already closed before she got there. She entered her code and stepped inside just in time to see the elevator glide shut. Standing back, she watched the floor numbers flicker one after another.

"Katherine?"

K.O. whirled around to discover LaVonne Young, her neighbor and friend. LaVonne was the only person who called her Katherine. "What are you doing, dear?"

K.O. pointed an accusing finger past the elegantly decorated lobby tree to the elevator.

LaVonne stood in her doorway with her huge tomcat, named predictably enough, Tom, tucked under her arm. She wore a long shapeless dress that was typical of her wardrobe, and her long graying hair was drawn back in a bun. When K.O. had first met her, LaVonne had reminded her of the character Auntie Mame. She still did. "Something wrong with the elevator?" LaVonne asked.

"No, I just saw a man…" K.O. glanced back and noticed that the elevator had gone all the way up to the penthouse suite. That shouldn't really come as a shock. His book sales being what they were, he could easily afford the penthouse.

LaVonne's gaze followed hers. "That must be Dr. Jeffries."

"You know him?" K.O. didn't bother to hide her interest. The more she learned, the better her chances of engaging him in conversation.

"Of course I know Dr. Jeffries," the retired accountant said. "I know everyone in the building."

"How long has he lived here?" K.O. demanded. She'd been in this building since the first week it was approved for occupation. So she should've run into him before now.

"I believe he moved in soon after the place was renovated. In fact, the two of you moved in practically on the same day."

That was interesting. Of course, there was a world of difference between a penthouse suite and the first-floor, one-bedroom unit she owned. Or rather, that the bank owned and she made payments on. With the inheritance she'd received from her maternal grandparents, K.O. had put a down payment on the smallest, cheapest unit available. It was all she could afford at the time—and all she could afford now. She considered herself lucky to get in when she did.

"His name is on the mailbox," LaVonne said, gesturing across the lobby floor to the mailboxes.

"As my sister would tell you, I'm a detail person." It was just the obvious she missed.

"He's a celebrity, you know," LaVonne whispered conspiratorially. "Especially since his book was published."

"Have you read it?" K.O. asked.

"Well, no, dear, I haven't, but then never having had children myself, I'm not too concerned with child-raising. However, I did hear Dr. Jeffries interviewed on the radio and he convinced me. His book is breaking all kinds of records. Apparently it's on all the bestseller lists. So there must be *something* to what he says. In fact, the man on the radio called Dr. Jeffries the new Dr. Spock."

"You've got to be kidding!" Jeffries's misguided gospel was spreading far and wide.

LaVonne stared at her. "In case you're interested, he's not married."

"That doesn't surprise me," K.O. muttered. Only a man without a wife and children could possibly come up with such ludicrous ideas. He didn't have a family of his own to test his theories on; instead he foisted them on unsuspecting parents like her sister, Zelda, and brother-in-law, Zach. The deterioration in the girls' behavior was dramatic, but Zelda insisted this was normal as they adjusted to a new regimen. They'd "find their equilibrium," she'd said, quoting the book. Zach, who worked long hours, didn't really seem to notice. The twins' misbehavior would have to be even more extreme to register on him.

"Would you like me to introduce you?" LaVonne asked.

"No," K.O. responded immediately. Absolutely not. Well, maybe, but not now. And not for the reasons LaVonne thought.

"Do you have time for tea?" LaVonne asked. "I wanted to tell you about the most recent class I attended. Fascinating stuff, just fascinating." Since her retirement, La-

Vonne had been at loose ends and signed up for a variety of workshops and evening classes.

"I learned how to unleash my psychic abilities."

"You're psychic?" K.O. asked.

"Yes, only I didn't know it until I took this class. I've learned so much," she said in wonder. "So much. All these years, my innate talent has lain there, unused and unfulfilled. It took this class to break it free and show me what I should've known all along. *I can see into the future.*" She spoke in a portentous whisper.

"You learned this after one class?"

"Madame Ozma claims I have been blessed with the sight. She warned me not to waste my talents any longer."

This *did* sound fascinating. Well…bizarre, anyway. K.O. would have loved to hear all about the class, but she really needed to start work. In addition to writing Christmas letters—which she did only in November and December—she was a medical transcriptionist by training. It paid the bills and had allowed her to put herself through college to obtain a public relations degree. Now she was searching for a job in PR, which wasn't all that easy to find, even with her degree. She was picky, too. She wanted a job with a salary that would actually meet her expenses. Over the years she'd grown accustomed to a few luxuries, like regular meals and flush toilets.

Currently her résumé was floating around town. Anytime now, she was bound to be offered the perfect job.

And in the meanwhile, these Christmas letters gave her some useful practice in creating a positive spin on some unpromising situations—like poor Bill Mulcahy's.

"I'd love a cup of tea, but unfortunately I've got to get to work."

"Perhaps tomorrow," LaVonne suggested.

"That would be great."

"I'll call upon my psychic powers and look into your future if you'd like." She sounded completely serious.

"Sure," K.O. returned casually. Perhaps LaVonne could let her know when she'd find a job.

LaVonne's eyes brightened. "I'll study my class notes and then I'll tell you what I *see* for you."

"Thanks." She reached over and scratched Tom's ears. The big cat purred with pleasure.

With a bounce in her step, LaVonne went into her condo, closing the door with a slam that shook her Christmas wreath, decorated with golden moons and silver stars. K.O. headed for her own undecorated door, which was across the hall. Much as she disapproved of her sister's hero, she could hardly wait to tell Zelda the news.

Chapter 2

K.O. waited until she'd worked two hours straight before she phoned her sister. Zelda was a stay-at-home mom with Zoe and Zara, who were identical twins. Earlier in the year Zelda and Zach had purchased the girls each a dog. Two Yorkshire terriers, which the two girls had promptly named Zero and Zorro. K.O. called her sister's home the Land of Z. Even now, she wasn't sure how Zelda kept the girls straight, let alone the dogs. Even their barks sounded identical. *Yap. Yap* and *yap* with an occasional *yip* thrown in for variety, as if they sometimes grew bored with the sound of their own yapping.

Zelda answered on the third ring, sounding frazzled and breathless. "Yes?" she snapped into the phone.

"Is this a bad time?" K.O. asked.

"Oh, hi." The lack of enthusiasm was apparent. In addition to everything else, Dr. Jeffries's theories had placed a strain on K.O.'s relations with her younger sister.

"Merry Christmas to you, too," K.O. said cheerfully. "Can you talk?"

"Sure."

"The girls are napping?"

"No," Zelda muttered. "They decided they no longer need naps. Dr. Jeffries says on page 125 of his book that children should be allowed to sleep when, and only when, they decide they're tired. Forcing them into regimented nap- and bedtimes, is in opposition to their biological natures."

"I see." K.O. restrained the urge to argue. "Speaking of Dr. Jeffries…"

"I know you don't agree with his philosophy, but this is the way Zach and I have chosen to raise our daughters. When you have a family of your own, you can choose how best to parent your children."

"True, but…"

"Sorry," Zelda cried. It sounded as if she'd dropped the phone.

In the background, K.O. could hear her sister shouting at the girls and the dogs. Her shouts were punctuated with the dogs' yapping. A good five minutes passed before Zelda was back.

"What happened?" K.O. asked, genuinely concerned.

"Oh, nothing."

"As I started to say, I saw Dr. Jeffries."

"On television?" Zelda asked, only half-interested.

"No, in person."

"Where?" All at once she had Zelda's attention.

"On Blossom Street. You aren't going to believe this, but he actually lives in my building."

"Dr. Jeffries? Get out of here!"

Zelda was definitely interested now. "Wait—I heard he moved to Seattle just before his book was published." She took a deep breath. "Wow! You really *saw* him?"

"Uh-huh."

"Oh, my goodness, did you talk to him? Is he as handsome in person as he is in his photo?"

Feeling about him the way she did, K.O. had to consider the question for a moment. "He's fairly easy on the eyes." That was an understatement but looks weren't everything. To her mind, he seemed stiff and unapproachable. Distant, even.

"Did you tell him that Zach and I both read his book and what a difference it's made in our lives?"

"No, but…"

"K.O., could you… Would it be too much to get his autograph? Could you bring it on the fifteenth?"

K.O. had agreed to spend the night with the twins while Zelda and Zach attended his company's Christmas party. Her sister and brother-in-law had made arrangements to stay at a hotel downtown, just the two of them.

"All the mothers at the preschool would *die* to have Dr. Jeffries's autograph."

"I haven't met him," K.O. protested. It wasn't like she had any desire to form a fan club for him, either.

"But you just said he lives in your building."

"Yes."

"Are you sure it's him?"

"It looks like him. Anyway, LaVonne said it was."

Zelda gave a small shout of excitement. "If LaVonne says it's him, then it must be. How could you live in the same building as Dr. Jeffries and not know it?" her sister cried as though K.O. had somehow avoided this critical knowledge on purpose. "This is truly amazing. I've *got* to have his autograph."

"I'll…see what I can do," K.O. promised. This was not good. She'd hoped to find common ground with her sister, not become a…a go-between so Zelda could get her hero's autograph. Some hero! K.O.'s views on just about everything having to do with parenting were diametrically opposed to those purveyed by Dr. Wynn Jeffries. She'd feel like a fraud if she asked for his autograph.

"One more thing," Zelda said when her excitement had died down. "I know we don't agree on child-rearing techniques."

"That's true, but I understand these are your daughters."

She took a deep breath. "How you raise them isn't really any of my business."

"Exactly," Zelda said emphatically. "Therefore, Zach and I want you to know we've decided to downplay Christmas this year."

"Downplay Christmas," K.O. repeated, not sure what that meant.

"We aren't putting up a tree."

"No Christmas tree!" K.O. sputtered, doing a poor job of hiding her disapproval. She couldn't imagine celebrating the holiday without decorating a tree. Her poor nieces would be deprived of a very important tradition.

"I might allow a small potted one for the kitchen table." Zelda seemed a bit doubtful herself. She *should* be doubtful, since a Christmas tree had always been part of their own family celebration. The fact that their parents had moved to Arizona was difficult enough. This year they'd decided to take a cruise in the South Pacific over Christmas and New Year's. While K.O. was happy to see her mother and father enjoying their retirement, she missed them enormously.

"Is this another of Dr. Jeffries's ideas?" K.O. had read enough of his book—and heard *more* than enough about his theories—to suspect it was. Still, she could hardly fathom that even Wynn Jeffries would go this far. Outlaw Christmas? The man was a menace!

"Dr. Jeffries believes that misleading children about Santa does them lasting psychological damage."

"The girls can't have Santa, either?" This was cruel and unusual punishment. "Next you'll be telling me that you're doing away with the tooth fairy, too."

"Why, yes, of course. It's the same principle."

K.O. knew better than to argue with her sister. "Getting back to Christmas..." she began.

"Yes, Christmas. Like I said, Zach and I are planning to make it a low-key affair this year. Anything that involves Santa is out of the question."

Thankfully her sister was unable to see K.O. roll her eyes.

"In fact, Dr. Jeffries has a chapter on the subject. It's called 'Bury Santa Under the Sleigh.' Chapter eight."

"He wants to bury Santa Claus?" K.O. had heard enough. She'd personally bury Dr. Jeffries under a pile of plowed snow before she'd let him take Christmas away from Zoe and Zara. As far as she was concerned, his entire philosophy was unacceptable, but this no-Santa nonsense was too much. Here was where she drew her line in the snow—a line Wynn Jeffries had overstepped.

"Haven't you been listening to *anything* I've said?" Zelda asked.

"Unfortunately, I have."

Her doorbell chimed. "I need to go," K.O. told her sister. She sighed. "I'll see what I can do about that autograph."

"Yes, please," Zelda said with unmistakable gratitude.

"It would mean the world to me if you could get Dr. Jeffries's autograph."

Sighing again, K.O. replaced the receiver and opened the door to find her neighbor LaVonne standing there. Although *standing* wasn't exactly the right word. LaVonne was practically leaping up and down. "I'm sorry to bother you but I just couldn't wait."

"Come in," K.O. said.

"I can't stay but a minute," the retired CPA insisted as she stepped over the threshold, clutching Tom. "I did it!" she exclaimed. "I saw the future." She squealed with delight and did a small jig. "I saw the future of your love life, K.O. It happened when I went to change the kitty litter."

"The…kitty litter." That was fitting, since it was where her love life happened to be at the moment. In some kind of toilet, anyway.

"Tom had just finished his business," LaVonne continued, gazing lovingly at her cat, "and there it was, plain as day."

"His business?" K.O. asked.

"No, no, the future. You know how some people with the *gift* can read tea leaves? Well, it came to me in the kitty-litter box. I know it sounds crazy but it's true. It was right there in front of me," she said. "You're going to meet the man of your dreams."

"Really?" K.O. hated to sound so disappointed. "I

don't suppose you happened to see anything in the kitty litter about me finding a job?"

LaVonne shook her head. "Sorry, no. Do you think I should go back and look again? It's all in the way it's arranged in the kitty litter," she confided. "Just like tea leaves."

"Probably not." K.O. didn't want to be responsible for her neighbor sifting through Tom's "business" any more than necessary.

"I'll concentrate on your job prospects next."

"Great." K.O. was far more interested in locating full-time employment than falling in love. At twenty-eight she wasn't in a rush, although it *was* admittedly time to start thinking about a serious relationship. Besides, working at home wasn't conducive to meeting men. Zelda seemed to think that as a medical transcriptionist K.O. would meet any number of eligible physicians. That, however, hadn't turned out to be the case. The only person in a white coat she'd encountered in the last six months had been her dentist, and he'd been more interested in looking at her X-rays than at her.

"Before I forget," LaVonne said, getting ready to leave. "I'd like you to come over tomorrow for cocktails and appetizers."

"Sure." It wasn't as if her social calendar was crowded. "Thanks."

"I'll see you at six." LaVonne let herself out.

"Concentrate on seeing a job for me," K.O. reminded her, sticking her head in the hallway. "The next time you empty the litter box, I mean."

LaVonne nodded. "I will," she said. As she left, she was mumbling to herself, something K.O. couldn't hear.

The following morning, K.O. set up her laptop on a window table in the French Café, determined to wait for Dr. Jeffries. Now she felt obliged to get his autograph, despite her disapproval of his methods. More importantly, she had to talk to him about Christmas. This clueless man was destroying Christmas for her nieces—and for hundreds of thousands of other kids.

She had no intention of knocking on his door. No, this had to seem unplanned. An accidental meeting. Her one hope was that Wynn Jeffries was hooked on his morning latte. Since this was Seattle, she felt fairly certain he was. Nearly everyone in the entire state of Washington seemed to be a coffee addict.

In an effort to use her time productively, K.O. started work on the Mulcahy Christmas letter, all the while reminding herself that he was paying her double. She had two ideas about how to approach the situation. The first was comical, telling the truth in an outlandish manner and letting the reader assume it was some sort of macabre humor.

Merry Christmas from the Mulcahys, K.O. wrote. She bit

her lip and pushed away a strand of long blond hair that had escaped from her ponytail. *Bill and I have had a challenging year. Mason sends greetings from the juvenile detention center where he's currently incarcerated. Julie is pregnant and we pray she doesn't marry the father. Bill, at least, is doing well, although he's worried about paying for the mental care facility where I'm receiving outpatient therapy.*

K.O. groaned. This *wasn't* humorous, macabre or otherwise. It was difficult to turn the Mulcahys' disastrous year into comedy, especially since the letter was purportedly coming from them.

She deleted the paragraph and tried her second approach.

Merry Christmas from the Mulcahys, and what an—interesting? unexpected? unusual?—*year it has been for our lovely family.* K.O. decided on *eventful. Bill and I are so proud of our children, especially now as they approach adulthood. Where have all the years gone?*

Mason had an opportunity he couldn't turn down and is currently away at school. Our son is maturing into a fine young man and is wisely accepting guidance from authority figures. Our sweet Julie is in her second year of college. She and her boyfriend have decided to deepen their relationship. Who knows, there might be wedding bells—and perhaps even a baby—in our daughter's future.

So intent was she on putting a positive spin on the sad details of Bill Mulcahy's year that she nearly missed Wynn

Jeffries. When she looked up, it was just in time to see Dr. Jeffries walk to the counter. K.O. leaped to her feet and nearly upset her peppermint mocha, an extravagance she couldn't really afford. She remained standing until he'd collected his drink and then straightening, hurried toward him.

"Dr. Jeffries?" she asked, beaming a winsome smile. She'd practiced this very smile in front of the mirror before job interviews. After her recent cleaning at the dentist's, K.O. hoped she didn't blind him with her flashing white teeth.

"Yes?"

"You are Dr. Jeffries, Dr. Wynn Jeffries?"

"I am." He seemed incredibly tall as he stood in front of her. She purposely blocked his way to the door.

K.O. thrust out her hand. "I'm Katherine O'Connor. We live in the same building."

He smiled and shook her hand, then glanced around her. He seemed eager to escape.

"I can't tell you what a surprise it was when La-Vonne pointed out that the author of *The Free Child* lived in our building."

"You know LaVonne Young?"

"Well, yes, she's my neighbor. Yours, too," K.O. added. "Would you care to join me?" She gestured toward her table and the empty chairs. This time of day, it was rare to find a free table. She didn't volunteer the fact that she'd set up shop two hours earlier in the hope of bumping into him.

He checked his watch as if to say he really didn't have time to spare.

"I understand *The Free Child* has hit every bestseller list in the country." Flattery just might work.

Wynn hesitated. "Yes, I've been most fortunate."

True, but the parents and children of America had been most *un*fortunate in her view. She wasn't going to mention that, though. At least not yet. She pulled out her chair on the assumption that he wouldn't refuse her.

He joined her, with obvious reluctance. "I think I've seen you around," he said, and sipped his latte.

It astonished her that he knew who she was, while she'd been oblivious to his presence. "My sister is a very big fan of yours. She was thrilled when she heard I might be able to get your autograph."

"She's very kind."

"Her life has certainly changed since she read your book," K.O. commented, reaching for her mocha.

He shrugged with an air of modesty. "I've heard that quite a few times."

"Changed for the *worse*," K.O. muttered.

He blinked. "I beg your pardon?"

She couldn't contain herself any longer. "You want to take Santa away from my nieces! *Santa Claus.* Where's your heart? Do you know there are children all over

America being deprived of Christmas because of *you?*"
Her voice grew loud with the strength of her convictions.

Wynn glanced nervously about the room.

K.O. hadn't realized how animated she'd become until
she noticed that everyone in the entire café had stopped
talking and was staring in their direction.

Wynn hurriedly stood and turned toward the door,
probably attempting to flee before she could embarrass
him further.

"You're no better than…than Jim Carrey," K.O. wailed.
She meant to say the Grinch who stole Christmas but it
was the actor's name that popped out. He'd played the
character in a movie a few years ago.

"Jim Carrey?" He turned back to face her.

"Worse. You're a…a regular Charles Dickens." She
meant Scrooge, darn it. But it didn't matter if, in the heat
of her anger, she couldn't remember the names. She just
wanted to embarrass him. "That man," she said, stabbing
an accusatory finger at Wynn, "wants to bury Santa Claus
under the sleigh."

Not bothering to look back, Wynn tore open the café
door and rushed into the street. "Good riddance!" K.O.
cried and sank down at the table, only to discover that
everyone in the room was staring at her.

"He doesn't believe in Christmas," she explained and
then calmly returned to the Mulcahys' letter.

Chapter 3

The confrontation with Wynn Jeffries didn't go well, K.O. admitted as she changed out of her jeans and sweater later that same afternoon. When LaVonne invited her over for appetizers and drinks, K.O. hadn't asked if this was a formal party or if it would be just the two of them. Unwilling to show up in casual attire if her neighbor intended a more formal event, K.O. chose tailored black slacks, a white silk blouse and a red velvet blazer with a Christmas tree pin she'd inherited from her grandmother. The blouse was her very best. Generally she wore her hair tied back, but this evening she kept it down, loosely sweeping up one side and securing it with a rhinestone barrette. A little lip gloss and mascara, and she was ready to go.

A few minutes after six, she crossed the hall and rang LaVonne's doorbell. As if she'd been standing there waiting, LaVonne opened her door instantly.

K.O. was relieved she'd taken the time to change. Her neighbor looked lovely in a long skirt and black jacket with any number of gold chains dangling around her neck and at least a dozen gold bangles on her wrists.

"Katherine!" she cried, sounding as though it'd been weeks since they'd last spoken. "Do come in and meet Dr. Wynn Jeffries." She stepped back and held open the door and, with a flourish, gestured her inside.

Wynn Jeffries stood in the center of the room. He held a cracker raised halfway to his mouth, his eyes darting to and fro. He seemed to be gauging how fast he could make his exit.

Oh, dear. K.O. felt guilty about the scene she'd caused that morning.

"I believe we've met," Wynn said stiffly. He set the cracker down on his napkin and eyed the door.

Darn the man. He looked positively gorgeous, just the way he did on the book's dust jacket. This was exceedingly unfair. She didn't *want* to like him and she certainly didn't want to be attracted to him, which, unfortunately she was. Not that it mattered. She wasn't interested and after their confrontation that morning, he wouldn't be, either.

"Dr. Jeffries," K.O. murmured uneasily as she walked into the room, hands clasped together.

He nodded in her direction, then slowly inched closer to the door.

Apparently oblivious to the tension between them, LaVonne glided to the sideboard, where she had wine and liquor bottles set on a silver platter. Sparkling wineglasses and crystal goblets awaited their decision. "What can I pour for you?" she asked.

"I wouldn't mind a glass of merlot, if you have it," K.O. said, all the while wondering how best to handle this awkward situation.

"I do." LaVonne turned to Wynn. "And you, Dr. Jeffries?"

He looked away from K.O. and moved to stand behind the sofa. "Whiskey on the rocks."

"Coming right up."

"Can I help?" K.O. asked, welcoming any distraction.

"No, no, you two are my guests." And then as if to clear up any misconception, she added, "My *only* guests."

"Oh," K.O. whispered. A sick feeling attacked the pit of her stomach. She didn't glance at Wynn but suspected he was no more pleased at the prospect than she was.

A moment later, LaVonne brought their drinks and indicated that they should both sit down.

K.O. accepted the wine and Wynn took his drink.

With her own goblet in hand, LaVonne claimed the overstuffed chair, which left the sofa vacant. Evidently Dr. Jeffries was not eager to sit; neither was K.O. Finally she chose one end of the davenport and Wynn sat as far from her as humanly possible. Each faced away from the other.

"Wynn, I see you tried the crab dip," LaVonne commented, referring to the appetizers on the coffee table in front of them.

"It's the best I've ever tasted," he said, reaching for another cracker.

"I'm glad you enjoyed it. The recipe came from Katherine."

He set the cracker down and brushed the crumbs from his fingers, apparently afraid he was about to be poisoned.

K.O. sipped her wine in an effort to relax. She had a feeling that even if she downed the entire bottle, it wasn't going to help.

"I imagine you're wondering why I invited you here this evening," LaVonne said. Phillip, her white Persian, strolled regally into the room, his tail raised, and with one powerful thrust of his hind legs, leaped into her lap. LaVonne ran her hand down the length of his body, stroking his long, white fur. "It happened again," she announced, slowly enunciating the words.

"What happened?" Wynn asked, then gulped his drink.

Dramatically, LaVonne closed her eyes. "The sight."

Obviously not understanding, Wynn glanced at K.O., his forehead wrinkled.

"LaVonne took a class this week on unleashing your psychic abilities," K.O. explained under her breath.

Wynn thanked her for the explanation with a weak smile.

LaVonne's shoulders rose. "I have been gifted with the sight," she said in hushed tones.

"Congratulations," Wynn offered tentatively.

"She can read cat litter," K.O. told him.

"That's not all," LaVonne said, raising one hand. "As I said, it happened again. This morning."

"Not with the litter box?" K.O. asked.

"No." A distant look came over LaVonne as she fixed her gaze on some point across the room.

Peering over her shoulder, K.O. tried to figure out what her neighbor was staring at. She couldn't tell—unless it was the small decorated Christmas tree.

"I was eating my Raisin Bran and then, all of a sudden, I knew." She turned slightly to meet K.O.'s eyes. "The bran flakes separated, and that was when two raisins bobbed to the surface."

"You saw…the future?" K.O. asked.

"What she saw," Wynn muttered, "was two raisins in the milk."

LaVonne raised her hand once more, silencing them. "I saw the *future*. It was written in the Raisin Bran even more clearly than it'd been in the cat litter." She pointed a finger at K.O. "Katherine, it involved *you*."

"Me." She swallowed, not sure whether to laugh or simply shake her head.

"And you." LaVonne's finger swerved toward Wynn. Her voice was low and intent.

"Did it tell you Katherine would do her utmost to make a fool of me at the French Café?" Wynn asked. He scooped up a handful of mixed nuts.

As far as K.O. was concerned, *nuts* was an appropriate response to her neighbor's fortune-telling.

LaVonne dropped her hand. "No." She turned to K.O. with a reproachful frown. "Katherine, what did you do?"

"I…" Flustered she looked away. "Did…did you know Dr. Jeffries doesn't believe in Santa Claus?" There, it was in the open now.

"My dear girl," LaVonne said with a light laugh. "I hate to be the one to disillusion you, but there actually *isn't* a Santa."

"There is if you're five years old," she countered, glaring at the man on the other end of the sofa. "Dr. Jeffries is ruining Christmas for children everywhere." The man deserved to be publicly ridiculed. Reconsidering, she revised the thought. "He should be censured by his peers for even *suggesting* that Santa be buried under the sleigh."

"It appears you two have a minor difference of opinion," LaVonne said, understating the obvious.

"I sincerely doubt Katherine has read my entire book."

"I don't need to," she said. "My sister quotes you chapter and verse in nearly every conversation we have."

"This is the sister who asked for my autograph?"

"Yes," K.O. admitted. Like most men, she concluded, Dr. Jeffries wasn't immune to flattery.

"She's the one with the children?"

K.O. nodded.

"Do you have children?"

LaVonne answered for her. "Katherine is single, the same as you, Wynn."

"Why doesn't that surprise me?" he returned.

K.O. thought she might have detected a smirk in his reply. "It doesn't surprise me that you're single, either," she said, elevating her chin. "No woman in her right mind—"

"My dears," LaVonne murmured. "You're being silly."

K.O. didn't respond, and neither did Wynn. "Don't you want to hear what I saw in my cereal?"

Phillip purred contentedly as LaVonne continued to stroke his fluffy white fur.

"The future came to me and I saw—" she paused for effect "—I saw the two of you. Together."

"Arguing?" Wynn asked.

"No, no, you were in love. Deeply, deeply in love."

K.O. placed her hand over her heart and gasped, and then almost immediately that remark struck her as the most comical thing she'd ever heard. The fact that La-Vonne was reading her future, first in cat litter and now Raisin Bran, was ridiculous enough, but to match K.O.

up with Wynn— It was too much. She broke into peals of laughter. Pressing her hand over her mouth, she made an effort to restrain her giggles.

Wynn looked at her curiously.

LaVonne frowned. "I'm serious, Katherine."

"I'm sorry. I don't mean to be rude. LaVonne, you're my friend and my neighbor, but I'm sorry, it'll never happen. Never in a million years."

Wynn straightened. "While Katherine and I clearly don't see eye to eye on any number of issues, I tend to agree with her on this."

LaVonne sighed expressively. "Our instructor, Madam Ozma, warned us this would happen," she said with an air of sadness. "Unbelievers."

"It isn't that I don't believe you," K.O. rushed to add. She didn't want to offend LaVonne, whose friendship she treasured, but at the same time she found it difficult to play along with this latest idea of hers. Still, the possibility of a romance with just about anyone else would have suited her nicely.

"Wynn?" LaVonne said. "May I ask how you feel about Katherine?"

"Well, I didn't officially meet her until this morning."

"I might've given him the wrong impression," K.O. began. "But—"

"No," he said swiftly. "I think I got the right impression. You don't agree with me and I had the feeling that for some reason you don't like me."

"True...well, not exactly. I don't know you well enough to like *or* dislike you."

LaVonne clapped her hands. "Perfect! This is just perfect."

Both K.O. and Wynn turned to her. "You don't really know each other, isn't that correct?" she asked.

"Correct," Wynn replied. "I've seen Katherine around the building and on Blossom Street occasionally, but we've never spoken—until the unfortunate incident this morning."

K.O. felt a little flustered. "We didn't start off on the right foot." Then she said in a conciliatory voice, "I'm generally not as confrontational as I was earlier today. I might've gotten a bit...carried away. I apologize." She did feel guilty for having embarrassed him and, in the process, herself.

Wynn's dark eyebrows arched, as if to say he was pleasantly surprised by her admission of fault.

"We all, at one time or another, say things we later regret," LaVonne said, smiling down on Phillip. She raised her eyes to K.O. "Isn't that right, Katherine?"

"Yes, I suppose so."

"And some of us," she went on, looking at Wynn, "make hasty judgments."

He hesitated. "Yes. However in this case—"

"That's why," LaVonne said, interrupting him, "I took

the liberty of making a dinner reservation for the two of you. Tonight—at seven-thirty. An hour from now."

"A dinner reservation," K.O. repeated. Much as she liked and respected her neighbor, there was a limit to what she was willing to do.

"It's out of the question," Wynn insisted.

"I appreciate what you're doing, but…" K.O. turned to Wynn for assistance.

"I do, as well," he chimed in. "It's a lovely gesture on your part. Unfortunately, I have other plans for this evening."

"So do I." All right, K.O.'s plans included eating in front of the television and watching *Jeopardy,* and while those activities might not be anything out of the ordinary, they did happen to be her plans.

"Oh, dear." LaVonne exhaled loudly. "Chef Jerome Ray will be so disappointed not to meet my friends."

If Wynn didn't recognize the name, K.O. certainly did. "You know Chef Jerome Ray?"

"Of Chez Jerome?" Wynn inserted.

"Oh, yes. I did his taxes for years and years. What most people don't realize is that Jerome is no flash in the pan, if you'll excuse the pun. In fact, it took him twenty years to become an overnight success."

The Seattle chef had his own cooking show on the Food Network, which had become an immediate hit. His techniques with fresh seafood had taken the country by storm. The last K.O. had heard, it took months to get a reservation at Chez Jerome.

"I talked to Jerome this afternoon and he said that as a personal favor to me, he would personally see to your dinner."

"Ah…" K.O. looked at Wynn and weighed her options.

"Dinner's already paid for," LaVonne said in an encouraging voice, "and it would be a shame to let it go to waste."

A nuked frozen entrée and *Jeopardy,* versus one dinner with a slightly contentious man in a restaurant that would make her the envy of her friends. "I might be able to rearrange my plans," K.O. said after clearing her throat. Normally she was a woman of conviction. But in these circumstances, for a fabulous free dinner, she was willing to compromise.

"I think I can do the same," Wynn muttered.

LaVonne smiled brightly and clapped her hands. "Excellent. I was hoping you'd say that."

"With certain stipulations," Wynn added.

"Yes," K.O. said. "There would need to be stipulations."

Wynn scowled at her. "We will *not* discuss my book or my child-rearing philosophies."

"All right," she agreed. That sounded fair. "And we'll…we'll—" She couldn't think of any restriction of her own, so she said, "We refuse to overcat." At Wynn's frown, she explained, "I'm sort of watching my weight."

He nodded as though he understood, which she was sure he didn't. What man really did?

"All I care about is that the two of you have a marvelous dinner, but I know you will." LaVonne smiled at them both. "The raisins have already assured me of that." She studied her watch, gently dislodged Phillip and stood. "You'll need to leave right away. The reservation's under my name," she said and ushered them out the door.

Before she could protest or comment, K.O. found herself standing in the hallway with Wynn Jeffries, her dinner date.

Chapter 4

If nothing else, K.O. felt this dinner would afford her the opportunity to learn about Wynn. Well, that and an exceptional dining experience, of course. Something in his background must have prompted a child-rearing ideology that in her opinion was completely impractical and threatened to create a generation of spoiled, self-involved brats. Although she didn't have children of her own, K.O. had seen the effect on her nieces ever since Zelda had read that darn book. She was astonished by how far her sister had been willing to go in following the book's precepts, and wondered if Zach understood the full extent of Zelda's devotion to *The Free Child*. Her brother-in-law was quite the workaholic. He was absorbed in his job and often stayed late into the evenings and worked weekends.

Chez Jerome was only a few blocks from Blossom Street, so K.O. and Wynn decided to walk. She retrieved a full-length red wool coat from her condo while Wynn waited outside the building. The moment she joined him, she was hit by a blast of cold air. A shiver went through her, and she hunched her shoulders against the wind. To her surprise, Wynn changed places with her, walking by the curb, outside the shelter of the buildings, taking the brunt of the wind. It was an old-fashioned gentlemanly action and one she hadn't expected. To be fair, she didn't know *what* to expect from him. With that realization came another. He didn't know her, either.

They didn't utter a single word for the first block.

"Perhaps we should start over," she suggested.

Wynn stopped walking and regarded her suspiciously. "You want to go back? Did you forget something?"

"No, I meant you and me."

"How so?" He kept his hands buried in the pockets of his long overcoat.

"Hello," she began. "My name is Katherine O'Connor, but most people call me K.O. I don't believe we've met."

He frowned. "We did earlier," he said.

"This is pretend." Did the man have to be so literal? "I want you to erase this morning from your memory and pretend we're meeting for the first time."

"What about drinks at LaVonne's? Should I forget that, too?"

"Well." She needed to think this over. That hadn't been such a positive experience, either. "Perhaps it would be best," she told him.

"So you want me to act as if this is a blind date?" he asked.

"A blind date," she repeated and immediately shook her head. "I've had so many of those, I need a Seeing Eye dog."

He laughed, and the sound of it was rich and melodious. "Me, too."

"You?" A man this attractive and successful required assistance meeting women?

"You wouldn't believe how many friends have a compulsion to introduce me to *the woman of my dreams.*"

"My friends say the same thing. *This* is the man you've been waiting to meet your entire life. Ninety-nine percent of the time, it's a disaster."

"Really? Even you?" He seemed a little shocked that she'd had help from her matchmaking friends.

"What do you mean *even you?*"

"You're blond and beautiful—I thought you were joking about those blind dates."

She swallowed a gasp of surprise. However, if that was the way he saw her, she wasn't going to argue.

He thrust out his hand. "Hello, Katherine, my name is Jim Carrey."

She laughed and they shook hands. They continued walking at a leisurely pace, and soon they were having a lively conversation, exchanging dating horror stories. She laughed quite a few times, which was something she'd never dreamed she'd do with Wynn Jeffries.

"Would you mind if I called you Katherine?" he asked.

"Not at all. Do you prefer Wynn or Dr. Jeffries?"

"Wynn."

"I've heard absolutely marvelous things about Chez Jerome," she said. Not only that, some friends of K.O.'s had recently phoned to make dinner reservations and were told the first available opening was in May.

"LaVonne is certainly full of surprises," Wynn remarked. "Who would've guessed she had a connection with one of the most popular chefs in the country?"

They arrived at the restaurant, and Wynn held the door for her, another gentlemanly courtesy that made her smile. This psychologist wasn't what she'd expected at all. After hearing his theories about Christmas, she'd been sure he must be a real curmudgeon. But in the short walk from Blossom Street to the restaurant, he'd disproved almost every notion she'd had about him. Or at least about his personality. His beliefs were still a point of contention.

When Wynn mentioned LaVonne's name to the maître d', they were ushered to a secluded booth. "Welcome to Chez Jerome," the man said with a dignified bow.

K.O. opened her menu and had just started to read it

when Jerome himself appeared at their table. "Ah, so you are LaVonne's friends."

K.O. didn't mean to gush, but this was a real honor. "I am so excited to meet you," she said. She could hardly wait to tell Zelda about this—even though her sister would be far more impressed by her meeting Wynn Jeffries than Jerome.

The chef, in his white hat and apron, kissed her hand. The entire restaurant seemed to be staring at them and whispering, wondering who they were to warrant a visit from the renowned chef.

"You won't need those," Jerome said and ostentatiously removed the tasseled menus from their hands. "I am preparing a meal for you personally. If you do not fall in love after what I have cooked, then there is no hope for either of you."

Wynn caught her eye and smiled. Despite herself, K.O. smiled back. After a bit of small talk, Jerome returned to the kitchen.

Once the chef had gone, Wynn leaned toward her and teased, "He makes it sound as if dinner is marinated in Love Potion Number Nine." To emphasize the point, he sang a few lines from the old song.

K.O. smothered a giggle. She hated to admit it, but rarely had she been in a more romantic setting, with the elegant linens, flattering candlelight and soft classical music. The mood was flawless; so was their dinner, all four courses, even though she couldn't identify the exact nature of everything they ate. The appetizer was some kind of soup, served in a martini glass, and it tasted a bit like melted sherbet. Later, when their waiter told them the soup featured sea urchin, K.O. considered herself fortunate not to have known. If she had, she might not have tasted it. But, in fact, it was delicious.

"Tell me about yourself," she said to Wynn when the soup dishes were taken away and the salads, which featured frilly greens and very tart berries, were delivered.

He shrugged, as though he didn't really have anything of interest to share. "What would you like to know?"

"How about your family?"

"All right." He leaned back against the luxurious velvet cushion. "I'm an only child. My mother died three years ago. My father is Max Jeffries." He paused, obviously waiting to see if she recognized the name and when she didn't, he continued. "He was a surfer who made a name for himself back in the late sixties and early seventies."

She shook her head. Surfing wasn't an activity she knew much about, but then she really wasn't into sports. Or exercise, either. "My dad's the captain of his bowling team," she told him.

He nodded. "My parents were hippies." He grinned. "True, bona fide, unreconstructed hippies."

"As in the Age of Aquarius, free love and that sort of thing?" This explained quite a bit, now that she thought about it. Wynn had apparently been raised without boundaries himself and had turned out to be a successful and even responsible adult. Maybe he figured that would be true of any child raised according to his methods.

Wynn nodded again. "Dad made it rich when he was awarded a patent for his surfboard wax. Ever heard of Max's Waxes?" He sipped his wine, a lovely mellow pinot gris. K.O. did, too, savoring every swallow.

"I chose my own name when I was ten," he murmured.

It was hardly necessary to say he'd lived an unconventional life. "Why did you decide on Wynn?" she asked, since it seemed an unusual first name.

"It was my mother's maiden name."

"I like it."

"Katherine is a beautiful name," he commented. "A beautiful name for a beautiful woman."

If he didn't stop looking at her like that, K.O. was convinced she'd melt. This romantic rush was more intense than anything she'd ever experienced. She wasn't even prepared to *like* Wynn, and already she could feel herself falling for this son of a hippie. In an effort to break his spell, she forced herself to look away.

"Where did you grow up?" she asked as their entrées were ceremoniously presented. Grilled scallops with wild rice and tiny Brussels sprouts with even tinier onions.

"California," he replied. "I attended Berkeley."

"I lived a rather conventional life," she said after swooning over her first bite. "Regular family, one sister, two parents. I studied to become a medical transcriptionist, worked for a while and returned to college. I have a degree in public relations, but I'm currently working from home as a transcriptionist while looking for full-time employment. I'd really like to work as a publicist, but those jobs are rare and the pay isn't all that great." She closed her eyes. "Mmm. I think this is the best meal I've ever had." And she wasn't referring *just* to the food.

He smiled. "Me, too."

A few minutes later, he asked, "Your sister is married with children?"

"Identical twin girls. Zoe and Zara. I'm their godmother." When she discussed the twins, she became animated, telling him story after story. "They're delightful," she finally said. Dessert and coffee arrived then. An unusual cranberry crème brûlée, in honor of the season, and cups of exquisite coffee.

"So you like children?" Wynn asked when they'd made serious progress with their desserts.

"Oh, yes," she said, then added a qualifier, "especially well-behaved children."

His eyebrows arched.

Seeing how easy it was to get sidetracked, she said, "I think children are a subject we should avoid."

"I agree." But Wynn's expression was good-natured, and she could tell he hadn't taken offense.

Even after a two-and-a-half-hour dinner, K.O. was reluctant to leave. She found Wynn truly fascinating. His stories about living in a commune, his surfing adventures—including an encounter with a shark off the coast of Australia—and his travels kept her enthralled. "This has been the most wonderful evening," she told him. Beneath the polished exterior was a remarkable human being. She found him engaging and unassuming and, shock of shocks, *likeable*.

After being assured by Jerome that their meal had already been taken care of, Wynn left a generous tip. After fervent thanks and a protracted farewell, they collected their coats. Wynn helped K.O. on with hers, then she wrapped her scarf around her neck.

When they ventured into the night, they saw that snow had begun to fall. The Seattle streets were decorated for the season with sparkling white lights on the bare trees. The scene was as festive as one could imagine. A horse-drawn carriage passed them, the horse's hooves clopping on the pavement, its harness jingling.

"Shall we?" Wynn asked.

K.O. noticed that the carriage was traveling in the opposite direction from theirs, but she couldn't have cared less. For as long as she could remember, she'd wanted a carriage ride. "That would be lovely." Not only was Wynn a gentleman, but a romantic, as well, which seemed quite incongruous with his free-and-easy upbringing.

Wynn hailed the driver. Then he handed K.O. into the

carriage before joining her. He took the lap robe, spread it across her legs, and slipped his arm around her shoulders. It felt like the most natural thing in the world to be in his embrace.

"I love Christmas," K.O. confessed.

Wynn didn't respond, which was probably for the best, since he'd actually put in writing that he wanted to bury Santa Claus.

The driver flicked the reins and the carriage moved forward.

"It might surprise you to know that I happen to feel the same way you do about the holidays."

"But you said—"

He brought a finger to her lips. "We agreed not to discuss my book."

"Yes, but I *have* to know…."

"Then I suggest you read *The Free Child*. You'll understand my philosophies better once you do. Simply put, I feel it's wrong to mislead children. That's all I really said. Can you honestly object to that?"

"If it involves Santa, I can."

"Then we'll have to agree to disagree."

She was happy to leave that subject behind. The evening was perfect, absolutely perfect, and she didn't want anything to ruin it. With large flakes of snow drifting down and the horse clopping steadily along, the carriage swaying, it couldn't have been more romantic.

Wynn tightened his arm around her and K.O. pressed her head against his shoulder.

"I'm beginning to think LaVonne knows her Raisin Bran," Wynn whispered.

She heard the smile in his voice. "And her cat litter," she whispered back.

"I like her cats," he said. "Tom, Phillip and…"

"Martin," she supplied. The men in her neighbor's life all happened to be badly spoiled and much-loved cats.

The carriage dropped them off near West Lake Center. Wynn got down first and then helped K.O. "Are you cold?" he asked. "I can try to find a cab if you'd prefer not to walk."

"Stop," she said suddenly. All this perfection was confusing, too shocking a contrast with her previous impressions of Dr. Wynn Jeffries.

He frowned.

"I don't know if I can deal with this." She started walking at a fast pace, her mind spinning. It was difficult to reconcile this thoughtful, interesting man with the hardhearted destroyer of Christmas Zelda had told her about.

"Deal with *what?*" he asked, catching up with her.

"You—you're wonderful."

He laughed. "That's bad?"

"It's not what I expected from you."

His steps matched hers. "After this morning, I wasn't sure what to expect from you, either. There's a big difference between the way you acted then and how you've been this evening. *I* didn't change. You did."

"I know." She looked up at him, wishing she understood what was happening. She recognized attraction when she felt it, but could this be real?

He reached for her hand and tucked it in the crook of his arm. "Does it matter?" he asked.

"Not for tonight," she said with a sigh.

"Good." They resumed walking, more slowly this time. She stuck out her tongue to catch the falling snow, the way she had as a child. Wynn did, too, and they both smiled, delighted with themselves and each other.

When they approached their building on Blossom Street, K.O. was almost sad. She didn't want the evening to end for fear she'd wake in the morning and discover it had all been a dream. Worse, she was afraid she'd find out it was just an illusion created by candlelight and gorgeous food and an enchanting carriage ride.

She felt Wynn's reluctance as he keyed in the door code. The warmth that greeted them inside the small lobby was a welcome respite from the cold and the wind. The Christmas lights in the lobby twinkled merrily as he escorted her to her door.

"Thank you for one of the most romantic evenings of my life," she told him sincerely.

"I should be the one thanking you," he whispered. He held her gaze for a long moment. "May I see you again?"

She nodded. But she wasn't sure that was wise. "When?"

K.O. leaned against her door and held her hand to her forehead. The spell was wearing off. *"I don't think this is a good idea."* That was what she'd *intended* to say. Instead, when she opened her mouth, the words that popped out were, "I'm pretty much free all week."

He reached inside his overcoat for a PDA. "Tomorrow?"

"Okay." How could she agree so quickly, so impulsively? Every rational thought told her this relationship wasn't going to work. At some point—probably sooner rather than later—she'd have to acknowledge that they had practically nothing in common.

"Six?" he suggested.

With her mind screaming at her to put an end to this *now,* K.O. pulled out her Day-Timer and checked her schedule. Ah, the perfect excuse. She already had a commitment. "Sorry, it looks like I'm booked. I have a friend who's part of the Figgy Pudding contest."

"I beg your pardon?"

"Figgy Pudding is a competition for singing groups. It's a fund-raising event," she explained, remembering that he was relatively new to the area. "I told Vickie I'd come and cheer her on." Then, before she could stop herself, she added, "Want to join me?"

Wynn nodded. "Sure. Why not."

"Great." But it wasn't great. During her most recent visit with Vickie, K.O. had ranted about Dr. Jeffries for at least ten minutes. And now she was going to be introducing her friend to the man she'd claimed was ruining America. Introducing him as her...*date?*

She had to get out of this.

Then Wynn leaned forward and pressed his mouth to hers. It was such a nice kiss, undemanding and sweet. Romantic, too, just as the entire evening had been. In that moment, she knew exactly what was happening and why, and it terrified her. She liked Wynn. Okay, *really* liked him. Despite his crackpot theories and their total lack of compatibility. And it wasn't simply that they'd spent a delightful evening together. A charmed evening. No, this had all the hallmarks of a dangerous infatuation. Or worse.

Wynn Jeffries! Who would've thought it?

Chapter 5

The phone woke K.O. out of a dead sleep. She rolled over, glanced at the clock on her nightstand and groaned. It was already past eight. Lying on her stomach, she reached for the phone and hoped it wasn't a potential employer, asking her to come in for an interview that morning. Actually, she prayed it *was* a job interview but one with more notice.

"Good morning," she said in her best businesslike voice.

"Katherine, it's LaVonne. I didn't phone too early, did I?"

In one easy motion, K.O. drew herself into a sitting position, swinging her legs off the bed. "Not at all." She rubbed her face with one hand and stifled a yawn.

"So," her neighbor breathed excitedly. "How'd it go?"

K.O. needed a moment to consider her response. La-Vonne was obviously asking about her evening with Wynn; however, she hadn't had time to analyze it yet. "Dinner was incredible," she offered and hoped that would satisfy her friend's curiosity.

"Of course dinner was incredible. Jerome promised me it would be. I'm talking about you and Wynn. He's very nice, don't you think? Did you notice the way he couldn't take his eyes off you? Didn't I tell you? It's just as I saw in the kitty litter and the Raisin Bran. You two are *meant* for each other."

"Well," K.O. mumbled, not knowing which question to answer first. She'd prefer to avoid them all. She quickly reviewed the events of the evening and was forced to admit one thing. "Wynn wasn't anything like I expected."

"He said the same about you."

"You've talked to him?" If K.O. wasn't awake before, she certainly was now. "What did he say?" she asked in a rush, not caring that LaVonne would realize how interested she was.

"Exactly that," LaVonne said. "Wynn told me you were nothing like he expected. He didn't know what to think when you walked into my condo. He was afraid the evening would end with someone calling the police—and then he had a stupendous night. That was the word he used—*stupendous.*"

"Really." K.O. positively glowed with pleasure.

"He had the look when he said it, too."

"What look?"

"The *look,*" LaVonne repeated, emphasizing the word, "of a man who's falling in love. You had a good time, didn't you?"

"I did." K.O. doubted she could have lied. She *did* have a wonderful evening. Shockingly wonderful, in fact, and that made everything ten times worse. She wanted to view Wynn as a lunatic confounding young parents, a grinch out to steal Christmas from youngsters all across America. How could she berate him and detest him if she was in danger of falling in love with him? This was getting worse and worse.

"I knew it!" LaVonne sounded downright gleeful. "From the moment I saw those raisins floating in the milk, I knew. The vision told me everything."

"Everything?"

"Everything," LaVonne echoed. "It came to me, as profound as anything I've seen with my psychic gift. You and Dr. Jeffries are perfect together."

K.O. buried her face in her hand. She'd fallen asleep in a haze of wonder and awakened to the shrill ring of her phone. She couldn't explain last night's feelings in any rational way.

She wasn't attracted to Wynn, she told herself. How could she be? The man who believed children should set their own rules? The man who wanted to eliminate Santa Claus? But she was beginning to understand what was going on here. For weeks she'd been stuck inside her condo, venturing outside only to meet Christmas-letter clients. If she wasn't transcribing medical records, she was filling out job applications. With such a lack of human contact, it was only natural that she'd be swept along on the tide of romance LaVonne had so expertly arranged for her.

"Wynn told me you were seeing him again this evening," LaVonne said eagerly.

"I am?" K.O. vaguely remembered that. "Oh, right, I am." Her mind cleared and her memory fell into place like an elevator suddenly dropping thirteen floors. "Yes, as it happens," she said, trying to think of a way out of this. "I invited Wynn to accompany me to the Figgy Pudding event at West Lake Plaza." She'd *invited* him. What was she thinking? *What was she thinking?* Mentally she slapped her hand against her forehead. Before this afternoon, she had to find an excuse to cancel.

"He's very sweet, isn't he?" LaVonne said.

"He is." K.O. didn't want to acknowledge it but he was. He'd done it on purpose; she just didn't know *why*. What was his purpose in breaking down her defenses?

She needed to think. She pulled her feet up onto the bed and wrapped one arm around her knees. He *had* been sweet and alarmingly wonderful. Oh, he was clever.

But what was behind all that charm? Nothing good, she'd bet.

"I have more to tell you," LaVonne said, lowering her voice to a mere whisper. "It happened again this morning." She paused. "I was feeding the boys."

K.O. had half a mind to stop her friend, but for some perverse reason she didn't.

"And then," LaVonne added, her voice gaining volume, "when I poured the dry cat food into their bowls, some of it spilled on the floor."

"You got a reading from the cat food?" K.O. supposed this shouldn't surprise her. Since LaVonne had taken that class, everything imaginable provided her with insight— mostly, it seemed, into K.O.'s life. Her love life, which to this point had been a blank slate.

"Would you like to know how many children you and Wynn are going to have?" LaVonne asked triumphantly.

"Any twins?" K.O. asked, playing along. She might as well. LaVonne was determined to tell her, whether she wanted to hear or not.

"Twins," LaVonne repeated in dismay. "Oh, my goodness, I didn't look that closely."

"That's fine."

LaVonne took her seriously. "Still, twins are definitely a possibility. Sure as anything, I saw three children. Multiple births run in your family, don't they? Because it might've been triplets."

"Triplets?" It was too hard to think about this without her morning cup of coffee. "Listen, I need to get off the phone. I'll check in with you later," K.O. promised.

"Good. You'll give me regular updates, won't you?"

"On the triplets?"

"No," LaVonne returned, laughing. "On you and Wynn. The babies come later."

"Okay," she said, resigned to continuing the charade. Everything might've been delightful and romantic the night before, but this was a whole new day. She was beginning to figure out his agenda. She'd criticized his beliefs, especially about Christmas, and now he was determined to change hers. It was all a matter of pride. *Male* pride.

She'd been vulnerable, she realized. The dinner, the wine, Chef Jerome, a carriage ride, walking in the snow. *Christmas.* He'd actually used Christmas to weaken her resolve. The very man who was threatening to destroy the holiday for children had practically seduced her in Seattle's winter wonderland. What she recognized now was that in those circumstances, she would've experienced the same emotions with just about any man.

As was her habit, K.O. weighed herself first thing and gasped when she saw she was up two pounds. That fabulous dinner had come at a price. Two pounds. K.O. had to keep a constant eye on her weight, unlike her sister. Zelda was naturally thin whereas K.O. wasn't. Her only successful strategy for maintaining her weight was to weigh herself daily and then make adjustments in her diet.

Even before she'd finished putting on her workout gear, the phone rang again. K.O. could always hope that it was a potential employer, but caller ID informed her it was her sister.

"Merry Christmas, Zelda," K.O. said. This was one small way to remind her that keeping Santa away from Zoe and Zara was fundamentally wrong.

"Did you get it?" Zelda asked excitedly. "Did you get Dr. Jeffries's autograph for me?"

"Ah…"

"You didn't, did you?" Zelda's disappointment was obvious.

"Not exactly."

"Did you even *talk* to him?" her sister pressed.

"Oh, yes, we did plenty of that." She recalled their conversation, thinking he might have manipulated that, too, in order to win her over to his side. The dark side, she thought grimly. Like Narnia without Aslan, and no Christmas.

A stunned silence followed. "Together. You and Dr. Jeffries were together?"

"We went to dinner…."

"You went to dinner with Dr. Wynn Jeffries?" Awe became complete disbelief.

"Yes, at Chez Jerome." K.O. felt like a name-dropper

but she couldn't help it. No one ate at Chez Jerome and remained silent.

Zelda gasped. "You're making this up and I don't find it amusing."

"I'm not," K.O. insisted. "LaVonne arranged it. Dinner was incredible. In fact, I gained two pounds."

A short silence ensued. "Okay, I'm sitting down and I'm listening really hard. You'd better start at the beginning."

"Okay," she said. "I saw Wynn, Dr. Jeffries, in the French Café."

"I already know that part."

"I saw him again." K.O. stopped abruptly, thinking better of telling her sister about the confrontation and calling him names. Not that referring to him as Jim Carrey and Charles Dickens was especially insulting, but still... "Anyway, it's not important now."

"Why isn't it?"

"Well, Wynn and I agreed to put that unfortunate incident behind us and start over."

"Oh, my goodness, what did you do?" Zelda demanded. "What did you say to him? You didn't embarrass him, did you?"

K.O. bit her lip. "Do you want to hear about the dinner or not?"

"Yes! I want to hear *everything*."

K.O. then told her about cocktails at LaVonne's and her

neighbor's connection with the famous chef. She described their dinner in lavish detail and mentioned the carriage ride. The one thing she didn't divulge was the kiss, which shot into her memory like a flaming dart, reminding her how weak she really was.

As if reading her mind, Zelda asked, "Did he kiss you?"

"Zelda! That's private."

"He did," her sister said with unshakable certainty. "I can't believe it. Dr. Wynn Jeffries kissed my sister! You don't even like him."

"According to LaVonne I will soon bear his children."

"What!"

"Sorry," K.O. said dismissively. "I'm getting ahead of myself."

"Okay, okay, I can see this is all a big joke to you."

"Not really."

"I don't even know if I should believe you."

"Zelda, I'm your sister. Would I lie to you?"

"Yes!"

Unfortunately Zelda was right. "I'm not this time, I swear it."

Zelda hesitated. "Did you or did you not get his autograph?"

Reluctant though she was to admit it, K.O. didn't have any choice. "Not."

"That's what I thought." Zelda bade her a hasty farewell and disconnected the call.

Much as she hated the prospect, K.O. put on her sweats and headed for the treadmill, which she kept stored under her bed for emergencies such as this. If she didn't do something fast to get rid of those two pounds, they'd stick to her hips like putty and harden. Then losing them would be like chiseling them off with a hammer. This, at least, was her theory of weight gain and loss. Immediate action was required. With headphones blocking outside distractions, she dutifully walked four miles and quit only when she was confident she'd sweated off what she'd gained. Still, a day of reduced caloric intake would be necessary.

She showered, changed her clothes and had a cup of coffee with skim milk. She worked on the Mulcahys' Christmas letter, munching a piece of dry toast as she did. After that, she transcribed a few reports. At one o'clock LaVonne stopped by with a request.

"I need help," she said, stepping into K.O.'s condo. She carried a plate of cookies.

"Okay." K.O. made herself look away from the delectable-smelling cookies. Her stomach growled. All she'd had for lunch was a small container of yogurt and a glass of V8 juice.

"I hate to ask," LaVonne said, "but I wasn't sure where else to turn."

"LaVonne, I'd do anything for you. You know that."

Her friend nodded. "Would you write my Christmas letter for me?"

"Of course." That would be a piece of cake. Oh, why did everything come down to food?

"I have no idea how to do this. I've never written one before." She sighed. "My life is pitiful."

K.O. arched her brows. "What do you mean, pitiful? You have a good life."

"I do? I've never married and I don't have children. I'm getting these Christmas letters from my old college friends and they're all about how perfect their lives are. In comparison mine is so dull. All I have are my three cats." She looked beseechingly at K.O. "Jazz up my life, would you? Make it sound just as wonderful as my girlfriends' instead of just plain boring."

"Your life is *not* boring." Despite her best efforts, K.O. couldn't keep her eyes off the cookies. "Would you excuse me?"

"Ah...sure."

"I'll be back in a minute. I need to brush my teeth."

Her neighbor eyed her speculatively as K.O. left the room.

"It's a trick I have when I get hungry," she explained, coming out of the bathroom holding her toothbrush, which was loaded with toothpaste. "Whenever I get hungry, I brush my teeth."

"You do what?"

"Brush my teeth."

Her friend regarded her steadily. "How many times have you brushed your teeth today?"

"Four…no, five times. Promise me you'll take those cookies home."

LaVonne nodded. "I brought them in case I needed a bribe."

"Not only will I write your letter, I'll do it today so you can mail off your cards this week."

Her friend's eyes revealed her gratitude. "You're the best."

Ideas were already forming in K.O.'s mind. Writing La-Vonne's Christmas letter would be a snap compared to finishing Bill Mulcahy's. Speaking of him… K.O. glanced at her watch. She was scheduled to meet him this very afternoon.

"I've got an appointment at three," she told her friend. "I'll put something together for you right away, drop it off, see Bill and then stop at your place on my way back."

"Great." LaVonne was still focused on the toothbrush. "You're meeting Wynn later?"

She nodded. "At six." She should be contacting him and canceling, but she didn't know how to reach him. It was a weak excuse—since she could easily ask LaVonne for his number. Actually, she felt it was time to own up to the truth. She wanted to see Wynn again, just so she'd have some answers. *Was* she truly attracted to him? *Did* he have some nefarious agenda, with the intent of proving himself right and her wrong? Unless she spent another evening with him, she wouldn't find out.

"Are you…" LaVonne waved her hand in K.O.'s direction.

"Am I what?"

LaVonne sighed. "Are you going to take that toothbrush with you?"

"Of course."

"I see." Her neighbor frowned. "My psychic vision didn't tell me anything about that."

"No, I don't imagine it would." K.O. proceeded to return to the bathroom, where she gave her teeth a thorough brushing. Perhaps if Wynn saw her foaming at the mouth, he'd know her true feelings about him.

Chapter 6

K.O. had fun writing LaVonne's Christmas letter. Compared to Bill Mulcahy's, it was a breeze. Her friend was worried about how other people, people from her long-ago past, would react to the fact that she'd never married and lacked male companionship. K.O. took care of that.

Merry Christmas to my Friends, K.O. began for LaVonne. *This has been an exciting year as I juggle my time between Tom, Phillip and Martin, the three guys in my life. No one told me how demanding these relationships can be. Tom won my heart first and then I met Phillip and how could I refuse him? Yes, there's a bit of jealousy, but they manage to be civil to each other. I will admit that things heated up after I started seeing Martin. I fell for him the minute we met.*

I'm retired now, so I have plenty of time to devote to the demands of these relationships. Some women discover love in their twenties. But it took me until I was retired to fall into this kind of happiness. I lavish attention and love on all three guys. Those of you who are concerned that I'm taking on too much, let me assure you—I'm woman enough to handle them.

I love my new luxury condo on Blossom Street here in Seattle. And I've been continuing my education lately, enhancing my skills and exploring new vistas.

K.O. giggled, then glanced at her watch. The afternoon had escaped her. She hurriedly finished with a few more details of LaVonne's year, including a wine-tasting trip to the Yakima Valley, and printed out a draft of the letter.

The meeting with Bill Mulcahy went well, and he paid her the balance of what he owed and thanked her profusely. "This is just perfect," he said, reading the Christmas letter. "I wouldn't have believed it, if I wasn't seeing it for myself. You took the mess this year has been and turned it all around."

K.O. was pleased her effort had met with his satisfaction.

LaVonne was waiting for her when she returned, the Christmas letter in hand. "Oh, Katherine, I don't know how you do it. I laughed until I had tears in my eyes. How can I ever thank you?"

"I had fun," she assured her neighbor.

"I absolutely insist on paying you."

"Are you kidding? No way." After everything LaVonne had done for her, no thanks was necessary.

"I love it so much, I've already taken it down to the printer's and had copies made on fancy Christmas paper. My cards are going out this afternoon, thanks to you."

K.O. shrugged off her praise. After all, her friend had paid for her dinner with Wynn at Chez Jerome and been a good friend to her all these months. Writing a simple letter was the least she could do.

K.O. had been home only a short while when her doorbell chimed. Thinking it must be LaVonne, who frequently stopped by, she casually opened it, ready to greet her neighbor.

Instead Wynn Jeffries stood there.

K.O. wasn't ready for their outing—or to see him again. She needed to steel herself against the attraction she felt toward him.

"Hi." She sounded breathless.

"Katherine."

"Hi," she said again unnecessarily.

"I realize I'm early," he said. "I have a radio interview at 5:30. My assistant arranged it earlier in the week and I forgot to enter it into my PDA."

"Oh." Here it was—the perfect excuse to avoid seeing him again. And yet she couldn't help feeling disappointed.

He must've known, as she did, that any kind of relationship was a lost cause.

"That's fine, I understand," she told him, recovering quickly. "We can get together another time." She offered this in a nonchalant manner, shrugging her shoulders, deciding this really was for the best.

His gaze held hers. "Perhaps you could come with me," he said.

"Come with you?" she repeated and instantly recognized this as a bad idea. In fact, as bad ideas went, it came close to the top. She hadn't been able to keep her mouth shut in the bookstore and had been banned for life. If she had to listen to him spout off his views in person, K.O. didn't know if she could restrain herself from grabbing the mike and pleading with people everywhere to throw out his book or use it for kindling. Nope, attending the interview with him was definitely *not* a good plan.

When she didn't immediately respond, he said, "After the interview, we could go on to the Figgy Pudding thing you mentioned."

She knew she should refuse. And yet, before she could reconsider it, she found herself nodding.

"I understand the radio station is only a few blocks from West Lake Plaza."

"Yes..." Her mouth felt dry and all at once she was nervous.

"We'll need to leave right away," he said, looking at his watch.

"I'll get my coat." She was wearing blue jeans and a long black sweater—no need to change.

Wynn entered her condo and as she turned away, he stopped her, placing one hand on her arm.

K.O. turned back and was surprised to find him staring at her again. He seemed to be saying he wasn't sure what was happening between them, either. Wasn't sure what he felt or why… Then, as if he needed to test those feelings, he lowered his mouth to hers. Slowly, ever so slowly… K.O. could've moved away at any point. She didn't. The biggest earthquake of the century could've hit and she wouldn't have noticed. Not even if the building had come tumbling down around her feet. Her eyes drifted shut and she leaned into Wynn, ready—no, more than ready—*eager* to accept his kiss.

To her astonishment, it was even better than the night before. This *couldn't* be happening and yet it was. Fortunately, Wynn's hands were on her shoulders, since her balance had grown unsteady.

When he pulled away, it took her a long time to open her eyes. She glanced up at him and discovered he seemed as perplexed as she was.

"I was afraid of that," he said.

She blinked, understanding perfectly what he meant. "Me, too."

"It was as good as last night."

"Better," she whispered.

He cleared his throat. "If we don't leave now, I'll be late for the interview."

"Right."

Still, neither of them moved. Apparently all they were capable of doing was staring at each other. Wynn didn't seem any happier about this than she was, and in some small way, that was a comfort.

K.O. forced herself to break the contact between them. She collected her coat and purse and was halfway to the door when she dashed into the bathroom. "I forgot my toothbrush," she informed him.

He gave her a puzzled look. "You brush after every meal?" he asked.

"No, before." She smiled sheepishly. "I mean, I didn't yesterday, which is why I have to do it today."

He didn't question her garbled explanation as she dropped her toothbrush carrier and toothpaste inside her purse.

Once outside the building, Wynn walked at a fast pace as if he already had second thoughts. For her part, K.O. tried not to think at all. To protect everyone's peace of mind, she'd decided to wait outside the building. It was safer that way.

By the time they arrived at the radio station, K.O. realized it was far too frigid to linger out in the cold. She'd wait in the lobby.

Wynn pressed his hand to the small of her back and guided her through the impressive marble-floored lobby toward the elevators.

"I'll wait here," she suggested. But there wasn't any seating or coffee shop. If she stayed there, it would mean standing around for the next thirty minutes or so.

"I'm sure they'll have a waiting area up at the station," Wynn suggested.

He was probably right.

They took the elevator together, standing as far away from each other as possible, as though they both recognized the risk for potential disaster.

The interviewer, Big Mouth Bass, was a well-known Seattle disk jockey. K.O. had listened to him for years but this was the first time she'd seen him in person. He didn't look anything like his voice. For one thing, he was considerably shorter than she'd pictured and considerably...rounder. If she had the opportunity, she'd share her toothbrush trick with him. It might help.

"Want to sit in for the interview?" Big Mouth asked.

"Thank you, no," she rushed to say. "Dr. Jeffries and I don't necessarily agree and—"

"No way." Wynn's voice drowned hers out.

Big Mouth was no fool. K.O. might've imagined it, but she thought a gleam appeared in his eyes. He hosted a live interview show, after all, and a little controversy would keep things lively.

"I insist," Big Mouth said. He motioned toward the hallway that led to the control booth.

K.O. shook her head. "Thanks, anyway, but I'll wait out here."

"We're ready for Dr. Jeffries," a young woman informed the radio personality.

"I'll wait here," K.O. said again, and before anyone could argue, she practically threw herself into a chair and grabbed a magazine. She opened it and pretended to read, sighing with relief as Big Mouth led Wynn out of the waiting area. The radio in the room was tuned to the station, and a couple of minutes later, Big Mouth's booming voice was introducing Wynn.

"I have with me Dr. Wynn Jeffries," he began. "As many of you will recall, Dr. Jeffries's book, *The Free Child,* advocates letting a child set his or her own boundaries. Explain yourself, Dr. Jeffries."

"First, let me thank you for having me on your show," Wynn said, and K.O. was surprised by how melodic he sounded, how confident and sincere. "I believe," Wynn continued, "that structure is stifling to a child."

"*Any* structure?" Big Mouth challenged.

"Yes, in my opinion, such rigidity is detrimental to a child's sense of creativity and his or her natural ability to develop moral principles." Wynn spoke eloquently, citing example after example showing how structure had a negative impact on a child's development.

"No boundaries," Big Mouth repeated, sounding incredulous.

"As I said, a child will set his or her own."

Just listening to Wynn from her chair in the waiting room, K.O. had to sit on her hands.

"You also claim a parent should ignore inappropriate talk."

"Absolutely. Children respond to feedback and when we don't give them any, the undesirable action will cease."

Big Mouth asked a question now and then. Just before the break, he said, "You brought a friend with you this afternoon."

"Yes…" All the confidence seemed to leave Wynn's voice.

"She's in the waiting area, isn't she?" Big Mouth continued, commenting more than questioning. "I gathered, during the few minutes in which I spoke to your friend, that she doesn't agree with your child-rearing philosophy."

"Yes, that's true, but Katherine isn't part of the interview."

Big Mouth chuckled. "I thought we'd bring her in after the break and get her views on your book."

"Uh…"

"Don't go away, folks—this should be interesting. We'll be right back after the traffic and weather report."

On hearing this, K.O. tossed aside the magazine and started to make a run for the elevator. Unfortunately Big Mouth was faster than his size had led her to believe.

"I...I don't think this is a good idea," she said as he led her by the elbow to the control booth. "I'm sure Wynn would rather not..."

"Quite the contrary," Big Mouth said smoothly, ushering her into the recording room, which was shockingly small. He sat her next to Wynn and handed her a headset. "You'll share a mike with Dr. Jeffries. Be sure to speak into it and don't worry about anything."

After the traffic report, Big Mouth was back on the air.

"Hello, Katherine," he said warmly. "How are you this afternoon?"

"I was perfectly fine until a few minutes ago," she snapped.

Big Mouth laughed. "Have you read Dr. Jeffries's book?"

"No. Well, not really." She leaned close to the microphone.

"You disagree with his philosophies, don't you?"

"Yes." She dared not look at Wynn, but she was determined not to embarrass him the way she had in the French Café. Even if they were at odds about the validity of his Free Child movement, he didn't deserve to be publicly humiliated.

"Katherine seems to believe I'm taking Christmas away from children," Wynn blurted out. "She's wrong, of course. I have a short chapter in the book that merely suggests parents bury the concept of Santa."

"You want to *bury Santa?*" Even Big Mouth took offense at that, K.O. noticed with a sense of righteousness.

"My publisher chose the chapter title and against my better judgment, I let it stand. Basically, all I'm saying is that it's wrong to lie to a child, no matter how good one's intentions."

"He wants to get rid of the Tooth Fairy and the Easter Bunny, too," K.O. inserted.

"That doesn't make me a Jim Carrey," Wynn said argumentatively. "I'm asking parents to be responsible adults. That's all."

"What does it hurt?" K.O. asked. "Childhood is a time of make-believe and fairy tales and fun. Why does everything have to be so serious?"

"Dr. Jeffries," Big Mouth cut in. "Could you explain that comment about Jim Carrey?"

"I called him that," K.O. answered on his behalf. "I meant to say the Grinch. You know, like in *How the Grinch Stole Christmas.* Jim Carrey was in the movie," she explained helplessly.

Wynn seemed eager to change the subject. He started to say something about the macabre character of fairy tales and how they weren't "fun," but Big Mouth cut him off.

"Ah, I see," he said, grinning from ear to ear. "You two have a love/hate relationship. That's what's *really* going on here."

K.O. looked quickly at Wynn, and he glared back. The

"hate" part might be right, but there didn't seem to be any "love" in the way he felt about her.

"Regrettably, this is all the time we have for today," Big Mouth told his audience. "I'd like to thank Dr. Jeffries for stopping by this afternoon and his friend Katherine, too. Thank you both for a most entertaining interview. Now for the news at the top of the hour."

Big Mouth flipped a switch and the room went silent. So silent, in fact, that K.O. could hear her heart beat.

"We can leave now," Wynn said stiffly after removing his headphones.

Hers were already off. K.O. released a huge pent-up sigh. "Thank goodness," she breathed.

Wynn didn't say anything until they'd entered the elevator.

"That was a disaster," he muttered.

K.O. blamed herself. She should never have accompanied him to the interview. She'd known it at the time and still couldn't resist. "I'm sorry. I shouldn't have gone on the air with you."

"You weren't given much choice," he said in her defense.

"I apologize if I embarrassed you. That wasn't my intention. I tried not to say anything derogatory—surely you could see that."

He didn't respond and frankly, she didn't blame him.

"The thing is, Katherine, you don't respect my beliefs."

"I don't," she reluctantly agreed.

"You couldn't have made it any plainer." The elevator doors opened and they stepped into the foyer.

"Perhaps it would be best if we didn't see each other again." K.O. figured she was only saying what they were both thinking.

Wynn nodded. She could sense his regret, a regret she felt herself.

They were outside the building now. The street was festive with lights, and Christmas music could be heard from one of the department stores. At the moment, however, she felt anything but merry.

The Figgy Pudding contest, which was sponsored by the Pike Market Senior Center and Downtown Food Bank as an annual fund-raiser, would've started by now and, although she didn't feel the least bit like cheering, she'd promised Vickie she'd show up and support her efforts for charity.

K.O. thrust out her hand and did her utmost to smile. "Thank you, Wynn. Last night was one of the most incredible evenings of my life," she said. "Correction. It was *the* most incredible night ever."

Wynn clasped her hand. His gaze held hers as he said, "It was for me, too."

People were stepping around them.

She should simply walk away. Vickie would be looking for her. And yet…she couldn't make herself do it.

"Goodbye," he whispered.

Her heart was in her throat. "Goodbye."

He dropped his hand, turned and walked away. His steps were slow, measured. He'd gone about five feet when he glanced over his shoulder. K.O. hadn't moved. In fact, she stood exactly as he'd left her, biting her lower lip—a habit she had when distressed. Wynn stopped abruptly, his back still to her.

"Wynn, listen," she called and trotted toward him. "I have an idea." Although it'd only been a few feet, she felt as if she was setting off on a marathon.

"What?" He sounded eager.

"I have twin nieces."

He nodded. "You mentioned them earlier. Their mother read my book."

"Yes, and loved it."

There was a flicker of a smile. "At least *someone* in your family believes in me."

"Yes, Zelda sure does. She thinks you're fabulous." K.O. realized she did, too—aside from his theories. "My sister and her husband are attending his company Christmas dinner next Friday, the fifteenth," she rushed to explain. "Zelda asked me to spend the night. Come with me. Show me how your theories *should* work. Maybe Zelda's doing it wrong. Maybe you can convince me that the Free Child movement makes sense."

"You want me to come with you."

"Yes. We'll do everything just as you suggest in your book, and I promise not to say a word. I'll read it this week, I'll listen to you and I'll observe."

Wynn hesitated.

"Until then, we won't mention your book or anything else to do with your theories."

"Promise?"

"Promise," she concurred.

"No more radio interviews?"

She laughed. "That's an easy one."

A smile came to him then, appearing in his eyes first. "You've got yourself a deal."

Yes, she did, and K.O. could hardly wait to introduce Zoe and Zara to Dr. Wynn Jeffries. Oh, she was sincere about keeping an open mind, but Wynn might learn something, too. The incorrigible twins would be the true crucible for his ideas.

K.O. held out her hand. "Are you ready for some Figgy Pudding?" she asked.

He grinned, taking her mittened hand as they hurried toward the Figgy Pudding People's Choice competition.

Chapter 7

The Figgy Pudding People's Choice event was standing room only when Wynn and K.O. arrived. Vickie and her friends hadn't performed yet and were just being introduced by a popular morning-radio host for an easy-listening station. K.O. and Vickie had been friends all through high school and college. Vickie had married three years ago, and K.O. had been in her wedding party. In fact, she'd been in any number of wedding parties. Her mother had pointedly asked whether K.O. was ever going to be a bride, instead of a bridesmaid.

"That's my friend over there," K.O. explained, nodding in Vickie's direction. "The one in the Santa hat."

Wynn squinted at the group of ladies huddled together

in front of the assembly. "Aren't they all wearing Santa hats?"

"True. The young cute one," she qualified.

"They're all young and cute, Katherine." He smiled. "Young enough, anyway."

She looked at Wynn with new appreciation. "That is such a sweet thing to say." Vickie worked for a local dentist as a hygienist and was the youngest member of the staff. The other women were all in their forties and fifties. "I could just kiss you," K.O. said, snuggling close to him. She looped her arm through his.

Wynn cleared his throat as though unaccustomed to such open displays of affection. "Any particular reason you suddenly find me so kissable?"

"Well, yes, the women with Vickie are…a variety of ages."

"I see. I should probably tell you I'm not wearing my glasses."

K.O. laughed, elbowing him in the ribs. "And here I thought you were being so gallant."

He grinned boyishly and slid his arm around her shoulders.

Never having attended a Figgy Pudding event before, K.O. didn't know what to expect. To her delight, it was enchanting, as various groups competed, singing Christmas carols, to raise funds for the Senior Center and Food Bank. Vickie and her office mates took second place, and

K.O. cheered loudly. Wynn shocked her by placing two fingers in his mouth and letting loose with a whistle that threatened to shatter glass. It seemed so unlike him.

Somehow Vickie found her when the singing was over. "I wondered if you were going to show," she said, shouting to be heard above the noise of the merry-go-round and the crowd. Musicians gathered on street corners, horns honked and the sights and sounds of Christmas were everywhere. Although the comment was directed at K.O., Vickie's attention was unmistakably on Wynn.

"Vickie, this is Wynn Jeffries."

Her friend's gaze shot back to K.O. "Wynn Jeffries? Not *the* Wynn Jeffries?"

"One and the same," K.O. said, speaking out of the corner of her mouth.

"You've got to be joking." Vickie's mouth fell open as she stared at Wynn.

For the last two months, K.O. had been talking her friend's ear off about the man and his book and how he was ruining her sister's life. She'd even told Vickie about the incident at the bookstore, although she certainly hadn't confided in anyone else; she wasn't exactly proud of being kicked out for unruly behavior. Thinking it might be best to change the subject, K.O. asked, "Is John here?"

"John?"

"Your husband," K.O. reminded her. She hadn't seen Wynn wearing glasses before, but she hoped his comment about forgetting them was sincere, otherwise he might notice the close scrutiny Vickie was giving him.

"Oh, *John,*" her friend said, recovering quickly. "No, he's meeting me later for dinner." Then, as if inspiration had struck, she asked, "Would you two like to join us? John got a reservation at a new Chinese restaurant that's supposed to have great food."

K.O. looked at Wynn, who nodded. "Sure," she answered, speaking for both of them. "What time?"

"Nine. I was going to do some shopping and meet him there."

They made arrangements to meet later and Vickie went into the mall to finish her Christmas shopping.

"I'm starving now," K.O. said when her stomach growled. Although she had her toothbrush, there really wasn't a convenient place to foam up. "After last night, I didn't think I'd ever want to eat again." She considered mentioning the two pounds she'd gained, but thought better of it. Wynn might not want to see her again if he found out how easily she packed on weight. Well, she didn't *really* believe that of him, but she wasn't taking any chances. Which proved that, despite everything, she was interested. In fact, she'd made the decision to continue with this relationship, see where their attraction might lead, almost without being aware of it.

"How about some roasted chestnuts?" he asked. A vendor was selling them on the street corner next to a musician who strummed a guitar and played a harmonica at the same time. His case was open on the sidewalk for anyone who cared to donate. She tossed in a dollar and hoped he used whatever money he collected to pay for music lessons.

"I've never had a roasted chestnut," K.O. told him.

"Me, neither," Wynn confessed. "This seems to be the season for it, though."

While Wynn waited in line for the chestnuts, K.O. became fascinated with the merry-go-round. "Will you go on it with me?" she asked him.

Wynn hesitated. "I've never been on a merry-go-round."

K.O. was surprised. "Then you have to," she insisted. "You've missed a formative experience." Taking his hand, she pulled him out of the line. She purchased the tickets herself and refused to listen to his excuses. He rattled off a dozen—he was too old, too big, too clumsy and so on. K.O. rejected every one.

"It's going to be fun," she said.

"I thought you were starving."

"I was, but I'm not now. Come on, be a good sport. Women find men who ride horses extremely attractive."

Wynn stopped arguing long enough to raise an eyebrow. "My guess is that the horse is generally not made of painted wood."

"Generally," she agreed, "but you never know."

The merry-go-round came to a halt and emptied out on the opposite side. They passed their tickets to the attendant and, leading Wynn by the hand, K.O. ushered him over to a pair of white horses that stood side by side. She set her foot in the stirrup and climbed into the molded saddle. Wynn stood next to his horse looking uncertain.

"Mount up, partner," she said.

"I feel more than a little ridiculous, Katherine."

"Oh, don't be silly. Men ride these all the time. See? There's another guy."

Granted, he was sitting on a gaudy elephant, holding a toddler, but she didn't dwell on that.

Sighing, Wynn climbed reluctantly onto the horse, his legs so long they nearly touched the floor. "Put your feet in the stirrups," she coaxed.

He did, and his knees were up to his ears.

K.O. couldn't help it; she burst out laughing.

Wynn began to climb off, but she stopped him by leaning over and kissing him. She nearly slid off the saddle in the process and would have if Wynn hadn't caught her about the waist.

Soon the carousel music started, and the horses moved up and down. K.O. thrust out her legs and laughed, thoroughly enjoying herself. "Are you having fun yet?" she asked Wynn.

"I'm ecstatic," he said dryly.

"Oh, come on, Wynn, relax. Have some fun."

Suddenly he leaned forward, as if he were riding for the Pony Express. He let out a cry that sounded like sheer joy.

"That *was* fun," Wynn told her, climbing down when the carousel stopped. He put his hands on her waist and she felt the heat of his touch in every part of her body.

"You liked it?"

"Do you want to go again?" he asked.

The line was much longer now. "I don't think so."

"I've always wanted to do that. I felt like a child all over again," he said enthusiastically.

"A Free Child?" she asked in a mischievous voice.

"Yes, free. That's exactly what my book's about, allowing children freedom to become themselves," he said seriously.

"Okay." She was biting her tongue but managed not to say anything more. Surely there were great rewards awaiting her in heaven for such restraint.

"Would you like to stop at the bookstore?" he asked. "I like to sign copies when I'm in the neighborhood."

"You mean an autographing?" She hoped it wouldn't be at the same bookstore that had caused all the trouble.

"Not exactly an autographing," Wynn explained. "The bookseller told me that a signed book is a sold book. When it's convenient, authors often visit bookstores to sign stock."

"Sort of a drive-by signing?" she asked, making a joke out of it.

"Yeah." They started walking and just as she feared, they were headed in the direction of *the* bookstore.

As they rounded the corner and the store came into sight, her stomach tightened. "I'll wait for you outside," she said, implying that nothing would please her more than to linger out in the cold.

"Nonsense. There's a small café area where you can wait in comfort."

"Okay," she finally agreed. Once she'd made it past the shoplifting detector K.O. felt more positive. She was afraid her mug shot had been handed out to the employees and she'd be expelled on sight.

Thankfully she didn't see the bookseller who'd asked her to leave. That boded well. She saw Wynn chatting with a woman behind the counter. He followed her to the back of the store. Some of the tension eased from K.O.'s shoulder blades. Okay, she seemed to be safe. And she didn't have to hide behind a coffee cup. Besides, she loved to read and since she was in a bookstore, what harm would it do to buy a book? She was in the mood for something entertaining. A romantic comedy, she decided, studying a row of titles. Without much trouble, she found one that looked perfect and started toward the cashier.

Then it happened.

Wynn was waiting up front, speaking to the very book-seller who'd banished K.O. from the store.

Trying to be as inconspicuous as possible, K.O. set the book aside and tiptoed toward the exit, shoulders hunched forward, head lowered.

"Katherine," Wynn called.

With a smile frozen in place, she turned to greet Wynn and the bookseller.

"It's you!" The woman, who wore a name tag that identified her as Shirley, glared at K.O.

She timidly raised her hand. "Hello again."

"You two know each other?" Shirley asked Wynn in what appeared to be complete disbelief.

"Yes. This is my friend Katherine."

The bookseller seemed to have lost her voice. She looked from Wynn to Katherine and then back.

"Good to see you again," K.O. said. She sincerely hoped Shirley would play along and conveniently forget that unfortunate incident.

"It *is* you," Shirley hissed from between clenched teeth.

"What's this about?" Wynn asked, a puzzled expression on his face. "You've met before?"

"Nothing," K.O. all but shouted.

"As a matter of fact, we have met." Shirley's dark eyes narrowed. "Perhaps your *friend* has forgotten. I, however, have not."

So it was going to be like that, was it? "We had a dif-ference of opinion," K.O. told Wynn in a low voice.

"As I recall, you were permanently banned from the store."

"Katherine was *banned* from the store?" Wynn asked incredulously. "I can't believe she'd do anything deserving of that."

"Maybe we should leave now," K.O. suggested, and tugged at his sleeve.

"If you want to know," Shirley began, but K.O. interrupted before she could launch into her complaint.

"Wynn, please, we should go," she said urgently.

"I'm sure this can all be sorted out," he murmured, releasing his coat sleeve from her grasp.

Shirley, hands on her hips, smiled snidely. She seemed to take real pleasure in informing Wynn of K.O.'s indiscretion.

"This *friend* of yours is responsible for causing a scene in this very bookstore, Dr. Jeffries."

"I'm sure no harm was meant."

K.O. grabbed his arm. "It doesn't matter," she said, desperate to escape.

"Katherine does tend to be opinionated, I agree," he said, apparently determined to defend her. "But she's actually quite reasonable."

"Apparently you don't know her as well as you think."

"I happen to enjoy Katherine's company immensely."

Shirley raised her eyebrows. "Really?"

"Yes, really."

"Then you might be interested to know that your so-called friend nearly caused a riot when she got into an argument with another customer over *your* book."

Wynn swiveled his gaze to K.O.

She offered him a weak smile. "Ready to leave now?" she asked in a weak whisper.

Chapter 8

K.O.'s doorbell chimed, breaking into a satisfying dream. Whatever it was about seemed absolutely wonderful and she hated to lose it. When the doorbell rang again, the sound longer and more persistent, the dream disappeared. She stumbled out of bed and threw on her flannel housecoat.

Reaching the door, she checked the peephole and saw that it was LaVonne. No surprise there. Unfastening the lock, K.O. let her in, covering a yawn.

"What time did you get home last night?" her neighbor cried as she hurried in without a cat—which was quite unusual. "I waited up as long as I could for you." La-

Vonne's voice was frantic. "I didn't sleep a wink all night," she said and plopped herself down on the sofa.

K.O. was still at the front door, holding it open. "Good morning to you, too."

"Should I make coffee?" LaVonne asked, leaping to her feet and flipping on the light as she swept into the kitchen. Not waiting for a response, she pulled out the canister where K.O. kept her coffee grounds.

K.O. yawned again and closed the front door. "What time is it?" Early, she knew, because her eyes burned and there was barely a hint of daylight through her living room windows.

"Seven-twenty. I didn't get you up, did I?"

"No, I had to answer the door anyway." Her friend was busy preparing coffee and didn't catch the joke. "How are the guys?" K.O. asked next. LaVonne usually provided her with daily updates on their health, well-being and any cute activities they'd engaged in.

"They're hiding," she said curtly. "All three of them." She ran water into the glass pot and then poured it in the coffeemaker.

Katherine wondered why the cats were in a snit but didn't have the energy to ask.

"You haven't answered my question," LaVonne said as the coffee started to drip. She placed two mugs on the counter.

"Which one?" K.O. fell into a kitchen chair, rested her arms on the table and leaned her head on them.

"Last night," LaVonne said. "Where were you?"

"Wynn and I were out—"

"*All* night?"

"You're beginning to sound like my mother," K.O. protested.

LaVonne straightened her shoulders. "Katherine, you hardly know the man."

"I didn't sleep with him, if that's what you think." She raised her head long enough to speak and then laid it down on her arms again. "We went out to dinner with some friends of mine after the Figgy Pudding contest."

"It must've been a very late dinner." LaVonne sounded as if she didn't quite believe her.

"We walked around for a while afterward and went out for a drink. The time got away from us. I didn't get home until one."

"I was up at one and you weren't home," LaVonne said in a challenging tone. She poured the first cup of coffee and took it herself.

"Maybe it was after two, then," K.O. said. She'd completely lost track of time, which was easy to do. Wynn was so charming and he seemed so interested in her and her friends.

Vickie's husband, John, was a plumbing contractor. Despite Wynn's college degrees and celebrity status, he'd fit in well with her friends. He'd asked intelligent questions, listened and shared anecdotes about himself that had them all laughing. John even invited Wynn to play poker with him and his friends after the holidays. Wynn had accepted the invitation.

Halfway through the meal Vickie had announced that she had to use the ladies' room. The look she shot K.O. said she should join her, which K.O. did.

"That's really Wynn Jeffries?" she asked, holding K.O.'s elbow as they made their way around tables and through the restaurant.

"Yes, it's really him."

"Does he know about the bookstore?"

K.O. nodded reluctantly. "He does now."

"You didn't tell him, did you?"

"Unfortunately, he found out all on his own."

Vickie pushed open the door to the ladies' as K.O. described the scene from the bookstore. "No way," her friend moaned, then promptly sank down on a plush chair in the outer room.

K.O.'s face grew red all over again. "It was embarrassing, to say the least."

"Was Wynn upset?"

What could he say? "He didn't let on if he was." In fact, once they'd left the store, Wynn seemed to find the incident highly amusing. Had their roles been reversed, she didn't know how she would've felt.

"He didn't blow up at you or anything?" Vickie had given her a confused look. "This is the guy you think should be banned from practicing as a psychologist?"

"Well, that might've been a bit strong," she'd said, re-considering her earlier comment.

Vickie just shook her head.

"He rode the merry-go-round with me," K.O. said aloud, deciding that had gone a long way toward redeeming him in her eyes. When she glanced up, she realized she was talking to LaVonne.

"He did what?" LaVonne asked, bringing her back to the present.

"Wynn did," she elaborated. "He rode the carousel with me."

"Until two in the morning?"

"No, before dinner. Afterward, we walked along the waterfront, then had a glass of wine. We started walking again and finally stopped for coffee at an all-night diner and talked some more." He seemed to want to know all about her, but in retrospect she noticed that he'd said very little about himself.

"Good grief," LaVonne muttered, shaking her head, "what could you possibly talk about for so long?"

"That's just it," K.O. said. "We couldn't *stop* talking." And it was even more difficult to stop kissing and to say good-night once they'd reached her condo. Because there was so much more to say, they'd agreed to meet for coffee at the French Café at nine.

LaVonne had apparently remembered that Katherine didn't have any coffee yet and filled her mug. "Just black," K.O. told her, needing a shot of unadulterated caffeine. "Thanks.

"Why were you waiting up for me?" she asked after her first bracing sip of coffee. Then and only then did her brain clear, and she understood that LaVonne must have something important on her mind.

"You wrote that fantastic Christmas letter for me," her neighbor reminded her.

"I did a good job, didn't I?" she said.

"Oh, yes, a good job all right." LaVonne frowned. "I liked it so much, I mailed it right away."

"So, what's the problem?"

"Well…" LaVonne sat down in the chair across from K.O. "It was such a relief to have something clever and… and exciting to tell everyone," LaVonne said, "especially my college friends."

So far, K.O. didn't see any problem at all. She nodded, encouraging her friend to get to the point.

LaVonne's shoulders sagged. "If only I'd waited," she moaned. "If only I'd picked up my own mail first."

"There was something in the mail?"

LaVonne nodded. "I got a card and a Christmas letter from Peggy Solomon. She was the president of my college sorority and about as uppity as they come. She married her college boyfriend, a banker's son. She had two perfect children and lives a life of luxury. She said she's looking forward to seeing me at our next reunion." There was a moment of stricken silence. "Peggy's organizing it, and she included the invitation with her card."

"That's bad?"

"Yes," LaVonne wailed. "It's bad. How am I supposed to show up at my forty-year college reunion, which happens to be in June, without a man? Especially *now*. Because of my Christmas letter, everyone in my entire class will think I've got more men than I know what to do with."

"LaVonne, you might meet someone before then."

"If I haven't met a man in the last forty years, what makes you think I will in the next six months?"

"Couldn't you say it's such a tricky balancing act you don't dare bring any of them?"

LaVonne glared at her. "Everyone'll figure out that it's all a lie." She closed her eyes. "And if they don't, Peggy's going to make sure she tells them."

Another idea struck K.O. "What about your psychic powers? Why don't you go check out the litter box again?" On second thought, maybe that wasn't such a great idea.

"Don't you think I would if I could?" she cried, becoming ever more agitated. "But I don't see anything about myself. Trust me, I've tried. So far, all my insights have been about you and Wynn. A lot of good my new-found talent has done *me*. You're being romanced night and day, and I've just made a complete fool of myself."

"LaVonne…"

"Even my cats are upset with me."

"Tom, Phillip and Martin?" K.O. had never understood why her neighbor couldn't name her feline companions regular cat names like Fluffy or Tiger.

"They think *I'm* upset with *them*. They're all hiding from me, and that's never happened before."

K.O. felt guilty, but she couldn't have known about the college reunion, any more than LaVonne did. "I'm sure everything will work out for the best," she murmured. She wished she had more than a platitude to offer, but she didn't.

"At this point that's all I can hope for." LaVonne expelled her breath and took another sip of coffee. That seemed to relax her, and she gave K.O. a half smile. "Tell me about you and Wynn."

"There's not much to say." And yet there was. She honestly liked him. Vickie and John had, too. Never would K.O. have guessed that the originator of the Free Child movement she so reviled would be this warm, compassionate and genuinely nice person. She would've been happy to settle for *one* of those qualities. Despite everything K.O. had done to embarrass him, he was attracted to her. And it went without saying that she found Wynn Jeffries compelling and smart and…wonderful. But she was afraid to examine her feelings too closely—and even more afraid to speculate about his.

"You've spent practically every minute of the last two days together," LaVonne said. "There's got to be something."

Shrugging, K.O. pushed her hair away from her face.

"You were with him until two this morning."

"And I'm meeting him at the café in about an hour and a half," she said as she glanced at the time on her microwave.

"So what gives?" LaVonne pressed.

"I like him," she said simply. K.O. hadn't been prepared to have any feelings for him, other than negative ones. But they got along well—as long as they didn't discuss his book.

Overjoyed by her confession, LaVonne clapped her hands. "I knew it!"

K.O. felt it would be wrong to let her friend think she really believed in this psychic nonsense. She'd cooperated with LaVonne's fantasy at first but now it was time to be honest. "Wynn said he asked you about me before you introduced us."

LaVonne looked away. "He did, but it was just in passing."

"He knew I lived in the building and had seen me around."

Her neighbor shifted in her seat. She cleared her throat before answering. "All right, all right, I was aware that he might be interested." She paused. "He asked me if you were single."

Really? Wynn hadn't told her that. "When was this?"

"Last week."

"Was it before or after you discovered your psychic talents?"

"Before."

Aha.

"Why didn't he just introduce himself?"

"I asked him that, too," LaVonne said. "Apparently he's shy."

"Wynn?"

LaVonne raised one shoulder. She frowned over at the phone on the counter. "You've got a message."

It'd been so late when she finally got to bed that K.O. hadn't bothered to check. Reaching over, she pressed the play button.

"K.O.," Zelda's voice greeted her. "Good grief, where are you? You don't have a date, do you?" She made it sound as if that was the last thing she expected. "Is there any chance it's with Dr. Jeffries? Call me the minute you get home." The message was followed by a lengthy beep and then there was a second message.

"Katherine," Zelda said more forcefully this time. "I don't mean to be a pest, but I'd appreciate it if you'd get back to me as soon as possible. You're out with Dr. Jeffries, aren't you?" Zelda managed to make that sound both accusatory and improbable.

Another beep.

"In case you're counting, this is the third time I've phoned you tonight. Where can you possibly be this late?"

No one ever seemed to care before, K.O. thought, and now her sister and LaVonne were suddenly keeping track of her love life.

Zelda gave a huge sigh of impatience. "I won't call again. But I need to confirm the details for Friday night. You're still babysitting, aren't you?"

"I'll be there," K.O. muttered, just as if her sister could hear. *And so will Wynn.*

Zelda added, "And I'd really like it if you'd get me that autograph."

"I will, I will," K.O. promised. She figured she'd get him to sign Zelda's copy of his book on Friday evening.

LaVonne drained the last of her coffee and set the mug in the sink. "I'd better get back. I'm going to try to coax the boys out from under the bed," she said with a resigned look as she walked to the door.

"Everything'll work out," K.O. assured her again—with a confidence she didn't actually feel.

LaVonne responded with a quick wave and left, slamming the door behind her.

Now K.O. was free to have a leisurely shower, carefully choose her outfit...and daydream about Wynn.

Chapter 9

Wynn had already secured a window table when K.O. arrived at the French Café. As usual, the shop was crowded, with a long line of customers waiting to place their orders.

In honor of the season, she'd worn a dark-blue sweater sprinkled with silvery stars and matching star earrings. She hung her red coat on the back of her chair.

Wynn had thoughtfully ordered for her, and there was a latte waiting on the table, along with a bran muffin, her favorite. K.O. didn't remember mentioning how much she enjoyed the café's muffins, baked by Alix Townsend, who sometimes worked at the counter. The muffins were a treat she only allowed herself once a week.

"Good morning," she said, sounding a little more breathless than she would've liked. In the space of a day, she'd gone from distrust to complete infatuation. Just twenty-four hours ago, she'd been inventing ways to get out of seeing Wynn again, and now...now she could barely stand to be separated from him.

She broke off a piece of muffin, after a sip of her latte in its oversize cup. "How did you know I love their bran muffins?" she asked. The bakery made them chock-full of raisins and nuts, so they were deliciously unlike blander varieties. Not only that, K.O. always felt she'd eaten something healthy when she had a bran muffin.

"I asked the girl behind the counter if she happened to know what you usually ordered, and she recommended that."

Once again proving how thoughtful he was.

"You had one the day you were here talking to some guy," he said flippantly.

"That was Bill Mulcahy," she explained. "I met with him because I wrote his Christmas letter."

Wynn frowned. "He's one of your clients?"

"I told you how I write people's Christmas letters, remember?" It'd been part of their conversation the night before. "I'll write yours if you want," she said, and then thinking better of it, began to sputter a retraction.

She needn't have worried that he'd take her up on the offer because he was already declining. He shook his head. "Thanks, anyway." He grimaced. "I don't want to offend you, but I find that those Christmas letters are typically a pack of lies!"

"Okay," she said mildly. She decided not to argue. K.O. sipped her coffee again and ate another piece of muffin, deciding not to worry about calories, either. "Don't you just love Christmas?" she couldn't help saying. The sights and sounds of the season were all around them. The café itself looked elegant; garlands draped the windows and pots of white and red poinsettias were placed on the counter. Christmas carols played, just loudly enough to be heard. A bell-ringer collecting for charity had set up shop outside the café and a woman sat at a nearby table knitting a Christmas stocking. K.O. had noticed a similar one displayed in A Good Yarn, the shop across the street, the day she'd followed Wynn. Christmas on Blossom Street, with its gaily decorated streetlights and cheerful banners, was as Christmassy as Christmas could be.

"Yes, but I had more enthusiasm for the holidays before today," Wynn said.

"What's wrong?"

He stared down at his dark coffee. "My father left a message on my answering machine last night." He hesitated as he glanced up at her. "Apparently he's decided—at the last minute—to join me for Christmas."

"I see," she said, although she really didn't. Wynn had only talked about his parents that first evening, at Chez

Jerome. She remembered that his parents had been hippies, and that his mother had died and his father owned a company that manufactured surfboard wax. But while she'd rattled on endlessly about her own family, he'd said comparatively little about his.

"He didn't bother to ask if I had other plans, you'll notice," Wynn commented dryly.

"Do you?"

"No, but that's beside the point."

"It must be rather disconcerting," she said. Parents sometimes did things like that, though. Her own mother often made assumptions about holidays, but it had never troubled K.O. She was going to miss her parents this year and would've been delighted if they'd suddenly decided to show up.

"Now I have to go to the airport on Sunday and pick him up." Wynn gazed out the window at the lightly falling snow. "As you might've guessed, my father and I have a rather…difficult relationship."

"I'm sorry." She wasn't sure what to say.

"The thing is," Wynn continued. "My father's like a big kid. He'll want to be entertained every minute he's here. He has no respect for my work or the fact that I have to go into the office every day." Wynn had told her he met with patients most afternoons; he kept an office in a medical building not far from Blossom Street.

"I'm sorry," she said again.

Wynn accepted her condolences with a casual shrug. "The truth is, I'd rather spend my free time with you."

He seemed as surprised by this as K.O. herself. She sensed that Wynn hadn't been any more prepared to feel this way about her than she did about him. It was all rather unexpected and at the same time just plain wonderful.

"Maybe I can help," K.O. suggested. "The nice thing about working at home is that I can choose my own hours." That left her open for job interviews, Christmas letters and occasional babysitting. "My transcription work is really a godsend while I'm on my job quest. So I can help entertain him if you'd like."

Wynn considered for a moment. "I appreciate your offer, but I don't know if that's the best solution." He released a deep sigh. "I guess you could say my father's not my biggest fan."

"He doesn't believe in your child-rearing ideas, either?" she teased.

He grinned. "I wish it was that simple. You'll know what I mean once you meet him," Wynn said. "I think I mentioned that at one time he was a world-class surfer."

"Yes, and he manufactures some kind of special wax."

Wynn nodded. "It's made him rich." He sighed again. "I know it's a cliché, but my parents met in San Francisco in the early 70s and I think I told you they joined a commune. They were free spirits, the pair of them. Dad hated what he called 'the establishment.' He dropped out of college, burned his draft card, that sort of thing. He didn't want any responsibility, didn't even have a bank account—until about fifteen years ago, when someone offered to mass-produce his surfboard wax. And then he grabbed hold with both hands."

K.O. wondered if he realized he was advocating his parents' philosophy with his Free Child movement. However, she didn't point it out.

"In the early days we moved around because any money Dad brought in was from his surfing, so the three of us followed the waves, so to speak. Then we'd periodically return to the commune. I had a wretched childhood," he said bleakly. "They'd called me Radiant Sun, Ray for short, but at least they let me choose my own name when I was older. They hated it, which was fine by me. The only real family I had was my maternal grandparents. I moved in with the Wynns when I was ten."

"Your parents didn't like your name?"

"No, and this came from someone who chose the name Moon Puppy for himself. Mom liked to be called Daffodil. Her given name was Mary, which she'd rejected, along with her parents' values."

"But you—"

"My grandparents were the ones who saw to it that I stayed in school. They're the ones who paid for my education. Both of them died when I was a college senior, but they were the only stable influence I had."

"What you need while your father is here," K.O. said, "is someone to run interference. Someone who can act as a buffer between you and your father, and that someone is me."

Wynn didn't look convinced.

"I want to help," she insisted. "Really."

He still didn't look convinced.

"Oh, and before I forget, my sister left three messages on my phone. She wants your autograph in the worst way. I thought you could sign her copy of *The Free Child* next Friday when—" It suddenly occurred to her that if Wynn's father was visiting, he wouldn't be able to watch the twins with her. "Oh, no," she whispered, unable to hide her disappointment.

"What's wrong?"

"I— You'll have company, so Friday night is out." She put on a brave smile. She didn't actually need his help, but this was an opportunity to spend time with him—and to prove that his theories didn't translate into practice. She might be wrong, in which case she'd acknowledge the validity of his Free Child approach, but she doubted it.

Wynn met her eyes. "I'm not going to break my commitment. I'll explain to my father that I've got a previous engagement. He doesn't have any choice but to accept it, especially since he didn't give me any notice."

"When does he arrive?" K.O. asked. She savored another piece of her muffin, trying to guess which spices Alix had used.

"At four-thirty," Wynn said glumly.

"It's going to work out fine." That was almost identical to what she'd told LaVonne earlier that morning.

Then it hit her.

LaVonne needed a man in her life.

Wynn was looking for some way to occupy his father.

"Oh, my goodness." K.O. stood and stared down at Wynn with both hands on the edge of the table.

"What?"

"Wynn, I have the perfect solution!"

He eyed her skeptically.

"LaVonne," she said, sitting down again. She was so sure her plan would work, she felt a little shiver of delight. "You're going to introduce your father to LaVonne!"

He frowned at her and shook his head. "If you're thinking what I suspect you're thinking, I can tell you right now it won't work."

"Yes, it will! LaVonne needs to find a man before her college reunion in June. She'd—"

"Katherine, I appreciate the thought, but can you honestly see LaVonne getting involved with an ex-hippie who isn't all that ex—and is also the producer of Max's Wax?"

"Of course I can," she said, refusing to allow him to

thwart her plan. "Besides, it isn't up to us. All we have to do is introduce the two of them, step back and let nature take its course."

Wynn clearly still had doubts.

"It won't hurt to try."

"I guess not..."

"This is what I'll do," she said, feeling inspired. She couldn't understand Wynn's hesitation. "I'll invite your father and LaVonne to my place for Christmas cocktails."

Wynn crossed his arms. "This is beginning to sound familiar."

"It should." She stifled a giggle. Turnabout was fair play, after all.

"Maybe we should look at the olives in the martinis and tell them we got a psychic reading," Wynn joked.

"Oh, that's good," K.O. said with a giggle. "A drink or two should relax them both," she added.

"And then you and I can conveniently leave for dinner or a movie."

"No...no," K.O. said, excitedly. "Oh, Wynn this is ideal! We'll arrange a dinner for *them*."

"Where?"

"I don't know." He was worrying about details too much. "We'll think of someplace special."

"I wonder if I can reach Chef Jerome and get a reservation there," Wynn murmured.

K.O. gulped. "I can't afford that."

"Not to worry. My father can."

"That's even better." K.O. felt inordinately pleased with herself. All the pieces were falling into place. Wynn would have someone to keep his father occupied until Christmas, and LaVonne might find a potential date for her class reunion.

"What are your plans for today?" Wynn asked, changing the subject.

"I'm meeting Vickie and a couple of other friends for shopping and lunch. What about you?"

"I'm headed to the gym and then the office. I don't usually work on weekends, but I'm writing a follow-up book." He spoke hesitantly as if he wasn't sure he should mention it.

"Okay." She smiled as enthusiastically as she could. "Would you like me to go to the airport with you when you pick up your father?"

"You'd do that?"

"Of course! In fact, I'd enjoy it."

"Thank you, then. I'd appreciate it."

They set up a time on Sunday afternoon and went their separate ways.

K.O. started walking down to Pacific Place, the mall where she'd agreed to meet Vickie and Diane, when her cell phone rang. It was Wynn.

"What day?" he asked. "I want to get this cocktail party idea of yours on my schedule."

"When would you suggest?"

"I don't think we should wait too long."

"I agree."

"Would Monday evening work for you?"

"Definitely. I'll put together a few appetizers and make some spiked eggnog. I'll pick up some wine—and gin for martinis, if you want." She smiled, recalling his comment about receiving a "psychic" message from the olives.

"Let me bring the wine. Anything else?"

"Could you buy a cat treat or two? That's in case La-Vonne brings Tom or one of her other cats. I want her to concentrate on Moon Puppy, not kitty."

Wynn laughed. "You got it. I'll put in a call to Chef Jerome, although I don't hold out much hope. Still, maybe he'll say yes because it's LaVonne."

"All we can do is try. And there are certainly other nice places."

Wynn seemed reluctant to end the conversation. "Katherine."

"Yes."

"Thank you. Hearing my father's message after such a lovely evening put a damper on my Christmas."

"You're welcome."

"Have fun today."

"You, too." She closed her cell and set it back in her purse. Her step seemed to have an extra bounce as she hurried to meet her friends.

Chapter 10

Saturday afternoon, just back from shopping, K.O. stopped at LaVonne's condo. She rang the doorbell and waited. It took her neighbor an unusually long time to answer; when she did, LaVonne looked dreadful. Her hair was disheveled, and she'd obviously been napping—with at least one cat curled up next to her, since her dark-red sweatshirt was covered in cat hair.

"Why the gloomy face?" K.O. asked. "It's almost Christmas."

"I know," her friend lamented.

"Well, cheer up. I have great news."

"You'd better come inside," LaVonne said without any real enthusiasm. She gestured toward the sofa, although it seemed to require all the energy she possessed just to lift her arm. "Sit down if you want."

"Wouldn't you like to hear my good news?"

LaVonne shrugged her shoulders. "I guess."

"It has to do with you."

"Me?"

"Yup. I met Vickie and Diane at Pacific Place, and we had lunch at this wonderful Italian restaurant."

LaVonne sat across from her, and Martin automatically jumped into her lap. Tom got up on the chair, too, and leisurely stretched out across the arm. She petted both cats with equal fondness.

"I ordered the minestrone soup," K.O. went on to tell her, maintaining her exuberance. "That was when it happened." She'd worked out this plan on her way home, inspired by Wynn's joke about the olives.

"What?"

"I had a psychic impression. Isn't that what you call it? Right there with my two friends in the middle of an Italian restaurant." She paused. "It had to do with romance."

"Really?" LaVonne perked up, but only a little.

"It was in the soup."

"The veggies?"

"No, the crackers," K.O. said and hoped she wasn't carrying this too far. "I crumbled them in the soup and—"

"What did you see?" Then, before K.O. could answer, LaVonne held out one hand. "No, don't tell me, let me guess. It's about you and Wynn," her neighbor said. "It must be."

"No...no. Remember how you told me you don't have the sight when it comes to yourself? Well, apparently I don't, either."

LaVonne looked up from petting her two cats. Her gaze narrowed. "What did you see, then?"

"Like I said, it was about *you,*" K.O. said, doing her best to sound excited. "You're going to meet the man of your dreams."

"I am?" She took a moment to consider this before her shoulders drooped once more.

"Yes, you! I saw it plain as anything."

"Human or feline?" LaVonne asked in a skeptical voice.

"Human," K.O. announced triumphantly.

"When?"

"The crackers didn't say exactly, but I felt it must be soon." K.O. didn't want to tell LaVonne too much, otherwise she'd ruin the whole thing. If she went overboard on the details, her friend would suspect K.O. was setting her up. She needed to be vague, but still implant the idea.

"I haven't left my condo all day," LaVonne mumbled, "and I don't plan to go out anytime in the near future. In fact, the way I feel right now, I'm going to be holed up in here all winter."

"You're overreacting."

Her neighbor studied her closely. "Katherine, you *really* saw something in the soup?"

"I did." Nothing psychic, but she wasn't admitting that. She'd seen elbow macaroni and kidney beans and, of course, the cracker crumbs.

"But you didn't take the class. How were you able to discover your psychic powers if you weren't there to hear the lecture from Madam Ozma?" she wanted to know.

K.O. crossed her fingers behind her back. "It must've rubbed off from spending all that time with you."

"You think so?" LaVonne asked hopefully.

"Sure." K.O. was beginning to feel bad about misleading her friend. She'd hoped to mention the invitation for Monday night, but it would be too obvious if she did so now.

"There might be something to it," LaVonne said, smiling for the first time. "You never know."

"True…one never knows."

"Look what happened with you and Wynn," LaVonne said with a glimmer of excitement. "The minute I saw those two raisins gravitate toward each other, I knew it held meaning."

"I could see that in the crackers, too."

This was beginning to sound like a church revival meeting. Any minute, she thought, LaVonne might stand up and shout *Yes, I believe!*

"Then Wynn met you," she burbled on, "and the instant he did, I saw the look in his eyes."

What her neighbor had seen was horror. LaVonne couldn't have known about their confrontation earlier that day. He'd clearly been shocked and, yes, horrified to run into K.O. again. Especially with the memory of her ranting in the café so fresh in his mind.

"You're right," LaVonne said and sat up straighter. "I shouldn't let a silly letter upset me."

"Right. And really, you don't even know how much of what your college friend wrote is strictly true." K.O. remembered the letter she'd written for Bill Mulcahy. Not exactly lies, but not the whole truth, either.

"That could be," LaVonne murmured, but she didn't seem convinced. "Anyway, I know better than to look to a man for happiness." LaVonne was sounding more like her old self. "Happiness comes from within, isn't that right, Martin?" she asked, holding her cat up. Martin dangled from her grasp, mewing plaintively. "I don't need a man to be complete, do I?"

K.O. stood up, gathering her packages as she did. Toys and books for the twins, wrapping paper, a jar of specialty olives.

"Thanks for stopping by," LaVonne said when K.O. started toward the door. "I feel a hundred percent better already."

"Keep your eyes open now," she told LaVonne. "The man in the soup could be right around the corner." Or on the top floor of their condo building, she added silently.

"I will," her neighbor promised and, still clutching Martin, she shut the door.

Sunday afternoon Wynn came to K.O.'s door at three, his expression morose.

"Cheer up," she urged. "Just how bad can it be?"

"Wait until you meet Moon Puppy. Then you'll know."

"Come on, is your father really *that* bad?"

Wynn sighed deeply. "I suppose not. He's lonely without my mother. At loose ends."

"That's good." She paused, hearing what she'd said. "It's not good that he's lonely, but… Well, you know what I mean." LaVonne might seem all the more attractive to him if he craved female companionship. LaVonne deserved someone who needed her, who would appreciate her and her cats and her…psychic talents.

"You ready?" he asked.

"Let me grab my coat."

"You don't have to do this, you know."

"Wynn, I'm happy to," she assured him, and she meant it.

The airport traffic was snarled, and it took two turns through the short-term parking garage to find an available space. Thankfully they'd allotted plenty of time.

Wynn had agreed to meet his father at baggage claim. No more than five minutes after they'd staked out a place near the luggage carousel, a man wearing a Hawaiian shirt, with long dark hair tied in a ponytail, walked toward them. He didn't have a jacket or coat.

K.O. felt Wynn stiffen.

"Wynn!" The man hurried forward.

Wynn met his father halfway, with K.O. trailing behind, and briefly hugged him. "Hello, Dad." He put his hand on K.O.'s shoulder. "This is my friend Katherine O'Connor. Katherine, this is my father, Moon Puppy Jeffries."

Moon Puppy winced. "Delighted to meet you, Katherine," he said politely. "But please, call me Max. I don't go by Moon Puppy anymore."

"Welcome to Seattle," K.O. said, shaking hands. "I'm sorry you didn't arrive to sunshine and warmer weather."

"Thank you. Don't worry, I've got a jacket in my bag."

In a few minutes Max had collected his suitcase and Wynn led the way to his car. "It's been unseasonably chilly," K.O. said, making small talk as they took the escalator to the parking garage. Max had retrieved his jacket by then.

At the car, Wynn took the suitcase from his father and stored it in the trunk. This gave K.O. an opportunity to study father and son. She glanced at Wynn and then back at his father. After the description Wynn had given her, she'd expected something quite different. Yes, Max Jeffries looked like an old hippie, as Wynn had said, but his hair was neatly trimmed and combed. He wore clean, pressed clothes and had impeccable manners. He was an older version of Wynn and just as respectable looking, she thought. Well, except for the hair.

"It was a surprise to hear you were coming for Christmas," Wynn commented when he got into the car.

"I figured it would be," his father said. "I didn't mention it earlier because I was afraid you'd find a convenient excuse for me not to come."

So Max Jeffries was direct and honest, too. A lot like his son. K.O. liked him even more.

They chatted on the ride into Seattle, and K.O. casually invited him for cocktails the following afternoon.

"I'd enjoy that," Wynn's father told her.

"Katherine wants to introduce you to her neighbor, LaVonne."

"I see," Max said with less enthusiasm and quickly changed the subject. "I understand your book is selling nicely."

"Yes, I'm fortunate to have a lot of publisher support."

"He's writing a second book," K.O. said, joining the conversation. It pleased her that Max seemed proud of his son.

"So, how long have you two been seeing each other?" Max asked, looking at K.O.

"Not long," Wynn answered for them. His gaze caught K.O.'s in the rearview mirror. "We met through a psychic," he said.

"We most certainly did not." K.O. was about to argue

when she realized Wynn was smiling. "We actually met through a mutual friend who believes she has psychic powers," she explained, not telling Max that her neighbor and this "psychic" were one and the same.

As they exited off the freeway and headed into downtown Seattle and toward Blossom Street, Max said, "I had no idea Seattle was this beautiful."

"Oh, just wait until nighttime," K.O. told him. It was fast becoming dark, and city lights had begun to sparkle. "There's lots to do at night. Wynn and I took a horse-drawn carriage ride last week and then on Friday night we went on a merry-go-round."

"My first such experience," Wynn said, a smile quivering at the edges of his mouth.

"Your mother and I never took you?" Max sounded incredulous.

"Never."

"I know I had some failings as a father," Max said despondently.

"Not getting to ride on a merry-go-round isn't exactly a big deal, Dad. Don't worry about it," Wynn muttered.

That seemed to ease his father's mind. "So what's on the agenda for tomorrow?" he asked brightly.

Wynn cast K.O. a look as if to say he'd told her so.

"I can take you on a tour of Pike Place Market," K.O. offered.

"That would be great." Max thanked her with a warm

smile. "I was hoping to get a chance to go up the Space Needle while I'm here, too."

"We can do that on Tuesday."

Max nodded. "Do you have any free time, Wynn?" he asked.

"Some," Wynn admitted with obvious reluctance. "But not much. In addition to my appointments and writing schedule, I'm still doing promotion for my current book."

"Of course," Max murmured.

K.O. detected a note of sadness in his voice and wanted to reassure him. Unfortunately she didn't know how.

Chapter 11

Wynn phoned K.O. early Monday morning. "I don't think this is going to work," he whispered.

"Pardon?" K.O. strained to hear.

"Meet me at the French Café," he said, his voice only slightly louder.

"When?" She had her sweats on and was ready to tackle her treadmill. After shedding the two pounds, she'd gained them again. It wasn't much, but enough to send her racing for a morning workout. She knew how quickly these things could get out of control.

"Now," he said impatiently. "Want me to pick you up?"

"No, I'll meet you there in ten minutes."

By the time she entered the café, Wynn had already

purchased two cups of coffee and procured a table. "What's wrong?" she asked as she pulled out the chair.

"He's driving me insane!"

"Wynn, I like your father. You made him sound worse than a deadbeat dad, but he's obviously proud of you and—"

"Do you mind if we don't list his admirable qualities just now?" He brought one hand to his temple, as if warding off a headache.

"All right," she said, doing her best to understand.

"The reason I called is that I don't think it's a good idea to set him up with LaVonne."

"Why not?" K.O. thought her plan was brilliant. She had everything worked out in her mind; she'd bought the liquor and intended to dust and vacuum this afternoon. As far as she was concerned, the meeting of Max and La-Vonne was destiny. Christmas romances were always the best.

"Dad isn't ready for another relationship," Wynn declared. "He's still mourning my mother."

"Shouldn't he be the one to decide that?" Wynn might be a renowned child psychologist but she believed everyone was entitled to make his or her own decisions, especially in matters of the heart. She considered it all right to lend a helping hand, however. That was fair.

"I can tell my father's not ready," Wynn insisted.

"But I invited him for drinks this evening and he accepted." It looked as if her entire day was going to be spent with Max Jeffries, aka Moon Puppy. Earlier she'd agreed to take him to Pike Place Market, which was a must-see for anyone visiting Seattle. It was always an entertaining place for tourists, but never more so than during the holiday season. The whole market had an air of festivity, the holiday mood infectious.

"What about LaVonne?" he asked.

"I'll give her a call later." K.O. hadn't wanted to be obvious about this meeting. Still, when LaVonne met Max, she'd know, the same way Wynn and K.O. had known, that they were being set up.

"Don't," he said, cupping the coffee mug with both hands.

"Why not?"

He frowned. "I have a bad feeling about this."

K.O. smothered a giggle. "Are you telling me you've found your own psychic powers?"

"Hardly," he snorted.

"Wynn," she said, covering his hand with hers in a gesture of reassurance. "It's going to work out fine, trust me." Hmm. She seemed to be saying that a lot these days.

He exhaled slowly, as if it went against his better judgment to agree. "All right, do whatever you think is best."

"I've decided to simplify things. I'm serving eggnog and cookies." And olives, if anyone wanted them. When she'd find time to bake she didn't know, but K.O. was determined to do this properly.

"Come around five-thirty," she suggested.

"That early?"

"Yes. You're taking care of arranging their dinner, right?"

"Ah…I don't think they'll get that far."

"But they might," she said hopefully. "You make the reservation, and if they don't want to go, then we will. Okay?"

He nodded. "I'll see what I can do." Wynn took one last swallow of coffee and stood. "I've got to get to the office." Slipping into his overcoat, he confided, "I have a patient this morning. Emergency call."

K.O. wondered what kind of emergency that would be—an ego that needed splinting? A bruised id? But she knew better than to ask. "Have a good day," was all she said. In his current mood, that was an iffy proposition. K.O. couldn't help wondering what Max had done to upset him.

"You, too," he murmured, then added, "And thank you for looking after Moon Puppy."

"His name is Max," K.O. reminded him.

"Maybe to you, but to me he'll always be the hippie surfer bum I grew up with." Wynn hurried out of the café.

By five that afternoon, K.O. felt as if she'd never left the treadmill. After walking for forty minutes on her machine, she showered, baked and decorated three dozen cookies and then met Wynn's father for a whirlwind tour of the Seattle waterfront, starting with Pike Place. She phoned LaVonne from the Seattle Aquarium. LaVonne had instantly agreed to drinks, and K.O. had a hard time getting off the phone. LaVonne chatted excitedly about the man in the soup, the man K.O. had claimed to see with her "psychic" eyes. Oh, dear, maybe this had gone a little too far....

Max was interested in absolutely everything, so they didn't get back to Blossom Street until after four, which gave K.O. very little time to prepare for *the meeting*.

She vacuumed and dusted and plumped up the sofa pillows and set out a dish of peppermint candies, a favorite of LaVonne's. The decorated sugar cookies were arranged on a special Santa plate. K.O. didn't particularly like sugar cookies, which, therefore, weren't as tempting as shortbread or chocolate chip would've been. She decided against the olives.

K.O. was stirring the rum into the eggnog when she saw the blinking light on her phone. A quick check told her it was Zelda. She didn't have even a minute to chat and told herself she'd return the call later.

Precisely at 5:30 p.m., just after she'd put on all her Christmas CDs, Wynn arrived without his father. "Where's your dad?" K.O. demanded as she accepted the bottle of wine he handed her.

"He's never on time if there's an excuse to be late," Wynn muttered. "He'll get here when he gets here. You noticed he doesn't wear a watch?"

K.O. had noticed and thought it a novelty. LaVonne wasn't known for her punctuality, either, so they had at least that much in common. Already this relationship revealed promise—in her opinion, anyway.

"How did your afternoon go?" Wynn asked. He sat down on the sofa and reached for a cookie, nodding his head to the tempo of "Jingle Bell Rock."

"Great. I enjoyed getting to know your father."

Wynn glanced up, giving her a skeptical look.

"What is it with you two?" she asked gently, sitting beside him.

Wynn sighed. "I didn't have a happy childhood, except for the time I spent with my grandparents. I resented being dragged hither and yon, based on where the best surf could be found. I hated living with a bunch of self-absorbed hippies whenever we returned to the commune, which was their so-called home base. For a good part of my life, I had the feeling I was a hindrance my father tolerated."

"Oh, Wynn." The unhappiness he still felt was at odds with the amusing stories he'd told about his childhood at Chez Jerome and during dinner with Vickie and John. She'd originally assumed that he was reflecting his own upbringing in his "Free Child" theories, but she now saw that wasn't the case. Moon Puppy Max might have been a hippie, but he'd imposed his own regimen on his son. Not much "freedom" there.

"Well, that's my life," he said stiffly. "I don't want my father here and I dislike the way he's using you and——"

"He's not using me."

He opened his mouth to argue, but apparently changed his mind. "I'm not going to let my father come between us."

"Good, because I'd feel terrible if that happened." This would be a near-perfect relationship—if it wasn't for the fact that he was Wynn Jeffries, author of *The Free Child.* And the fact that he hadn't forgiven his father, who'd been a selfish and irresponsible parent.

His eyes softened. "I won't let it." He kissed her then, and K.O. slipped easily into his embrace. He wrapped his arms around her and they exchanged a series of deep and probing kisses that left K.O.'s head reeling.

"Katherine." Wynn breathed harshly as he abruptly released her.

She didn't want him to stop.

"You'd better answer your door," he advised.

K.O. had been so consumed by their kisses that she hadn't heard the doorbell. "Oh," she breathed, shaking her head to clear away the fog of longing. This man did things to her heart—not to mention the rest of her—that even a romance novelist couldn't describe.

Wynn's father stood on the other side of the door, wearing another Hawaiian flowered shirt, khaki pants and flip-flops. From the way he'd dressed, he could be on a tropical isle rather than in Seattle with temperatures hovering just above freezing. K.O. could tell that Max's choice of clothes irritated Wynn, but to his credit, Wynn didn't comment.

Too bad the current Christmas song was "Rudolph," instead of "Mele Kiliki Maka."

K.O. welcomed him and had just poured his eggnog when the doorbell chimed again. Ah, the moment she'd been waiting for. Her friend had arrived. K.O. glided toward the door and swept it open as if anticipating Santa himself.

"LaVonne," she said, leaning forward to kiss her friend's cheek. "How good of you to come." Her neighbor had brought Tom with her. The oversize feline was draped over her arm like a large furry purse.

"This is so kind of you," LaVonne said. She looked startled at seeing Max.

"Come in, please," K.O. said, gesturing her inside. She realized how formal she sounded—like a character in an old drawing room comedy. "Allow me to introduce Wynn's father, Max Jeffries. Max, this is LaVonne Young."

Max stood and backed away from LaVonne. "You have a cat on your arm."

"This is Tom," LaVonne said. She glanced down lovingly at the cat as she stepped into the living room. "Would you like to say hello?" She held Tom out, but Max shook his head adamantly.

By now he'd backed up against the wall. "I don't like cats."

"What?" She sounded shocked. "Cats are magical creatures."

"Maybe to you they are," the other man protested. "I don't happen to be a cat person."

Wynn shared an I-told-you-so look with K.O.

"May I get you some eggnog?" K.O. asked, hoping to rescue the evening from a less-than-perfect beginning.

"Please," LaVonne answered just as "Have Yourself a Merry Little Christmas" began.

Eager for something to do, K.O. hurried into the kitchen and grabbed the pitcher of eggnog.

She heard Tom hiss loudly and gulped down some of her own eggnog to relax.

"Your cat doesn't like me," Max said as he carefully approached the sofa.

"Oh, don't be silly. Tom's the friendly one."

"You mean you have *more* than one?"

"Dad," Wynn said, "why don't you sit down and make yourself comfortable. You're quite safe. Tom is very well-behaved."

"I don't like cats," Max reiterated.

"Tom is gentle and loving," LaVonne said.

Max slowly approached the sofa. "Then why is he hissing at me?"

"He senses your dislike," LaVonne explained. She gave Max a dazzling smile. "Pet him, and he'll be your friend for life."

"See, Dad?" Wynn walked over to LaVonne, who sat with Tom on her lap. He ran his hand down Tom's back and the tabby purred with pleasure.

"He likes you," Max said.

"He'll like you, too, as soon as you pet him." LaVonne was still smiling happily, stroking the cat's head.

Max came a bit closer. "You live in the building?" he asked, making his way, step by careful step, toward LaVonne.

"Just across the hall," she answered.

"Your husband, too?"

"I'm single. Do you enjoy cards? Because you're welcome to stop by anytime."

K.O. delivered the eggnog. This was going even better than she'd hoped. Max was already interested and LaVonne was issuing invitations. She recognized the gleam in the other man's eyes. A sense of triumph filled her and she cast a glance in Wynn's direction. Wynn was just reaching into his pocket, withdrawing a real-looking catnip mouse.

Relaxed now, Max leaned forward to pet Tom.

At that very moment, chaos broke out. Although La-

Vonne claimed she'd never known Tom to take a dislike to anyone, the cat clearly detested Max. Before anyone could react, he sprang from her lap and grabbed Max's bare arm. The cat's claws dug in, drawing blood. He wasn't about to let go, either.

"Get him off," Max screamed, thrashing his arm to and fro in an effort to free himself from the cat-turned-killer. Wynn was desperately—and futilely—trying to distract Tom by waving the toy mouse. It didn't help.

"Tom, Tom!" LaVonne screeched at the top of her lungs. Blood spurted onto the carpet.

In a panic, Max pulled at Tom's fur. The cat then sank his teeth into Max's hand and Max yelped in pain.

"Don't hurt my cat," LaVonne shrieked.

Frozen to the spot, K.O. watched in horror as the scene unfolded. Wynn dropped the mouse, and if not for his quick action, K.O. didn't know what would have happened. Before she could fully comprehend how he'd done it, Wynn had disentangled Tom from his father's arm. LaVonne instantly took her beloved cat into her embrace and cradled him against her side.

At the sight of his own blood, Max looked like he was about to pass out. K.O. hurriedly got him a clean towel, shocked at the amount of blood. The scratches seemed deep. "Call 911," Max shouted.

Wynn pulled out his cell phone. "That might not be a bad idea," he said to K.O. "Cat scratches can get infected."

"Contact the authorities, too," Max added, glaring at LaVonne. He stretched out his good arm and pointed at her. "I want that woman arrested and her animal destroyed."

LaVonne cried out with alarm and hovered protectively over Tom. "My poor kitty," she whispered.

"You're worried about the *cat?*" Max said. "I'm bleeding to death and you're worried about your cat?"

Wynn replaced his phone. "The medics are on their way."

"Oh...good." K.O. could already hear sirens in the background. She turned off her CD player. Thinking she should open the lobby door, she left the apartment, and when the aid car arrived, she directed the paramedics. Things had gotten worse in the short time she was gone. Max and LaVonne were shouting at each other as the small living room filled with people. Curious onlookers crowded the hallway outside her door.

"My cat scratched him and I'm sorry, but he provoked Tom," LaVonne said stubbornly.

"I want that woman behind bars." Max stabbed his finger in LaVonne's direction.

"Sir, sir, we need you to settle down," instructed the paramedic who was attempting to take his blood pressure.

"While she's in jail, declaw her cat," Max threw in.

Wynn stepped up behind K.O. "Yup," he whispered. "This is a match made in heaven, all right."

Then, just when K.O. was convinced nothing more could go wrong, her phone started to ring.

Chapter 12

"Don't you think you should answer that?" the paramedic treating Max's injuries asked.

K.O. was too upset to move. The romantic interlude she'd so carefully plotted couldn't have gone worse. At least Wynn seemed to understand her distress.

"I'll get it," Wynn said, and strode into the kitchen. "O'Connor residence," he said. At the way his eyes instantly shot to her, K.O. regretted not answering the phone herself.

"It's your sister," he said, holding the phone away from his ear.

Even above the racket K.O. could hear Zelda's high-pitched excitement. Her idol, Dr. Wynn Jeffries, had just spoken to her. The last person K.O. wanted to deal with just then was her younger sister. However, she couldn't subject Wynn to Zelda's adoration.

She took the phone, but even before she had a chance to speak, Zelda was shrieking, "Is it *really* you, Dr. Jeffries? Really and truly?"

"Actually, no," K.O. informed her sister. "It's me."

"But Dr. Jeffries is with you?"

"Yes."

"Keep him there!"

"I beg your pardon?"

"Don't let him leave," Zelda said, sounding even more excited. "I'm calling on my cell. I'm only a few minutes away." She took a deep breath. "I need to talk to him. It's urgent. Zach and I just had the biggest argument *ever,* and I need to talk to Dr. Jeffries."

"Zelda," K.O. cut in. "Now is not the best time for you to visit."

"Didn't you hear me?" her sister cried. "This is an emergency."

With that, the phone went dead. Groaning, K.O. replaced the receiver.

"Is something wrong?" Wynn asked as he stepped around the paramedic who was still looking after Max.

"It's Zelda. She wants—no, *needs*—to talk to you. According to her it's an emergency." K.O. felt the need to warn him. "She's already on her way."

"Now? You mean she's coming now?"

K.O. nodded. "Apparently so." Zelda hadn't mentioned what this argument with Zach was about. Three guesses said it had to do with Christmas and Wynn's theories. Oh, great. Her sister was arriving at the scene of a disaster.

"Are you taking him to the h-hospital?" LaVonne sobbed, covering her mouth with both hands.

"It's just a precaution," the medic answered. "A doctor needs to look at those scratches."

"Not that dreadful man!" LaVonne cried, pointing at Max. "I'm talking about my cat."

"Oh." The paramedic glanced at his companion. "Unfortunately, in instances such as this, we're obliged to notify Animal Control."

"You're hauling my Tom to…jail?"

"Quarantine," he told her gently.

For a moment LaVonne seemed about to faint. Wynn put his arm around the older woman's shoulders and led her to the sofa so she could sit down. "This can't be happening," LaVonne wailed. "I can't believe this is happening to my Tom."

"Your cat should be—"

Wynn cast his father a look meaningful enough to silence the rest of whatever Max had planned to say.

"I'm going to be scarred for life," Max shouted. "I just hope you've got good insurance, because you're going to pay for this. And you're going to pay big."

"Don't you dare threaten me!" LaVonne had recovered enough to shout back.

With his arm stretched out in front of him, Max Jeffries followed the paramedic out of the condo and past the crowd of tenants who'd gathered in the hallway outside K.O.'s door.

"That...that terrible man just threatened me," LaVonne continued. "Tom's never attacked anyone like this before."

"Please, please, let me through."

K.O. heard her sister's voice.

Meanwhile LaVonne was weeping loudly. "My poor Tom. My poor, poor Tom. What will become of him?"

"What on earth is going on here?" Zelda demanded as she made her way into the apartment. The second paramedic was gathering up his equipment and getting ready to leave. The blood-soaked towels K.O. had wrapped around Max's arm were on the floor. The scene was completely chaotic and Zelda's arrival only added to the mayhem.

"Your f-father wants to s-sue me," LaVonne stuttered, pleading with Wynn. "*Do* something. Promise me you'll talk to him."

Wynn sat next to LaVonne and tried to comfort her. "I'll do what I can," he said. "I'm sure that once my father's settled down he'll listen to reason."

LaVonne's eyes widened, as though she had trouble believing Wynn. "I don't mean to insult you, but your father doesn't seem like a reasonable man to me."

"Whose blood is that?" Zelda asked, hands on her hips as she surveyed the room.

K.O. tried to waylay her sister. "As you can see," she said, gesturing about her, "this *really* isn't a good time to visit."

"I don't care," Zelda insisted. "I need to talk to Dr. Jeffries." She thrust his book at him and a pen. "Could you sign this for me?"

Just then a man wearing a jacket that identified him as an Animal Control officer came in, holding an animal carrier. The name Walt was embroidered on his shirt.

Wynn quickly signed his name, all the while watching the man from Animal Control.

LaVonne took one look at Walt and burst into tears. She buried her face in her hands and started to rock back and forth.

"Where's the cat?" Walt asked.

"We've got him in the bathroom," the paramedic said.

"Please don't hurt him," LaVonne wept. "Please, please…"

Walt raised a reassuring hand. "I handle situations like this every day. Don't worry, Miss, I'll be gentle with your pet."

"Dr. Jeffries, Dr. Jeffries." Zelda slipped past K.O. and climbed over LaVonne's knees in order to reach Wynn. She plunked herself down on the coffee table, facing him. "I really do need to talk to you."

"Zelda!" K.O. was shocked by her sister's audacity.

"Zach and I never argue," Zelda said over her shoulder, glaring at K.O. as if that fact alone should explain her actions. "This will only take a few minutes, I promise. Once I talk to Dr. Jeffries, I'll be able to tell Zach what he said and then he'll understand."

LaVonne wailed as Walt entered the bathroom.

K.O. heard a hiss and wondered if her shower curtain was now in shreds. She'd never seen a cat react to anyone the way Tom had to Wynn's father. Even now she couldn't figure out what had set him off.

"This'll only take a minute," Zelda went on. "You see, my husband and I read your book, and it changed everything. Well, to be perfectly honest, I don't know if Zach read the whole book." A frown crossed her face.

"LaVonne, perhaps I should take you home now," K.O. suggested, thinking it might be best for her neighbor not to see Tom leave the building caged.

"I can't leave," LaVonne said. "Not until I know what's happening to Tom."

The bathroom door opened and Walt reappeared with Tom safely inside the cat carrier.

"Tom, oh, Tom," LaVonne wailed, throwing her arms wide.

"Dr. Jeffries, Dr. Jeffries," Zelda pleaded, vying for his attention.

"Zelda, couldn't this wait a few minutes?" K.O. asked.

"Where are you taking Tom?" LaVonne demanded.

"We're just going to put him in quarantine," Walt said in a soothing voice.

"Tom's had all his shots. My veterinarian will verify everything you need to know."

"Good. Still, we're legally required to do this. I guarantee he'll be well looked after."

"Thank you," K.O. said, relieved.

"Can I speak to Dr. Jeffries now?" Zelda asked impatiently. "You see, I don't think my husband really did read your book," she continued, picking up where she'd left off. "If he had, we wouldn't be having this disagreement."

"I'll see LaVonne home," K.O. said. She closed one arm around her friend's waist and steered her out of the condo.

Wynn looked at Zelda and sent K.O. a beseeching glance.

"I'll be back as soon as I can," she promised.

He nodded and mouthed the word *hurry*.

K.O. rolled her eyes. As she escorted LaVonne, the sound of her sister's voice followed her into the hallway, which was fortunately deserted. It didn't take long to get LaVonne settled in her own place. Once she had Phillip and Martin with her, she was comforted, since both seemed to recognize her distress and lavished their mistress with affection.

When she returned to her condo, K.O. found that her

sister hadn't moved. She still sat on the coffee table, so close to Wynn that their knees touched. Judging by the speed with which Zelda spoke, K.O. doubted he'd had a chance to get a word in edgewise.

"Then the girls started to cry," Zelda was saying. "They want a Christmas tree and Zach thinks we should get one."

"I don't believe—" Wynn was cut off before he could finish his thought.

"I know you don't actually condemn Christmas trees, but I didn't want to encourage the girls about this Santa thing, and I feel decorating a tree would do that. If we're going to bury Santa under the sleigh—and I'm in complete agreement with you, Dr. Jeffries—then it makes sense to downplay everything else having to do with Christmas, too. Certainly all the commercial aspects. But how do I handle the girls' reaction when they hear their friends talking about Santa?"

Wynn raised a finger, indicating that he'd like to comment. His request, however, was ignored.

"I feel as you do," Zelda rushed on breathlessly, bringing one hand to her chest in a gesture of sincerity. "It's wrong to mislead one's children with figures of fantasy. It's wrong, wrong, wrong. Zach agreed with me—but only in principle, as it turns out. Then we got into this big fight over the Christmas tree and you have to understand that my husband and I hardly ever argue, so this is all very serious."

"Where's Zach now?" K.O. asked, joining Wynn on the sofa.

As if to let her know how much he appreciated having her back, Wynn reached for her hand. At Zelda's obvious interest, he released it, but the contact, brief as it was, reassured her.

Zelda lowered her head. "Zach's at home with the girls. If you must know, I sort of left my husband with the twins."

"Zoe and Zara," K.O. said under her breath for Wynn's benefit.

"Despite my strong feelings on the matter, I suspect my husband is planning to take our daughters out to purchase a Christmas tree." She paused. "A *giant* one."

"Do you think he might even decorate it with Santa figurines and reindeer?" K.O. asked, pretending to be scandalized.

"Oh, I hope not," Zelda cried. "That would ruin everything I've tried so hard to institute in our family."

"As I recall," Wynn finally said. He waited a moment as if to gauge whether now was a good time to insert his opinions. When no one interrupted him, he continued. "I didn't say anything in my book against Christmas trees, giant or otherwise."

"Yes, I know that, but it seems to me—"

"It seems to *me* that you've carried this a bit further than advisable," Wynn said gently. "Despite what you and K.O.

think, I don't want to take Christmas away from your children or from you and your husband. It's a holiday to be celebrated. Family and traditions are important."

K.O. agreed with him. She felt gratified that there was common ground between them, an opinion on which they could concur. Nearly everything she'd heard about Wynn to this point had come from her sister. K.O. was beginning to wonder if Zelda was taking his advice to extremes.

"Besides," he said, "there's a fundamental contradiction in your approach. You're correct to minimize the element of fantasy—but your children are telling you what they want, aren't they? And you're ignoring that."

K.O. wanted to cheer. She took Wynn's hand again, and this time he didn't let go.

"By the way," Zelda said, looking from Wynn to K.O. and staring pointedly at their folded hands. "Just when did you two start dating?"

"I told you—"

"What you said," her sister broke in, "was that Dr. Jeffries lived in the same building as you."

"I told you we went to dinner a couple of times."

"You most certainly did not." Zelda stood up, an irritated expression on her face. "Well, okay, you did mention the one dinner at Chez Jerome."

"Did you know that I'm planning to join Katherine this Friday when she's watching the twins?" Wynn asked.

"She's bringing you along?" Zelda's eyes grew round

with shock. "You might've said something to me," she burst out, clearly upset with K.O.

"I thought I had told you."

"You haven't talked to me in days," Zelda wailed. "It's like I'm not even your sister anymore. The last I heard, you were going to get Dr. Jeffries's autograph for me, and you didn't, although I specifically asked if you would."

"Would you prefer I not watch the twins?" Wynn inquired.

"Oh, no! It would be an honor," Zelda assured him, smiling, her voice warm and friendly. She turned to face K.O. again, her eyes narrowed. "But my own sister," she hissed, "should've told me she intended on having a famous person spend the night in my home."

"You're not to tell anyone," K.O. insisted.

Zelda glared at her. "Fine. I won't."

"Promise me," K.O. said. Wynn was entitled to his privacy; the last thing he needed was a fleet of parents in SUVs besieging him about his book.

"I promise." Without a further word, Zelda grabbed her purse and made a hasty exit.

"Zelda!" K.O. called after her. "I think we need to talk about this for a minute."

"I don't have a minute. I need to get home to my husband and children. We'll talk later," Zelda said in an ominous tone, and then she was gone.

Chapter 13

"I'd better leave now, as well," Wynn announced, getting his coat. "Dad'll need me to drive him back from the emergency room." K.O. was glad he didn't seem eager to go.

For her part, she wanted him to stay. Her nerves were frayed. Nothing had worked out as she'd planned and now everyone was upset with her. LaVonne, her dear friend, was inconsolable. Zelda was annoyed that K.O. hadn't kept her updated on the relationship with Wynn. Max Jeffries was just plain angry, and while the brunt of his anger had been directed at LaVonne, K.O. realized he wasn't pleased with her, either. Now Wynn had to go. Reluctantly K.O. walked him to the door. "Let me know how your father's doing, okay?" she asked, looking up at him.

"Of course." Wynn placed his hands on her shoulders. "You know I'd much rather be here with you."

She saw the regret in his eyes and didn't want to make matters worse. "Thank you for being so wonderful," she said and meant it. Wynn had been the voice of calm and reason throughout this entire ordeal.

"I'll call you about my father as soon as I hear."

"Thank you."

After a brief hug, he hurried out the door.

After a dinner of eggnog and peanut butter on crackers, K.O. waited up until after midnight, but no word came. Finally, when she couldn't keep her eyes open any longer, she climbed between the sheets and fell instantly asleep. This surprised her; she hadn't anticipated sleeping easily or well. When she woke the following morning, the first thoughts that rushed into her mind were of Wynn. Something must have happened, something unexpected and probably dreadful, or he would've called.

Perhaps the hospital had decided to keep Max overnight for observation. While there'd been a lot of blood involved, K.O. didn't think any of the cuts were deep enough to require stitches. But if Max had filed a police report, that would cause problems for LaVonne and might explain Wynn's silence. Every scenario that roared through her head pointed to trouble.

Even before she made her first cup of coffee, K.O.'s stomach was in knots. As she headed into the kitchen, she discovered a sealed envelope that had been slipped under her door.

It read:

Katherine,
I didn't get back from the hospital until late and I was afraid
you'd already gone to bed. Dad's home and, other than being
cantankerous, he's doing fine, so don't worry on his account.
The hospital cleaned and bandaged his arm and said he'd
be good as new in a week or so. Please reassure LaVonne.
The cuts looked worse than they actually were.

Could you stop by my office this afternoon? I'm at the
corner of Fourth and Willow, Suite 1110. Does one o'clock
work for you? If you can't fit it into your schedule, please
contact my assistant and let her know. Otherwise, I'll look
forward to seeing you, then.

Wynn

Oh, she could fit it in. She could *definitely* fit it in. K.O. was ready to climb Mount Rainier for a chance to see Wynn. With purpose now, she showered and dressed and then, on the off chance Max might need something, she phoned Wynn's condo.

His father answered right away, which made her wonder if he'd been sitting next to the phone waiting for a call.

"Good morning," she said, striving to sound cheerful and upbeat—all the while hoping Max wasn't one to hold grudges.

"Who is this?"

"It's K.O.," she told him, her voice faltering despite her effort to maintain a cheery tone.

He hesitated as if he needed time to place who she might be. "Oh," he finally said. "The woman from downstairs. The woman whose *friend* caused me irreparable distress." After another pause, he said, "I'm afraid I might be suffering from trauma-induced amnesia."

"Excuse me?" K.O. was sure she'd misunderstood.

"I was attacked yesterday by a possibly rabid beast and am fortunate to be alive. I don't remember much after that vicious animal sank its claws into my arm," he added shakily.

K.O. closed her eyes for a moment. "I'm so sorry to hear that," she said, going along with it. "But the hospital released you, I see."

"Yes." This was said with disdain; apparently, he felt the medical profession had made a serious error in judgment. "I'm on heavy pain medication."

"Oh, dear."

"I don't know where my son's gone," he muttered fretfully.

If Wynn hadn't told his father he was at the office, then K.O. wasn't about to, either. She suspected Wynn had good reason to escape.

"Since you live in the building…" Max began.

"Uh…" She could see it coming. Max wanted her to sit and hold his uninjured hand for the rest of the day.

"I do, but unfortunately I'm on my way out."

"Oh."

It took K.O. a few more minutes to wade through the guilt he was shoveling in her direction. "I'll drop by and check on you later," she promised.

"Thank you," he said, ending their conversation with a groan, a last shovelful of guilt.

K.O. hung up the phone, groaning, too. This was even worse than she'd imagined and she had a fine imagination. Max was obviously playing this incident for all it was worth. Irreparable distress. Rabid beast. Trauma-induced amnesia! Oh, brother.

Wanting to leave before Max decided to drop by, she hurried out the door and stopped at the French Café for a mocha and bran muffin. If ever she'd deserved one, it was now. At the rate her life was going, there wouldn't be enough peppermint mochas in the world to see her through another day like yesterday.

Rather than linger as she normally did, K.O. took her drink and muffin to go and enjoyed a leisurely stroll down Blossom Street. A walk would give her exercise and clear her mind, and just then clarity was what she needed. She admired the evergreen boughs and garlands decorating the storefronts, and the inventive variations on Christmas themes in every window. The weather remained unseasonably cold with a chance of snow flurries. In December Seattle was usually in the grip of gloomy winter rains, but that hadn't happened yet this year. The sky was already a clear blue with puffy clouds scattered about.

By the time she'd finished her peppermint mocha, K.O. had walked a good mile and felt refreshed in both body and mind. When she entered her building, La-Vonne—wearing a housecoat—was stepping out of her condo to grab the morning paper. Her eyes were red and puffy and it looked as if she hadn't slept all night. She bent over to retrieve her paper.

"LaVonne," K.O. called out.

Her friend slowly straightened. "I thought I should see if there's a report in the police blotter about Tom scratching that…that man," she spat out.

"I doubt it."

"Is he…back from the hospital?"

"Max Jeffries is alive and well. He sustained a few scratches, but it isn't nearly as bad as we all feared." Wynn's father seemed to be under the delusion that he'd narrowly escaped with his life, but she didn't feel the need to mention that. Nor did K.O. care to enlighten LaVonne regarding Max's supposed amnesia.

"I'm so glad." LaVonne sounded tired and sad.

"Is there anything I can get you?" K.O. asked, feeling partially to blame.

"Thanks for asking, but I'm fine." She gave a shuddering sob. "Except for poor Tom being in jail…"

"Call if you need me," K.O. said before she returned to her own apartment.

The rest of the morning passed quickly. She worked for a solid two hours and accomplished more in that brief time than she normally did in four. She finished a medical report, sent off some résumés by e-mail and drafted a Christmas letter for a woman in Zach's office who'd made a last-minute request. Then, deciding she should check on Max Jeffries, she went up for a quick visit. At twelve-thirty, she grabbed her coat and headed out the door again. With her hands buried deep in her red wool coat and a candy-cane striped scarf doubled around her neck, she walked to Wynn's office.

This was her first visit there, and she wasn't sure what to expect. When she stepped inside, she found a comfortable waiting room and thought it looked like any doctor's office.

A middle-aged receptionist glanced up and smiled warmly. "You must be Katherine," she said, extending her hand. "I'm Lois Church, Dr. Jeffries's assistant."

"Hello," K.O. said, returning her smile.

"Come on back. Doctor is waiting for you." Lois led her to a large room, lined with bookshelves and framed degrees. A big desk dominated one end, and there was a sitting area on the other side, complete with a miniature table and chairs and a number of toys.

Wynn stood in front of the bookcase, and when K.O. entered the room, he closed the volume he'd been reading and put it back in place.

Lois slipped quietly out of the room and shut the door.

"Hi," K.O. said tentatively, wondering at his mood.

He smiled. "I see you received my note."

"Yes," she said with a nod. She remained standing just inside his office.

"I asked you to come here to talk about my father. I'm afraid he's going a little overboard with all of this."

"I got that impression myself."

Wynn arched his brows. "You've spoken to him?"

She nodded again. "I stopped by to see how he's doing. He didn't seem to remember me right away. He says he's suffering from memory loss."

Wynn groaned.

"I hate to say this, but I assumed that hypochondria's what he's really suffering from." She paused. "Either that or he's faking it," she said boldly.

Wynn gave a dismissive shrug. "I believe your second diagnosis is correct. It's a recurring condition of his," he said with a wry smile.

K.O. didn't know quite what to say.

"He's exaggerating, looking for attention." Wynn motioned for her to sit down, which she did, sinking into the luxurious leather sofa. Wynn took the chair next to it. "I don't mean to sound unsympathetic, but for all his easygoing hippie ways, Moon Puppy—Max—can be quite the manipulator."

"Well, it's not like LaVonne did it on purpose or anything."

There was a moment's silence. "In light of what happened yesterday, do you still want me to accompany you to your sister's?" he asked.

K.O. would be terribly disappointed if he'd experienced a change of heart. "I hoped you would, but if you need to bow out because of your father, I understand."

"No," he said decisively. "I want to do this. It's important for us both, for our relationship."

K.O. felt the same way.

"I've already told my father that I have a business appointment this weekend, so he knows I'll be away."

That made K.O. smile. This *was* business. Sort of.

"I'd prefer that Max not know the two of us will be together. He'll want to join us and, frankly, dealing with him will be more work than taking care of the kids."

"All right." Despite a bit of residual guilt, K.O. was certainly willing to abide by his wishes. She was convinced that once Wynn spent time with Zoe and Zara, he'd know for himself that his theories didn't work. The twins and their outrageous behavior would speak more eloquently than she ever could.

"I'm afraid we might not have an opportunity to get together for the rest of the week."

She was unhappy about it but understood. With his injuries and need for attention, Max would dominate Wynn's time.

"Are you sure your father will be well enough by Friday for you to leave?" she asked.

"He'd better be," Wynn said firmly, "because I'm going. He'll survive. In case you hadn't already figured this out, he's a little…immature."

"Really?" she asked, feigning surprise. Then she laughed out loud.

Wynn smiled, too. "I'm going to miss you, Katherine," he said with a sigh. "I wish I could see you every day this week, but between work and Max…"

"I'll miss you, too."

Wynn checked his watch and K.O. realized that was her signal to go. Wynn had appointments.

They both stood.

"Before I forget," he said casually. "A friend of mine told me his company's looking for a publicist. It's a small publisher, Apple Blossom Books, right in the downtown area, not far from here."

"They are?" K.O.'s heart raced with excitement. A small publishing company would be ideal. "Really?"

"I mentioned your name, and Larry asked if you'd be willing to send in a résumé." Wynn picked up a business card from his desk and handed it to her. "You can e-mail it directly to him."

"Oh, Wynn, thank you." In her excitement, she hugged him.

That seemed to be all the encouragement he needed to keep her in his arms and kiss her. She responded with equal fervor, and it made her wonder how she could possibly go another three days until she saw him again.

They smiled at each other. Wynn threaded his fingers through her hair and brought his mouth to hers for another, deeper kiss.

A polite knock at the door was followed by the sound of it opening.

Abruptly Wynn released her, taking a step back. "Yes, Lois," he said, still looking at K.O.

"Your one-thirty appointment has arrived."

"I'll be ready in just a minute," he said. As soon as the door was shut, he leaned close, touching his forehead to hers. "I'd better get back to work."

"Me, too." But it was with real reluctance that they drew apart.

As K.O. left, glancing at the surly teen being ushered into his office, she felt that Friday couldn't come soon enough.

Chapter 14

On Thursday afternoon, LaVonne invited K.O. for afternoon tea, complete with a plate of sliced fruitcake. "I'm feeling much better," her neighbor said as she poured tea into mugs decorated with cats in Santa costumes. "I've been allowed to visit Tom, and he's doing so well. In a couple of days, he'll be back home where he belongs." She frowned as if remembering Wynn's father. "No thanks to that dreadful man who had Tom taken away from me."

K.O. sat on the sofa and held her mug in one hand and a slice of fruitcake in the other. "I'm so pleased to hear Tom will be home soon." Her conscience had been bothering her, and for the sake of their friendship, K.O. felt the need to confess what she'd done.

"The best part is I haven't seen that maniac all week," LaVonne was saying.

K.O. gave her neighbor a tentative smile and lowered her gaze. She hadn't seen Max, either. Or Wynn, except for that brief visit to his office, although they'd e-mailed each other a couple of times. He'd kept her updated on his father and the so-called memory loss, from which Max had apparently made a sudden recovery. In fact, he now remembered a little too much, according to Wynn. But the wounds on his arm appeared to be healing nicely and Max seemed to enjoy the extra attention Wynn paid him. Wynn, meanwhile, was looking forward to the reprieve offered by their visit to Zelda's.

"I owe you an apology," K.O. said to LaVonne.

"Nonsense. You had no way of knowing how Tom would react to Mr. Jeffries."

"True, but…" She swallowed hard. "You should know…" She started again. "I didn't really have a psychic experience."

LaVonne set down her mug and stared at K.O. "You didn't actually see a man for me in the soup? You mean to say there *wasn't* any message in the cracker crumbs?"

"No," K.O. admitted.

"Oh."

"It might seem like I was making fun of you and your psychic abilities, but I wasn't, LaVonne, I truly wasn't I thought that if you believed a man was coming into your life, you'd be looking for one, and if you were expecting to meet a man, then you just might, and I hoped that man would be Wynn's father, but clearly it wasn't…isn't." This was said without pausing for breath.

A short silence ensued, followed by a disappointed, "Oh."

"Forgive me if I offended you."

LaVonne took a moment to think this through. "You didn't," she said after a while. "I've more or less reached the same conclusion about my psychic abilities. But—" she smiled brightly "—guess what? I've signed up for another class in January." She reached for a second slice of fruitcake and smiled as Martin brought K.O. the catnip mouse Wynn had given Tom that ill-fated evening.

"Another one at the community college?" K.O. asked.

LaVonne shook her head. "No, I walked across the street into A Good Yarn and decided I'd learn how to knit."

"That sounds good."

"Want to come, too?" LaVonne asked.

Every time her friend enrolled in a new course, she urged K.O. to take it with her. Because of finances and her job search, K.O. had always declined. This time, however, she felt she might be able to swing it. Not to mention the fact that she owed LaVonne… "I'll see."

"Really?" Even this little bit of enthusiasm seemed to delight LaVonne. "That's wonderful."

"I had a job interview on Wednesday," K.O. told her, squelching the desire to pin all her hopes on this one interview. Apple Blossom Books, the publisher Wynn had recommended, had called her in almost immediately. She'd met with the president and the marketing manager, and they'd promised to get back to her before Christmas. For the first time in a long while, K.O. felt optimistic. A publishing company, even a small one, would be ideal.

"And?" LaVonne prompted.

"And…" K.O. said, smiling. "I'm keeping my fingers crossed."

"That's just great! I know you've been looking for ages."

"The Christmas letters are going well, too," she added. "I wrote another one this week for a woman in Zach's office. She kept thinking she had time and then realized she didn't, so it was a rush job."

"You might really be on to something, you know. A little sideline business every Christmas."

"You aren't upset with me about what I did, are you?" K.O. asked, returning to her apology. "You've been such a good friend, and I wouldn't do anything in the world to hurt you."

"Nah," LaVonne assured her, petting Phillip, who'd jumped into her lap. "If anyone's to blame it's that horrible man. As far as I'm concerned, he's a fruitcake." That said, she took another bite of the slice she'd been enjoying.

* * *

Wynn had devised a rather complicated plan of escape. On Friday afternoon he would leave his office at three-thirty and pick K.O. up on the corner of Blossom Street and Port Avenue. Because he didn't want to risk going inside and being seen by his father, she'd agreed to wait on the curb with her overnight bag.

K.O. was packed and ready long before the time they'd arranged. At three, her phone rang. Without checking caller ID, she knew it had to be her sister.

"I can't believe Dr. Wynn Jeffries is actually coming to the house," she said and gave a shrill cry of excitement. "You can't *imagine* how jealous my friends are."

"No one's supposed to know about this," K.O. reminded her.

"No one knows exactly when he'll be here, but I did mention it to a few close friends."

"Zelda! You promised."

"I know, I know. I'm sorry, but I couldn't keep this to myself. You just don't understand what an honor it is to have Dr. Jeffries in my home."

"But…"

"Don't worry, no one knows it's this weekend," Zelda told her.

"You're *sure?*"

"I swear, all right?"

It would be a nightmare if a few dozen of Zelda's closest friends just happened to drop by the house unannounced. Unfortunately, K.O. didn't have any choice but to believe her.

"How are the girls?" K.O. asked, hoping the twins were up to their usual antics. She didn't want Zoe and Zara to be on their best behavior. That would ruin all her plans.

"They're fine. Well, mostly fine. Healthwise, they're both getting over ear infections."

Oh, dear. "You might've told me this before!" K.O. cried. Her mind shifted into overdrive. If the girls were sick, it would throw everything off. Wynn would insist their behavior was affected by how they were feeling.

"They've been on antibiotics for the last two weeks," Zelda said, breaking into her thoughts. "The doctor explained how important it is to finish the medicine, and they only have a couple of doses left. I wrote it all down for you and Dr. Jeffries, so there's no need to worry."

"Fine," K.O. said, relieved. "Anything else you're not telling me?"

Her sister went silent for a moment. "I can't think of anything. I've got a list of instructions for you and the phone numbers where we can be reached. I do appreciate this, you know."

K.O. in turn appreciated the opportunity to spend this time with the twins—and to share the experience with Wynn. At least they'd be able to stop tiptoeing around the subject of the Free Child movement.

"We have a Christmas tree," Zelda murmured as if she were admitting to a weakness of character. "Zach felt we needed one, and when I spoke to Dr. Jeffries last Monday he didn't discourage it. So I gave in, although I'm still not sure it's such a good idea."

"You made the right choice," K.O. told her.

"I hope so."

K.O. noticed the clock on her microwave and was shocked to see that it was time to meet Wynn. "Oh, my goodness, I've got to go. I'll see you in about thirty minutes."

K.O. hung up the phone and hurried to put on her long wool coat, hat and scarf. Grabbing her purse and overnight bag, she rushed outside. Traffic was heavy, and it was already getting dark. She'd planned to be waiting at the curb so when Wynn pulled up, she could quickly hop inside his car. Then they'd be on their way, with no one the wiser.

No sooner had she stepped out of the building than she saw Max Jeffries walking toward her. His cheeks were ruddy, as if he'd been out for a long stroll.

"Well, hello there, Katherine," he said cheerfully. "How are you this fine cold day?"

"Ah…" She glanced furtively around. "I'm going to my sister's tonight," she said when he looked pointedly at her small suitcase.

"Wynn's away himself."

"Pure coincidence," she told him and realized how guilty she sounded.

Max chuckled. "Business trip, he said."

She nodded, moving slowly toward the nearby corner of Blossom and Port. She kept her gaze focused on the street, fearing she was about to give everything away.

"I'm healing well," Max told her conversationally. "I had a couple of rough days, but the pain is much better now."

"I'm glad to hear it."

"Yes, me, too. I never want to see that crazy cat woman again as long as I live."

It demanded restraint not to immediately defend her friend, but K.O. managed. "I see your memory's back," she said instead, all the while keeping a lookout for Wynn.

"Oh, yes, it returned within a day or two. In some ways," he sighed, "I wished it hadn't. Because now all I can think about is how that vicious feline latched on to my arm."

Not wanting to give Max an excuse to continue the conversation, K.O. threw him a vague smile.

"Have you ever seen so much blood in your life?" he said with remarkable enthusiasm.

"Uh, no," she murmured. Since it was her towels that had cleaned it up, she had to confess there'd been lots.

"My son seems to be quite taken with you," Max said next.

As badly as she wanted to urge Max to go about his

business, K.O. couldn't ignore that particular comment. Not when Max dropped this little morsel at her feet—much as Martin had presented her with the catnip mouse. "He does? Really?"

Max nodded.

"He talks about me?"

"Hmm. It's more a question of what he doesn't say than what he does. He was always an intense child. As a youngster… Well, I'm sure you don't have time to go into that right now."

K.O. thought she could see Wynn's car. "I don't… I'm sorry."

"Take my word for it, Wynn's interested in you."

K.O. felt like dancing in the street. "I'm interested in him, too," she admitted.

"Good, good," Max said expansively. "Well, I'd better get back inside. Have a nice weekend."

"I will. Thank you." It did look like Wynn's car. His timing was perfect—or almost. She hoped that when he reached the curb, his father would be inside the building.

Just then the front doors opened and out stepped La-Vonne. She froze in midstep when she saw Wynn's father. He froze, too.

K.O. watched as LaVonne's eyes narrowed. She couldn't see Max's face, but from LaVonne's reaction, she assumed he shared her resentment. They seemed unwilling to walk past each other, and both stood there, looking wildly in all directions except ahead. If it hadn't been so sad, it would've been laughable.

K.O. could see that it was definitely Wynn's car. He smiled when he saw her and started to ease toward the curb. At the same moment, he noticed his father and La-Vonne and instantly pulled back, merging into traffic again. He drove straight past K.O.

Now LaVonne and Max were staring at each other. They still hadn't moved, and people had to walk around them as they stood in the middle of the sidewalk.

K.O. had to find a way to escape without being de-tected. As best as she could figure, Wynn had to drive around the block. With one-way streets and heavy traf-fic, it might take him ten minutes to get back to Blos-som. If she hurried, she might catch him on Port Avenue or another side street and avoid letting Max see them to-gether.

"I think my ride's here," she said, backing away and dragging her suitcase with her.

They ignored her.

"Bye," she said, waving her hand.

This, too, went without comment. "I'll see you both later," she said, rushing past them and down the sidewalk.

Again there was no response.

K.O. didn't dare look back. Blossom Street had never seemed so long. She rounded the corner and walked some distance down Port, waiting until she saw Wynn's car again. Raising her arm as if hailing a taxi, she managed to catch his attention.

Wynn pulled up to the curb, reached over and opened the passenger door. "That was a close call," he murmured as she climbed inside.

"You have no idea," she said, shaking her head.

"Is everything all right?" he asked.

"I don't know and, frankly, I don't want to stick around and find out."

Wynn chuckled. "I don't, either," he said, rejoining the stream of traffic.

They were off on what she hoped would be a grand adventure in the land of Z.

Chapter 15

"This is Zoe," K.O. said as her niece wrapped one arm around her leg. After a half-hour of instructions, Zelda was finally out the door, on her way to meet Zach at the hotel. The twins stood like miniature statues, dressed in jean coveralls and red polka-dot shirts, with their hair in pigtails. They each stared up at Wynn.

"No, I'm Zara."

K.O. narrowed her eyes, unsure whether to believe the child. The twins were identical and seemed to derive great satisfaction from fooling people, especially their parents.

"Zoe," K.O. challenged. "Tell the truth."

"I'm hungry."

"It'll be dinnertime soon," K.O. promised.

Zoe—and she felt sure it *was* Zoe—glared up at her. "I'm hungry *now*. I want to eat *now*." She punctuated her demand by stamping her foot. Her twin joined in, shouting that she, too, was hungry.

"I want dinner *now*," Zara insisted.

Wynn smiled knowingly. "Children shouldn't be forced to eat on a schedule. If they're hungry, we should feed them no matter what the clock says."

Until then, the girls had barely acknowledged Wynn. All of a sudden, he was their best friend. Both beamed brilliant smiles in his direction, then marched over and stood next to him, as though aligning themselves with his theories.

"What would you like for dinner?" he asked, squatting down so he was at eye level with them.

"Hot dogs," Zoe said, and Zara agreed. The two Yorkies, Zero and Zorro, seemed to approve, because they barked loudly and then scampered into the kitchen.

"I'll check the refrigerator," K.O. told him. Not long ago, Zelda hadn't allowed her daughters anywhere near hot dogs. She considered them unhealthy, low-quality fare that was full of nitrates and other preservatives. But nothing was off limits since Zelda had read *The Free Child* and become a convert.

"I'll help you look," Zara volunteered and tearing into the kitchen, threw open the refrigerator door and peered inside.

Not wanting to be left out, Zoe dragged over a

kitchen chair and climbed on top. She yanked open the freezer and started tossing frozen food onto the floor. Zero and Zorro scrambled to get out of the way of flying frozen peas and fish.

"There aren't any hot dogs," K.O. said after a few minutes. "Let's choose something else." After all, it was only four o'clock and she was afraid that if the girls ate too early, they'd be hungry again later in the evening.

"I *want* a hot dog," Zara shouted.

"Me, too," Zoe chimed in, as though eating wieners was a matter of eternal significance.

Wynn stood in the kitchen doorway. "I can run to the store."

K.O. couldn't believe her ears. She hated to see him cater to the whims of Zoe and Zara, but far be it from her to object. If he was willing to go to those lengths to get the twins the meal they wanted, she'd let him do it.

"Isn't that nice of Dr. Jeffries?" K.O. asked her nieces.

Both girls ignored her and Wynn.

K.O. followed him into the other room, where Wynn retrieved his jacket from the hall closet. "I'll be back soon," he said.

"I'll put together a salad and—"

"Let the girls decide if they want a salad," Wynn interrupted. "Given the option, children will choose a well-balanced diet on their own. We as adults shouldn't be making these decisions for them."

K.O. had broken down and bought a copy of *The Free Child* at a small bookstore that had recently opened on Blossom Street. She'd skimmed it last night, so she knew this advice was in the book, stated in exactly those words. She might not approve, but for tonight she was determined to follow his lead. So she kept her mouth shut. Not that it was easy.

While the girls were occupied, he planted a gentle kiss on her lips, smiled and then was out the door.

It was now three days since they'd been able to spend time together. With that one short kiss, a lovely warmth spread through her. She closed the door after him and was leaning against it when she noticed that the twins had turned to stare at her. "While we're waiting for Wynn to get back, would you like me to read you a story?" she asked. The salad discussion could wait.

The girls readily agreed, and the three of them settled on the sofa. She was only a few pages into the book when both Zoe and Zara slumped over, asleep. Before Zelda left, she'd said the twins had been awake since five that morning, excited about Katherine's visit. Apparently they no longer took naps. This was something else Wynn had advised. Children would sleep when they needed to, according to him. Regimented naptimes stifled children's ability to understand their internal clocks. Well, Zoe and Zara's clocks had obviously wound down—and K.O. was grateful.

The quiet was so blissful that she leaned her head back

and rested her own eyes. The tranquility didn't last long, however. In less than fifteen minutes, Wynn was back from the store, carrying a plastic bag with wieners and fresh buns. The dogs barked frantically as he entered the house, waking both children.

"Here they are," he announced as if he brandished an Olympic gold medal.

Zara yawned. "I'm not hungry anymore."

"Me, neither," Zoe added.

It probably wasn't the most tactful thing to do, but K.O. smiled triumphantly.

"That's okay. We can wait until later," Wynn said, completely unfazed.

He really was good with the girls and seemed to enjoy spending time with them. While K.O. set the kitchen table and cleared away the clutter that had accumulated everywhere, Wynn sat down and talked to the twins. The girls showed him the Christmas tree and the stockings that hung over the fireplace and the nativity scene set up on the formal dining room table.

K.O. heard Zoe mention her imaginary horse named Blackie. Not to be outdone, Zara declared that *her* imaginary horse was named Brownie. Wynn listened to them seriously and even scooted over to make room for the horses on the sofa. K.O. was grateful that Wynn was sharing responsibility for the girls, whose constant demands quickly drained her.

"I'm hungry now," Zoe informed them half an hour later.

"I'll start the hot dogs," K.O. said, ready for dinner herself.

"I want pancakes."

"With syrup," Zara said. Zoe nodded.

K.O. looked at Wynn, who shrugged as if it was no big deal.

"Then pancakes it is," K.O. agreed. She'd let him cope with the sugar high. For the next ten minutes she was busy mixing batter and frying the pancakes. The twins wanted chocolate syrup and strawberry jam on top, with bananas and granola. Actually, it didn't taste nearly as bad as K.O. had feared.

According to her sister's instructions, the girls were to be given their medication with meals. After dinner, Zoe and Zara climbed down from their chairs. When K.O. asked them to take their plates to the sink, they complied without an argument or even a complaint.

"Time for your medicine," K.O. told them next. She removed two small bottles filled with pink antibiotic from the refrigerator.

The two girls raced about the kitchen, shrieking, with the dogs yapping at their heels. They seemed incapable of standing still.

"Girls," K.O. ordered sternly. "Take your medicine and then you can run around." The way they were dashing back and forth, it was difficult to see who was who.

Zara skidded to a stop and dutifully opened her mouth. Carefully measuring out the liquid, K.O. filled the spoon and popped it into the child's mouth. Immediately afterward, the twins took off in a frenzied race around the kitchen table.

"Zoe," K.O. said, holding the second bottle and a clean spoon and waiting for the mayhem to die down so she could dispense the correct dose to her other niece. "Your turn."

The twin appeared in front of her, mouth open. K.O. poured medicine onto the spoon. About to give it to Zoe, she hesitated. "You're not Zoe. You're Zara."

"I'm Zoe," she insisted. Although the girls were identical, K.O. could usually tell one from the other, partly by their personalities. Zara had the stronger, more dominant nature. "Are you sure?" she asked.

The little girl nodded vigorously. Uncertain, K.O. reluctantly gave her the medication. The twins continued to chase each other about the kitchen, weaving their way around and between Wynn and K.O. The dogs dashed after them, yapping madly.

Wynn asked, "Is everything all right?"

K.O. still held the empty spoon. "I have a horrible feeling I just gave two doses to the same girl."

"You can trust the twins to tell you the truth," Wynn pronounced. "Children instinctively know when it's important to tell the truth."

"Really?" K.O. couldn't help worrying.

"Of course. It's in the book," Wynn said as if quoting Scripture.

"You didn't feed Blackie and Brownie," Zara cried when K.O. tossed the leftover pancakes in the garbage.

"Then we must." Wynn proceeded to remove the cold pancakes and tear them into small pieces. Zero and Zorro leaped off the ground in an effort to snatch up the leftovers. Zoe and Zara sat on the floor and fed the dogs and supposedly their imaginary pets, as well.

The yapping dogs were giving K.O. a headache. "How about if I turn on the television," she suggested, shouting to be heard above the racket made by the girls and the dogs.

The twins hollered their approval, but the show that flashed onto the screen was a Christmas cartoon featuring none other than Santa himself. Jolly old soul that he was, Santa laughed and loaded his sleigh while the girls watched with rapt attention. Knowing how her sister felt, K.O. figured this was probably the first time they'd seen Santa all season. K.O. glanced at Wynn, who was frowning back.

"Let's see what else is on," K.O. said quickly.

"I want to watch Santa," Zoe shouted.

"Me, too," Zara muttered.

Wynn sat on the sofa between them and wrapped his arms around their small shoulders. "This show is about a character called Santa Claus," he said in a solicitous voice.

Both girls were far too involved in the program to be easily distracted by adult conversation.

"Sometimes mommies and daddies like to make believe, and while they don't mean to lie, they can mislead their children," he went on.

Zoe briefly tore her gaze away from the television screen. "Like Santa, you mean?"

Wynn smiled. "Like Santa," he agreed.

"We know he's not real," Zoe informed them with all the wisdom of a five-year-old.

"Santa is really Mommy and Daddy," Zara explained. "*Everyone* knows that."

"They do?"

Both girls nodded.

Zoe's eyes turned serious. "We heard Mommy and Daddy fighting about Santa and we almost told them it doesn't matter 'cause we already know."

"We like getting gifts from him, though," Zara told them.

"Yeah, I like Santa," Zoe added.

"But he's not real," Wynn said, sounding perfectly logical.

"Mommy's real," Zara argued. "And Daddy, too."

"Yes, but..." Wynn seemed determined to argue further, but stopped when he happened to glance at K.O. He held her gaze a moment before looking away.

K.O. did her best to keep quiet, but apparently Wynn

realized how difficult that was, because he clammed up fast enough.

The next time she looked at the twins, Zara had slumped over to one side, eyes drooping. K.O. gently shook the little girl's shoulders but Zara didn't respond. Still fearing she might have given one twin a double dose of the antibiotic, she knelt down in front of the other child.

"Zoe," she asked, struggling to keep the panic out of her voice. "Did you get your medicine or did Zara swallow both doses?"

Zoe grinned and pantomimed zipping her mouth closed.

"Zoe," K.O. said again. "This is important. We can't play games when medicine is involved." So much for Wynn's theory that children instinctively knew when it was necessary to tell the truth.

"Zara likes the taste better'n me."

"Did you take your medicine or did Zara take it for you?" Wynn asked.

Zoe smiled and shook her head, indicating that she wasn't telling.

Zara snored, punctuating the conversation.

"Did you or did you not take your medicine?" Wynn demanded, nearly yelling.

Tears welled in Zoe's eyes. She buried her face in K.O.'s lap and refused to answer Wynn.

"This isn't a joke," he muttered, clearly losing his patience with the twins.

"Zoe," K.O. cautioned. "You heard Dr. Jeffries. It's important for us to know if you took your medication."

The little girl raised her head, then slowly nodded. "It tastes bad, but I swallowed it all down."

"Good." Relief flooded K.O. "Thank you for telling the truth."

"I don't like your friend," she said, sticking her tongue out at Wynn. "He yells."

"I only yelled because...you made me," Wynn countered. He marched to the far side of the room, and K.O. reflected that he didn't sound so calm and reasonable anymore.

"Why don't we all play a game?" she suggested.

Zara raised her head sleepily from the sofa edge. "Can we play Old Maid?" she asked, yawning.

"I want to play Candyland," Zoe mumbled.

"Why don't we play both?" K.O. said, and they did. In fact, they played for two hours straight, watched television and then drank hot chocolate.

"Shall we take a bath now?" K.O. asked, hoping that would tire the girls out enough to want to go to bed. She didn't know where they got their stamina, but her own was fading rapidly.

The twins were eager to do something altogether different and instantly raced out of the room.

Wynn looked like he could use a break—and he hadn't even seen them at their most challenging. All in all, the girls were exhibiting good behavior, or what passed for good in the regime of the Free Child.

"I'll run the bath water," K.O. told Wynn as he gathered up the cards and game pieces. Had she been on her own, K.O. would have insisted the twins pick up after themselves.

While the girls were occupied in their bedroom, she put on a Christmas CD she particularly liked and started the bath. When she glanced into the living room, she saw Wynn collapsed on the sofa, legs stretched out.

"It hasn't been so bad," he said, as though that was proof his theories were working well. "As soon as the twins are down, we can talk," he murmured, "about us..."

K.O. wasn't ready for that, feeling he should spend more time with the girls. She felt honor-bound to remind Wynn of what he'd written in his book. "Didn't you say that children know when they need sleep and we as adults should trust them to set their own schedules?"

He seemed about to argue with her, but then abruptly sat up and pointed across the room. "What's that?"

A naked dog strolled into the living room. Rather, a hairless dog.

"Zero? Zorro?" K.O. asked. "Oh, my goodness!" She dashed into the bathroom to discover Zara sitting on the floor with Wynn's electric shaver. A pile of brown-and-black dog hair littered the area.

"What happened?" Wynn cried, hard on her heels. His mouth fell open when he saw the girls intent on their task. They'd gone through his toiletries, which were spread across the countertop next to the sink. K.O. realized that the hum of the shaver had been concealed by the melodious strains of "Silent Night." "What are you doing?"

"We're giving haircuts," Zara announced. "Do you want one?"

Chapter 16

Two hours later, at ten-thirty, both Zoe and Zara were in their beds and asleep. This was no small accomplishment. After half a dozen stories, the girls were finally down for the night. K.O. tiptoed out of the room and as quietly as possible closed the door. Wynn was just ahead of her and looked as exhausted as she felt.

Zero regarded K.O. forlornly from the hallway. The poor dog had been almost completely shaved. He stared up at her, hairless and shivering. Zorro still had half his hair. The Yorkshire terrier's left side had been sheared before K.O. managed to snatch the razor out of her niece's hand. Last winter Zelda had knit tiny dog sweaters, which K.O. found, and with Wynn's help slipped over the two terriers. At least they'd be warm, although neither dog seemed especially grateful.

K.O. sank down on the sofa beside Wynn, with the dogs nestled at their feet. Breathing out a long, deep sigh, she gazed up at the ceiling. Wynn was curiously quiet.

"I feel like going to bed myself," she murmured when she'd recovered enough energy to speak.

"What time are your sister and brother-in-law supposed to return?" Wynn asked with what seemed to require an extraordinary amount of effort.

"Zelda said they should be home by three."

"That late?"

K.O. couldn't keep the grin off her face. It was just as she'd hoped. She wouldn't have to argue about the problem with his Free Child theories, since he'd been able to witness for himself the havoc they caused.

Straightening, K.O. suggested they listen to some more music.

"That won't disturb them, will it?" he asked when she got up to put on another CD. Evidently he had no interest in anything that might wake the girls.

"I should hope not." She found the Christmas CD she'd given to Zelda two years earlier, and inserted it in the player. It featured a number of pop artists. Smiling over at Wynn, she lowered the volume. John Denver's voice reached softly into the room, singing "Joy to the World."

Wynn turned off the floor lamp, so the only illumination came from the Christmas-tree lights. The mood was cheerful and yet relaxed.

For the first time in days they were alone. The incident with Wynn's father and the demands of the twins were the last things on K.O.'s mind.

Wynn placed his arm across the back of the sofa and she sat close to him, resting her head against his shoulder. All they needed now was a glass of wine and a kiss or two. Romance swirled through the room with the music and Christmas lights. Wynn must've felt it, too, because he turned her in his arms. K.O. started to close her eyes, anticipating his kiss, when she caught a movement from the corner of her eye.

She gasped.

A mouse…a rodent ran across the floor.

Instantly alarmed, K.O. jerked away from Wynn.

He bolted upright. "What is it?"

"A mouse." She hated mice. "There," she cried, covering her mouth to stifle a scream. She pointed as the rodent scampered under the Christmas tree.

Wynn leaped to his feet. "I see it."

Apparently so did Zero, because he let out a yelp and headed right for the tree. Zorro followed.

K.O. brought both feet onto the sofa and hugged her knees. It was completely unreasonable—and so clichéd—to be terrified of a little mouse. But she was. While logic told her a mouse was harmless, that knowledge didn't help.

"You have to get it out of here," she whimpered as panic set in.

"I'll catch it," he shouted and dived under the Christmas tree, toppling it. The tree slammed against the floor, shattering several bulbs. Ornaments rolled in all directions. The dogs ran for cover. Fortunately the tree was still plugged in because it offered what little light was available.

Unable to watch, K.O. hid her eyes. She wondered what Wynn would do if he did manage to corner the rodent. The thought of him killing it right there in her sister's living room was intolerable.

"Don't kill it," she insisted and removed her hands from her eyes to find Wynn on his hands and knees, staring at her.

The mouse darted across the floor and raced under the sofa, where K.O. just happened to be sitting.

Zero and Zorro ran after it, yelping frantically.

K.O. screeched and scrambled to a standing position on the sofa. Not knowing what else to do, she bounced from one cushion to the other.

Zero had buried his nose as far as it would go under the sofa. Zorro dashed back and forth on the carpet. As hard as she tried, K.O. couldn't keep still and began hopping up and down, crying out in abject terror. She didn't care if she woke the girls or not, there was a mouse directly beneath her feet…somewhere. For all she knew, it could have crawled into the sofa itself.

That thought made her jump from the middle of the sofa, over the armrest and onto the floor, narrowly missing Zero. The lamp fell when she landed, but she was able to catch it seconds before it crashed to the floor. As she righted the lamp, she flipped it on, provided a welcome circle of light.

Meanwhile, Barry Manilow crooned out "The Twelve Days of Christmas."

Still on all fours, Wynn crept across the carpet to the sofa, which he overturned. As it pitched onto its back, the mouse shot out.

Directly at K.O.

She screamed.

Zero yelped.

Zorro tore fearlessly after it.

K.O. screamed again and grabbed a basket in which Zelda kept her knitting. She emptied the basket and, more by instinct than anything else, flung it over the mouse, trapping him.

Wynn sat up with a shocked look. "You got him!"

Both dogs stood guard by the basket, sniffing at the edges. Zero scratched the carpet.

Zelda's yarn and needles were a tangled mess on the floor but seemed intact. Breathless, K.O. stared at the basket, not knowing what to do next. "It had a brown tail," she commented.

Wynn nodded. "I noticed that, too."

"I've never seen a mouse with a brown tail before."

"It's an African brown-tailed mouse," he said, sounding knowledgeable. "I saw a documentary on them."

"African mice are here in the States?" She wondered if Animal Control knew about this.

He nodded again. "So I gather."

"What do we do now?" Because Wynn seemed to know more about this sort of thing, she looked to him for the answer.

"Kill it," he said without a qualm.

Zero and Zorro obviously agreed, because they both growled and clawed at the carpet, asking for the opportunity to do it themselves.

"No way!" K.O. objected. She couldn't allow him to kill it. The terriers, either. Although mice terrified her, K.O. couldn't bear to hurt any of God's creatures. "All I want you to do is get that brown-tailed mouse out of here." As soon as Zelda returned, K.O. planned to suggest she call a pest control company to inspect the entire house. Although, if there were other mice around, she didn't want to know it....

"All right," Wynn muttered. "I'll take it outside and release it."

He got a newspaper and knelt down next to the dogs.

Carefully, inch by inch, he slid the paper beneath the up-ended basket. When he'd finished that, he stood and carried the whole thing to the front door. Zero and Zorro followed, leaping up on their hind legs and barking wildly.

K.O. hurried to open first the door and then the screen. The cold air felt good against her heated face.

Wynn stepped onto the porch while K.O. held back the dogs by closing the screen door. They both objected strenuously and braced their front paws against the door, watching Wynn's every movement.

K.O. turned her back as Wynn released the African brown-tailed mouse into the great unknown. She wished the critter a pleasant life outside.

"Is it gone?" she asked when Wynn came back into the house, careful to keep Zero and Zorro from escaping and racing after the varmint.

"It's gone, and I didn't even need to touch it," he assured her. He closed the door.

K.O. smiled up at him. "My hero," she whispered.

Wynn playfully flexed his muscles. "Anything else I can do for you, my fair damsel?"

Looping her arms around his neck, K.O. backed him up against the front door and rewarded him with a warm, moist kiss. Wynn wrapped his arms about her waist and half lifted her from the carpet.

"You *are* my hero," she whispered between kisses. "You saved me from that killer mouse."

"The African brown-tailed killer rat."

"It was a *rat?*"

"A small one," he murmured, and kissed her again before she could ask more questions.

"A baby rat?" That meant there must be parents around and possibly siblings, perhaps any number of other little rats. "What makes you think it was a rat?" she demanded, fast losing interest in kissing.

"He was fat. But perhaps he was just a fat mouse."

"Ah…"

"You're still grateful?"

"Very grateful, but—"

He kissed her again, then abruptly broke off the kiss. His eyes seemed to focus on something across the room.

K.O. tensed, afraid he'd seen another mouse. Or rat. Or rodent of some description.

It took genuine courage to glance over her shoulder, but she did it anyway. Fortunately she didn't see anything—other than an overturned Christmas tree, scattered furniture and general chaos brought about by the Great Brown-Tailed Mouse Hunt.

"The fishbowl has blue water," he said.

"Blue water?" K.O. dropped her arms and stared at the counter between the kitchen and the living room, where the fishbowl sat. Sure enough, the water was a deep blue.

Wynn walked across the room.

Before K.O. could ask what he was doing, Wynn

pushed up his sweater sleeve and thrust his hand into the water. "Just as I thought," he muttered, retrieving a gold pen.

After she'd found the twins with Wynn's electric shaver, she realized, they'd opened his overnight case.

"This is a gold fountain pen," he told her, holding up the dripping pen. "As it happens, this is a *valuable* gold fountain pen."

"With blue ink," K.O. added. She didn't think it could be too valuable, since it was leaking.

She picked up the bowl with both hands and carried it into the kitchen, setting it in the sink. Scooping out the two goldfish, she put them in a temporary home—a coffee cup full of fresh, clean water—and refilled the bowl.

Wynn was pacing the kitchen floor behind her.

"Does your book say anything about situations like this?" she couldn't resist asking.

He glared at her and apparently that was all the answer he intended to give.

"Aunt Katherine?" one of the twins shouted. "Come quick." K.O. heard unmistakable panic in the little girl's voice.

Soon the two girls were both crying out.

Hurrying into the bedroom with Wynn right behind her, K.O. found Zoe and Zara weeping loudly.

"What's wrong?" she asked.

"Freddy's gone," Zoe wailed.

"Freddy?" she repeated. "Who's Freddy?"

"Our hamster," Zoe explained, pointing at what K.O. now recognized as a cage against the far wall. "He must've figured out how to open his cage."

A chill went through her. "Does Freddy have a brown tail and happen to be a little chubby?" she asked the girls.

Hope filled their eyes as they nodded eagerly.

K.O. scowled at Wynn. African brown-tailed mouse, indeed.

Chapter 17

Thankfully, Wynn rescued poor Freddy, who was discovered shivering in a corner of the porch. The girls were relieved to have their hamster back, and neither mentioned the close call Freddy had encountered with certain death. After calming the twins, it took K.O. and Wynn an hour to clean up the living room. By then, they were both cranky and tired.

Saturday morning, Zoe and Zara decided on wieners for breakfast. Knowing Wynn would approve, K.O. cooked the hot dogs he'd purchased the night before. However, the unaccustomed meat didn't settle well in Zoe's tummy and she threw up on her breakfast plate.

Zara insisted that all she wanted was orange juice poured over dry cereal. So that was what she got.

For the rest of the morning, Wynn remained pensive and remote. He helped her with the children but didn't want to talk. In fact, he seemed more than eager to get back to Blossom Street. When Zelda and Zach showed up that afternoon, he couldn't quite hide his relief. The twins hugged K.O. goodbye and Wynn, too.

While Wynn loaded the car, K.O. talked to Zelda about holiday plans. Zelda asked her to join the family for Christmas Eve dinner and church, but not Christmas Day, which they'd be spending with Zach's parents. K.O. didn't mind. She'd invite LaVonne to dinner at her place. Maybe she'd include Wynn and his father, too, despite the disastrous conclusion of the last social event she'd hosted for this same group. Still, when she had the chance, she'd discuss it with Wynn.

On the drive home, Wynn seemed especially quiet.

"The girls are a handful, aren't they?" she asked, hoping to start a conversation.

He nodded.

She smiled to herself, remembering Wynn's expression when Zoe announced that their hamster had escaped. Despite his reproachful silence, she laughed. "I promise not to mention that rare African brown-tailed mouse again, but I have to tell LaVonne."

"I never said it was rare."

"Oh, sorry, I thought you had." One look told her Wynn wasn't amused. "Come on, Wynn," she said, as they merged with the freeway traffic. "You have to admit it was a little ridiculous."

He didn't appear to be in the mood to admit anything. "Are you happy?" he asked.

"What do you mean?"

"You proved your point, didn't you?"

So that was the problem. "If you're referring to how the girls behaved then, yes, I suppose I did."

"You claimed that after your sister read my book, they changed into undisciplined hellions."

"Well…" Wasn't it obvious? "They're twins," she said, trying to sound conciliatory, "and as such they've always needed a lot of attention. Some of what happened on Friday evening might have happened without the influence of your child-rearing theories. Freddy would've escaped whether Zelda read your book or not."

"Very funny."

"I wasn't trying to be funny. Frankly, rushing to the store to buy hot dogs because that's what the girls wanted for dinner is over the top, in my opinion. I feel it teaches them to expect that their every whim must be met."

"I beg to differ. My getting the dinner they wanted showed them that I cared about their likes and dislikes."

"Two hours of sitting on the floor playing Old Maid said the same thing," she inserted.

"I let you put them to bed even though they clearly weren't ready for sleep."

"I beg to differ," she said, a bit more forcefully than she'd intended. "Zoe and Zara were both yawning when they came out of the bath. I asked them if they wanted to go to bed."

"What you asked," he said stiffly, "was if they were *ready* for bed."

"And the difference is?"

"Two hours of storytime while they wore us both out."

"What would you have done?" she asked.

His gaze didn't waver from the road. "I would've allowed them to play quietly in their room until they'd tired themselves out."

Quietly? He had to be joking. Wynn seemed to have conveniently forgotten that during the short time they were on their own, Zoe and Zara had gotten into his overnight bag. Thanks to their creative use of his personal things, the goldfish now had a bluish tint. The two Yorkies were nearly hairless. She could argue that because the girls considered themselves *free,* they didn't see anything wrong with opening his bag. The lack of boundaries created confusion and misunderstanding.

"Twins are not the norm," he challenged. "They encourage ill behavior in each other."

"However, before Zelda read your book, they were reasonably well-behaved children."

"Is that a fact?" He sounded as though he didn't believe her.

"Yes," she said swiftly. "Zoe and Zara were happy and respectful and kind. Some would even go so far as to say they were well-adjusted. Now they constantly demand their own way. They're unreasonable, selfish and difficult." She was only getting started and dragged in another breath. "Furthermore, it used to be a joy to spend time with them and now it's a chore. And if you must know, I blame you and that blasted book of yours." There, she'd said it.

A stark silence followed.

"You don't mince words, do you?"

"No…"

"I respect that. I wholeheartedly disagree, but I respect your right to state your opinion."

The tension in the car had just increased by about a thousand degrees.

"After this weekend, you still disagree?" She was astonished he'd actually said that, but then she supposed his ego was on the line.

"I'm not interested in arguing with you, Katherine."

She didn't want to argue with him, either. Still, she'd hoped the twins would convince him that while his theories might look good on paper, in reality they didn't work.

After Wynn exited the freeway, it was only a few short

blocks to Blossom Street and the parking garage beneath their building. Wynn pulled into his assigned slot and turned off the engine.

Neither moved.

K.O. feared that the minute she opened the car door, it would be over, and she didn't want their relationship to end, not like this. Not now, with Christmas only nine days away.

She tried again. "I know we don't see eye to eye on everything—"

"No, we don't," he interrupted. "In many cases, it doesn't matter, but when it comes to my work, my livelihood, it does. Not only do you not accept my theories, you think they're ludicrous."

She opened her mouth to defend herself, then realized he was right. That was exactly what she thought.

"You've seen evidence that appears to contradict them and, therefore, you discount the years of research I've done in my field. The fact is, you don't respect my work."

Feeling wretched, she hung her head.

"I expected there to be areas in which we disagree, Katherine, but this is more than I can deal with. I'm sorry, but I think it would be best if we didn't see each other again."

If that was truly how he felt, then there was nothing left to say.

"I appreciate that you've been honest with me," he continued. "I'm sorry, Katherine—I know we both would've liked this to work, but we have too many differences."

She made an effort to smile. If she thought arguing with him would do any good, she would have. But the hard set of his jaw told her no amount of reasoning would reach him now. "Thank you for everything. Really, I mean that. You've made this Christmas the best."

He gave her a sad smile.

"Would it be all right—would you mind if I gave you a hug?" she asked. "To say goodbye?"

He stared at her for the longest moment, then slowly shook his head. "That wouldn't be a good idea," he whispered, opening the car door.

By the time K.O. was out of the vehicle, he'd already retrieved her overnight bag from the trunk.

She waited, but it soon became apparent that he had no intention of taking the elevator with her. It seemed he'd had about as much of her company as he could stand.

She stepped into the elevator with her bag and turned around. Before the doors closed, she saw Wynn leaning against the side of his car with his head down, looking dejected. K.O. understood the feeling.

It had been such a promising relationship. She'd never felt this drawn to a man, this attracted. If only she'd been able to keep her mouth shut—but, oh, no, not her. She'd wanted to prove her point, show him the error of his ways. She still believed he was wrong—well, mostly wrong—but now she felt petty and mean.

When the elevator stopped at the first floor, the doors slid open and K.O. got out. The first thing she did was collect her mail and her newspapers. She eyed the elevator, wondering if she'd ever see Wynn again, other than merely in passing, which would be painfully unavoidable.

After unpacking her overnight case and sorting through the mail, none of which interested her, she walked across the hall, hoping to talk to LaVonne.

Even after several long rings, LaVonne didn't answer her door. Perhaps she was doing errands.

Just as K.O. was about to walk away, her neighbor opened the door just a crack and peered out.

"LaVonne, it's me."

"Oh, hi," she said.

"Can I come in?" K.O. asked, wondering why LaVonne didn't immediately invite her inside. She'd never hesitated to ask her in before.

"Ah...now isn't really a good time."

"Oh." That was puzzling.

"How about tomorrow?" LaVonne suggested.

"Sure." K.O. nodded. "Is Tom back?" she asked.

"Tom?"

"Your cat."

"Oh, oh...that Tom. Yes, he came home this morning."

K.O. was pleased to hear that. She dredged up a smile. "I'll talk to you tomorrow, then."

"Yes," she agreed. "Tomorrow."

K.O. started across the hall, then abruptly turned back. "You might care to know that the Raisin Bran got it all wrong."

"I beg your pardon?" LaVonne asked, narrowing her gaze.

"I think you might've read the kitty litter wrong, too. But then again, that particular box accurately describes my love life."

LaVonne opened the door a fraction of an inch wider. "Do you mean to tell me you're no longer seeing Wynn?"

K.O. nodded. "Apparently we were both wrong in thinking Wynn was the man for me."

"He is," LaVonne said confidently.

K.O. sighed. "I wish he was. I genuinely like Wynn. When I first discovered he was the author of that loony book my sister read…" Realizing what she'd just said, K.O. began again. "When I discovered he wrote the book she'd read, I had my doubts."

"It *is* a loony book," LaVonne said.

"I should never have told him how I felt."

"You were honest."

"Yes, but I was rude and hurtful, too." She shook her head mournfully. "We disagree on just about every aspect of child-rearing. He doesn't want to see me again and I don't blame him."

LaVonne stared at her for an intense moment. "You're falling in love with him."

"No, I'm not," she said, hoping to make light of her feelings, but her neighbor was right. K.O. had known it the minute Wynn dived under the Christmas tree to save her from the not-so-rare African brown-tailed mouse. The minute he'd waved down the horse-drawn carriage and covered her knees with a lap robe and slipped his arm around her shoulders.

"Don't try to deny it," LaVonne said. "I don't really know what I saw in that Raisin Bran. Probably just raisins. But all along I've felt that Wynn's the man for you."

"I wish that was true," she said as she turned to go home. "But it's not."

As she opened her own door, she heard LaVonne talking. When she glanced back, she could hear her in a heated conversation with someone inside the condo. Unfortunately LaVonne was blocking the doorway, so K.O. couldn't see who it was.

"LaVonne?"

The door opened wider and out stepped Max Jeffries. "Hello, Katherine," he greeted her, grinning from ear to ear.

K.O. looked at her neighbor and then at Wynn's father. The last she'd heard, Max was planning to sue LaVonne for everything she had. Somehow, in the past twenty-four hours, he'd changed his mind.

"Max?" she said in an incredulous voice.

He grinned boyishly and placed his arm around LaVonne's shoulders.

"You see," LaVonne said, blushing a fetching shade of red. "My psychic talents might be limited, but you're more talented than you knew."

Chapter 18

K.O. was depressed. Even the fact that she'd been hired by Apple Blossom Books as their new publicist hadn't been enough to raise her spirits. She was scheduled to start work the day after New Year's and should've been thrilled. She was, only…nothing felt right without Wynn.

It was Christmas Eve and it should have been one of the happiest days of the year, but she felt like staying in bed. Her sister and family were expecting her later that afternoon, so K.O. knew she couldn't mope around the condo all day. She had things to do, food to buy, gifts to wrap, and she'd better get moving.

Putting on her coat and gloves, she walked out of her

condo wearing a smile. She refused to let anyone know she was suffering from a broken heart.

"Katherine," LaVonne called the instant she saw her. She stood at the lobby mailbox as if she'd been there for hours, just waiting for K.O. "Merry Christmas!"

"Merry Christmas," K.O. returned a little too brightly. She managed a smile and with her shoulders squared, made her way to the door.

"Do you have any plans for Christmas?" her neighbor called after her.

K.O.'s mouth hurt from holding that smile for so long. She nodded. "I'm joining Zelda, Zach and the girls this evening, and then I thought I'd spend a quiet Christmas by myself." Needless to say, she hadn't issued any invitations, and she'd hardly seen LaVonne in days. Tomorrow she'd cook for herself. While doing errands this morning, she planned to purchase a small—very small—turkey. She refused to mope and feel lonely, not on Christmas Day.

"Have dinner with me," LaVonne said. "It'll just be me and the boys."

When K.O. hesitated, she added, "Tom, Phillip and Martin would love to see you. I'm cooking a turkey and all the fixings, and I'd be grateful for the company."

"Are you sure?"

"Of course I'm sure!"

K.O. didn't take long to consider her friend's invitation. "I'd love to, then. What would you like me to bring?"

"Dessert," LaVonne said promptly. "Something yummy and special for Christmas."

"All right." They agreed on a time and K.O. left, feeling better than she had in days. Just as she was about to step outside, she turned back.

"How's Max?" she asked, knowing her neighbor was on good terms with Wynn's father. Exactly how good those terms were remained to be seen. She wondered fleetingly what the Jeffrieses were doing for Christmas, then decided it was none of her business. Still, the afternoon K.O. had found Max in LaVonne's condo, she'd been shocked to say the least. Their brief conversation the following day hadn't been too enlightening but maybe over Christmas dinner LaVonne would tell her what had happened—and what was happening now.

Flustered, LaVonne lowered her eyes as she sorted through a stack of mail that seemed to be mostly Christmas cards. "He's completely recovered. And," she whispered, "he's apologized to Tom."

A sense of pleasure shot through K.O. at this...and at the way LaVonne blushed. Apparently this was one romance that held promise. Her own had fizzled out fast enough. She'd come to truly like Wynn. More than like... At the thought of him, an aching sensation pressed down on her. In retrospect, she wished she'd handled the situation differently. Because she couldn't resist, she had to ask, "Have you seen Wynn?"

Her friend nodded but the look in LaVonne's eyes told K.O. everything she dreaded.

"He's still angry, isn't he?"

LaVonne gave her a sad smile. "I'm sure everything will work out. I know what I saw in that Raisin Bran." She attempted a laugh.

"When you see him again, tell him…" She paused. "Tell him," she started again, then gave up. Wynn had made his feelings clear. He'd told her it would be best if they didn't see each other again, and he'd meant it. Nine days with no word told her he wasn't changing his mind. Well, she had her pride, too.

"What would you like me to tell him?" LaVonne asked.

"Nothing. It's not important."

"You could write him a letter," LaVonne suggested.

"Perhaps I will," K.O. said on her way out the door, but she knew she wouldn't. It was over.

Blossom Street seemed more alive than at any other time she could remember. A group of carolers performed at the corner, songbooks in their hands. An elderly gentleman rang a bell for charity outside the French Café, which was crowded with customers. Seeing how busy the place was, K.O. decided to purchase her Christmas dessert now, before they completely sold out.

After adding a donation to the pot as she entered the café, she stood in a long line. When her turn finally came to order, she saw that one of the bakers was helping at the counter. K.O. knew Alix Townsend or, at least, she'd talked to her often enough to know her by name.

"Merry Christmas, K.O.," Alix said.

"Merry Christmas to you, too." K.O. surveyed the sweet delicacies behind the glass counter. "I need something that says Christmas," she murmured. The decorated cookies were festive but didn't seem quite right. A pumpkin pie would work, but it wasn't really special.

"How about a small Bûche de Noël," Alix said. "It's a traditional French dessert—a fancy cake decorated with mocha cream frosting and shaped to look like a Yule log. I baked it myself from a special recipe of the owner's."

"Bûche de Noël," K.O. repeated. It sounded perfect.

"They're going fast," Alix pointed out.

"Sold," K.O. said as the young woman went to collect one from the refrigerated case. It was then that K.O. noticed Alix's engagement ring.

"Will there be anything else?" Alix asked, setting the pink box on the counter and tying it with string.

"That diamond's new, isn't it?"

Grinning, Alix examined her ring finger. "I got it last week. Jordan couldn't wait to give it to me."

"Congratulations," K.O. told her. "When's the wedding?"

Alix looked down at the diamond as if she could hardly take her eyes off it. "June."

"That's fabulous."

"I'm already talking to Susannah Nelson—she owns the flower shop across the street. Jacqueline, my friend, insists we hold the reception at the Country Club. If it was up to me, Jordan and I would just elope, but his family would never stand for that." She shrugged in a resigned way. "I love Jordan, and I don't care what I have to do, as long as I get to be his wife."

The words echoed in K.O.'s heart as she walked out of the French Café with a final "Merry Christmas." She didn't know Alix Townsend all that well, but she liked her. Alix was entirely without pretense. No one need doubt how she felt about any particular subject; she spoke her mind in a straightforward manner that left nothing to speculation.

K.O. passed Susannah's Garden, the flower shop, on her way to the bank. The owner and her husband stood out front, wishing everyone a Merry Christmas. As K.O. walked past, Susannah handed her a sprig of holly with bright red berries.

"Thank you—this is so nice," K.O. said, tucking the holly in her coat pocket. She loved the flower shop and the beauty it brought to the street.

"I want to let the neighborhood know how much I appreciate the support. I've only been in business since September and everyone's been so help ful."

"Here, have a cup of hot cider." Susannah's husband was handing out plastic cups from a small table set up beside him. "I'm Joe," he said.

"Hello, Joe. I'm Katherine O'Connor."

Susannah slid one arm around her husband's waist and gazed up at him with such adoration it was painful for K.O. to watch. Everywhere she turned, people were happy and in love. A knot formed in her throat. Putting on a happy, carefree face was getting harder by the minute.

Just then the door to A Good Yarn opened and out came Lydia Goetz and a man K.O. assumed must be her husband. They were accompanied by a young boy, obviously their son. Lydia paused when she saw K.O.

Lydia was well-known on the street.

"Were you planning to stop in here?" she asked, and cast a quick glance at her husband. "Brad convinced me to close early today. I already sent my sister home, but if you need yarn, I'd be happy to get it for you. In fact, you could even pay me later." She looked at her husband again, as if to make sure he didn't object to the delay. "It wouldn't take more than a few minutes. I know what it's like to run out of yarn when you only need one ball to finish a project."

"No, no, that's fine," K.O. said. She'd always wanted to learn to knit and now that LaVonne was taking a class, maybe she'd join, too.

"Merry Christmas!" Lydia tucked her arm in her husband's.

"Merry Christmas," K.O. returned. Soon they hurried down the street, with the boy trotting ahead.

Transfixed, K.O. stood there unmoving. The lump that had formed in her throat grew huge. The whole world was in love, and she'd let the opportunity of her life slip away. She'd let Wynn go with barely a token protest, and that was wrong. If she believed in their love, she needed to fight for it, instead of pretending everything was fine without him. Because it wasn't. In fact, she was downright miserable, and it was time she admitted it.

She knew what she had to do. Afraid that if she didn't act quickly, she'd lose her nerve, K.O. ran back across the street and into her own building. Marching to the elevator, she punched the button and waited.

She wasn't even sure what she'd tell Wynn; she'd figure that out when she saw him. But seeing him was a necessity. She couldn't spend another minute like this. She'd made a terrible mistake, and so had he. If there was any chance of salvaging this relationship, she had to try.

Her heart seemed to be pounding at twice its normal rate as she rode the elevator up to Wynn's penthouse condominium. She'd only been inside once, and then briefly.

By the time she reached his front door, she was so dizzy she'd become light-headed. That didn't deter her from ringing the buzzer and waiting for what felt like an eternity.

Only it wasn't Wynn who opened the door. It was Max.

"Katherine," he said, obviously surprised to find her at his son's door. "Come in."

"Is Wynn available?" she asked, as winded as if she'd climbed the stairs instead of taking the elevator. Talking to Wynn—*now*—had assumed a sense of urgency.

Wynn stepped into the foyer and frowned when he saw her. "Katherine?" She could see the question in his eyes.

"Merry Christmas," Max said. He didn't seem inclined to leave.

"Could we talk?" she asked. "Privately?" She was terrified he'd tell her that everything had already been said, so she rushed to add, "Really, this will only take a moment and then I'll leave."

Wynn glanced at his father, who took the hint and reluctantly left the entryway.

K.O. remained standing there, clutching her purse with one hand and the pink box with the other. "I was out at the French Café and I talked to Alix."

"Alix?"

"She's one of the bakers and a friend of Lydia's—and Lydia's the lady who owns A Good Yarn. But that's not important. What *is* important is that Alix received an engagement ring for Christmas. She's so happy and in love, and Lydia is, too, and Susannah from the flower shop and just about everyone on the street. It's so full of Christmas out there, and all at once it came to me that…that I couldn't let this Christmas pass with things between us the way they are." She stopped to take a deep breath.

"Katherine, I—"

"Please let me finish, otherwise I don't know if I'll have the courage to continue."

He motioned for her to speak.

"I'm so sorry, Wynn, for everything. For wanting to be right and then subjecting you to Zoe and Zara. Their behavior *did* change after Zelda read your book and while I can't say I agree with everything you—"

"This is an apology?" he asked, raising his eyebrows.

"I'm trying. I'm sincerely trying. Please hear me out."

He crossed his arms and looked away. In fact, he seemed to find something behind her utterly fascinating.

This wasn't the time to lose her courage. She went on, speaking quickly, so quickly that the words practically ran together. "Basically, I wanted to tell you it was rude of me to assume I knew more than you on the subject of children. It was presumptuous and self-righteous. I was trying to prove how wrong you were…are, and that I was right. To be honest, I don't know what's right or wrong. All I know is how much I miss you and how much it hurts that you're out of my life."

"I'm the one who's been presumptuous and self-righteous," Wynn said. "You *are* right, Katherine, about almost everything. It hasn't been easy for me to accept that, let alone face it."

"Oh, for heaven's sake, aren't you two going to kiss and make up?" Max demanded, coming back into the foyer.

Apparently he'd been standing in the living room, out of sight, and had listened in on every word. "Wynn, if you let this woman walk away, then you're a fool. An even bigger fool than you know."

"I—I…" Wynn stuttered.

"You've been in love with her for weeks." Max shook his head as if this was more than obvious.

Wynn pinned his father with a fierce glare.

"You love me?" K.O. asked, her voice rising to a squeak. "Because I'm in love with you, too."

A light flickered in his eyes at her confession. "Katherine, I appreciate your coming. However, this is serious and it's something we both need to think over. It's too important—we can't allow ourselves to get caught up in emotions that are part of the holidays. We'll talk after Christmas, all right?"

"I can't do that," she cried.

"Good for you," Max shouted, encouraging her. "I'm going to phone LaVonne. This calls for champagne."

"What does?" Wynn asked.

"Us," she explained. "You and me. I love you, Wynn, and I can't bear the thought that I won't see you again. It's tearing me up. I don't *need* time to think about us. I already know how I feel, and if what your father says is true, you know how you feel about me."

"Well, I do need to think," he insisted. "I haven't figured out what I'm going to do yet, because I can't continue promoting a book whose theories I can no longer wholly support. Let me deal with that first."

"No," she said. "Love should come first." She stared into his eyes. "Love changes everything, Wynn." Then, because it was impossible to hold back for another second, she put down her purse and the Yule log and threw her arms around him.

Wynn was stiff and unbending, and then his arms circled her, too. "Are you always this stubborn?" he asked.

"Yes. Sometimes even more than this. Ask Zelda."

Wynn kissed her. His arms tightened around her, as if he found it hard to believe she was actually there in his embrace.

"That's the way to handle it," Max said from somewhere behind them.

Wynn and K.O. ignored him.

"He's been a real pain these last few days," Max went on. "But this should improve matters."

Wynn broke off the kiss and held her gaze. "We'll probably never agree on everything."

"Probably."

"I can be just as stubborn as you."

"That's questionable," she said with a laugh.

His lips found hers again, as if he couldn't bear not to kiss her. Each kiss required a bit more time and became a bit more involved.

"I don't believe in long courtships," he murmured, his eyes still closed.

"I don't, either," she said. "And I'm going to want children."

He hesitated.

"We don't need all the answers right this minute, do we, Dr. Jeffries?"

"About Santa—"

She interrupted him, cutting off any argument by kissing him. What resistance there was didn't last.

"I was about to suggest we could bring Santa out from beneath that sleigh," he whispered, his eyes briefly fluttering open.

"Really?" This was more than she'd dared hope.

"Really."

She'd been more than willing to forgo Santa as long as she had Wynn. But Santa *and* Wynn was better yet.

"No hamsters, though," he said firmly.

"Named Freddy," she added.

Wynn chuckled. "Or anything else."

The doorbell chimed and Max hurried to answer it, ushering LaVonne inside. The instant she saw Wynn and K.O. in each other's arms, she clapped with delight. "Didn't I tell you everything would work out?" she asked Max.

"You did, indeed."

LaVonne nodded sagely. "I think I may have psychic powers, after all. I saw it all plain as day in the leaves of my poinsettia," she proclaimed. "Just before Max called, two of them fell to the ground—together."

Despite herself, K.O. laughed. Until a few minutes ago, her love life had virtually disappeared. Now there was hope, real hope for her and Wynn to learn from each other and as LaVonne's prophecy—real or imagined—implied, grow together instead of apart.

"Champagne, anyone?" Max asked, bringing out a bottle.

Wynn still held K.O. and she wasn't objecting. "I need to hire you," he whispered close to her ear.

"Hire me?"

"I'm kind of late with my Christmas letter this year and I wondered if I could convince you to write one for me."

"Of course. It's on the house." With his arms around her waist, she leaned back and looked up at him. "Is there anything in particular you'd like me to say?"

"Oh, yes. You can write about the success of my first published book—and explain that there'll be a retraction in the next edition." He winked. "Or, if you prefer, you could call it a compromise."

K.O. smiled.

"And then I want you to tell my family and friends that I'm working on a new book that'll be called *The Happy Child,* and it'll be about creating appropriate boundaries within the Free Child system of parenting."

K.O. rewarded him with a lengthy kiss that left her

knees weak. Fortunately, he had a firm hold on her, and she on him.

"You can also mention the fact that there's going to be a wedding in the family."

"Two weddings," Max inserted as he handed LaVonne a champagne glass.

"Two?" LaVonne echoed shyly.

Max nodded, filling three more glasses. "Wynn and K.O.'s isn't the only romance that started out rocky. The way I figure it, if I can win Tom over, his mistress shouldn't be far behind."

"Oh, Max!"

"Is there anything else you'd like me to say in your Christmas letter?" K.O. asked Wynn.

"Oh, yes, there's plenty more, but I think we'll leave it for the next Christmas letter and then the one after that." He brought K.O. close once more and hugged her tight.

She loved being in his arms—and in his life. Next year's Christmas letter would be from both of them. It would be all about how happy they were...and every word would be true.

The Perfect Christmas

To
Gary and Marsha Roche
and
Bob Mullen
who have shared their love of
Civil War history
with Wayne and me

Chapter 1

"Who mails out Christmas cards before Thanksgiving?" Cassie Beaumont lamented to her best friend.

Angie Barber looked up from her microscope and seemed to take an extra moment to consider what Cassie had just said. "You got a Christmas card? Already?"

Cassie wheeled her chair back to her station. "Can you believe it?"

"Who from?"

"An old college friend. You wouldn't know her." Cassie shrugged. "Jill married Tom two weeks after we graduated."

"They have children?"

Cassie caught the wisp of longing in Angie's voice and

answered with a nod. "Two, a boy and a girl, and of course they're adorable."

"Of course," Angie echoed.

The Christmas card photo showed the four of them in matching outfits of green and red. The mother and daughter wore full-length green dresses with red-and-green plaid skirts. Father and son had on three-piece suits with vests in the same fabric as the dress skirts. It was too adorable for words.

"There was a letter, as well."

"Everything in their lives is perfect, right?" Angie asked.

"Perfect in every way," Cassie grumbled. The unfairness of it all was too much. Jill, who worked as a financial planner, held down a forty-hour-a-week job, kept a meticulous house and *still* managed to be a terrific wife and mother. Despite all the demands on her time, she'd mailed out her Christmas cards a full month in advance.

"Is there a reason the perfect Jill sent her Christmas cards so soon?" Angie asked.

"Jill and Tom just moved into a new home and wanted to update family and friends with their address change. Oh, and there was a photo of the house and it was—"

"Perfect," Angie finished for her.

"Perfect doesn't begin to describe it."

Angie watched her closely. "Do I detect a slight note of envy?" she asked.

"Slight envy? Me?" Cassie asked, exaggerating the

words. "Heavens, no. What you're hearing is a full-blown case of jealousy. The green-eyed monster is alive and well." Cassie rolled her chair to the end of a counter filled with an assortment of microscopes, test tubes, slides and other equipment, then stood, hands propped on her hips. "Do you realize how long it's been since I've been on a real date?"

"You went out with Greg last week," Angie reminded her.

"Greg isn't a man," Cassie blurted out. "I mean, he is, but not in the sense of someone I'm interested in," she said. "Greg's…completely unsuitable as marriage material." She didn't need to explain that, at thirty-four, the ticking of her biological clock got louder by the year.

Angie sighed. "I agree."

He was eligible in practically every way but he happened to be divorced and in love with his ex-wife. Unfortunately, he hadn't figured that out yet. The entire date, if it could even be called a date, was spent rehashing the tragedy of his divorce. He went on and on about how much he missed his three kids—and his ex-wife, if the number of times he mentioned her name was any indication. The night had been sheer drudgery for Cassie. It was her first and last date with Greg.

"The problem is, we don't meet many guys here at work," Angie said. Cassie was well aware of that. Since they were holed up in a lab eight to ten hours a day, working as biochemists for a plastics company, the opportunities to socialize outside the job were limited.

"What really hit home," Cassie said, "after receiving that Christmas card, is how badly I want a family of my own."

"I know." The longing was back in Angie's voice, too.

"I don't understand why it's so hard to meet men. I'm reasonably attractive, right?"

Angie nodded enthusiastically. "Yes."

"Thirty-four isn't so old, is it?"

"Not really."

Cassie shook her head and wondered why she was still single. She *wanted* to be married, and she liked to think she had the full package—five-five, dark hair, dark eyes. She was attractive, as Angie had confirmed, and she was smart, with a successful career, an engaging personality (if she did say so herself) and plenty of friends. "I blame my mother for this."

"Your mother?"

"I blame my father, too, even if he didn't stick around all that long."

"Or maybe *because* he didn't stick around."

"Yeah, I guess. After the divorce, my mother was so down on marriage, the whole idea terrified me."

"But it doesn't anymore, does it?"

"No. I want a husband and I'd really like children." She grinned. "The ironic thing is, my mother's remarried."

"Marriage seems to terrify your brother, too. Shawn

should be married by now, don't you think? He's older than you are."

"I'm not so sure about Shawn." Cassie sometimes wondered if Angie might be interested in her brother. There was actually nothing to indicate that, but every once in a while Cassie had this *feeling*.... "He travels so much that maintaining a long-term relationship would be difficult for him."

"True," Angie said.

Shawn was a well-known artist who painted murals all over the country. Brother and sister were close and kept in touch, calling each other two and three times a week. Currently Shawn was in Boca Raton, Florida, painting the side of a building that stood next to the freeway. He'd sent her photos of the mural from his cell phone— an ocean scene, which Cassie knew was his favorite. Whales rising up out of the crashing waves. Dolphins and sea turtles and all kinds of fish frolicked in the sparkling blue water. His murals made headlines wherever he went and huge crowds showed up to watch him paint.

"Shawn's a different case," Cassie said. In her opinion, that summed up the situation pretty accurately.

"But if you were married, I bet he'd show some interest in finding a wife," Angie commented.

Cassie had never thought of their family dynamic in those terms. Perhaps, in some obscure way, Shawn *was* waiting for her to make the leap first. Angie might be right. It wasn't that Shawn followed her lead—far from it. They'd both been traumatized by the divorce and by their mother's reaction. Their father, who wanted his kids to call him Pete, had been in and out of their lives. Mostly out and yet…yet he'd had a powerful influence on his children, whom he rarely recognized as such.

"Shawn won't feel marriage is safe until he sees *you* happily married," Angie went on to say.

Cassie scowled at her friend. "What makes you so smart?"

"Just an observation," Angie said. "I may not be correct, but it seems to me that you and Shawn are afraid of love."

"Me afraid of love? Hardly." Not if the longing in her heart was anything to go by. Like her friend Jill, she wanted it all.

"Whenever you meet a man—no matter how perfect he is—you find fault with him," Angie said.

Now, *that* was categorically untrue. "Not so," Cassie argued.

"Oh, it's all wine and roses in the beginning, but then it's over before you even have a chance to really know the guy."

"How can you say that?"

"Well, mostly," Angie told her softly, "I can say it because I've seen you do it again and again."

"You're not talking about me and Jess, are you? The

man had no class. He scratched his private parts in public!"

"Not Jess."

"Who do you mean, then?"

"Rod."

Cassie cocked her head. "Rod? Rod who?"

"I don't remember his last name. You went out with him a year ago."

"Not Rod Showers? Good grief, he was so cheap I had to pay for my half of the meal and tip the valet because he refused to do it."

"What about Charles…"

Cassie got the point quickly enough. "Okay, okay, so I have standards."

"High standards."

"Okay, fine. High standards." Cassie had made the effort, though. "I've *tried* to meet men."

"We both have."

"I had hopes for that online dating service." The advertisements had looked so promising. Cassie and Angie had signed up together and then waited expectantly to meet their perfect matches.

It didn't happen.

"I had real hopes for that, too," Angie returned sadly. "I thought for sure we'd meet really wonderful husbands."

Cassie sighed. That had been an expensive venture. Her expectations had been great and her disappointment greater. Angie's too. In fact, Angie was the one who'd suggested trying the Internet.

"The church singles group was a good idea," she said now.

"A great idea," Cassie concurred, "if there'd been any men involved." They'd gone there to discover the group consisted of thirty women and two men—both close to retirement age.

Angie nodded. "The pickings were few and far between."

"We've read all the right books," Cassie said. "*Dating for Dummies. How to Find a Man in Five Easy Lessons.* My personal favorite was *Lasso Yourself a Husband and Other Ways to Make a Man Notice You.*"

"The only thing we managed to lasso was a hundred-dollar credit-card bill for all those books."

"Divided two ways," Cassie reminded her.

"They did make for interesting reading."

"They would've been a lot more interesting if we'd been able to make any of them work," Cassie said in acerbic tones.

"Yeah…"

"We've tried everything."

"I'm not giving up," Angie insisted. "And I won't let you give up, either."

Cassie sighed.

She was close to it. The Christmas card from Jill and

Tom was the final straw. For too long she'd been convinced that one day soon, she'd be mailing glossy Christmas cards to all *her* friends and relatives. She, too, would have a photograph that showed the perfect husband, the perfect children, a boy and a girl, all looking forward to the perfect Christmas. But year after year it was the same. No husband. No children. And each Christmas with her embittered mother more depressing than the one before.

The time had come to step forward and find a man, she decided with new resolve. Maybe she did need to lower her standards. She couldn't allow another Christmas to pass without—

"There's something, or rather someone, you *haven't* tried," Angie said, cutting into Cassie's thoughts.

Cassie perked up. "Oh?"

Angie grew strangely quiet.

Cassie frowned. "Don't hold out on me now, Angie."

"He's expensive."

"How expensive? No, wait, don't tell me." She paused. "Who is this *he?*"

"A matchmaker."

"A matchmaker," Cassie repeated slowly. "I didn't know there was such a thing in this day and age."

"There is." Angie avoided eye contact. "In fact, more and more people are turning to professional matchmakers. It works, too—most of the time."

"Now tell me how expensive he is."

"Thirty thousand dollars."

"What?"

"You heard me—and apparently he's worth it."

"And you know about him because…" Cassie let the question hang between them.

"Because I went to him."

Cassie slapped her hands against her sides. "Clearly you wasted your money."

"It didn't cost me a dime."

"And why is that?"

Angie's gaze darted in every direction except Cassie's. "He wouldn't accept me as a client."

"He rejected you?" The man was nuts! Angie was lovely and smart and a thousand other adjectives that flew through her mind. "What's wrong with this guy, anyway?"

"He was right…. I'm not a good candidate and I would've been wasting my money."

"Why didn't you tell me about him before?"

"I…I didn't want anyone to know I'd been turned down."

"If he rejected you, then he'll probably reject me, too."

"No…he said he couldn't accept me because I have feelings for someone else."

"Do you?"

"I did—a long time ago," she said without elaborating further. "But don't let my experience dissuade you. Check him out. Like you said earlier, you've tried everything else. At least make an appointment and see what he has to say."

Cassie was tempted to ask more about this man Angie had feelings for, but her friend had clearly signalled an unwillingness to talk about it. As far as the matchmaker went, she wasn't convinced. "He actually does this for a living?"

"Yes. He has an office and an assistant. I asked him for his credentials and he has an advanced degree in psychology and—" Angie stared directly at her "—he guarantees his work."

"Guarantees?"

"Yes. If he doesn't find you a husband, you get a full refund. So make an appointment and see for yourself. Remember—nothing ventured, nothing gained."

"I'll consider it," Cassie said. She hated to admit that the idea intrigued her. Then again, it *was* rather archaic. Besides, if this man had rejected Angie, he couldn't be any good. Still it was an opportunity, and nothing else had presented itself.

When she got to her condo building that evening, Cassie stopped at her mailbox in the lobby and immediately noticed that her newspaper was missing. No surprise there. It vanished every Tuesday when the shopping ads came out. Her neighbor Mrs. Mullinex, took it, although Cassie hadn't been able to prove that yet. On Wednesday mornings, her paper mysteriously reappeared with the coupons clipped out. Twice now, Cassie had met her neighbor in the lobby. The grandmotherly woman didn't resemble a thief and would've been above suspicion if not for the handful of coupons she clutched in her gloved fingers.

Grumbling under her breath, Cassie headed for her apartment. She tossed the mail on the kitchen counter without looking. The picture of Jill, Tom and their two children smiled at her from the refrigerator door.

The perfect family having the perfect Christmas.

Jill's smile seemed to be telling Cassie "All this could be yours, too."

"A matchmaker?" Cassie said aloud. "Am I really resorting to this?"

Angie had given Cassie his business card and then for good measure a hug and parting words of advice. "Just do it. I don't think you'll be sorry."

Cassie hesitated and glanced over at the perfect family posed in front of the world's most beautiful Christmas tree. Oh, for heaven's sake, what would it hurt?

After rummaging around the bottom of her purse, she found the engraved card that read: Dr. Simon Dodson, Professional Matchmaker.

Heart pounding, Cassie reached for the phone.

Chapter 2

Simon says: A good matchmaker *always* knows his clients—especially after a background check!

Cassie had to wait a week before she could get an appointment with Simon Dodson. He made sure she understood that he was doing her a favor by squeezing her in at the end of the day. All right, to be fair, his personal assistant, Ms. Snelling, a rather unpleasant woman, made it sound as if an appointment was a terrible inconvenience. Frankly Cassie didn't hold out much hope for this, and who could blame her? The matchmaking psychologist had declined to accept Angie, who was probably the most decent, kindest person Cassie had ever known.

The day of the appointment, Cassie went home to change clothes. She dressed carefully, choosing a suit that made her look confident but not formal, and she refreshed her makeup. When she walked into his office, it was with her head held high. She'd done her homework and was keeping an open mind. She'd checked two references the Snelling woman had passed on and felt she knew what to expect. Both couples had raved about Simon. The wives had warned her that Dr. Dodson wasn't the "warm and fuzzy" type. One of them had suggested that Cassie should be patient and not take offense. Hmm…that was unusual advice.

"Dr. Dodson will see you shortly," his assistant informed her primly after Cassie announced herself. The office had modern art decorating the walls, large green plants in the corners and soft leather furniture in a deep shade of brown.

"You filled out the paperwork I e-mailed you and brought it in?"

"Yes, I have it here." Cassie thought applying for a job at the CIA would've been easier. Simon was interested in every aspect of her background, from the name of her first-grade teacher to her current shoe size. Okay, maybe that was an exaggeration—a slight one—but she didn't see how most of the questions were relevant. Really, why did Simon need a list of any allergies she might have?

She handed the lengthy application form to the assistant, who scanned it, then took it into the inner office. Ms. Snelling reappeared a couple of minutes later and gave her a thorough once-over. Then, to Cassie's surprise, the woman offered her a reassuring smile.

Cassie studied the assistant. She guessed Ms. Snelling was in her late fifties; she seemed efficient and no-nonsense. Cassie sat with her hands politely folded in her lap. This might be the most important appointment of her entire life. The best Christmas present she'd ever get—even if it was from herself. A husband for Christmas. Hmm…

The great Dr. Simon Dodson kept her waiting a full thirty minutes. Cassie knew because she glanced at her watch every five minutes, crossed and uncrossed her legs and flipped through three magazines. By then, she'd grown impatient and irritable and had started to wonder if she'd made a mistake—or, worse, fallen for a scam. She wasn't accustomed to being ignored. She had better things to do than sit in a waiting room on what might turn out to be a fool's errand, a complete waste of time. She trusted that wasn't the case; still, the longer she waited, the less hope she had.

A buzzer made her jump. Ms. Snelling got smoothly to her feet, obviously used to such a peremptory summons. "Dr. Dodson will see you now," she said. She motioned toward the massive double doors that led into his office.

Cassie walked inside and her gaze went instantly to the man standing behind the large desk. The Internet research she'd done hadn't included any photos, so she hadn't been sure what to expect—but not someone relatively young with shockingly good looks. He was easily six-two and loomed above her.

"Ms. Beaumont?"

"That would be me," she said, straining to sound cool and collected.

"Please don't sit down."

"Uh…" The door closed behind her.

"Walk to the far side of my office and then walk back."

Cassie paused, which apparently he didn't like because he gestured for her to comply.

"Do I need to say, 'Mother, may I?'" she asked.

He didn't so much as crack a smile. "That won't be necessary."

"Okay." She did as he requested and felt his eyes burning into her with every step she took.

"You could stand to lose five pounds."

"I beg your pardon?" What a jerk!

"You heard me and you agree with me, only I doubt you'd admit it."

Okay, maybe she *could* shed a few pounds, but her figure looked fine the way it was.

He continued to study her and his frown deepened. "That color doesn't flatter you."

How dare he! "I happen to like navy blue." This was her favorite suit and she'd purchased it at a closeout sale for seventy percent off.

He frowned. "Pale blue would be better." He came out from behind his desk and walked around her. "You should let your hair grow, as well. That style is becoming but you need more length."

"I'm glad you think there's *something* attractive about me."

"I didn't say that."

This man was too much! Cassie was tempted to turn around and leave. She might have, only she decided to see how many other ways he could find to insult her. It was becoming a game to her.

"Sit," he said.

"Please?" Someone needed to teach this man some manners.

"Sit," he repeated, more loudly this time.

"Sit, *please,*" she returned pointedly.

A flicker of a smile showed in his dark brown eyes. "All right, sit, *please.*"

"Don't mind if I do," she said pleasantly, taking the chair across from his desk.

After a moment he said, "I've read your application." He sat down across from her, reached for the papers and leafed through them. "Tell me about your father."

"Why are you asking about him?"

He lifted his shoulder in a nonchalant shrug. "It's my experience that most women want to marry a man just like their father."

"Not me. Pete's a poor excuse for a father. I want as little to do with him as possible."

Simon immediately made a lengthy notation on a pad in front of him.

Cassie moved to the edge of the cushion. "What did you write?"

Simon looked up, a frown darkening his face. Clearly she'd offended him. She could only suppose he wasn't accustomed to anyone questioning his actions. "What did you say?" he said frostily.

"I asked if you'd tell me what you wrote down." She pointed at his notepad. "It was about me and my nonrelationship with my father, wasn't it?"

He flattened his hands on the desk. "These are my notes. I don't share them with clients."

The urge to stand and simply walk out the door was nearly overwhelming. Gritting her teeth, she said, "Has anyone ever told you you're rude?"

He grinned as if the comment pleased him. "As a matter of fact, yes. Several people have taken delight in revealing their opinions." He shook his head. "It has more to do with them and their hurt feelings than with me."

"What others think doesn't bother you?"

He gave a bored sigh. "Not particularly. Why should it? Now listen, Ms...." He glanced down at the application in an apparent effort to locate her name.

"Beaumont," she supplied.

"Ms. Beaumont," he said impatiently. "This is my office and *I* ask the questions here. Kindly refrain from interrupting me."

She leaned back in the chair. "By all means, ask away." She waved in his direction as though granting him permission to continue.

He narrowed his eyes. "In as few words as possible, explain to me why you aren't married."

That was easy enough to answer. She thought of what Angie had said a few days earlier. "I've been told my standards are too high."

He raised his eyes from the page, his expression startled.

"I guess you could say I'm choosy," she amended. "I'm looking for a perfect match. Someone who's just right—for me. The perfect man, the perfect marriage…and," she added, almost in a whisper, "the perfect Christmas."

He didn't respond. "You're how old?" he asked, instead. He ran his finger down the application.

"Thirty-four. How old are you?"

He exhaled. "As I requested earlier, kindly refrain from asking questions. My age is not your concern."

"Answer me one question, and then I promise not to ask anything else."

He glared at her.

"Just one," she cajoled. "You can't imagine how uncomfortable it is to sit here and have you scrutinize me. It's only fair that I should know something about you."

Sighing, he set the application aside, but before he could speak, she blurted out, "Are you married?"

His eyebrows arched. "*That's* your one question?"

"Yes, and it's important."

"Why is that?"

"Well, first, if you haven't been able to find yourself a wife, what qualifies you to find me a husband?"

"All I will say is that a doctor doesn't need to have a disease in order to cure it. I'm good at what I do. If I wasn't, I wouldn't be willing to offer a refund if I'm unsuccessful in locating a husband for you."

"Are you always so stiff and formal—as if your underwear's been starched?"

He stood abruptly. "I believe that will be all for this afternoon."

"You're sending me away?" She blinked, disappointed. Cassie was just starting to enjoy this. His typical clients were probably more respectful, if not downright obsequious.

"This interview is over."

"Did I pass?" She'd rather know now than be left hanging. She guessed not. She wouldn't be surprised if he didn't take her on. And yet, disagreeable though he was, Simon Dodson intrigued her.

He hesitated. "I'll be in touch later this week."

This was a line Cassie had heard before. "In other words, don't call me, I'll call you."

"Precisely."

Cassie recognized her marching orders. She bent down for her purse and reluctantly stood.

As she drove back to her condo, she tried to make sense of her short interview. On her way up, she collected her mail and noticed once again that the Tuesday paper was missing. Mrs. Mullinex, no doubt.

She ran for the elevator and saw Mr. Oliver, who lived on the same floor, standing inside. Looking her right in the eye, he let the doors close instead of holding them for her. This wasn't the first time, either. He was an unsociable man; the most she'd been able to coax out of him was a muffled greeting, as if he begrudged every word he was forced to speak.

When she got to her condo, she saw that she had company.

"Shawn!" Her brother had made himself at home and was wolfing down a sandwich while standing over her kitchen sink.

"Hey, it's about time you got home. Where were you?"

Rather than explain, Cassie walked over and hugged her big brother. "I had an appointment. How long are you here?" she asked.

"Two days, maybe three."

Shawn often had only a few days' rest before he flew to some other town where another commission awaited him. She knew he was headed to Phoenix, Arizona, next.

He had his own home in Portland, but every now and then he dropped in on her. In an effort to encourage his visits, she'd given him a key to her condo.

"I take it you're hungry."

"Starved."

"Let me fix you something decent." Cassie checked the contents of her refrigerator, then reached for a frying pan. She loved to cook and had a small repertoire of favorite dishes. This was one. "How does taco salad sound?"

"Like ambrosia from the gods." He sat on the stool and watched her move about the compact kitchen. "You're going to make some man a wonderful wife."

She whirled around to face him. "Funny you should say that."

Shawn went still. "You've met someone?"

"I would've told you!" They weren't in the habit of keeping secrets from each other. "My appointment this afternoon was with a professional matchmaker."

Her brother's head went back as if the announcement had shocked him. "Get out of here! A matchmaker?"

"I had my first appointment with the great and mighty Dr. Simon Dodson."

"How'd it go?"

Cassie set the onion on the chopping board and paused. "I'm not sure. Simon's pretty rude, but apparently he knows his stuff."

"Simon, is it?"

In her mind it was. "Yeah. He's not a medical doctor, even though he has a bunch of letters behind his name."

Her brother looked unconvinced. "You checked his references?"

"I did. I spoke with two couples who met through him. I was warned in advance that he isn't the most likeable fellow on the face of the earth, but they say he has this gift."

"How'd you hear about him?"

"Through Angie."

"Angie?" Her brother appeared as astonished by this as Cassie had been. "I wouldn't think she'd need a matchmaker. Did she go to him?"

Cassie nodded.

"When?"

"A little while ago. She didn't really say. What I don't get is why Simon rejected her."

"That's crazy! Angie's great."

"And I'm not?" she asked, her hand on her hip.

Shawn chuckled. "I'm staying as far away from that question as I can. What did the matchmaker say? If he rejected Angie, then what about you?"

That was the thirty-thousand-dollar question. "I don't know if Simon will accept me as a client or not. He said he'd phone, but…" The rest of her sentence was drowned out by loud rap music coming from the condo to the right of hers.

"Good grief, what's that?" Shawn covered his ears.

"My new neighbor," Cassie shouted back. She walked over to the kitchen wall and banged hard three times. Within half a minute, the music had been turned down to a more respectable volume.

"Jalapeño?" she asked next, hardly missing a beat.

"Might as well. My life could do with a bit of spicing up."

"Mine, too."

"So tell me more about this matchmaker. Do you like him?"

Cassie began tearing lettuce industriously. "The truth is, I don't. He's arrogant, snooty and definitely not my type. I'm not his, either. Not that it matters… But he doesn't like to be questioned or challenged. I could tell I irritated him."

"You heard he's successful, though, right?"

"Yeah." Until that moment, Cassie hadn't realized how much she hoped Simon would agree to work with her. "I don't know if he's ready for someone like me."

"What do you mean?"

She waved a lettuce leaf in his direction. "Like I said, I questioned his actions and his decisions. He didn't like it."

"I wonder why he rejected Angie," Shawn mused. "I mean, she's not annoying or—"

"Hey, stop right there."

Shawn laughed and leaned his elbows on the counter

where he sat. "Who's that picture of on the fridge?" he asked.

Although she didn't need to turn and look, Cassie did. She tensed slightly as she stared at the photograph of Jill and Tom and their perfect Christmas. "That, brother dearest, is my inspiration."

Chapter 3

A few minutes later, Cassie reached for her phone on impulse and dialed Angie's number.

"Hello? Oh, Cassie, I was hoping you'd call. How'd the appointment go?"

"Do you like taco salad?" Cassie asked rather than answering.

"Is there any food group I don't like?" Her friend had a smile in her voice.

"Silly question. Come join us."

"Us?"

"Yes, Shawn stopped by. I'm making a taco salad and if you have fresh tomatoes bring one. If not, we'll do without."

"Shawn's there? Your brother?"

"That's what I just said. Are you coming or not?"

"I'm on my way, and I've got a tomato," Angie said, "but when I get there, I want details about the meeting with Dr. Dodson."

Shawn grabbed an orange from her fruit bowl and tossed it in the air, juggling it with an apple and doing a poor job. The orange hit the floor and rolled into the living room. "I'm glad you invited Angie. How's she doing?"

"You know Angie. She's always in a good mood."

Her brother retrieved the orange. "Well…it'll be nice to see her again."

Cassie nodded absently as she began to sauté the ground beef.

By the time Angie arrived, Cassie had the hamburger with taco sauce simmering together. The salad fixings were in a large bowl, awaiting Angie's tomato. Shawn was grating the cheese.

Angie brightened the moment she walked into the room. "Shawn, it's great to see you."

"You, too." He set the cheese down long enough to give her a brief hug. Cassie always forgot how tiny her friend was until Angie stood next to her brother, who was well over six feet.

While Cassie got out the bag of tortilla chips and assembled the rest of the salad, Angie set the table and Shawn filled their water glasses. "Sorry I don't have any sangria," Cassie said as she carried the large wooden bowl to the table. Smaller bowls of meat, cheese and chips followed.

"This looks wonderful," Angie told her.

"Allow me." Shawn pulled out Angie's chair. Then he hurried around to the other side of the table to do the same for Cassie.

"Since when have you acquired gentlemanly manners?" Cassie asked.

Jokingly Shawn checked his watch. "About five minutes ago."

"Perfect timing."

"I'm dying to hear how everything went this afternoon," Angie said, her fork poised over the salad. "How was the meeting with...Dr. Dodson?" She glanced toward Shawn as if she wasn't sure she should say any more.

"It's okay." Cassie nodded. "He knows all about it."

Shawn rolled his eyes. "Personally I think she's nuts. So, what's the story with you and this matchmaker?"

Angie ignored the question and returned her attention to Cassie. "Don't keep me in suspense. What was your impression when you met him?"

"He's abrupt and ill-mannered, don't you agree?"

"That's putting it mildly." She turned to Shawn. "He rejected me. I didn't make it past the initial interview. I'll admit it was a blow to my ego but I felt I had to tell Cassie about him."

"I can't believe he'd reject you." Shawn looked genuinely outraged on Angie's behalf. "I don't understand why either of you would have any interest in someone who seems to enjoy insulting you."

"Why?" Cassie answered. "We're getting desperate, that's why. It's not easy to meet decent men, you know!"

"Not at our age," Angie added.

"See that picture of Jill and Tom?" Cassie said, pointing to her refrigerator. "She has the perfect life, the perfect family and is about to have the perfect Christmas. I want all that."

"Me, too," Angie murmured fervently. "And so far I haven't even come close."

Shawn blinked. "You two are actually serious?"

"Serious enough to pay thirty thousand bucks to find the right man."

Shawn's eyebrows shot up. "*How* much?"

Cassie didn't feel like repeating it. "You heard me."

Shaking his head, Shawn muttered something about being in the wrong business.

Angie sighed. "It's a ridiculous amount of money, I know, but from what I understand, it's worth every penny—if you're accepted, that is. Now, Cassie, tell me about your meeting with Dr. Dodson."

Mentally reviewing the appointment, Cassie suffered more than a few doubts. "I don't think I went over well."

"But you have a second appointment, right?"

"Supposedly." Cassie shrugged. "He said he'd call...."

"Cassie, that's great! Dr. Dodson read my application, took one look at me and said he didn't have anyone who'd suit me."

That wasn't precisely what Angie had told her earlier. Simon had apparently said she already held feelings for someone. If that *was* the case, Cassie didn't have any idea who it might be. She wished she'd questioned her further, but at the time she'd been too interested in hearing about this matchmaker and now didn't seem appropriate. Especially since Angie was obviously reluctant to talk about her own situation. The man in question must've been someone she'd met years ago, which was what Angie had implied. It certainly wasn't anyone Cassie knew, and they'd worked together for six years.

"Tell us what he said," Angie urged.

"Simon was pretty rude," Cassie said between bites of her salad. She added another layer of crushed tortilla chips to the lettuce.

"How?" Shawn asked. "I want specifics."

"Well, he didn't seem to like a single thing about me. Not my body type, not my choice of clothes or the color of my suit."

"I love that suit!" Angie cried.

"I did, too," Cassie said, immediately noting that she'd used the past tense. Hard as it was to admit, he was right about that. She would've preferred it in a soft robin's-egg blue, but the only available color had been navy.

"Didn't he have *anything* nice to say?" Angie asked.

"Well…he did mention that my hairstyle suited me but it needed more length. That was as close to a compliment as he got."

"But you made it past the first interview," Angie said again, as though Cassie had managed a feat of unparalleled skill.

"What I don't understand," Shawn said, pushing back in his chair, "is why you'd allow this man to insult you. I mean, everything he said was just a matter of opinion. *His* opinion." He raised both hands as the women started to protest. "Okay, I understand you're feeling desperate—to quote you—but I don't get it."

Cassie and Angie shared a look.

"I think it's the promise," Cassie said.

"The promise," Shawn repeated. "What promise?"

Angie leaned forward, folding her arms on the table. "Dr. Dodson guarantees that he'll find you a match."

"Someone who'll be a perfect match…"

"Someone who's as eager to meet us as we are them," Angie explained.

"The thing is," Cassie said, "I can't help wondering if the man of my dreams is actually out there."

"Of course he is," Shawn insisted. "Frankly I think all of this is nonsense. How can anyone *guarantee* that he'll find you a *perfect match?*" Sarcasm dripped from his words. "I can't believe you're willing to pay the guy that much money when you're completely capable of finding yourself a husband."

"Where?" Cassie asked, opening her arms and gesturing widely. "Tell me where he is and I'll send a search party to bag him."

"I'll volunteer," Angie said. "Maybe there'll be an extra man hanging around for me."

"Where?" Shawn ignored their teasing. "There are men, decent men, everywhere. You can meet him at work—" they shook their heads simultaneously "—well, then, at...at the grocery store. Or on the street. Or in a bookstore. Or..."

Angie cocked one finely shaped eyebrow. "Did you hear what I just heard?"

"I did," Cassie confirmed.

"What?" Shawn looked from one woman to the other.

"You used the word *meet,*" Cassie told him.

"Not marry," Angie said.

"Now, just a minute—" Shawn started to speak but Cassie cut him off.

"You're a prime example of what we're talking about."

"Me?" Shawn placed a hand over his heart. "I'm too busy for a wife and family. I'm constantly on the road. That's no life for kids."

"You don't feel the need for companionship, then?" Angie asked.

"Not really."

"Men don't," Cassie complained. "They don't know they're miserable until we tell them."

"So I'm miserable now?" Shawn laughed as if she'd made a joke. "Too bad I've never noticed."

Cassie wasn't about to argue with him. "Men aren't on the same timetable women are, and when they finally wake up and realize they want the same things we do, *they* can still father children."

"A woman has biological limitations," Angie said, "if she wants kids."

Her brother's look sobered. "You two aren't kidding."

"No way," Cassie said. "In fact, we're willing to put up with the criticism and scrutiny of someone like Simon Dodson in the hope of finding a good man we can share our lives with."

Shawn grew thoughtful. "I don't understand why he'd reject *you,* Angie. It seems to me you'd be an ideal candidate."

"Well, he did, and it's his prerogative," she said briskly. Then she smiled at Cassie. "I can hardly wait until you have your next appointment."

"Now, just a minute," Shawn said again. "You should've asked me to set you up before you went to all this trouble."

Cassie's eyes widened. "You have someone you want me to meet?"

"Well, sure. I know a dozen eligible men. I could've introduced you."

Cassie glanced at Angie. "He only thinks to mention this now?"

Angie frowned. "Do you really trust your brother to find you a husband?"

Cassie shook her head. "My idea of what I want and what he has to offer might be worlds apart."

"Hey, you two," Shawn said, breaking into their conversation. "I'm sitting right here. If you have any doubts, you can address them to me directly and not to each other."

"Okay," Cassie said. "Tell me about one such man."

"All right." He appeared to be deep in thought.

"I don't think he can scrounge up even one," Cassie whispered, raising her eyebrows.

"Give me a minute, would you," he snapped.

"Notice how testy he gets when challenged."

Her brother silenced her with a look.

"There's Riley," he declared triumphantly. He beamed a smile at Angie and then Cassie.

"I've always liked the name Riley," Angie said.

"Riley." Cassie threw back her head. "You're joking!"

"What's wrong with Riley?" Angie wanted to know.

"He's an artist friend of Shawn's. He's got two ex-wives, a gambling problem and he drinks too much. You're scraping the bottom of the frying pan if you're suggesting either of us should marry *Riley.*"

"He's reformed."

"Yeah, right. And when did this happen?"

Shawn seemed unsure. "Not too long ago. He said he's through messing up his life. What he needs now is a good woman."

Cassie exhaled slowly. "Tell him to talk to one of his ex-wives, then."

"Sorry," Angie said, "I'm not interested, either."

"You're going to have to try harder than that," Cassie informed her brother.

"What about Larry Upjohn? You couldn't meet a nicer guy if you tried."

"Do you know Larry?" Angie asked her.

Cassie nodded. "He's Shawn's CPA and in a word… *b-o-r-i-n-g.*"

"You didn't say you were looking for a stand-up comic," Shawn said, obviously annoyed.

"Call me superficial, but I don't want to date a man who wears knee-high socks with his sandals and a pocket protector in his pajamas."

"A little personality would be helpful," Angie said in a defeated voice. "As you can tell, it's not as easy as it seems."

"Warren!" Shawn's face lit up. "What about Warren?"

Once more Angie turned to Cassie.

She nodded, but without enthusiasm. "Warren's a… possibility."

"What's wrong with Warren?" Shawn cried.

Cassie shrugged. "Nothing really. He just doesn't ring my bells. He might Angie's, though."

Shawn leaned back, throwing out his arms in an expansive gesture. "I can introduce you, if you like."

"Tell me about him first," Angie said.

"He's Shawn's agent," Cassie explained. "He's a nice guy."

"Nice isn't a word I'd use to describe Warren," Shawn commented. "He's a tough negotiator."

"But a real kitten on the inside," Cassie said. "He's also divorced. Recently, if I remember."

"He and Clare split last year. I don't know many guys your age who aren't divorced."

"That's reassuring," Cassie muttered. Warren was the best of the rather shallow pool of Shawn's male friends and acquaintances. Shallow pools, as everyone knew, were usually the slimiest, too. This was exactly why she'd decided on the matchmaker.

"Warren's got a couple of kids. His wife has custody."

"Thanks, big brother, but I'll stick with Dr. Dodson."

"I appreciate the suggestion," Angie said, "but I'll pass on Warren, too."

"If I think of anyone else, I'll give you a call."

"You do that," Cassie said, although she didn't expect he would. "On second thought, phone Angie."

Chapter 4

Simon says: I can find the right mate for everyone. Even you!

Simon kept Cassie waiting forty-five minutes on her next visit. His assistant, Ms. Snelling, had called the day after her first appointment. It was now Friday. Since she'd been on pins and needles for three whole days, an additional forty-five minutes didn't bother her. Today would be when he'd announce whether he'd found her a match.

She couldn't figure out how, based on their brief conversation, Simon would be able to match her up with the perfect man. Maybe, as Angie said, it really was all about his ability as a psychologist, his scientific study of her lengthy questionnaire.

For three nights now, she'd been like a kid at Christmas—only instead of sugar plums dancing around in her head she saw men's faces. Men who were enthralled with her. Men who'd go through the same insulting rigmarole she had for the chance to meet her. Men who were just as eager for the very things she wanted—a home and family, security, a sense of belonging and a lifetime filled with love. And one of those men would be her perfect match.

"Dr. Dodson will see you now," Ms. Snelling said in the same crisp tone she'd used on Cassie's first visit.

Cassie bounded up from the chair as though she'd been ejected. Despite her eagerness, she tried to move slowly and calmly. When she entered his office, she found Simon sitting at his desk.

Without looking up, he gestured for her to sit, too.

Cassie did, perching on the very edge. She didn't expect an apology for being kept waiting and wasn't disappointed. When Simon eventually looked up, she noticed streaks of gray in his hair that had escaped her notice previously.

"What are your plans for Christmas?" he asked.

Of all the things Cassie had expected him to say, this wasn't it. "Ah…I'm not sure yet."

"Family plans?"

"Not really." She hadn't talked to her brother yet. Her mother and stepfather lived in Hawaii and it was unlikely that they'd fly in for the holidays. Her father…well, she hadn't spent Christmas with him since she was five or six. "There's just Shawn and me."

"And Shawn is?"

"My brother. It's on the questionnaire. He's—"

"Ah, yes," Simon broke in. "What did you do last Christmas?"

"Well, let me see…" She tried to remember where she'd been and with whom. Was it last year that Angie—

"This shouldn't be so difficult," he said.

"It was eleven months ago," she snapped. His attitude irritated her. "As I recall, Shawn and I went out to eat. Angie, a friend of mine, was supposed to join us but at the last minute she couldn't and we—"

"Yes, yes," he said, interrupting her again.

"And what exactly were *you* doing?" she demanded.

His eyes widened. "I beg your pardon?"

"Where were you last Christmas?"

"As I indicated during our previous session, I'm the one asking the questions."

Cassie made an effort to hold her temper. "I guess that slipped my mind. But I was allowed one question then, so I assume that's the case today, and I'm asking it now." She took a deep—and necessary—breath. "Where were *you* last Christmas?"

He exhaled slowly. "Right here in Seattle."

"With friends and loved ones?"

"That's more than one question." He looked pointedly in her direction. "Shall we continue or not? The choice is yours."

Knowing she was fighting a losing battle, Cassie tried to regain her equilibrium. "Yes, let's continue, although I don't understand what last Christmas has to do with anything."

"That's not your concern."

"Are you always this dictatorial?" She realized she was asking yet another question, but she couldn't stop herself.

"I am when I feel I can find the right match for a client. An exasperating one, I might add."

"Really?" That was worth all the insults he could issue, Cassie decided. She slid so far to the edge of the chair that she was in danger of falling onto the carpet. "You actually have someone in mind?"

"I do." This was said in a clipped, businesslike way.

She waited, but he wasn't any more forthcoming than that.

"Before I introduce you, there are a few matters we need to attend to."

"Fine." Her heart felt as if it had moved into her throat.

"My fee is thirty thousand dollars."

"Yes, I know… That's a lot of money."

Simon glanced up. "I thought you were aware of my

fee. If you can't afford me, then I suggest you leave now and save us both a lot of time and trouble."

The money was safely tucked in Cassie's savings account. "I put it aside for a wedding, but obviously there won't be one without a groom. I'm willing to make the investment."

"Good. Then I'll introduce you to John."

"His name is John?" John was a solid name, implying that he was a solid man; she liked him already.

"Before I introduce you—"

"There's a money-back guarantee, right?"

"I'll explain that in a moment."

"Okay, sorry, I didn't mean to interrupt." She wanted to capture every single detail of this meeting so she could repeat it all to Angie.

"I have three tasks I want you to complete first."

"Excuse me?" She wondered if she'd misheard him. Cassie was waiting to hear about her perfect mate, and he was talking about *tasks?* What was this, homework?

"These are qualifying tasks," he was saying. "I need to be sure you're the woman for John."

"But…no one said anything about needing to qualify."

He ignored her outburst. "Once you've fulfilled these three *simple* tasks, I will introduce you to John. The choice is easy—do what I ask and meet the man of your dreams or keep your money and walk away now." He sat back in his chair and clasped his hands, clearly regarding this as a take-it-or-leave-it proposition.

Cassie's head reeled. "Do you ask this of all your clients?" she cried, almost positive he didn't. Her nerves were quickly fraying.

"How often do I need to tell you? I'm not in the habit of answering questions." He paused and looked her straight in the eye. "However, I'll admit that I don't ask this of every client. Only certain ones."

"What made me so lucky?"

"Your motives. You expect to find the perfect husband, the perfect marriage and the perfect Christmas, correct?"

She remembered having said as much. She nodded.

"You're asking for the impossible."

"But…isn't that what you promised?"

"No. If you'll examine my Web site, you'll see that I promise the *right* mate. The most suitable spouse. But that's just the beginning. A happy marriage is about much more than the appearance of perfection."

Others had found true love. Jill and Tom had, so why couldn't she? "I can dream, can't I?" she muttered.

"Yes, you can dream as long as your dreams are rooted in reality."

"And you consider it your duty to drag me out of my happy fantasy and into the real world," she said sarcastically.

"What I consider my duty is to match you up with someone who'll spend the rest of his life thinking he's the most fortunate man alive to be with you."

"Oh." She swallowed tightly.

"Do you accept the three tasks or not?"

She hesitated. She needed more information before she agreed to anything. "What are they?"

"I'm not asking you to swim in shark-infested waters, if that's what you're worried about. It's nothing life-threatening."

"I won't have to eat anything disgusting, will I?"

He cringed. "Good grief, no. As I said, these are simple, ordinary tasks. It sounds as if you've been watching too much reality television."

"Actually, I don't. My friend Angie watches that stuff and then tells me about it the next day."

He ignored her explanation and reached for a slip of paper on his desk. "Here's your first task. I need you to volunteer for a four-hour shift as a bell ringer in front of the Southcenter Mall near Kent. Do you know it?"

"I know every mall within a two-hundred-mile radius of Seattle."

"I have no doubt of that."

Really, how difficult could a four-hour shift be? "Sure, that won't be a problem."

"It's the weekend after Thanksgiving."

"Great. The mall will be hopping."

"There's a quota the charity expects you to make, but I don't think you'll have any trouble with that."

"Okay. What's the second task?" The first one didn't

seem too hard; the next one was probably along similar lines.

"You said on the application form that you're interested in a man who wants children."

"I am."

"Good. I'm going to give you the opportunity to spend an entire afternoon with the little darlings. You'll be one of Santa's elves for a picture-taking session at the Tacoma Mall."

"An elf?"

"There's a costume. I apologize, but it's one of the requirements."

"Okay, fine, I can be an elf." She didn't like the idea of wearing some silly outfit with tights and pointed shoes but she could cope. "And the final task?"

He reached for another slip of paper. "I also saw on your application that you enjoy cooking."

"I do." And she was pretty good at it if she did say so herself.

"Excellent. For your third task, I want you to cook Christmas dinner. Turkey, stuffing, mashed potatoes with gravy, salad, vegetables…that sort of thing. Oh, and two different kinds of homemade pie."

"And who's going to be eating this huge meal?"

"Your neighbors."

"Ah." She raised her index finger in protest. "I don't have the friendliest neighbors…."

"Invite them, anyway."

"And who's going to check up to see if I've completed these tasks?" she asked. She suspected Simon hadn't thought this completely through.

"I'll be checking in on you during the first two tasks."

"You might as well come to Christmas dinner, then. Can I invite my brother and best friend, too?"

"Of course," he said, but he didn't respond to her admittedly reluctant invitation.

"Can they bring a contribution?" She was thinking Shawn could scrounge up a cooked turkey somewhere and even Angie could manage stuffing out of a box.

"No, you will be providing the entire meal."

Cassie was afraid of that.

"Now that you know the tasks, do you feel you can handle them?"

"I guess so—but what exactly is the point?"

He smiled—a glimmer of a smile. "Each task will tell me something about you. Something important. However, you don't seem very confident. Can you or can't you? A yes or no will suffice."

Lifting her hand to her brow she saluted him smartly. "Aye, aye, sir."

Her gesture failed to amuse him, but he did relax somewhat. "Now that we've squared away that portion of our discussion, it's time to finalize the paperwork."

"All right. Oh—do I get to ask three things of you— small, easy-to-perform tasks?"

He sent her a withering look.

"Obviously I don't," she said under her breath.

"Let's make this clear," he said with exaggerated patience. "*You're* the one who sought me out. You came to me because of your desire for a husband and a family. I don't advertise. I didn't ask you to step into this office. You came of your own free will."

"I did," she concurred.

"Then we play this by my rules."

She resisted rolling her eyes for fear he'd demand she leave. "Rules," she repeated softly. "Is this a game to you?"

"No, this is life, yours and John's. He's a good man who wants the same things you do."

"Okay, I accept your rules."

"Thank you."

"Can I at least see his photograph?"

"No. You will meet when it's time. There will be no information exchanged before that official meeting."

Cassie didn't like it, but she didn't have any alternative. She nodded.

Simon opened a side drawer and withdrew a contract. "I advise you to have your attorney look this over before you sign it. This is a standard contract, stating what you can expect for your thirty thousand dollars."

"What if John and I don't gel? If we aren't a good fit?"

"That occasionally happens and it's a fair question. Your money will be refunded to both of you in full."

"In that case, will you introduce me to another potential mate?"

"No."

"No. No?"

"This is a one-shot deal."

"One-shot?" That sounded risky.

"If I offered choices, my clients would be wondering who else might be available. When I pick a mate for you, it's the best match I can find, someone I believe will complement your strengths, share your values and fulfill your desires—within reasonable parameters."

"And your success rate is?"

"High. I don't accept a client unless I'm confident I have the right person for him or her. It's as simple as that."

Cassie stared down at the contract. She'd feel better if she liked Simon more. The man was rude, arrogant and short-tempered.

It was as if he'd read her thoughts. "You don't need to like me, Cassie," he said. "In fact, it's preferable that you don't."

"Really?"

"Yes, really," he returned. "The last thing I want or need is for a client to fall in love with me. It only complicates matters, and I don't like unnecessary complications. Understood?"

"Now who's dreaming?"

A smile came and went. A smile that charmed her despite everything he'd said and done.

Chapter 5

Simon says: Maybe money can't buy love—but it can get you practically everything else.

On the Saturday morning after Thanksgiving, which she'd spent with Angie and her family, Cassie headed for Southcenter Mall. This was the venue for her first task and she was eager to prove herself to Simon, obviously a curmudgeon. Spending four hours soliciting money for charity couldn't possibly be that difficult.

Since she'd be standing outside, Cassie dressed in wool pants and a hand-knit sweater over her long-sleeved blouse. Between the shirt and sweater, she could barely get her arms inside the sleeves of her coat. She added a hat, gloves and a scarf, dressing for the cold. When she met her one true love, she wanted to make sure she didn't have a runny nose and a sore throat.

Cassie showed up at the mall at the required time and met the other charity bell ringers. Standing with her colleagues, she glanced around. Some were being paid and frankly she thought they looked kind of shifty. Others, like her, were volunteers.

"Smile and greet everyone," the leader instructed. "Be friendly even if someone walks past you."

Filled with enthusiasm, Cassie could hardly wait to be assigned her post.

"Make eye contact" was the second bit of advice. "And ring that bell. Remind shoppers of those less fortunate."

"Got it," Cassie said aloud.

"This is one of the busiest shopping weekends of the year, so you shouldn't have any problem making your quota."

In the back of her mind, she recalled Simon's casually mentioning something about collecting a certain dollar amount and the way he'd made light of it. The recommended donation amount turned out to be $60 an hour. That was a dollar a minute! How was she supposed to know how much money she'd collected when the red pot was securely locked? It wasn't as if she could pry the lid off and count the cash.

"Are we ready?" their helpful leader called out.

Cassie's shout blended in with the others'. "Ready!"

One by one, they received their assignments. Cassie was told to stand in front of the Target store, which had an outside entrance. With bell in hand, she headed toward her designated post. This wasn't so bad. Not only was she helping the underprivileged but she was moving toward the man of her dreams.

She waited eagerly as a couple walked up. Smiling sweetly, she jerked her hand several times in succession, making the bell jangle. "Merry Christmas," she greeted them.

The couple avoided eye contact and entered the store via the door farthest from Cassie.

Their lack of generosity—and appreciation for her efforts—didn't faze her.

Not much later, a grandmotherly type approached her. "Do you have change for a five?" the woman asked.

"Sorry, we can't make change."

"Oh, dear," she said regretfully, "then perhaps I can give you something on my way out."

"Don't worry," Cassie said cheerfully, "I'll be here."

In her first thirty minutes, Cassie estimated that she'd collected less than five dollars, which wasn't even close to her hourly goal. She stomped her feet to ward off the cold. In an effort to liven things up a bit, she attempted to ring the tunes of popular Christmas songs.

She gave that up during "Frosty the Snowman" when

a teenage boy walked past and reached for his cell phone. He said, "Hello. Hello. Hello," before he realized it was her bell and not his cell. He stopped in front of her and glared.

"Sorry," she said, and gasped when the youth shot her the finger.

"Well, Merry Christmas to you, too." Of all the nerve! After an hour Angie came by and mercifully handed her a cup of steaming hot coffee.

"God love you," she said, gratefully accepting it.

"How's it going?"

If it'd been Simon rather than Angie, she would have declared that this was the most wonderful, rewarding experience of her life. With Angie she felt compelled to tell the truth. "I can't feel my nose."

"Can I get you anything else?" her friend asked, her expression concerned.

"Put some money in the pot. I'm nowhere near my quota."

"Oh, sure." Angie put in a hefty donation.

"Thank you."

"Do you want me to stand in for you? You look like you could use a break."

"No way." Simon Dodson was sure to find out about it and consider her unworthy of John. Cassie wasn't willing to risk that.

"You have a donation quota?"

Cassie nodded. "I bet that guy at the other entrance isn't having this problem," she muttered. Her breath made small whiffs of fog. Her nose wasn't the only body part in danger of frostbite. Even the knit cap wasn't enough to completely protect her ears. She'd swear those weren't earrings dangling from her lobes, but tiny icicles.

"I'll come and see you again later," Angie promised.

"Great, and thanks for the coffee." Cassie wondered whether anyone would notice if she stuck her nose in the hot liquid.

Angie disappeared inside the mall and Cassie rang her bell with renewed enthusiasm. It helped to remember that in less than three hours she would have completed one of the tasks that would bring her closer to meeting John.

In retrospect she wished she'd pushed Simon to show her John's photograph. Then again, she didn't want any predetermined impressions of him. He was already bigger than life in her mind. She pictured him at the head of a boardroom table or the helm of a sailboat. Or...

Suddenly, she noticed the scruffily dressed middle-aged man standing in front of her. He looked like he belonged to a motorcycle gang. He had on a worn leather jacket that barely zipped up over his protruding belly and a bandanna around his head. His hair, long and greasy and tied in a ponytail, reached to the middle of his back. He made a beeline for Cassie as if destiny had called him to her side.

Her bell ringing became a whole lot less enthusiastic.

He looked her slowly up and down. Then he smiled as if to say her waiting days were over; *he* had arrived. "Hello, there, pretty lady."

Cassie managed a weak smile in return. "Happy holidays." This guy didn't strike her as the charitable type.

"I bet you're real cold standing out here all by yourself."

She didn't respond but his gaze lingered on her, which gave her a decidedly uncomfortable feeling.

"I could find ways to keep us both warm."

"Ah…actually I'm warm as toast," she said. An outright lie. She hoped he didn't notice that, by this time, her nose was probably blue.

A mother and daughter scurried past her. Cassie thrust out her arm and rang the bell as if sounding an alarm during the great San Francisco fire. When the pair resolutely ignored her, she rang the bell using both hands. Still they walked past. In fact, it seemed to Cassie that they went out of their way to avoid her. In other words, she was on her own with the biker.

"We'd be grateful for a donation," she told him.

"I was thinking you could give me one."

"Me? What could I possibly give you?" As soon as she asked the question, Cassie realized her mistake. "Forget I asked that," she said.

"What are you doing after this stint?" he asked.

Cassie could hardly believe this was happening and let

her bell-holding hand fall to her side. "Are you trying to pick me up?" she asked incredulously. "You're old enough to be my father." She did her best to hide her revulsion.

"Hey, you can't blame a guy for trying."

"Yes, I can. Now kindly move along. You're discouraging donations." She scowled at him, letting him know she didn't appreciate that he was cutting into her hourly quota.

He chuckled as though amused. "You have no idea what you're missing."

Frankly, Cassie was grateful for the escape. She heaved a sigh of relief when he sauntered off. Her one hope was that when he left the mall he'd use a different exit.

As soon as Mr. Easy Rider was gone, donations picked up. Still, as far as she could figure, Cassie wasn't even close to making the recommended quota, despite her cheerful greetings.

Distracted, she didn't notice another man approaching.

"You should be ashamed of yourself," he said angrily.

Taken aback, she blinked, then asked, "I beg your pardon?" Obviously *he* wasn't the one standing in the cold, ringing his heart out, seeking donations for the poor.

"It isn't even December."

"And your point is?" she challenged, which she recognized almost immediately was a mistake. She didn't want to invite an argument, which she'd inadvertently done.

"Christmas is far too commercial."

"Ah…"

"Everyone's got their hand out. I've had it up to here," he said, slicing the air over his head, "with greedy beggars asking for handouts."

"Greedy beggars?" she repeated, growing agitated. "Don't you have any compassion for others? Where's your Christmas spirit?"

"It doesn't come out until December. Look at these shops! Most of them had their Christmas displays up before Halloween. All they're after is the almighty dollar."

"Go complain to them, not me," she urged, hoping to send Scrooge on his way. "And when you do, say hello to Tiny Tim for me."

"Who?"

"Never mind."

"Those greedy shop owners spoil the true meaning of Christmas. And you're no better than corporate America, stopping people as they're going into the store. Irritating them with that stupid bell."

"I'm not asking you for anything. The bell is to remind shoppers of the less fortunate. I didn't *stop* you—you're the one who came up to me. Furthermore…" She halted midsentence as it occurred to her that this man might be a plant of Simon's, that he'd purposely headed right over to chat with her.

Cassie eyed him warily. "Simon sent you, didn't he?"

"Simon? Who's Simon?"

"This is a test, isn't it?"

"Lady, I don't know what you're talking about."

"You can't fool me! Simon sent you to see how I'd respond. Well, you can tell him I saw through your little charade and it didn't work." She felt downright smug that Simon hadn't outsmarted her.

Scrooge stared at her, wearing a puzzled look. Then his eyes narrowed. "Lady, I suggest you seek counseling."

"Thank you, but I suggest you make an appointment first. You can tell Simon I said that, okay?"

He backed away from her as if he suddenly suspected she carried an infectious disease.

Donations were few and far between, and Cassie glanced toward her counterpart at the other end of the mall with envy. He had more business than he knew what to do with. She, on the other hand, felt like the Little Match Girl. Using her foot, she eased the red kettle ever so slightly toward the department store entrance. She was about halfway between the two when the other charity collector noticed.

Cassie eased her foot away from the pot and gazed in the opposite direction.

"Hey, you!" he shouted, pointing an accusing finger at her. "You stay in your half of the mall and I'll stay in mine."

Playing innocent, Cassie pressed her gloved hand to her chest. "Are you speaking to me?" she called.

"You drag that kettle one step closer, sister, and you'll live to regret it."

Cassie opened her mouth, then closed it. She'd been caught. There was nothing to do but drag the kettle back, one step at a time.

Eventually Cassie returned to her original spot and figured she'd probably lost thirty minutes in this attempt to find more fertile ground. With no option other than to follow her original plan, she continued to greet the shoppers, doing her best to display a cheerful holiday spirit.

A young couple approached from the mall parking lot and Cassie made eye contact with the man. The woman, who carried a cup of takeout coffee, didn't appear to see her, but he looked friendly enough, so Cassie rang the bell with renewed energy. These people seemed like the kind who'd dig deep into their wallets in order to help the less fortunate.

As they neared the store, just as Cassie had hoped, the man reached in his back pocket for his wallet. This was a good sign. Cassie smiled encouragingly.

The woman walked toward the store entrance, while the man paused in front of Cassie and slipped a twenty-dollar bill into the pot.

The woman quickly rejoined her husband. "How much did you put in there?" she demanded.

"Come on, Alicia, it's for charity."

"Charity begins at home. We've been through this, re-member? We're on a Christmas budget. We don't have extra money to be giving away."

The man grimaced apologetically.

"It's for a good cause," Cassie reminded the woman.

"As for you," Alicia said menacingly. "I saw the way you were flirting with my husband. You didn't think I noticed, did you?"

Cassie was too stunned to react. "I wasn't—"

"Don't bother denying it. I have eyes. Maybe the two of you are old *friends*."

"Alicia," the man snapped.

"That's it, we're finished. It's over." In a fit of anger she tossed the cup of coffee at Cassie.

She gasped and leaped back but not in time to avoid hav-ing coffee splash the front of her caramel-colored wool coat.

The man looked horrified, whispered something Cas-sie couldn't hear, then hurried after his wife. "Alicia, Ali-cia…"

In shock and denial, Cassie stared down at her coat. Some very unladylike comments formed in her mind. However, she didn't express them since that would reflect poorly on the charitable organization. Within minutes she was glad she'd kept her mouth shut. Because, to Cassie's astonishment, donations started to increase dramatically following the incident. She glanced at the other bell ringer, who was scowling at her. He rang his bell louder and harder.

Cassie retaliated with an all-out rendition of "Deck the Halls" and soon had a short line, everyone waiting to drop in donations. She wasn't sure what had changed but clearly there'd been a reversal. Perhaps her bell ringing was superior. Or perhaps that section of the parking lot had filled up. Whatever the cause, she was taking full advantage of it.

Toward the end of her shift, a sweet old lady sidled up to Cassie with a benevolent smile. She stuffed something inside her coat pocket and leaned close to whisper, "Use this to buy yourself a decent coat, dear. You poor thing."

That was it? People thought she was a charity case and had taken pity on her. Too bad the coffee incident had happened at the end of her four hours. Who knew how much she would've collected if it had occurred earlier.

She nearly laughed aloud when she realized one glove was missing. Cassie didn't have a clue when that had disappeared or how.

Precisely four hours into her assignment, when she was about ready to hand in her kettle and bell, she saw Dr. Simon Dodson. He was walking across the parking lot and headed directly toward her. And he was frowning.

Chapter 6

Simon says: The best match for you is the one *I*
arrange.

Just as Simon approached, an elderly gentleman stepped
up to the pot and inserted a folded bill.

"Thank you and Merry Christmas," Cassie told him
cheerfully.

"No, thank *you*," the old man returned. "You see, I
was on a troop train in World War II and your organization met us at the station as we disembarked and
handed out doughnuts and coffee. That small kindness
meant the world to those of us going off to war. I've
never forgotten it."

Cassie hardly knew what to say.

"A lot of us didn't come home from the war, but I'll bet you those of us who did will always remember the friendly smiles and support you gave us. I'm an old man now and I don't have many more years left." He grew teary-eyed as he spoke. "Merry Christmas, young lady," he whispered, gently squeezing her hand, "and thank you again for the sacrifice you're making on behalf of others."

Now it was Cassie who had tears in her eyes. She brushed them aside as Simon came closer. The old man had disappeared inside the mall by the time he arrived.

"How was it?" he asked.

Cassie tried to swallow the lump in her throat. "My grandfather was in the Second World War, too."

"I beg your pardon?"

"That elderly gentleman," she said, sniffling, "the one who was just here. He told me about something that happened when he went off to war and thanked me as if I was the one who'd been kind to him."

"I didn't see any old man."

"You didn't? He was here a minute ago and was...just wonderful." She didn't understand how Simon could have missed him. It was unlikely that he'd have eyes only for her.

"What happened to your coat?" Simon asked, apparently not interested in hearing about the man who had touched her so deeply.

"Oh, that," she said, glancing down. "That was a lucky

break. Well, to be honest, it didn't seem like it at the time, but I collected a lot of pity donations as a result."

He didn't ask her to elaborate. "Your shift is over. You can leave now."

"What about my substitute?" Cassie wasn't about to be lured away from her duty station until the next person was firmly in place.

"That would be me," a cheerful middle-aged woman said from behind Simon, the supervisor at her side.

Cassie handed over the bell, and the supervisor took her full kettle and replaced it with an empty one. "Good luck," Cassie told the new bell ringer and meant every word. She nearly added that the woman was going to need it.

"You didn't tell me how your morning went," Simon said. He walked into the mall with her.

Cassie stood just inside the sliding glass doors for a moment, soaking in the blast of warm air. Until now she hadn't fully realized how utterly cold she'd been. Four hours had felt like forever.

"You don't want to know," she said. Her teeth had only now stopped chattering.

"I don't ask questions if I don't want an answer."

"Okay, fine. I misplaced a glove, and my nose lost feeling in the first half hour." She looked at him and muttered, "It's still there, isn't it? My nose, I mean."

"Yes." His mouth twitched, but he didn't admit he was amused.

"My feet feel like blocks of ice. A jealous wife threw coffee on me and some sweet old lady slipped a fifty-dollar bill into my coat pocket because she felt sorry for me. I threw it in the pot," she added righteously.

Simon arched his brows. That apparently was his only comment.

"Furthermore, I recognized your plant."

"My...plant?"

"The man you sent. Okay, so I made that remark about saying hello to Tiny Tim. Oh, and about seeing a shrink. I probably shouldn't have, but I couldn't help it. He was obnoxious. Did you pay him extra for being rude?" she asked. That sounded like something Simon would do.

He eyed her speculatively, but didn't respond one way or the other.

"He told you, didn't he?" Cassie could easily picture Scrooge running to Simon to tattle on her.

As they walked past a Starbucks, Cassie stopped abruptly. "I would kill for a latte," she said and veered back into the store.

Simon followed, and they stood in line together. When they reached the counter, Cassie ordered her vanilla latte, along with two shortbread cookies. It was after two, and she hadn't had lunch yet.

Simon ordered a large black coffee and paid their bill. Although the small area was crowded, a couple left just then and they were able to secure a table.

Cassie sank gratefully into the chair. She crossed her legs, and removed one boot so she could rub feeling back into her toes, pausing occasionally to sip her latte. It tasted like heaven.

"About this, uh, plant you mentioned."

"Oh, him. Not to worry, I caught on fast enough. Well, maybe not as fast as I should have, but it was obvious that you sent him. He didn't try very hard to hide it, either."

"Not *that* obvious," Simon said mildly. "Because I didn't send anyone."

"Oh, come on. There's no need to carry on this charade."

He regarded her sternly. "I am not in the habit of lying."

She studied him—and realized he just might be telling the truth.

"I will repeat myself this once. I did not send anyone to test you."

"Oh." The man with all the complaints had been so unpleasant that it was a natural assumption.

To hide her embarrassment, Cassie tore the cellophane off her cookies and gobbled them both down.

"What did you learn from the experience?" Simon asked.

She rolled her eyes. "You didn't tell me there'd be an exam."

"It's not an exam. I asked a straightforward question."

"Well…" Cassie took a sip of her latte, then removed

her other boot. "For one thing, I will never pass someone standing in the cold ringing a bell and not leave a donation. You wouldn't believe how many people simply look the other way."

"But you've ignored a bell ringer now and then, haven't you?"

"Okay, I may have, but I won't again. I don't think I've ever worked harder at anything."

The merest hint of a smile showed in his eyes.

"You find that funny? Why don't *you* stand out in the cold for four hours and see how you like it?"

"I prefer to write a check."

"Of course you would. It's much easier."

"Agreed. That's the point. Anything else?"

"Well, there was the lovely old man." She turned an angry look on Simon. "You must've chased him away."

"Like I said, I didn't notice any old man and I certainly didn't chase one away."

"He was definitely there. He reminded me of my grandfather. Grampa died when I was young, but I remember him so well." She grew introspective. "He was in the war, too. That old man made everything that happened today worthwhile."

She gestured at her stained coat and her stocking feet, then tentatively at her nose. "I think I'm finally thawing out."

"I'm glad to hear it."

He didn't sound glad. In fact, he sounded bored.

"Tell me about John," she urged.

Simon's deep sigh informed her that she was becoming tiresome. "What do you want to know?"

"Something. Anything. Did you assign him three tasks like you did me? What are they?"

"I won't discuss my other clients with you." The way he said it suggested she'd committed a major faux pas.

She forged ahead despite that. "Has John asked about me?"

Another sigh. "I should never have mentioned his name."

"But you did and now I'm curious. Come on, Simon, have a heart. Give me one small detail, one tiny tidbit, about my hero."

He glanced at her coat and, seeing the huge coffee stain, must have taken pity on her. "All right, if you have to know, he's an engineer."

"An engineer?" she repeated slowly.

"Your children will be left-brain geniuses."

"Children." Overwhelmed with excitement she grasped Simon's hand.

"Restrain yourself, please."

"Oh, Simon, loosen up a little, would you?"

He looked at her coldly, as though her comment didn't merit a response.

"Has John asked about me?"

He nodded.

Rubbing her palms together, she blurted out, "And what did you say?" After asking, she quickly changed her mind. "No, don't tell me—I'd rather not know."

"It wasn't unflattering, if that's what you're implying." This was promising. "Really?"

"Are you looking for compliments, Cassie?"

"No…well, maybe." Then, because she was curious and she couldn't resist, she asked, "Do you like me, Simon?"

He regarded her for a moment, as though carefully weighing his response. "Not particularly. Wait—let me re-phrase that. I don't have any feelings for you whatsoever. Except for the appropriate reactions of a professional to-ward his client, of course."

What would it have cost him to smile and say some-thing nice? "You really are a dolt."

He stiffened. "I beg your pardon?"

"You heard me. You know, if you smiled more often you might look human. You're supposed to be a psy-chologist—haven't you heard that a smile is a positive way of interacting?"

"I don't see any reason to—"

"Forget it. You are who you are, and I am who I am."

"That was profound." He seemed to be making fun of her.

Cassie didn't care. Simon was a means to an end, and if he found her a decent man she could love for the rest of her life, then it didn't matter if he liked her or not.

"When can I complete the second task?" she asked, eager to hurry the process along. From the sound of it, John was equally excited about meeting her.

"I'm making the final arrangements next week. I'll be in touch as soon as everything's set."

"Okay." Cassie finished her latte and dabbed at the crumbs left over from her shortbread cookies. "You're not very good at relationships, are you? Personally, I mean, not professionally."

Acting as if she hadn't spoken, Simon shoved back his chair and seemed about to leave. "As I said earlier, I'll be in touch."

"Before you go, I'd like to ask how you came to this line of work."

"You already know I don't answer personal questions. This isn't about me."

"But it is."

"*Au contraire.* You came to me for services rendered. Do you interrogate your dentist about his background—or private life?"

"No, but—"

"You let him do his job and you walk away satisfied when he's finished. It's the same with me, or it should be. I perform a service, nothing more. I'm good at what I do and I enjoy my work."

"Always?"

"Some matches are more difficult than others. Some

clients more trying." He looked pointedly in her direction.

"At least you can take comfort from knowing that once I meet John, you won't ever need to see me again."

"Yes, there is that…."

Cassie couldn't help it; she burst out laughing.

Simon seemed genuinely puzzled. "Why is that funny?"

"It wouldn't have been if you hadn't been so honest about it. You'll be happy to get rid of me, won't you?"

He stood and tossed his empty coffee container in the proper receptacle. "You did very well today, Cassie."

For a moment, she thought her ears had deceived her. "Was that a compliment, an actual *compliment,* from the great Dr. Simon Dodson?"

"Not really," he said soberly. "It was a statement of fact. The truth is, I didn't expect you to last all four hours. You surprised me."

"I want to meet John," she told him, disregarding the implied insult in his words.

"So I gathered, and soon you shall."

Ten minutes later, they left Starbucks together and exchanged civil goodbyes.

Cassie could hardly wait to get back to her condo so she could talk to Angie. The minute she'd showered and changed, she reached for the phone and hit speed dial.

After several rings, she was connected to voice mail. That was odd. Angie hadn't said anything about going out—but then it wasn't as if Cassie was her parole officer.

Much later that afternoon she heard from Angie.

"Where were you?" Cassie asked right away.

"Shopping. 'Tis the season, you know?" Her friend seemed to be in high spirits.

"Did you find any bargains?"

"Lots. How'd the morning go?"

"Simon said I surprised him."

"You saw Dr. Dodson?"

"Yeah, he showed up to check on me. We had coffee afterward."

"You and...Dr. Dodson? Simon?"

"What's so odd about that?"

"I don't know," Angie said. "I just can't picture it."

"It wasn't like a date or anything," Cassie insisted. "More of a...debriefing. He said he'd be in touch next week with the details about my next task. I get to be an elf. That *has* to be easier than what I did this morning."

"I wouldn't be so sure of that," Angie warned her.

Chapter 7

Her arms loaded down with groceries, Cassie hurried over to the elevator. "Mr. Oliver, hold that door for me!" she cried frantically, trying not to drop the quart of milk dangling from her index finger.

Mr. Oliver pretended not to hear, and the doors glided shut in her face.

Cassie ground her teeth in frustration. This wasn't the first time Mr. Oliver had purposely let the elevator close as she ran toward it. She'd watched him do the same thing with other residents. Obviously it gave him some kind of thrill. She might have imagined it, but Cassie swore she saw a glimmer of sadistic humor in his eyes as the doors slid closed.

She lowered one bag to the floor and pushed the call button. While she waited, she went to collect her newspaper, only to discover the slot was empty—and it wasn't even Tuesday. Apparently Mrs. Mullinex was now clipping coupons from the Sunday edition, as well.

Perhaps it was time to confront the retired schoolteacher.

Cassie took the elevator up to the fifth floor, brought her groceries to the kitchen, and walked down the hallway to Mrs. Mullinex's unit. Outside her neighbor's door, she rang the bell until she heard footsteps on the other side.

"Hold your horses," Mrs. Mullinex called out.

She answered the door, wearing her housecoat and slippers. Her head was covered in pink curlers and wrapped with a bandanna knotted directly above her forehead. It wasn't a look Cassie saw very often these days—if ever.

"Why, Cassie, how nice of you to stop by," she said pleasantly. "Can I offer you a glass of eggnog?"

"Oh, no, thank you." Cassie made an attempt to be neighborly or at least polite. "Uh, I believe you have my newspaper."

Her neighbor seemed startled, as if the suggestion that she might have taken something not hers was a devastating insult. Mrs. Mullinex raised one hand to her mouth in a gesture of innocence. "Oh, dear, was that *your* paper?"

Cassie held out her hand.

The older woman slowly retrieved the thick weekend edition and reluctantly placed it in Cassie's outstretched hand. "I was wondering, dear, if you wouldn't mind letting me have the section with the *New York Times* crossword puzzle."

Cassie clutched the paper to her chest.

"Only when you're finished with it, of course."

"I happen to enjoy doing the crossword puzzle, Mrs. Mullinex."

"Oh."

Wondering if she'd been a little too inflexible, Cassie returned to her own condo, put away her groceries and made a cup of coffee. She sat down with the paper, prepared to relax. She'd just turned to the middle section, grabbed a pen—doing the crossword puzzle in pen was a matter of pride—when the rap music started next door. The whole room seemed to vibrate. Cassie groaned. There was no question: the fates were conspiring against her.

Getting up from her chair, Cassie pounded her fist against the kitchen wall hard enough to rattle her dishes. She had to repeat the pounding twice before the music was lowered to a tolerable level.

Settled once more, she rested her feet on the ottoman, crossed her ankles and savored the first sip of coffee when her doorbell rang.

"Oh, for the love of heaven," she muttered, tossing

down the pen. If it turned out to be one of her annoying neighbors—whom she'd be having dinner with all too soon, according to Simon—she didn't know what she'd say.

To her astonishment, it was her brother, toting a five-foot Christmas tree.

"Shawn, what are you doing here?" Normally she'd be fortunate to see him twice in four months, and this was his second visit to Seattle in as many weeks.

"Are you complaining?"

"Of course not!"

"I come bearing gifts." He thrust the Christmas tree into the room.

"So I noticed."

Shawn grinned. "I thought you could use a bit of Christmas cheer." He stepped into the condo and leaned the tree against the living room wall. "This also seemed like a good excuse to stop by so you could tell me how everything went yesterday."

Had it only been the day before that she'd stood in the cold, soliciting donations? That didn't seem possible, and yet Cassie hadn't stopped thinking about the experience. What remained uppermost in her mind was the time she'd spent with Simon at the coffee shop. He'd been frank, unemotional, honest. She amended that to *brutally* honest. When she'd met him, she'd considered him rude and arrogant, but since then she'd had a change of heart.

Simon, she decided, was simply…direct. He said what he felt and didn't moderate his opinions in deference to other people's flimsy egos. She'd never met anyone quite like him.

"Well?" Shawn prodded her.

"Who do you want to hear about first—Mr. Scrooge, who *wasn't* sent by Simon as a test," she added, "or would you rather I told you about the woman who threw coffee at me because she thought I'd flirted with her husband?"

Shawn flopped down on the sofa. "Both, and while you're up, I'll take a cup of that coffee."

"Sure," she said, while she got a mug and filled it to the brim. "You won't believe what he said to me."

"Scrooge?"

"No, Simon. I asked if he liked me and he said 'not particularly.' What's so funny is the fact that—"

"Funny? You thought this was funny?"

"Not at first," she admitted. "The thing with Simon is that he wasn't being intentionally rude. He's the most plainspoken man I've ever encountered."

"Sounds like a bore to me."

"I called him a dolt." She smiled at the memory. "He didn't much like that."

"So he can dish it out, but he can't take it?"

"Well, he certainly isn't used to it."

They chatted for a while, until Shawn eventually said,

"I hope you realize that all you've done is talk about Simon. I've yet to hear a word about anyone else."

"Really?" Caught up in her musing, Cassie hadn't noticed.

"I think you might be falling for him."

"For Simon?" The suggestion was ludicrous. "Oh, hardly! If I'm focusing on him, it's because he's the man who holds the key to my happiness. He's going to introduce me to John—and I have high hopes for John. He's my perfect—oops, *most suitable,* which is what Simon calls it—match."

"Just in time for the perfect—or should I say, *most suitable*—Christmas."

Cassie suspected Shawn was mocking her a little, but she was too hopeful and too happy to care.

All at once he grew serious. "Don't build your expectations too high, Cassie. What if you and this John character don't really connect?"

"But we will. That's the beauty of it. Simon studied our profiles and concluded that we're ideal for each other. I think his success lies in the fact that he can be emotionally detached and even clinical. It's all quite scientific, you know."

"Uh-huh." Shawn nodded wryly.

"Did I mention Simon refuses to talk about himself? That's probably why he's so brilliant at this. He doesn't want to cloud the relationship between him and his clients. His sole focus is on finding the right person for them."

"Seems to me you've got him all figured out."

"I think I just might. Now wipe that smirk off your face," she said. Now that she'd thought seriously about Simon, and she'd been doing that for the past twenty-four hours, it all made a crazy kind of sense.

Simon made sense.

Simply put, he wasn't encumbered with the need to please others. His skill at matchmaking was based on his knowledge of psychology, as he claimed, but he obviously had good instincts, too. His success rate was impressive, and if he honestly felt John-the-engineer would make her a good husband, then Cassie didn't doubt it for an instant.

"He's an engineer," she murmured.

"Simon?"

"No, my match. Simon offered me a crumb of information yesterday."

"An engineer," Shawn echoed. "I guess your kids will be left-brained."

"That's what Simon said," she returned excitedly.

Shawn looked surprised. "You told him about your IQ?"

"No, but it was on the questionnaire." In high school, her high IQ had been an embarrassment rather than an asset. She always used to insist that scoring well on a test didn't make her any different from everyone else. She still felt that way—although it did get her through two chemistry degrees in four years instead of six.

"Mom was always proud of your intelligence," Shawn reminded her.

"It didn't matter to our father, though, did it?" As a child, Cassie had thought it was her fault their father had left the family. Although it made no sense for a seven-year-old to assume that kind of blame, she had. Later, she'd learned this was fairly typical in situations like this. They'd all been devastated, but she'd unconsciously taken on the role of scapegoat.

"Speaking of Dad…"

Cassie already knew what was coming. "He called you?"

Shawn nodded.

"His yearly sojourn into fatherhood! Lucky you. This year it was your turn to receive the great gift of his phone call. What did he have to say?"

"He saw one of my murals and wanted to tell me he was impressed."

Cassie shrugged. "That was nice."

"A surprise, actually."

Cassie knew how long Shawn had waited for any praise from their father. They rarely discussed him; the subject was still too painful for them both.

"Where was he?" The last she'd heard, he was living aboard his sailboat somewhere in the Caribbean.

"Hawaii."

Cassie chuckled. "Really? Wouldn't it be amusing if he ran into Mom on the streets of Honolulu?"

Shawn shook his head. "She's over him. She forgave him a long time ago."

"Mom's a better woman than I am." Talking about their father depressed her. "Can't we discuss something else? Something more cheerful—like bank foreclosures?"

Shawn snorted. "Very funny."

"I don't know why he bothers," she said.

"I thought we weren't going to discuss Dad."

"Right. Sorry."

Shawn drank the last of his coffee and stood. "I've gotta go."

"You mean you aren't going to stay and help me trim the tree?"

"Can't. I've got an…appointment."

From the gleam in his eyes, this so-called appointment involved a woman. "You've got a date."

"I'm not telling."

It really wasn't fair. Cassie had to pay tens of thousands of dollars to meet men, and her brother had women falling all over him. It must be those piercing blue eyes of his—plus, of course, the fact that he was talented, rich and eligible.

Cassie walked him to the door.

"Are you coming back here tonight?" she asked.

"Nope. I'm taking the red-eye to Phoenix."

"Will I see you at Christmas?"

"Sure. Where else would I go?"

"Call me, okay?"

"Will do. Besides, I want to hear all about Simon."

"John," she corrected. "Simon's the matchmaker."

"Right." That gleam was back in his eyes and Cassie suspected the slip had been intentional.

An hour later, Cassie had the Christmas tree in its stand and set by the window that overlooked the city. The big star above Macy's glowed in the dim light of late afternoon. She dragged her ornaments out from the guest room closet and decided to give Angie a call. Trimming a tree all alone wasn't any fun.

Her friend answered immediately. "Come on over," Cassie invited her. "Shawn stopped by to drop off a Christmas tree and then abandoned me to decorate it by myself. I've got hot apple cider and popcorn popping in the microwave."

"Oh, Cassie, I'd love to but I can't."

"Are you off shopping again?"

"No, I'm meeting an old friend. Sort of a last-minute thing. You could join us if you want."

"Anyone I know?"

"Um, not really."

"Oh, well, I've got an appointment with a box of ornaments, a bowl of popcorn and the DVD of *The Bishop's Wife*."

Angie sounded regretful. "I hate the thought of you trimming the tree alone."

"Oh, I don't mind." And that was true. She was in a good mood; in fact, she planned to give Mrs. Mullinex the Sunday paper when she'd finished—and she'd leave the crossword untouched.

"Think of next year," Angie urged. "You'll most likely be married by then."

"John and me." She filled her head with happy thoughts of a Christmas photo in front of next year's tree, the two of them smiling blissfully into the camera. The perfect Christmas. The first card she mailed out would be to Jill and Tom.

"You might even be pregnant by then."

"Whoa, you're moving a little too fast."

"Why? You're getting the best husband money can buy, aren't you?"

Cassie laughed. She hadn't thought of it in those terms but Angie was right. She was paying top dollar to meet John-the-engineer; by the same token, he'd been willing to pay top dollar to meet her.

And the one walking away with fistfuls of cash was Simon Dodson.

As far as Cassie was concerned, he would have earned every penny.

Chapter 8

A t the end of their brief telephone conversation, Angie had said she'd call Cassie once she got home Sunday evening. Although it'd been an offhand comment, Cassie was surprised when she didn't hear from her. Apparently Angie's last-minute meeting with her friend had turned into more of an event.

Cassie didn't think much about it until Angie showed up at the lab Monday morning. Her friend's face radiated...joy. Unmistakable joy.

"Well, well, well," Cassie said, watching Angie closely. Something was up, and it didn't take Sherlock Holmes to figure out that a man was involved. Clearly Angie had met someone special. The "old friend" from yesterday evening?

"Stop looking at me like that," Angie said, blushing.

"You're in love, aren't you?"

Angie's eyes widened. "You can tell? Really?"

Cassie nodded. "You've got the happy look. You know, the one we all get when we first realize we're falling for someone." She knew it had to be the "friend" Angie had seen last night.

Angie shyly glanced away. "The most incredible feeling came over me this morning." Her voice fell to a whisper. "It's like…a sixth sense, a knowledge, that this man could be the one."

"That's the feeling I'm talking about." Cassie had never experienced it herself, but she'd seen it again and again with her friends.

A wistful happiness shone from Angie's eyes, but she didn't say anything else.

After several minutes Cassie couldn't stand it anymore. "Well?" she asked.

The reflective look disappeared and was instantly replaced by one that was far more guarded. "Well, what?"

"Aren't you going to give me details?"

Angie hesitated. "Of course…but not yet."

This confused Cassie. First, there was very little they didn't tell each other—except for Angie's meeting with the matchmaker and it was easy to understand why her friend hadn't mentioned that, since Simon had rejected her as a client. If it'd happened to her, Cassie wouldn't have announced it, either. But this was an entirely different matter. For some reason, Angie preferred to remain tight-lipped about this man in her life. Well, so be it. When necessary, Cassie could be patient. If Angie wanted to keep this mystery man to herself for a while, Cassie would respect that.

"I'll tell you everything soon," Angie said. "It's just that I'd like to hold on to this feeling for a little longer."

Still, Cassie couldn't help being curious. "Would it hurt to let me know how you met?"

Angie's face relaxed into a warm smile. "You'll love that part. We sort of stumbled upon each other. We dated for a while ages ago and decided it wasn't going to work. Or rather, he did, not me. So I began the search again."

"So this is the guy you've been in love with all along?"

Angie nodded. "You'll meet him," she said a second time. "I promise."

"Will you be seeing him soon?"

"No. It's a bit…complicated at the moment."

"Complicated?" Cassie didn't like the sound of that. "He's not married or anything, is he?"

Angie shook her head. "Oh, no! Nothing like that."

"Good." Cassie smiled, then glanced down at her feet. "Actually," she said in a low voice, "I was hoping to chat with you last night. I had a couple of questions."

"What kind of questions?"

"I wanted to ask you about Simon."

"What about him?"

"Basically…I was curious. Other than the information on his Web site, what do you know?"

Angie shrugged. "Not much."

"How did you hear about him?"

"He was a birthday gift—at least, the first consultation was."

"Who from?"

"My mother. She wants grandchildren and knew how brokenhearted I was when…this other relationship ended. She heard about Simon when he did a radio interview."

"Simon did a radio interview?"

"I don't think he does them often. This was around Valentine's Day a few years back."

"Oh."

Angie cocked her head to one side. "Why this interest in Dr. Dodson all of a sudden?"

Cassie didn't want Angie or anyone to suspect how intrigued she was by the matchmaker. She found her thoughts drifting toward him far more often than was comfortable. She told herself that once her curiosity was satisfied, he'd drift into the background where he belonged.

While she'd gone on to his Web site—the address was noted on his business card—she hadn't searched further.

That evening, she did. She logged on to the Internet and immediately typed his name into Google. There wasn't a *lot,* but enough to answer some of her questions. He'd been a Rhodes scholar, attending Cambridge —after Harvard. He'd taught at a prestigious East Coast college. He'd written political articles for the *Wall Street Journal* and the *New York Times.* Just as she'd realized earlier, he had opinions about everything and didn't mind sharing them…in unvarnished prose.

According to Wikipedia, Simon had never been married. She found that…interesting.

Intent as she was on reading her computer screen, the phone startled her. "Yes," Cassie said, snatching it up. Her gaze stayed on the screen for fear she'd miss a single detail.

"Ms. Beaumont?" The female voice was vaguely familiar. "This is Dr. Dodson's office."

A chill raced down her spine. Simon knew she was online, reading about him! He was about to inform her that she'd forfeited her thirty thousand dollars. "I won't do it again!" she blurted without thinking.

"Excuse me?"

"Were you phoning because—" Cassie stopped abruptly, aware of how absurd she'd been. How paranoid. "Can I help you?" she asked sweetly.

By now Ms. Snelling sounded utterly confused. "Would it be convenient for you to stop by tomorrow afternoon at four-thirty?" she asked.

"Ah, sure." That meant leaving work a bit early, which wasn't really a problem.

"Thank you. Dr. Dodson will see you then."

Rattled as she was, Cassie had hung up before she thought to ask what the meeting was about. She assumed Simon would be giving her the information regarding her second task. But why not call? Maybe he had her elf costume, although that seemed unlikely.

She felt a sense of expectation. She had to admit that Simon fascinated her, although she didn't especially like him—any more than he liked her. Perhaps he represented a challenge and she couldn't resist trying to make him aware of her as a woman. *Everyone* needed to be liked and appreciated, even Simon. That was probably what had led him into the matchmaking business. Certainly the couples she'd spoken to had expressed their appreciation—if not liking—for him. So maybe he couldn't achieve romantic satisfaction for himself but he could for others. It all seemed rather lonely.

On Tuesday, she kept checking her watch. Angie, who might otherwise have commented, was preoccupied, as well. Cassie had decided not to question her about this new, or rather resumed, relationship. When Angie was ready to tell her, she would. Cassie could only hope this man turned out to be everything Angie believed he was. Perhaps they could have a double wedding!

Because Simon had kept her waiting at their previous appointments, Cassie didn't bother to show up until four forty-five. His assistant's disapproval was obvious. When

Cassie stepped up to the desk, the older woman regarded her with distaste. "You're late."

"Well, yes… Simon, Dr. Dodson, was late the past two times and—"

"And you felt turnabout was fair play," he said, standing in the doorway leading to his office. "If you'll forgive the cliché." His arms were crossed and he looked more amused than annoyed.

It'd been four days since she'd last seen him and it struck her again how attractive he was.

He arched his brows. "You have nothing to say? Generally I can't get you to shut up and now you act as if we've never met."

"No…I figured you'd be late and—and I didn't want to waste time sitting here…" she stammered, embarrassed that he'd caught her staring.

"Don't let it happen again."

"Then don't keep me waiting again," she returned.

His shoulders relaxed. "Ah, I see the Cassie I recognize is back. Follow me. We have business to discuss." He walked into his office, Cassie close behind him.

Without waiting for an invitation, she took the visitor's chair across from his desk. She leaned back, legs crossed, trying to appear confident.

Looking stiff and formal once more, Simon sat down. "I asked to see you because I have the information concerning your agreement to work as Santa's helper."

She nodded. "Okay, but you could've phoned—unless you have my outfit."

"Outfit?"

"For my elf job."

Simon shook his head, and for the first time since she'd arrived, he seemed edgy. "There's been a small change in plans."

"Change? What do you mean?"

"The mall has experienced a decline in the number of parents bringing their children to meet Santa."

"Does this mean Santa won't be requiring my help, after all?" She did her best to keep her enthusiasm to a minimum. She wouldn't mind getting out of this; she liked children—in fact, she loved them—but if her tasks were limited to two instead of three, she'd be done that much sooner. Then Simon could introduce her to John.

Despite herself, she felt a twinge of regret at the idea of never seeing Simon again. But once he'd made the official introduction, his role would be over, his job done. She realized she'd miss his acerbic responses....

Simon frowned at her. "What are you thinking?" he asked.

Cassie answered a bit more sharply than she'd intended. "I'm sure you're not interested in my thoughts."

Again his brows shot toward his hairline. "I wonder how long it will take you to learn that I do not ask questions unless I *am* interested in the answer."

Cassie threw back her head. "All right, fine. I was just thinking that you're a very odd man. I find I'm rather… intrigued by you. Not in any romantic way, of course."

"Of course," he said dryly. "I can't tell you what a relief that is."

"It's more like…driving past a car wreck. Horrible though it is, you can't stop yourself from looking."

His frown deepened. "I can assure you my life is no wreck—nor is my car."

"Yes, well, I'm sure there's nothing wrong with your car." Ignoring her comment and its implication, Simon picked up a piece of paper. "As I was saying, I heard from the Tacoma Mall regarding your assignment. There's been a slight change."

"Is this because of what you said earlier—that there's a decline in the number of children visiting Santa?"

"Yes. But here's what—"

"Oh, wait, I have a question," Cassie broke in.

Simon looked up at the ceiling as though his patience, which was always in short supply, had been sorely tested yet again. "No."

"That's rather dictatorial," she said. "How could a question hurt?"

"If you'd let me get a word in edgewise… I'm trying to give you some important information."

"About helping Santa?" Simon acted as if she'd have to smuggle top secret papers to the north pole.

"This relates directly to your assignment," he said, avoiding eye contact. "I need to know if you're afraid of heights."

How could that possibly pertain to her working as an elf? "Not really. Why?"

Simon paused. "Maybe you should ask me your question, after all, before I explain."

"I'd rather hear what you have to say first."

He sighed loudly. "I talked to the mall and—"

"Yes, yes, we've been through this."

"I did mention that a uniform—a costume—is required."

"Yes." His reluctance to get to the point was beginning to concern her.

"I wasn't aware anything like this would be asked of you, but I'm encouraged that you don't have any fear of heights."

"I don't have to swing from the top of the Space Needle, do I?"

"No…" He exhaled slowly, staring down at his desk. "The mall wants the first elf—that would be you—to arrive by wire."

Cassie swallowed hard. "You're not referring to a telegram, are you?"

"No."

"A wire…from where?"

Again he avoided meeting her gaze. "The ceiling."

Cassie frowned, attempting to picture it. "You mean they want me to fly in like Peter Pan?"

"Exactly."

"You're joking!" This was the most preposterous idea she'd ever heard.

"The reindeer will follow you."

"*Live* reindeer?"

"They're plastic, but the mall wants to make a real production of Santa's arrival."

"And," she said, swallowing again since her mouth was so dry, "I'm part of the production."

"Yes. Are you willing to do this?" he asked.

Cassie's fingers tightened around her purse strap. "Would I still meet John if I decline?"

Simon hesitated. "This wasn't part of our original agreement, so I'd need to find a replacement task. That might take a few weeks."

"I don't want to wait any longer than I already have to."

"Then I'll inform the mall there won't be a problem and they can expect you on Saturday morning around nine."

Her complete lack of reaction must have alerted Simon to the fact that she was having second thoughts.

"No need to worry," Simon assured her. "I've been told it's quite safe. The wire will hold up to four hundred pounds."

"Oh." Cassie couldn't believe she'd agreed to this. When she glanced up, she thought, just for a moment, that she saw a smile on Simon's face. She leaned forward. "Were you smiling?"

"Pardon me?"

"You were smiling, weren't you? You're enjoying this." The man should be arrested for deriving pleasure from her humiliation.

His mouth quivered, but Simon had the good grace to look away. "Actually, I was thinking you're going to manage this quite well. You're a woman who's destined for high places."

Unfortunately, his vote of confidence didn't excite her. And his joke didn't amuse her.

Chapter 9

Simon says: The best match for you is the one I arrange—because I know you better than you know yourself.

"This must be a joke," Cassie said, staring at the limp green tights. No way was she going to stuff her hips and thighs into those.

"Dr. Dodson gave us your size, miss," said an elderly woman, whose name tag identified her as Daisy.

"He did?" Well, if he assumed she wore a size four, then who was she to enlighten him with the truth? Besides, the material did stretch.

Daisy handed her the elf costume, which consisted of

a short green dress, like a skater's, with white faux fur edging the hem and a wide red belt. A green Santa-style hat with a white fur ball dangling from the end completed the outfit. But the pièce de résistance was a gold-painted pair of slippers with curled-up toes.

"The changing room is this way," Daisy said as she guided her down the dimly lit mall corridor.

Cassie followed, clutching the uniform, the hat and shoes.

"I can't tell you how pleased we are that you agreed to do this," Daisy was telling her. "You already have an audience of children waiting."

This wasn't news Cassie wanted to hear. "Where will Santa be while I'm floating through the air?"

"Oh, he'll be right behind you."

"Great." So she wouldn't be doing a solo flight. If she was going to descend from the clouds, Santa should do the same.

"Only…Santa will be on ground level," Daisy explained.

This was unfair.

The woman stopped and, frowning, bent down to pick up an empty beer can. "Oh, dear," she grumbled. "I'm afraid Floyd's been at it again."

"And who is Floyd?" Cassie asked a bit fearfully.

Daisy's voice was a low whisper. "He's Santa."

Was she saying Santa was a *drunk?* Outrageous!

"Santa?" Cassie cried.

"Don't misunderstand me," Daisy hurried to say. "Floyd's a wonderful Santa and the kids love him. The problem is, the children can be a bit wearing…as you'll discover for yourself in a few minutes." Daisy led her through a dark tunnel to some kind of alleyway deep inside the mall. "There's a ladies' room back here where you can change into your costume. I'll wait outside and once you're done, I'll have one of the technicians help you into the harness."

Cassie gaped at her.

"We want you to be as safe as possible," Daisy said in a confiding voice. "The wire will lower you from the top level of the mall to the ground floor."

"Oh." Cassie couldn't recall if the mall was two or three levels. One thing was guaranteed—she'd have her eyes closed the entire flight.

As if reading her mind, Daisy added, "You have to play this up, you know."

"Play this up?" Cassie asked skeptically. "What do you mean?"

"To the crowd. We want you to yell out that Santa's on his way and all the boys and girls will be getting a gift from him."

"We're giving them gifts?"

"Candy canes. The children look forward to receiving those."

A cheap candy cane was a gift? That seemed to be an exaggeration—but who was Cassie to quibble over truth in advertising?

They finally got to the ladies' room and Cassie went inside. She removed her shoes and then her jeans and sweater. She hung what she could on the hook of the stall door, then sat on the toilet in order to slip on the tights. *Force* them on was more accurate.

The fit was so tight, they felt like an extra skin. Unfortunately they didn't reach all the way to her waist. One wrong move, and Cassie feared they'd roll down and reveal features—like her butt—that she'd rather keep private. It helped a little to jump up and down and then prance around, pulling on the waistband as she did. She also did a couple of squats. Still, the tights didn't stretch quite as far as she would've liked.

"Is everything all right in there, dear?" Daisy asked.

"Just fine," Cassie told her. Thankfully, the minidress fit. The shoes were good, too. She adjusted the hat in the bathroom mirror and realized she'd need to secure it for the flight. Digging around the bottom of her purse, she located two paper clips, which worked—sort of. How long those paper clips had been there and where they'd come from would forever remain a mystery. Cassie could only be grateful for their presence.

She opened the restroom door, feeling more than a little foolish.

Daisy stood back and brought both hands to her face. "Oh, this is just perfect."

"I look okay?"

"You look *wonderful*. The children are going to be so excited." Daisy glanced at her watch, then led Cassie to an elevator. Silently they rode to the second floor, where a crew of men seemed to be waiting for her. Eight—or was it nine?—life-size plastic reindeer were lined up against the wall beside an authentic-looking sleigh.

Before Cassie had a chance to ask any questions, two of the men stepped forward and strapped her into a harness. They moved her arms, each grasping one, lifting them up and down.

One of the men murmured something in Spanish. She couldn't understand what he'd said, but got the gist of it when he made the sign of the cross and raised his eyes heavenward.

"Don't look down," the other man advised her tersely.

"You don't have a thing to worry about," Daisy said with a grandmotherly smile.

Suddenly a voice came over the loudspeaker system. "Boys and girls, moms and dads—is that Santa's sleigh I hear?"

The man next to her jingled bells and everyone looked up to where Cassie stood.

"Okay, boys," Daisy whispered and stepped back.

Suddenly Cassie was hoisted from the ground. Her feet

made running movements as she scrabbled to find her footing and instead found only air.

"Play to the crowd," Daisy instructed in a loud stage whisper.

"Santa's on his way!" Cassie called out, doing her best to sound enthusiastic although she was absolutely terrified. "I can see him now! Look, here comes Santa."

And then it happened. Cassie gasped as her tights rolled down, catching on her thighs. She didn't know what to do. The tights slid farther down and everyone in the entire mall seemed to be staring up at her.

"I can see the elf's underpants," a little boy called, pointing at her.

Suspended above the ground, Cassie watched as several mothers covered their children's eyes.

"Get her to the ground fast," Cassie heard Daisy hiss.

The men released the rope and Cassie plunged downward. "Yiiiiiii!" she screamed, all the while struggling to pull up her tights. She'd partially succeeded—then saw that she was about to make a crash landing.

Just when it seemed she was destined to slam into the ground, a tall man emerged from the crowd and deftly caught her in his arms. The impact would have been enough to send them both sprawling to the floor if not for the fact that he'd braced his feet. Together they staggered backward until her hero recovered his balance.

Cassie opened her eyes to see that the stranger who'd

rescued her wasn't a stranger at all. Her startled eyes met Simon's, and they both breathed a sigh of relief. For a long moment, they stared at each other. Cassie's arms were tightly wrapped around his neck. It took time for her to find her voice and, when she did, it came out in a high-pitched squeal.

"You're paying for this," she told him, her pulse hammering in her ears. Why she'd ever agreed to this ridiculous scenario she'd never know. One thing was for sure; there wouldn't be a repeat performance.

Simon lowered her to the ground. "A simple thank-you will suffice," he said calmly.

Fortunately the audience was distracted by the flying reindeer, and no one could hear her X-rated response. Santa made his appearance, slipping out from behind a curtain. Santa Floyd carried a large bag over his shoulder, presumably filled with candy canes.

Santa ascended to his special chair, a huge cushioned monstrosity set up on the curtained dais, and Cassie took her place beside him. She looked around for Simon but he was nowhere in sight. The boys and girls lined up with their parents, and the photographer was ready with his camera.

The first boy clung to his mother. "He's a little scared," the woman explained, prying her son loose from her leg.

The poor kid was panic-stricken. Cassie couldn't understand why the mother felt it was so important to make him sit on Santa's lap.

"There's no need to be frightened." Cassie crouched down and tried to reassure the boy, who couldn't have been more than four years old.

"Go away!" he shouted.

Cassie straightened and stepped back. Her timing was perfect. The boy, without even a hint of warning, vomited on one of her shoes.

"Oh, dear. I'm so sorry," the mother said a dozen times. "I had no idea Jason was going to do that."

Cassie hopped around on one foot until the photographer produced a small towel. If Jason was any indication of what she should expect, Cassie could only imagine the rest of her day.

"Why don't you sit on Santa's lap with your son," the photographer suggested. The mother appeared eager to do anything that would remove attention from Cassie and the results of her son's queasy stomach. She clambered onto Floyd's lap, her son dangling from her arms.

After cleaning off her shoe, Cassie returned to her duties. The next few children had obviously had prior experience. They all told Santa their Christmas wishes, rattling off everything on their lists.

The line moved relatively well for the next half hour or so. There was the occasional crying baby and one pair of twins who took up more time than allotted, but all in all, it was a smooth-running operation.

Cassie had worked about two hours of her three-hour

shift and was just beginning to think this job was tolerable. A lot of the children, while frightened, were eager to meet Santa. "Who are *you?*" a little girl asked as she waited patiently for her turn some time later. Cassie's shift was almost over by then, and there were only a few more kids in line. Other than a harrowing entrance and one small boy with a queasy stomach, it hadn't worked out so badly.

"Who am I?" Cassie repeated the question. "I'm one of Santa's helpers," she said as she handed the child a candy cane.

"Are you really an elf?"

Cassie nodded.

"You don't look like an elf."

"I don't?" Cassie said, surprised.

"You look more like a—"

"You pushed in front of me," the child's mother protested, elbowing the woman ahead of her in line.

"I most certainly did not!" The second woman elbowed the other one back as her son watched, eyes wide.

"Mommy, I have to pee." This plaintive declaration came from the first combatant's daughter, aged four or five.

"We are not getting out of this line now. I'll find you a restroom as soon as we're done," she said and shoved her way to the front, dragging the little girl.

"Would you kindly tell this person that I was ahead of

her?" The comment was directed at Cassie by the other woman. The shoving match continued.

"Sorry," Cassie said, coming to stand between the two mothers. "I really wasn't paying attention, but if this goes on, I'm afraid I'll have to ask you both to leave." She said this with great authority and was rather proud of herself.

"Mommy," the little girl cried, her voice urgent now. "I can't wait anymore."

That was when Cassie felt the warm liquid soak into the top of her foot. She glanced down and saw a small waterfall raining down, ruining her undamaged shoe—the one unstained by vomit.

Letting out a yell, she leaped back and automatically shook her foot.

"Orange!" the woman shouted.

"It's okay. I don't have to pee anymore."

"Oh, dear…"

"Your daughter's name is Orange?" the other woman asked.

The first woman nodded. "We're from Florida."

The second mother backed away from the puddle on the floor, clutching her son's hand—and leaving Orange at the head of the line.

"I have a tissue." Orange's mother—Grapefruit? Cassie thought hysterically—offered her a crumpled wad.

"I'm fine," Cassie muttered. She intended to burn these tights once her shift was over. The shoes were probably goners, too. She wondered if Simon could possibly have known what this stint would entail.

After the two squabbling mothers had finished with Santa, a young girl, the very last one in line, approached Cassie all by herself.

"She hasn't paid," the photographer said as he returned his camera to its case.

Pleading eyes were raised to Cassie's. "I need to talk to Santa for just a minute," the girl whispered. "You don't have to give me a candy cane."

"How old are you?" Cassie asked, bending down so they were eye-to-eye.

"Eight."

Just a bit too old to believe in Santa Claus. And yet the child was so intent, Cassie didn't feel she could turn her away.

"Forget about the picture," she said when the photographer cast her a dirty look.

"Ho. Ho. Ho. And who do we have here?" Santa asked, ignoring the other man. He held out his arms to the child.

"Catherine," the child said softly. She walked up to Santa but didn't sit on his lap.

"And what would you like for Christmas?" he asked, playing his role to the hilt.

Staring down at the carpet, the child said, "I want my daddy to come home." Huge tears welled in her eyes. "He left and now my mommy says they're getting a divorce. All I want for Christmas is my daddy back.'"

Cassie felt tears burning in her own eyes. She looked at Floyd and wondered how he'd handle this.

"That's a mighty big order, Catherine," he said.

"I don't want anything else. I don't need toys but I need my daddy."

"Catherine?" A woman's voice echoed through the mall.

"I'm here, Mommy!"

The child's mother rushed up the steps to Santa's throne and fell to her knees in front of her daughter. She seemed about to burst into tears. "I looked *everywhere* for you," she cried. She threw her arms around her daughter's waist.

"I told you I was going to talk to Santa," Catherine reminded her. "I had to wait in line."

"I'm sorry if Catherine caused a problem," her mother said and, standing, took the little girl by the hand—but not before Santa whispered a few words in the child's ear.

"We're finished," Santa said as Catherine's mother led her daughter away.

Cassie must have looked as upset as she felt because Floyd gently patted her back. "Those are the tough ones. You did a great job."

Cassie doubted that.

"What did you say to her?" she asked him.

"I said her daddy still loves her and that he'll always love her. That it's not her fault he left." He stretched his arms high above his head. "Now this Santa has an appointment with Mr. Budweiser. Want to join me?"

"Thanks…but no thanks."

"Then you're free to go. Another elf will take over for you this afternoon."

Cassie nodded, eager to make her escape. As she started for the changing room, Simon appeared beside her.

Cassie realized she wasn't going to be able to control her emotions. Tears streamed down her face.

"What is it?" he asked. He seemed genuinely concerned.

"I was that little girl once," she said with difficulty. "All I wanted for Christmas was for my daddy to come home." She covered her mouth with both hands, trying to stifle her sobs.

They reached the doorway that led to the mall interior. Simon held open the door and Cassie slipped into the darkened hallway. Once inside, she leaned against the wall and let the tears flow unrestrained.

Simon stood next to her for several minutes, then tentatively placed his arms around her.

Cassie didn't care who he was; she needed his comfort. She rested her face against him, sobbing into his expensive wool jacket.

His hold relaxed and, after an awkward moment, he spoke soothingly into her ear. She couldn't make out what he was saying. It didn't matter.

As if by instinct, she lifted her head and gazed up at him. He whispered something else, something that sounded like "It wasn't your fault." Then his lips, warm and tender, descended on hers.

Chapter 10

Simon says: If you're the woman he's looking for, I will find you.

Simon's gentleness consoled her as he held her close. Cassie didn't want him to ever stop, and he didn't seem inclined to let her go. Time lost meaning, and Cassie didn't know how long he held her against him.

Then, just when she was least prepared, he seemed to snap to attention, become aware of his surroundings. He dropped his arms and stepped away. His movements were so abrupt that she nearly stumbled. She might have if he hadn't clasped her shoulders to steady her.

Speechless, she stared up at him, unable to make sense

of what had happened in the past few minutes. Under normal conditions, Cassie didn't give way to emotion, and certainly not in public. But Christmas, that little girl and the memory of losing her own father had struck her hard and there'd been no stopping the barrage of deeply buried feelings. She told herself she was *not* going to react to that kiss.

"I need a cup of coffee," she murmured. Despite her tears her throat was parched.

Simon nodded.

"I'll change clothes and be right back." She was sure her voice sounded strained and unnatural. She hurried inside the ladies' room; once the door was closed she leaned against it and covered her face. Her whole body was trembling. Eventually, when she felt composed again, she straightened and began to dress.

To the best of her knowledge, this was the first time she'd ever cried over her father. Peter Beaumont had simply walked out of their lives one day as if it meant nothing. As if *they* meant nothing. The event had forever marked her and Shawn and their mother, as well. And yet he seemed oblivious to the anguish he'd inflicted on his wife and children. His excuse was that he needed to "find himself." Apparently he couldn't manage that and be a husband and father at the same time. His was a solitary path, and it didn't seem to matter how many hearts he crushed along the way. Cassie made every effort to cast all thoughts of him out of her mind. But he was there, as much as she wanted to deny his existence.

When Cassie had finished dressing, she left her outfit neatly on a ledge near the sink and wrote Daisy a note explaining why the shoes and tights were in the garbage. Then she brushed her hair and repaired her makeup. Simon was pacing in the hallway outside the door. He stopped when he saw her and even in the dimly lit hallway she could see that he wasn't quite himself, either.

With his hand at her elbow, he escorted her back into the mall and toward an exit. "There's a place close by where we can have coffee." He reached inside his pocket for his car keys. "I'll drive."

Cassie didn't know what was wrong with the restaurants that were within walking distance. However, she didn't have the energy to argue, so she just followed him.

She wasn't surprised to see that he drove a black sedan with a black interior, which was meticulously maintained; she wouldn't have expected anything less. Simon wasn't the type of man who'd have hamburger wrappings and stale French fries littering his vehicle.

They didn't speak; he glanced at her for approval, then flipped on a CD. She recognized the calming strains of a Bach piano concerto. Again, she wasn't surprised, although she couldn't have identified the piece. She leaned back, eyes shut, letting the music flow over her. The restaurant wasn't really all that close, she noted a little later.

It was perhaps a fifteen-minute drive along the Tacoma waterfront before he pulled into an exclusive housing development. He turned down several streets, then entered a driveway.

"This isn't a restaurant," Cassie said.

"No, it's my home."

"Your home?"

"I felt we'd both appreciate privacy for this discussion." He was probably right.

Simon ushered her inside. The house was spotless. It looked like one of those model homes with everything carefully arranged and color-coordinated, not a thing out of place. No Christmas decorations. Nor did she see a single photograph, and that seemed almost unnatural. Surely there were people in his life, people he loved and cared about. Family. Friends. Then again, maybe he preferred to keep his distance from others. Maybe he felt his job required it.

"Make yourself comfortable," he said and gestured toward the sofa. Then he disappeared into the kitchen through a swinging door.

Cassie looked out over Commencement Bay, although her thoughts still churned and she hardly noticed the beauty before her. She had a distinct feeling that their professional agreement was about to come to an end.

Other than one brief interchange—when he asked how she liked her coffee—all was silent.

After a few minutes, Simon reappeared with two cups of coffee. He handed her one, careful to avoid physical contact, before taking a seat as far away as the room allowed. He stared down at his coffee. "I would like to know what happened back at the mall," he said after a tense moment.

"Okay." It wasn't as if they could ignore the episode. "Which part do you want to discuss?"

"What were those tears about?"

Now Cassie stared into her coffee. "My father," she began, then shook her head. "The last child in line."

"The little girl who was by herself?"

"Yes. She came to Santa because..." The lump in her throat made it necessary to pause and swallow before she could continue. "She didn't want toys or clothes or gifts, she...she wanted her daddy back."

"Ah." Simon's eyes softened with understanding and what looked like sympathy. "She reminded you of yourself at that age. You said as much, didn't you?"

Cassie nodded. "My father left during the holidays. So he not only broke our hearts, he made sure Christmas would never be the same."

"He sounds like a real jewel of a human being," Simon said disdainfully.

But Cassie didn't wish her father ill. He'd paid for his mistakes; in his late sixties now, he was essentially alone. While she liked to think she'd put all the bitterness behind her, she didn't really have a relationship with him, nor did she seek one. Every so often, Pete made the effort to contact her, but they had nothing in common, nothing to talk about, nothing to share. The conversation typically lasted a few minutes. Invariably Cassie felt sad afterward.

"I don't want you to assume I'm the kind of woman who breaks into tears at the drop of a hat. I… It was like seeing myself all those years ago. Like feeling pain so raw it tore my heart out." Her voice quavered and she tried to conceal it by sipping coffee.

"Pain and the memory of pain—which often amounts to the same thing—don't really go away," Simon said. "That's why we have to learn to assimilate it."

She nodded.

Simon didn't say anything else for some time. "I believe it would be best if we…"

He stopped speaking, which made Cassie look at him.

"That kiss," he murmured, shifting his weight.

Seeing Simon ill at ease was so unusual she couldn't help enjoying it, although that was probably unkind of her. At least it was a distraction from her own painful past. "Yes, the kiss."

He frowned. "I want to assure you I don't make a habit of kissing my clients."

She instinctively recognized that as the truth.

"Weeping women don't generally affect me like that, either. I don't have any excuse and I wish to apologize."

His gaze held hers and she couldn't doubt the sincerity of his words. "I was as much at fault as you," she felt obliged to admit. "I—"

"I will refund your money," he said, cutting her off.

It was what she'd been afraid of. "But why?"

"I stepped over the line. This is the only way I can rectify the...incident."

Cassie bit her lip. She conceded that the kiss shouldn't have happened. But that wasn't a good reason to ruin everything. "Will I still meet John?" she asked, then held her breath, almost afraid of what he'd say. She was practically gasping for air by the time he replied.

"Considering that I was the one who initiated the... incident, I feel honor-bound to hold up my part of the bargain."

"If that's the case, then that kiss just cost you thirty thousand dollars."

He didn't look any too pleased with himself, but merely shrugged. "So be it. This was a lesson well learned."

"I don't feel I can let you do that." Tempting as it was for Cassie to accept, fair was fair. She hadn't exactly pushed him away. In fact, she'd welcomed his kiss, welcomed his comfort.

"I am not in the habit of arguing with my clients."

"Or with anyone, it seems."

He blinked as if it took him a moment to comprehend what she'd said. "Or with anyone," he agreed.

She sighed. "I appreciate the offer, Simon, really I do, but you weren't the only one who learned a lesson. How about if we both forget it ever happened and just move forward?"

"Fine," he said curtly. "I would like your promise that you'll never mention our kiss again. Can you do that?"

She nodded. "Yes. Of course."

"Good. I'll undertake to do the same thing."

She mimed zipping her lips closed. "It's gone, forgotten, cast into the deepest part of the ocean." The thought flashed into her mind that the ocean was filled with treasures—treasures no one even knew were there. When it happened, Simon's kiss had felt like treasure, unexpected and…beautiful.

"My plan for the third task is to have you cook Christmas dinner," he reminded her.

Cassie raised her hand. "Yes, I wanted to talk to you about that."

"What about it?"

She might as well be blunt. "Like I told you before, I don't have the best neighbors."

"What precisely is the problem?"

Cassie sat up straighter. The Simon she recognized was back. He wasn't interested in listening to any excuses—except that in this instance excuses were necessary. Cassie couldn't possibly invite her neighbors to Christmas dinner. She didn't really know these people, and what she did know unnerved her.

"Out with it, Cassie. I don't have all day."

Hiding her smile would have been impossible.

"What's that silly grin for?" he demanded in the gruff voice she'd grown accustomed to.

"You. You're back!"

"I never left."

"But you did," she said. "A few minutes ago, while we were discussing—you know, what we promised never to mention again—you seemed...almost human."

His left brow rose, mocking her. "*Almost,* you say?"

"Yes—and I rather liked it."

"Don't get used to it."

"Oh, not to worry. I won't." She set her coffee aside and sat on her hands. "Anyway, continue."

"We were discussing your third task."

"I feel you should know that one of my neighbors, Mrs. Mullinex, is a thief."

"She has a police record?"

"I... No, I don't think so. But who knows? Anyone who'd purposely take my newspaper..."

"Your *newspaper?*"

"Yes, that's what she's been stealing for the last few months." Then, stricken by an attack of conscience, Cassie went on to explain. "To be honest, Mrs. Mullinex does return it, but she clips out the coupons. Then, a couple of weeks back, she went so far as to take the Sunday edition, and get this—she likes to do the Sunday *New York*

Times crossword puzzle. *My* crossword puzzle." She narrowed her eyes. "I wouldn't have to invite her, would I?"

"Oh, yes."

"And Mr. Oliver?"

"What's wrong with Mr. Oliver?"

Cassie had no qualms about detailing her other neighbor's faults. "First, he's rude. More than once, Mr. Oliver has deliberately allowed the elevator doors to close on me." She wagged her index finger at Simon. "I'm positive he could see me, too. I saw that gleam in his eyes. The Sunday before last he left me standing there, loaded down with groceries, and he *enjoyed* it."

"I...see." Once more he seemed unimpressed by her tales of woe.

"Then there's the guy whose condo's next to mine. I don't know his name and I don't want to. He plays his music so loud it shakes my whole kitchen. It's horrible music, too. Rap and heavy metal." She paused. "Now here's the interesting part."

"I can hardly wait."

Simon might be making fun of her, but Cassie forged on. "I saw him in the hallway for the first time this week. All along I'd assumed that whoever he was, he must be college age. This guy was *old*. He had to be sixty if he was a day."

Having laid out her case, Cassie felt certain that Simon would understand why she wouldn't want to go to all that effort for these people. "So you'll reconsider?" she asked him.

"Reconsider what?"

"Giving me a different third task. Surely even you can see it would be impossible to put on a festive dinner for my neighbors."

"No, after hearing this, I believe the third task will be perfect."

Chapter 11

Simon says: The perfect neighbor is the one who's never home.

"You mean you *won't* reconsider?" Cassie sputtered. Simon was being totally unreasonable.

"Did you or did you not agree to host this dinner?"

"Well, yes," she admitted with some reluctance, "but that was before I realized I'd be obliged to fly through the air with my underwear showing." A little guilt on his part might not be amiss.

"A small wardrobe malfunction."

He said it with a straight face and Cassie stared at him,

wondering if this was meant to be a joke. "I suppose you could call it that."

"At least you didn't have a television audience."

She rolled her eyes. "Yeah, that makes it better."

"Regardless, you are still required to complete a third task."

Cassie made a face. "You're a cruel man, Dr. Dodson."

"You were well aware of the conditions of our agreement before you signed the contract. However…"

"Yes?" Hope filled her.

"However, I believe it might be advantageous if you served this dinner *prior* to Christmas. In other words, not on Christmas Day itself as I originally specified."

"Advantageous how?"

"If you agree to this new stipulation, I'll arrange for you to meet John before the twenty-fifth."

"Oh." Cassie had her suspicions. "And when did you make this decision?" She wasn't fooled; Simon wanted her gone and on her way to marital bliss so he wouldn't have to deal with her anymore.

"Why the dirty look? I would think you'd be grateful."

"I'd be a whole lot more grateful if I didn't distrust your motives."

Simon watched her steadily. "And what is wrong with my motives?"

Irritated, Cassie stood. She wasn't sure why his latest suggestion upset her—the opposite *should* be true. It should thrill her, since she'd be that much closer to meeting John. But it didn't. She walked over to the picture window. "You want me out of your life," she mumbled, her back to him.

"I didn't say that."

"You didn't need to."

"Listen, Cassie, and this is important. Don't fall in love with me. I'm not good husband material. Furthermore—"

"Oh, please," she snapped. "You're in greater danger of falling for me!"

"Don't flatter yourself." He went into the kitchen with their coffee cups. When he came back, she guessed it was time to leave. Her clue was that he'd put on his coat and scarf.

On the return trip to the mall, there was silence between them, no music, not even the radio. When they arrived, Cassie told him where to drop her off. Simon pulled up behind her parked car.

"Please let me know when you intend to serve the Christmas meal," he said.

"Can I get back to you?"

He kept his hands on the steering wheel and gazed straight ahead. "Fine. But remember that all three tasks must be completed to my satisfaction. So far, you've done well."

Was that praise? From the high and mighty Simon Dodson? She could hardly believe it. He *must* have an ulterior motive, no matter how much he claimed otherwise. Although, now that she considered it, he hadn't exactly denied her accusation. "I'll call you later in the week with the date."

"Good. I thought you'd come around."

She opened the passenger door, then climbed out and banged it shut. *"Good,"* she mimicked. Seeing someone waiting eagerly for her parking space, Cassie hurriedly got into her car and backed out.

On the drive home she did her best to analyze why someone she disliked could affect her so profoundly. It troubled her that she'd enjoyed Simon's touch and his kiss, that she felt invigorated by his—occasionally annoying—conversation.

Not until the following Wednesday was Cassie able to work out a date that was agreeable to all her neighbors, as well as Angie and Shawn. Dinner was scheduled for the Sunday before Christmas.

To her credit, Mrs. Mullinex seemed pleased by the invitation and offered to bring her special pickled brussels sprouts. Her mother's recipe, she said. Cassie declined, saying she'd take care of everything.

Mr. Oliver gave a one-word answer. "Why?"

"It's just an invitation to dinner," Cassie said. "I'm doing all the cooking and…and it seemed neighborly to have a Christmas celebration." The explanation struck her as a bit lame, but she could hardly tell him her *real* reason.

"Who else are you inviting?"

She told him.

"I suppose I could come," he said and closed the door. He made it sound as if he was doing her a favor. In retrospect, maybe he was.

The rap-music man was harder to catch. She rang his doorbell several times, then pounded hard, but either he didn't want to answer or he was so deaf he couldn't hear her. In the end she slipped a note under his door.

He responded in kind, placing a message under her door that said he'd be delighted to join her for dinner. He signed it *Bob,* which seemed a rather inoffensive name for someone who listened to such belligerent music.

Now that the arrangements were made, Cassie was ready to contact Simon. She knew he kept evening hours a couple of days a week for the benefit of working clients, and this was one of those days.

"He's not in the office," Ms. Snelling informed her. "I don't see your name on the appointment list."

"He asked me to call." Or maybe she'd volunteered; Cassie couldn't remember.

"I see. Do you wish to leave a message for him?"

"No." Cassie was emphatic about that. She preferred to speak to him personally. In her opinion, it was time that he learned the art of compromise. She was going to ask for one small concession, and if Simon had any common sense at all, he'd agree.

"Can you tell me when he'll be available?"

"Oh, dear, I'm afraid I can't. Dr. Dodson is home sick with the flu."

Simon was sick? Cassie felt immediate sympathy. "How long has he been out?"

"Two days, and when he phoned in, he sounded absolutely dreadful."

"Poor man." Cassie hung up and went about her business. Her apartment looked Christmassy, thanks primarily to her brother's tree. She'd draped it with merrily twinkling lights that brought a festive quality to the dark evening. Cassie had added a trio of angels to the fireplace mantel. A lovely wreath hung on the inside, rather than the outside, of her door because she didn't trust her neighbors (one in particular) not to steal it.

Even with Christmas music playing in the background and cookbooks strewn across the kitchen counter, all Cassie could think about was Simon, sick and in bed. He was alone. He'd never mentioned family. She didn't know about friends, either. As far as she could tell, there was no one to check up on him. If she'd had a special recipe for chicken noodle soup she would've made him a pot of it.

Then it came to her—why *not* make him some soup? Medicinal soup for a friend. Simon might not consider her a friend, but Cassie couldn't ignore the fact that he might need someone. She began paging through her cook-books....

She didn't fool herself into believing Simon would appreciate the effort. But even knowing he'd probably resent her dropping off the soup wasn't enough to change her mind.

"You're going to a lot of trouble for him," Angie told her the next morning at work, when Cassie brought in a full quart of her concoction.

"That's true," she said, finding space in the lunchroom fridge for her plastic container.

"Why would you care? He's such a difficult man. I bet he'll bite your head off for making him get out of bed to answer the door."

Cassie nodded.

"How do you know where he lives, anyway?"

Rather than launch into the whole complicated tale, she said, "It's a long story. I'll save it for when we have more time."

"I'm holding you to that."

Fortunately, two colleagues joined them for lunch, so Cassie was spared the necessity of telling Angie what had happened on Saturday, when she'd been an elf. After work she called Simon's office and learned he was still sick. Her decision made, Cassie drove to Tacoma. She had no problem locating the neighborhood but had to drive around numerous streets before she found his house.

By then, it was completely dark and the rain fell in sheets. Racing from the car to his front door, carrying her quart container, she shook the moisture out of her hair before she rang his doorbell. When no one answered, she was tempted to leave the soup on his porch and drive away.

Just as she turned to do exactly that, the door opened and Simon stood there in his housecoat and slippers. He looked even worse than she might have imagined, with a pale face, rumpled hair and rheumy eyes. Her sympathy was instantly aroused and it was all she could do not to reach out and test his brow for fever.

"Cassie?"

She hadn't planned what she'd say, and now her tongue seemed to twist itself into knots. "I heard you were sick.... I—I brought you some homemade chicken noodle soup."

He stared at her as if he wasn't sure whether he was hallucinating.

"How are you feeling?" she asked, although the answer was obvious.

"Terrible." He stepped aside, silently inviting her into the house.

Cassie hadn't expected that. In fact, she'd been sure that he'd be angry. She'd expected him to growl and demand that she leave.

"I can't stay long. Like I said, I wanted to drop off the soup and tell you the turkey dinner's set for Sunday."

Simon covered his mouth and coughed. It resembled

a dog's barking and seemed to rack his entire body. She wondered if he had pneumonia.

"Have you seen a doctor?" she asked urgently.

"I'll be fine. Don't fuss, Cassie."

"Someone should. Now, lie down and I'll heat up this soup." Taking charge, she walked past him and into his kitchen, which to her shock was untidy. Dishes littered the counter and pots were stacked in the sink. She could see that he'd made an effort to straighten up but had either grown too tired or was too sick to continue.

Before she started heating the soup, she placed the dirty dishes in the dishwasher and turned it on. Her soup warmed on the stove as she cleaned up the kitchen. Simon had disappeared and now returned dressed in slacks and a sweater. He'd apparently showered, because his hair was wet and combed.

"This is thoughtful of you." He actually sounded grateful.

Dishcloth in hand, Cassie regarded him suspiciously. "You mean to say you're not angry?"

"Why would I be angry?"

"I'm invading your privacy."

He acknowledged that with a slight tilt of his head.

The soup began to boil and Cassie removed the pan from the burner, poured some in a bowl and set it on the kitchen table with a spoon.

While Simon had his soup, she made them both cups

of strong, hot tea, then sat across from him at the table. She declined his suggestion of soup, since she was too nervous to eat.

"This might surprise you, but I quite like you when you're sick."

He set the spoon next to his bowl and studied her warily. "I beg your pardon?"

That must have sounded strange. "You're more human when you're vulnerable." He didn't respond.

Cassie was gratified to see that he finished the entire bowlful of soup.

"Shall we have our tea in the living room?" she asked, noting that the television was on, the volume low.

Simon nodded. "I've watched more television in the past three days than the previous three years."

"Oh, *Jeopardy!*'s just starting. That's my favorite game show," she said, sitting on the couch. Simon sat beside her, a careful distance away—not too close and not too far.

He picked up the remote and turned up the volume. The thirty minutes passed quickly. She couldn't resist shouting out answers—"What is the Battle of Gettysburg?" "Who are Sacco and Vanzetti?" "What is silver nitrate?" She was pleased that she was almost always right, although she noticed that Simon didn't participate at all. He must be feeling very ill.

"I should leave," she said after Final Jeopardy ("Who was St. Nicholas?") and started to stand.

Simon reached for her hand. "Stay a while longer, if you don't mind."

"I don't..." The sudden surge of tenderness she felt shocked her. What shocked her even more was that his hand continued to hold hers. His touch was light, but sometime during the next thirty minutes he intertwined their fingers. It was hard to concentrate on the rerun of *Frasier*—a Christmas episode she'd already seen—when her whole body was focused on his hand holding hers. Innocent enough on the surface, his action was highly sensual in its effect. She felt his touch in every part of her, in every sensitized nerve, every cell. She needed all her self-control not to turn into his arms and beg him to kiss her.

"My brother might be at the dinner," she said, hoping she didn't sound as breathless as she felt.

"I'd enjoy meeting him."

"You would? Angie might be able to come, too."

"Angie?"

"My best friend. You met her—and rejected her."

"Ah, yes, I remember her now."

"I wish you'd given her a chance," Cassie murmured.

"I couldn't. She was in love with someone and refused to admit it."

"How do you know?" she asked.

"It's my job. That's the point of such a detailed questionnaire. I explore people's responses and I read between the lines." He looked at her sternly, their hands still linked. "You know I can't discuss this with you."

"Oh." Her mouth had gone dry. If Simon could read others so well, she wondered if he was aware of the intense sensation she was experiencing. Did he feel it, too?

"Will you come for dinner?" she asked. This was the concession she'd intended to request. She wasn't quite sure why. She'd told herself it was so he'd be able to judge the way she handled the third task, which would expedite her introduction to John. But now...

He didn't answer.

"Please?"

He rubbed his thumb along hers and it was all Cassie could do not to faint. Her eyes drifted shut.

"I'll be there," he finally agreed.

"Thank you."

The argument between Frasier and Niles on the TV seemed to fade into the background. "I should go," she said.

"Yes," he said in a whisper. "You should." He released her and she clenched her fist to keep from grabbing his hand again.

"I'll see you at three o'clock on Sunday," she said hoarsely, staggering to her feet.

He nodded.

He didn't walk her to the door.

Chapter 12

Simon says: The perfect match lights a lasting fire.

Cassie pored over every cookbook she owned. They were all full of wonderful recipes. Even more encouraging, the instructions didn't seem too difficult. She had her menu set for this all-important dinner: roast turkey with a traditional stuffing, mashed potatoes and gravy, fresh green beans with butter and sliced almonds, two different salads and three kinds of pie, apple, pumpkin and pecan. Her grocery list was two pages long.

Angie had offered to help with the shopping; she'd also volunteered to set the table. This was by far the most elaborate meal Cassie had ever undertaken.

Her brother, too, seemed eager to help. Luckily, Shawn was in town for a benefit and he'd promised to hand-letter the place cards. He said he'd also do small drawings on each, which were sure to be highly collectible—if any of her neighbors recognized her brother as the famous mural artist. Well, even if they didn't, they were bound to like the personal touch.

Reading over the stuffing recipe one last time, Cassie rested her elbows on the kitchen counter.

Unfortunately, her mind kept wandering from the page. She hadn't seen Simon since she'd visited him in his home. He'd fully recovered from his bout with the flu and gone back to work.

Cassie knew that because she'd phoned and chatted briefly with his assistant who'd told her Simon was indeed in the office. But when Ms. Snelling asked if Cassie wished to speak to him, she'd declined and hurriedly got off the phone.

Simon hadn't called to thank her for the soup, not that she expected him to. He was coming to dinner on Sunday and she almost dreaded seeing him; at the same time, she could hardly wait.

She hardly thought of John—John the engineer, John the perfect man—anymore. Only Simon seemed to inhabit her mind. And her heart?

Something was very wrong.

The doorbell rang and Cassie left her kitchen. Angie

breezed into the room as though floating on air. This wasn't unusual these days. Her friend was in love. Angie seemed like a different person; nothing upset her, nothing annoyed her. In fact, she glowed with happiness. And yet she remained secretive about this new man in her life. Still, Cassie had begun to have her suspicions. In retrospect, the night of her solitary tree-decorating should have been a giveaway.

"You ready?" Angie asked.

"Shawn phoned earlier," Cassie said and carefully watched her friend's expression.

Angie revealed nothing.

"Oh, he's in town?"

"My brother seems to have a fair amount of business in the Pacific Northwest lately," Cassie said, playing along. "He said he was here for some benefit, but if you ask me, the one who's benefiting is my brother."

Angie turned away and walked into the kitchen. She set down her purse, then removed her coat and draped it over the back of a kitchen chair. "This is your menu for tomorrow?" she said, still avoiding eye contact. She studied the paper on which Cassie had written her menu ideas. "Three different pies seems a bit ambitious, don't you think?"

"I wanted there to be choices." It didn't escape Cassie's notice how quickly Angie had diverted the subject from Shawn.

"Simon agreed to come, right?"

Switching the topic to Simon was a clever move. "Yes." Before she could expand or hint further about Shawn, the doorbell chimed again. Cassie opened the door to her brother, who hugged her enthusiastically. His eyes gleamed with a merriment that was due to more than the season, Cassie thought. When he saw Angie his expression sobered. He greeted her politely, even rather distantly.

"This dinner is becoming quite the affair," Shawn said, handing her the place cards. The artwork—small watercolors, all individual, of Christmas trees and bells and stars—was beautiful.

"Thanks!" Cassie kissed his cheek. "Okay, you two, sit down," she ordered. She indicated the sofa. "Before you say anything, I want you to know that I arranged for you to be here at the same time."

Shawn and Angie took opposite sides of the sofa while Cassie stood directly in front of them, her arms crossed. "You aren't fooling me, you know. I suspected the two of you were seeing each other."

"We wanted to tell you," Angie blurted out. "Well, I did, but Shawn felt we should wait."

"We weren't sure this was going anywhere," Shawn explained, glancing at Angie.

"We wanted to keep it to ourselves for a while," Angie said in a small voice, glancing back at Shawn.

"If you're upset, blame me," Shawn said, quick to defend Angie.

"Why wouldn't you want me to know?" Cassie asked, directing the question to both of them. "I'm happy for you!"

"It just kind of happened."

"We dated for a while a year ago after we met at your birthday party, and it didn't work out," Shawn said.

"For him, maybe, but it worked for me. I fell in love with Shawn." Angie looked down at her hands, which were neatly folded in her lap.

"Oh, my goodness!" Cassie brought one hand to her mouth. "Simon wouldn't take you on as a client because you were in love with someone else. That someone was my brother, wasn't it?"

Angie's ears turned red as she nodded. "Shawn and I went out last year, like he said, and just when everything seemed to be going well…I didn't hear from him."

"I was traveling a lot," he said. "A relationship's hard when I'm on the road so much. Besides, I was falling for Angie and it scared me. I'd dated plenty of women but I didn't feel about them the way I did about Angie—and I panicked."

"I was distraught when we broke up," Angie whispered. "I wanted to tell you, but Shawn—"

"You never said a word." Cassie was embarrassed that she'd been so oblivious. "Before *or* after you called it quits."

Angie shrugged apologetically.

"I like my privacy," Shawn said. "You know that."

Cassie couldn't help being a little hurt. "For crying out loud, I'm your sister."

"I'm sorry." Shawn did appear regretful. "Neither of us meant to offend you or anything."

"After we broke it off, I tried to move on," Angie said. "Which is why I agreed when my mother wanted me to meet the matchmaker."

"I made an effort to get over Angie, too," Shawn confessed, smiling at her, "but I couldn't get her out of my mind."

"Then we met again just before Thanksgiving."

"Here," Angie clarified. They both nodded.

"And I realized how much I'd missed Angie," he went on, "and how foolish I'd been to let our relationship end."

"And *I* realized that Simon was right and despite everything, I was still in love with Shawn."

They slid closer on the couch and Shawn took Angie's hand. They stared into each other's eyes.

Cassie wanted to kick them both for being so foolish, for not understanding what they had the first time around. They deserved a second kick for keeping it a secret from her.

"We've been so happy," Angie told her, "and I was afraid that if we said anything, you'd feel left out."

"Left out? If I feel left out it's because you guys—two

of the most important people in my life—didn't let me in on something as big as this!"

"We did plan to tell you," Angie said.

"And when would that have been?"

"After the big dinner party."

Cassie laughed. "So that's why it was so easy to convince you to make an appearance."

Shawn nodded. "Now that you know, we don't have to show up, do we? Angie and I have better things to do than attend this crazy dinner party of yours."

"Shawn," Angie chastised.

The hopeful expression on his face was enough to make Cassie laugh. "No, you two are excused. Angie, you don't need to help with the shopping."

"I'll come if you want," Angie said.

She would, too, but Cassie could see that she'd rather be alone with Shawn than spend the day in a crowded grocery store.

"I'll be fine. Do something productive with your time, though—like shopping for an engagement ring."

Angie blushed again and Shawn cleared his throat. "As it happens, I have a ring picked out."

"You do?" Angie asked with tears in her voice.

"I'm not letting you get away from me again," Shawn said. "There's still plenty to discuss, but I can't see—"

"Yes."

"Yes, what?" he asked.

"Yes, I'll marry you and, yes, there's a lot still to be decided. But there's no obstacle the two of us can't overcome."

They left a few minutes later, so in love they couldn't keep their hands off each other.

Cassie had difficulty wiping the grin off her face. Shawn and Angie were perfect together. She wondered why she hadn't thought of it before—or noticed what was going on. Angie would probably move away from Seattle once they were married, which was the only disadvantage to an otherwise ideal situation.

All of a sudden it became crucial to talk to Simon. She had his office number and as she suspected he had an answering service.

"Would you please ask Mr. Dodson to return my call? It's…an emergency."

She didn't have to wait long for him to call back. When his name flashed across caller ID, Cassie exhaled a huge sigh of relief.

"Simon?" she said.

"Yes."

Cassie smiled at his gruff, unfriendly tone. She felt better already.

"There's been a change in our dinner plans."

"That's why you phoned?"

"Yes. My brother and Angie won't be attending."

"That's your emergency?"

"This might not be earth-shattering to you but—"

"Cassie…"

"I knew they were secretly involved, or at least I guessed they were. It's wonderful for them. They make a fabulous couple. I couldn't be happier, even if it means I'm going to lose my best friend."

Her outburst was followed by a short silence. "I don't quite understand why you called me. And I suggest you think of it as gaining a sister-in-law," he advised wryly, "not losing a friend."

"Yes, that's true, but she'll leave Seattle and the lab.… Anyway," she said in a more cheerful voice, "I wanted to let you know you were right about her being in love."

"Of course I was right. Did you seriously doubt it?"

"Well, perhaps not." She paused. "I shouldn't have called. You must consider me a nuisance."

"We can agree on that," he murmured.

"I know you regret taking me on as a client and I apologize for being such a pest."

"I've dealt with worse clients."

Funny how reassuring Cassie found even that faint encouragement.

He exhaled slowly. "You're upset. Is it because of your friend and your brother? Anything that upsets the status quo—even a good thing like this—takes time to accept."

Cassie wasn't sure why she'd felt such an overwhelming urge to hear his voice. His certainty was comforting, she supposed. He always had an answer, a reason, a solution.

"How can I help?" he asked, his tone almost gentle.

"I...I don't know."

"I have an idea," he said, his voice brightening.

"What?"

"I'll tell you something else about John."

"John?"

"The man I've matched you with."

"Oh. Yes." The man she'd paid thirty thousand dollars to meet. He'd completely slipped her mind.

"Okay," he said. "Let me think about it."

"What were you doing?" She felt guilty at the thought of interrupting him. "Before I called."

"What was I doing?" he repeated. "Why do you ask?"

"If I'm being too much of a bother, I'll hang up." She viewed him as someone who operated with purpose. Someone whose day was filled with constant demands. He had too many responsibilities to be interrupted by such mundane matters as her doubts and insecurities.

"I'm watching a college football game."

"You watch football?" He couldn't have shocked her more had he said he was on an aircraft headed for the moon. Practically every day Simon surprised her with how...*human* he was.

"Why would you find that unusual?"

"I didn't think football would interest you. It's so...so normal."

He laughed. "I am normal, Cassie. I'm like every other man."

"No, you aren't," she insisted. "You aren't like any

other man I've ever known, and now I'm seeing this whole other side of you and it's confusing."

He muttered something under his breath; it sounded as if he'd said he was confused himself, but Cassie couldn't be sure of that.

"About John," he said, changing the subject.

"I don't want to hear about John right now."

"Maybe you should. It'll adjust your focus."

"No, thanks. I'll be meeting him soon, won't I?"

"I can arrange the meeting for Monday afternoon if you like. When I last spoke to him about scheduling a face-to-face, John was ecstatic. He's *very* eager to make your acquaintance."

"Oh."

"He called it an early Christmas gift."

"Oh, yes, Christmas."

Silence stretched between them.

"I'll get to your condo a few minutes early," Simon said, filling the empty space. "I have your address. From your application—and the check."

The thirty-thousand-dollar check…

"See you then," he added.

"Yes, for dinner." Not until she'd hung up her phone, did she wonder why he wanted to come early.

Chapter 13

Cassie was up half the night baking pies and getting everything ready for her final task. Her alarm went off at six on Sunday morning. She staggered from her bed, got the turkey out of the refrigerator and nearly dropped it on the kitchen floor. Who knew twenty pounds would be so heavy?

Because she'd methodically planned every detail of the dinner preparations, she was right on schedule. She stuffed the turkey and it was in the oven and roasting nicely an hour later. She started on the salads next. The dining room table was set with a crisp white linen cloth. There were sprigs of holly beside each place card for a festive accent. She'd arranged every detail with the hope of impressing Simon. She'd dressed in a red and black velvet pantsuit and taken care with her makeup. For a final holiday touch she wore a ring with a large red stone.

He arrived a full hour before her guests were due, carrying a huge, perfect poinsettia for the centerpiece.

He handed it to her almost as if he was grateful to be rid of it.

"How lovely," she said delightedly. "Thank you."

She put the poinsettia on the table and stepped back to examine it.

"I love it, Simon." Rising onto the tips of her toes, she kissed his cheek.

He was frowning when she stepped back. "That was inappropriate," he said disapprovingly.

She didn't point out that he'd kissed her a few weeks ago. But to prove how wrong he was, she kissed his cheek a second time.

However, when she started to move away, Simon clasped her by the shoulders and pulled her into his embrace. Then he lowered his mouth to hers. Before she could account for her response, she threw her arms around his neck and kissed him back.

They both seemed to realize at precisely the same moment what they'd done. They leaped apart; Simon shoved his hands in his pockets, while Cassie turned around in an effort to regain her composure.

As they faced each other again, Cassie made a sweeping gesture toward the table, hoping to bring some levity to the situation. "Well, what do you think?" she asked.

He nodded. "You've done a wonderful job."

"Would you like to see the turkey?" she asked.

"If you wish."

"I do. You're the one who told me I had to do this... and in retrospect I'm glad you did." She led him into the kitchen, grabbed one of her oven mitts and opened the door. She basted the turkey and noted with pride how crisp and brown it looked. According to her calculations, it would be finished in forty minutes. Simon could remove it from the oven and it would sit for an additional fifteen minutes before being carved.

"Very nice," he said, when she closed the oven door. "Smells delicious, too."

"Have I surprised you?" she asked and knew she had, which was what she'd hoped.

He smiled. "I admit that you're one surprise after another." Which was exactly the thought she'd so recently had about him....

She managed to restrain herself from dancing a small, gleeful jig.

She poured Simon a glass of eggnog while they waited for the rest of her company. "Store-bought," she confessed as she joined him in the living room. They sat on opposite ends of the sofa.

That wasn't the only similarity to the way Shawn and

Angie had behaved the previous day. Like her brother and her friend, Simon and Cassie hardly looked at each other. Neither seemed inclined toward conversation, either.

"I was thinking…" Cassie began.

"It seems to me…" Simon said.

They both stopped, then Simon gestured toward her to speak.

"No, you first," she insisted.

"Please," he said.

Cassie didn't get a chance because the doorbell rang just then. Eager to break the unexplained tension between them, she hurried to answer. As she might have guessed, Mrs. Mullinex arrived first. She stood in the hallway dressed in her finest. For the first time in Cassie's memory, her hair wasn't in curlers. In fact, this was the first time she'd seen her neighbor's hair, period. It was…curly.

"This is so nice of you," the older woman chirped. Her eyes flew instantly to Simon and widened with womanly appreciation.

"This is…" Cassie wasn't sure how to introduce him. "Simon. My friend. Simon Dodson, Mrs. Mullinex."

"How do you do?" her neighbor cooed sweetly. "Please call me Phyllis."

"Phyllis," Cassie repeated. She'd lived in the building for three years and hadn't been aware of Mrs. Mullinex's first name, which didn't appear on the mailbox, not even as an initial. Her neighbor had never seen fit to share it with Cassie.

"I didn't realize Cassie had a male friend," Mrs. Mullinex said ever so coyly. "She is a sly one."

Cassie excused herself and disappeared inside the kitchen while she prepared the hors d'oeuvres. She'd leave Simon to fend for himself. When she heard the two of them chatting amicably, Cassie sighed. Simon possessed a few social graces, after all—but none that he was willing to display for *her* benefit.

Mr. Oliver showed up next. "The Seahawks game starts at four. This isn't going to take longer than that, is it?" he asked as he barreled past her and into the condo. He looked around and when he saw Phyllis Mullinex, a frown darkened his face.

"Mr. Oliver," Mrs. Mullinex greeted him stiffly.

"Phyllis."

They glared at each other like alley cats with hackles raised, each waiting for the other to make the first move.

"So…you two know each other," Cassie commented, watching them carefully.

"No," said Mrs. Mullinex.

"Oh, yes, we know each other very well," Mr. Oliver countered. "Would you mind if I turned the TV on?" he asked as he claimed the most comfortable chair. Not waiting for a response, he reached for the remote, leaned forward and pressed the on button. The television screen lit up and he immediately found the station he wanted. It featured another football game—not the Seahawks.

"I'd like to introduce my friend Dr. Simon Dodson," Cassie said, speaking loudly enough to be heard above the roar of the sports announcer.

Mr. Oliver acknowledged Simon with a disinterested nod of his head.

Her doorbell rang again. Grateful for an excuse to escape, Cassie rushed forward to answer. Bob, the rap aficionado from next door, stood on the other side. He'd apparently gone to some effort with his appearance; he'd greased his graying hair back from his forehead and donned a fresh pair of jeans and a sweater. He grinned when he saw her and handed her a lone rose.

"Welcome," Cassie said and brought him into the room.

When he saw the others, Bob's face fell. "You didn't say there'd be anyone else here," he said.

"Oh...sorry. I assumed you knew."

"So, dinner isn't just for the two of us?"

"Ah...no. I'm sure you've met Mrs. Mullinex and Mr. Oliver," Cassie said, motioning toward her guests.

"No, and I don't particularly care to," he grumbled.

"This is my friend Dr. Simon Dodson."

Bob's frown deepened. "You have a...friend?"

"Well, yes, sort of." The last thing she needed was for Bob to think she was interested in his attentions. If avoiding *that* trap meant stretching the truth, then so be it.

The oven timer went off, and Cassie took the opportunity to leave and close the kitchen door behind her. After all her hard work, this meal was going to be a disaster. None of these people liked one another.

Simon followed her into the kitchen. "Should the turkey come out yet?" he asked.

"Yes," she said distractedly as he slipped his hands into her Santa-face oven mitts.

"Simon," she pleaded. "What are we going to do?"

"About what?"

"Can't you see?" she cried. "Mrs. Mullinex and Mr. Oliver can barely stand to look at each other, and Bob thought this dinner was going to be a private affair between him and me."

"It'll be fine," he said soothingly.

Cassie sincerely doubted that.

Simon lifted the turkey out of the oven and set it on top of the stove.

Cassie thanked him. "According to my cookbook, the turkey should sit for no less than fifteen minutes before being carved."

"Do you need help with anything else?"

"No." She'd seen to everything before the guests were due. "I just have to get the food into the serving dishes."

Bowls lined the counter. Cassie was pleased with her organizational abilities. The potatoes were cooked and ready to be mashed. Green beans simmered on the stovetop. She drained off the liquid, added the melted butter and almonds and placed them in the bowl she'd chosen.

Simon returned to the living room with the others.

Then, picking up the bowl in which she planned to put the stuffing, she noticed something wrong. For a moment, all Cassie could do was stare at her hand.

No! Oh, dear. Now what?

Putting down the bowl, she opened the door slightly and peered out of the kitchen. "Simon," she called in a deceptively casual voice. "Would you come in here for a minute?"

He gave her an odd look but did as she requested.

The instant he set foot in the kitchen, she took his arms and pulled him all the way in. "Houston, we have a problem," she said in an urgent whisper.

"What kind of problem?"

"A very big one." Splaying her fingers, she held out her hand. "My ring is missing."

"Your ring."

"Yes, my ring."

He seemed unconcerned. "I'm sure it's around here somewhere. Can't you look for it later?"

"No."

"And why not?" he asked.

"Because the last time I saw it, I was stuffing the turkey."

"In other words..."

"Yes. In other words it's inside the bird."

"You're positive?"

"No, but where else would it be?"

Simon rolled his eyes toward the ceiling.

"What am I going to do?" A dozen scenarios played in her mind, none of them the least bit amusing. If someone bit into it and broke a tooth… "I'll be sued!" she said hoarsely, covering her eyes. "Someone might choke on it. My neighbors don't deserve to die, even if my newspapers do turn up missing now and then."

"Dish the stuffing into the bowl. You might find it."

"Okay, okay."

"And don't panic."

"Easy for you to say," she muttered as she transferred stuffing into the bowl, inspecting each spoonful closely.

"Mrs. Mullinex is a sweet lady," he was saying. "I don't know why you think she'd want to cause you any trouble."

"And Mr. Oliver?"

"He probably wouldn't even notice if he bit into the ring, especially if you left the football game on."

"And Bob?"

"He'd assume you were proposing marriage."

"Very funny."

"Oh, Cassie, I just—"

Mrs. Mullinex stuck her head into the kitchen. "Anything I can do, dear?"

"Ah, no, thanks. Everything's fine," Cassie assured her.

"Simon, come back and sit with me," the older woman wheedled.

Simon turned away from the counter and offered Mrs. Mullinex his arm, then threw Cassie a look that told her she was on her own.

A lot of help *he'd* been.

No sooner had Simon left than the door opened again. This time it was Bob.

"So," he said, leaning against the kitchen counter. "It's just the two of us now."

"Yes, well…" Cassie inserted the spoon inside the turkey to finish taking out the stuffing, but with Bob watching every move, she couldn't make a huge production of plowing through it, searching for her ring.

"I've always loved stuffing."

"Oh, me, too, but I'm not sure this turned out that well. I was thinking I wouldn't serve it."

"Let me taste." Before she could protest, he took her spoon and helped himself to a sample. After blowing on it, he popped it into his mouth. He smiled widely in approval. "This is fabulous! The best I've ever tasted."

"You're just being kind."

"Not at all. Here, I'll take it out for you."

"No," she cried and made an effort to stop him, but to no avail. Bob carried the bowl into the dining area.

When she followed with the salads, she saw that he'd

taken a forkful to Mrs. Mullinex. "Cassie says the stuffing didn't turn out to her liking. I disagree. What do you think?"

Mrs. Mullinex gave it a dainty taste. "Perfection," she said. "You're being modest, Cassie."

Mr. Oliver stood. "What's a turkey dinner without stuffing?"

"I didn't want to ruin anyone's diet," Cassie said, searching for an excuse, any excuse, to get the stuffing off the table.

Mr. Oliver raised his hand. "I'm on a low-carb diet myself."

"Then you won't want any of the stuffing," Cassie said thankfully.

"I thought I'd make an exception, this being Christmas and all."

"Oh…"

"Let's all help," Mrs. Mullinex suggested cheerfully. "We can bring out the rest of the serving dishes. We shouldn't leave all the work to Cassie."

Cassie sent a pleading glance in Simon's direction. He, however, was looking elsewhere.

Chapter 14

Simon says: A good matchmaker stays in the background, just like Santa's little helper, then swoops in at the opportune moment.

Cassie couldn't swallow a single bite as she carefully studied her guests enjoying their turkey with all the trimmings. Every time she saw a forkful of stuffing heading toward someone's mouth she had to restrain herself from leaping to her feet and yanking it away.

Simon revealed no such concern. Mrs. Mullinex had him engaged in a lengthy conversation. Judging by the attention he paid her, anyone would think she was the wittiest, prettiest woman on the face of the earth. Every once in a while, the older woman released a girlish trill that sounded, to Cassie's somewhat jaundiced ear, like a songbird strangling on too much seed.

"Mighty fine dinner," Bob told Cassie, eyeing her with far more appreciation than his meal.

"Thank you." She quickly looked away and offered Mr. Oliver more beans. More salad. More anything.

"Do you always cook like this?" Mr. Oliver asked. Before she could answer, he continued. "You probably have plenty of leftovers. No need to let 'em go to waste."

"That'd be a shame," Bob threw in. "I'd be happy to come over and help you finish them a few times a week."

Cassie felt it was important to set *him* straight right away. "Since I work and there's only me to cook for, I generally don't go to this much trouble." *Generally—like never!*

Bob glanced at Mr. Oliver, whose plate was heaped high with large portions of mashed potatoes and gravy. "I thought you said you were watching your weight?"

"Low-carb's the only way to go." He reached across the table for the butter, which he slathered on a roll.

"Cassie, dear," Mrs. Mullinex said in the same high-pitched bird voice she'd used since meeting Simon. "It's been such a long time since I made gravy. Does yours always have these lumps in it?"

Cassie stiffened her shoulders at the frightening thought that the ring might have slipped into the gravy. Then she realized her neighbor was denigrating her gravy-making skills, although she wasn't sure why. Her gravy was flawless, and if there were any lumps, which there weren't, it was a fluke. "No, I added them for your benefit," she answered in an equally saccharine voice.

Simon's gaze narrowed.

"Oh." Mrs. Mullinex blinked as if gauging whether or not to be offended.

"I'm joking, Mrs. Mullinex," Cassie said, feeling slightly guilty. "I apologize if there are lumps in the gravy."

"You can put lumps in my gravy anytime you want," Bob told her. He winked at her, then jiggled his eyebrows. Disgusting! The man was old enough to be her father.

"I believe I'll have some more of that stuffing," Simon said.

Cassie sprang from her chair and grabbed hold of the bowl. "I was going to take it back to the kitchen."

"Gimme that when you're finished," Mr. Oliver said, grinning broadly.

"Ah…" Cassie looked helplessly at Simon, who gently pried the bowl from her hands. "I'm not sure there's enough."

"There's plenty for everyone," Simon said and took a huge spoonful before passing it across the table to Mr. Oliver. "Let me hand it around."

"Doesn't anyone want to save room for pie?" Cassie asked brightly. She described each one, highlighting the fine qualities of the apple, pumpkin and pecan fillings.

"I don't know if I dare," Mrs. Mullinex trilled. "One must watch one's waistline." She paused, gazing around as if waiting for someone to tell her she needn't worry about such things.

Cassie volunteered in the hope that if her neighbor accepted the pie, she'd skip the extra stuffing, which, to her horror, was being passed around the table. "Why, Mrs. Mullinex, you have a very good figure."

"Pleasingly plump," Bob seconded.

The smile faded from the other woman's face. "Plump?"

"*Pleasingly* plump," Cassie said. "That's another way of saying—"

"I'm fat," Mrs. Mullinex cut in, frowning now.

"I like to be direct," Mr. Oliver said, glaring at the older woman. "Plump is plump, no matter how you try to fancy it up."

"Leave it to you to insult me, Harry," she snapped.

"You always were quick to take offense," Mr. Oliver snapped back. "A man makes a simple comment and you jump all over him and ruin a perfectly fine friendship."

"Ah…" Cassie raised her index finger, trying to get a comment in before the confrontation broke into a full-fledged argument.

"I don't know how anyone could even imply that you're overweight," Simon said, pouring everyone a little more wine.

Cassie managed a smile at his smooth handling of what was rapidly becoming an awkward situation. It also gave her an opportunity to make off with the stuffing unobserved.

"I'll put on a pot of coffee," Cassie said, jumping up from the table. She grabbed the stuffing bowl and practically ran into the kitchen, convinced she was about to have a nervous breakdown. Once inside, she leaned against the wall and breathed deeply, wanting nothing more than this dinner to be over.

When she returned, Simon had collected the dinner plates. Cassie reached for the gravy boat and stared down at it. Lumps, indeed! She couldn't find a single one!

Thankfully, after coffee and dessert, Cassie started to relax. Again Mrs. Mullinex damned her with faint praise regarding the pie, but by then Cassie didn't care. Besides, she had to agree—the apples were unevenly sliced.

"Don't you have anything good to say?" Mr. Oliver muttered. "I thought the pies were great. All of 'em."

"Excellent meal," Bob told her and tried to take her hand.

Cassie snatched it away before he had the chance. As far as she was concerned, the man should be arrested.

"I'll have you know, *Mr.* Oliver, I've paid Cassie several compliments," Mrs. Mullinex said righteously.

If that was the case, they'd flown right over Cassie's head.

By the time she saw her last neighbor to the door, Cassie was exhausted. As soon as Bob left—with obvious reluctance—she collapsed into a chair.

"You look a bit out of sorts," Simon commented.

"You think?" The man had mastered the art of understatement.

He grinned and sat on the sofa across from her. "Actually, the meal went well."

"You have got to be kidding. It was a disaster!"

"You're being too hard on yourself. You did an admirable job, and while it might not seem that your neighbors fully appreciated what you did, I believe they had an enjoyable afternoon."

She gave him a weak smile. "I don't know if I should be glad the ring didn't show up or not."

"Is it valuable?"

"Not really. I bought it in Hawaii a few years back. I hate to lose it, though." She raised her shoulders in a shrug. "But if it hasn't turned up by now, I doubt it ever will. For all I know, it might be in Mr. Oliver's digestive system."

"I'm sure it's not."

"What makes you say that?"

Reaching inside his suit pocket, Simon pulled out the ring, displaying it proudly between index finger and thumb. "Is this the ring you misplaced?"

Speechless, all Cassie could do was stare at him. Once the shock wore off, she lunged forward and grabbed the ring. "You're telling me you found it?"

"I did."

"Where?"

"On the kitchen counter. You must've taken it off and forgotten. I tried to get your attention in the kitchen and then at dinner but you ignored me."

"I didn't take it off." Cassie would've remembered that.

"Then it must have fallen off before you stuffed the turkey."

Cassie held the ring in one cupped hand, her relief overwhelming. Then, slowly, her suspicions started to rise. "Exactly when did you find this?"

"Just before Phyllis came into the kitchen. As I said, I tried to tell you but you were too flustered to notice."

"Phyllis?" she echoed. "Mrs. Mullinex is now Phyllis to you?"

"She's a delightful mature woman."

"Hmm. Then again, she isn't stealing *your* newspapers."

"I suggest you purchase her a subscription for Christmas."

"I'll think about it," Cassie muttered. Then, remembering the ring, she glared at him. "That was cruel and unusual punishment, letting me worry that someone was going to swallow this ring."

"I *tried* to tell you I'd found it," Simon said in his own defense. "Why else do you think I was passing the stuffing around?"

Well, there was that. "I'm too tired to argue with you." She stretched her legs out and let her hands dangle at her sides. Unable to prevent it, she yawned.

Taking that as his cue to leave, Simon stood. "I'd better go."

Cassie realized with a start that she wanted him to stay. "Don't go yet," she urged.

"Do you want help with the cleanup?"

"No."

"A drink or more coffee?"

She shook her head. "There's a football game on," she said.

Cassie could see he was tempted. Smiling up at him, she hoped that was enough incentive to get him to change his mind.

"I should get home," he finally said.

"Why?"

"I just should. And don't forget I'll be seeing you tomorrow," he reminded her.

"Tomorrow?"

"In my office. Late afternoon."

She couldn't recall an appointment, but if they had one, she'd certainly keep it.

"John will be there."

Oh, my goodness. Cassie had forgotten she was supposed to meet John. "Cancel it," she said hurriedly.

Simon frowned.

"I'm not ready to meet John."

"You've completed your three tasks to my satisfaction. I don't understand why you're hesitating. You've worked hard and waited for quite a while, and so has John. I hate to disappoint him."

Cassie's head was spinning with doubt and fear. "I need to talk to you first."

"Talk to me now," he said, none too patiently.

"I can't—I'm tired, and besides, I...I need to think."

He continued to frown, and she could see he wasn't happy with her. He left soon after.

Cassie sat on the sofa for at least an hour, trying to make sense of her relationship with Simon. Her feelings for him and her original expectations of John were scrambled in her mind. Eventually, when her whole life felt like a hopeless tangle, she called Angie.

Thankfully her friend was home.

"I need help," Cassie whispered.

"Cassie?" Angie said. "What's wrong?"

"I've done something foolish."

"What?"

She said the words out loud for the very first time. "I've fallen in love with Simon."

Chapter 15

Simon says: There's a perfect match for you; it just isn't me.

By the time Cassie reached Simon's office, she'd worked everything out. She'd rehearsed her speech all day. Her one hope was that Simon would own up to the fact that he shared her feelings.

His assistant greeted her warmly. "Hello, Ms. Beaumont. It's good to see you again."

"You, too, Ms. Snelling. Oh, nice tree."

That was the extent of the Christmas decorating in Simon's office—a small Norfolk pine on the credenza, draped with tiny white lights. Simple, classy, elegant.

Given her previous experiences visiting his office, Cassie automatically took a seat and picked up a magazine.

"Dr. Dodson will see you now."

"Already?"

"Yes, he told me I was to bring you into his office as soon as you arrived."

Cassie set the magazine aside and stood. It was now or never. The only thing left to do was forge ahead and pray they could discuss this with openness and honesty.

Ms. Snelling held the door for her. "Ms. Beaumont," she said, announcing Cassie.

As he had at their first meeting, Simon sat behind his desk, studying a periodical. He glanced up, acknowledging her with a nod, then resumed reading.

Cassie took a seat, crossed her legs, uncrossed them, then folded her hands as she waited. She knew Simon now and was familiar with his ways.

When he did finally look up, Cassie could see that he was on edge. She wondered if he'd managed to sleep after he'd left her apartment and suspected he'd tossed and turned, the same as she had.

"You said you wanted to speak to me." His voice was expressionless.

"Yes, please."

He checked his watch. "You have ten minutes."

That dictatorial approach didn't fool her. He wasn't

going to intimidate her, nor was he going to scare her into being silent.

"Ten minutes," she said softly. "I doubt it'll take that long."

He leaned back and Cassie leaned forward. "If you'll recall, it was my friend Angie who suggested I make an appointment with you."

He indicated with a slight nod that he remembered.

"You turned her down, right?"

"Yes." He sounded bored. "You know very well I did."

"For an excellent reason," she said, "as you and I are both aware."

He checked his watch again, as if to point out that the minutes were ticking away.

"Even though you rejected her, Angie thought highly enough of your skills as a matchmaker to recommend you to me."

"I know my business, Cassie."

"You won't get any argument from me." She grinned and looked down at her hands, surprised by how calm and controlled she sounded. While her heart continued to beat at an accelerated rate, she remained outwardly collected. "At first I thought the idea of those three tasks was ridiculous, but I complied. In fact, I was willing to do just about anything to prove my value as a wife."

Once more he glanced at his watch.

"I understand now why you chose the tasks you did.

Each one served a specific purpose. You knew all the facts I could list on a sheet of paper, and as a psychologist you could discern a great deal from that, but you didn't know the real me." She'd given much thought to his motives. "You didn't know my heart."

"Yes, well…"

"You wanted to find out how I interact with strangers as a volunteer. You wanted to see how well I deal with children and then you were interested in my homemaking skills."

"Practical aspects of any good marriage. But these tasks also told me that you have compassion and flexibility and a sense of humor."

She bowed her head to hide her pleasure at his words.

"John is looking for a woman who's willing to have children with him. A woman who enjoys socializing and wants to be part of a community. You are all those things."

He'd introduced the subject of John, so she'd better get that out of the way right now. "Oh, yes. John, the match you chose on my behalf. I do hope you cancelled the appointment."

"Per your request I did. However, I feel you should know John was extremely disappointed, as I expected he would be."

"I would've been, too, if I'd been waiting to meet my perfect match. Or as you'd probably say, my most *suitable* match," she said with a grin.

"And you aren't?" Simon challenged.

"No, unfortunately I've already made his acquaintance."

Simon's eyes narrowed. "Before you say anything else, I want you to think this through very carefully."

"I have," she said.

"I beg to differ." Simon spoke in the same unfriendly tones she'd heard at the beginning of their relationship.

"I brought up Angie's name for a specific reason. You knew after reading her answers to your questionnaire, and during your initial meeting, that she was in love with someone else." She paused. "As I told you on Saturday, that someone happens to be my brother. As I also told you, I was impressed by your insight in recognizing her feelings for Shawn so easily."

"As I've repeatedly said, I'm good at my job."

"You knew it would be wrong to introduce her to another man when she loved my brother."

"Yes."

"It would be just as wrong to introduce me to John when I'm in love with…you."

Simon briefly closed his eyes, then stood. "I've said it before and I'll say it again. Don't do this, Cassie. I'm off-limits."

"I can't keep still. I wish I could, but I can't."

He reclaimed his seat. Looking exasperated, he informed her, "This happens far more often than you realize. I've lost count of the number of women who believe they've fallen in love with me."

"I'm sure that's true." Simon was an attractive man. He had a strong sensual appeal and would turn heads wherever he went. She didn't assume for an instant that she was the only woman ever to fall for him.

"The thing you seem to forget is that you've paid thirty thousand dollars to meet the man I've chosen as your match."

Cassie hadn't forgotten.

"I held up my part of the bargain," he said.

"Yes, you did."

"I've deposited the check and it's cleared your bank."

She nodded.

"If you voluntarily decide not to meet your match, you should know there'll be no refund."

"I didn't think there would be."

"If you walk away now, without meeting John, you'll forfeit your money." He said it again, as if he felt it necessary to remind her of what was at risk.

"I'm aware of that."

"It would be foolish for you to do this."

"I've been called a fool for lesser things," she said calmly.

He shook his head. "I wouldn't have expected you to be an unreasonable woman."

"Really?" She smiled, just a little.

He looked pointedly at his watch. "Your time's about up. Is there anything else you'd care to say...in closing?"

This last part was said with emphasis, as though he was eager to usher her out the door.

"I'm almost finished," she told him.

He sighed.

"I'm not telling you how I feel so you can laugh at me, Simon."

His gaze held hers. "I would never do that," he said, then added, "any more than I did with the other women."

She tried to disguise a smile. "Nor do I wish to be humiliated."

He agreed with a nod.

"I have reason to believe you share my feelings."

"You—"

"Do you kiss other female clients?" she asked, interrupting him.

He was silent.

"I didn't think so. How many have you taken to your home?"

"None," he admitted from between clenched teeth.

"That's what I thought," she said. To her relief, he was being honest.

"I've never had a woman…a client break down in tears and turn to me for comfort. Yes, I stepped over the line. I regretted it immediately and, if you recall, I apologized."

"You did."

"I realized it was a mistake to allow any client access to

my personal life after you showed up at my home later with the soup. I should never have invited you inside."

"Why did you?"

He refused to meet her eyes. "I'd been ill for several days and my resistance was weak."

"Resistance to me?"

"No," he countered sharply, "resistance to impropriety."

"Ah." So that was the excuse he'd chosen.

"Afterward, I was afraid you might have read more into that evening than was warranted, and I see now that you have. I'm sorry I didn't address the subject earlier. I wish I had. As I feared, you've got the wrong impression."

"I see."

"It would be best if we could forget that evening entirely, put it out of our minds."

"I'm sorry," she said. "I can't forget that night. I can't make myself regret it, either. It was after our evening together that I knew, Simon. I'd fallen in love with you."

Simon met her look unflinchingly and yielded no emotion. "Please don't continue. This is embarrassing for you *and* for me."

"I have one other comment," she said, striving to remain unemotional. "Actually, it's more of a question than a comment."

"Then out with it, and let this matter be laid to rest."

She thanked him with a brief nod. "I can accept that a distraught female weeping on your shoulder might have caused you to offer comfort in a way you normally wouldn't."

"Thank you. I appreciate your understanding."

"I can even accept the fact that your resistance was low when I dropped by your home that evening."

Once more he nodded.

"But how do you account for the way you kissed me on Sunday?"

"Sunday?" he repeated. The color seemed to drain from his face.

"Can you tell me what prompted that kiss?" she asked.

He didn't answer for a long moment. "I have no excuse," he finally said.

"I'm not looking for excuses, Simon, I'm looking for honesty. It hasn't been easy to lay out my heart for you. If I've misread the situation, then I apologize. In that case, I'll walk out your door right now and you'll never hear from me again."

"That would...be a shame."

"Yes, it would," she agreed, hope seeping in for the first time since she'd entered his office.

"You've paid me a lot of money and I'd feel bad if you allowed this opportunity to slip by. John is awaiting an introduction, and I hate to disappoint him."

Cassie closed her eyes, struggling to hold on to her poise. After a moment, she opened them and met his look head-on. "I'm not meeting John or any other man you deem the right mate for me. Or my 'suitable' mate or whatever word you want to use. I've already found him and it's you."

Simon didn't acknowledge that comment in any way.

"*Have* I misread your feelings, Simon?" she asked softly.

He refused to answer.

Reluctantly she stood; she'd gone past her allotted ten minutes. "I won't embarrass you further—or myself for that matter. But before I go, I have one simple request."

"Fine," he said tersely.

"Look me in the eyes and tell me you don't love me. Do that and I'll leave and never trouble you again."

"I'm not playing word games with you, Cassie."

"This isn't a game. It's my life, my future—our future."

He squinted up at the ceiling. "Why do women have such a flair for the dramatic? I suppose you're going to spend the rest of your life pining away for me."

"No, I won't," she told him. "I love you and it's up to you to accept or reject that love. It'll hurt me, but I know I'll get over you in time. In every likelihood I'll marry someone else one day and perhaps even have children. Rest assured that if you reject me, I won't leap off a bridge."

"That's a relief."

She moved away from the chair, her heart pounding so hard she was astonished it didn't echo through the room. She gave him ample opportunity to stop her.

He didn't.

With her hand on the door, she turned back to look at Simon one last time. He sat at his desk, reading. She wasn't fooled. He might not admit it, but he loved her.

"Merry Christmas, Simon."

He glanced up and his eyes flared as though he was surprised to see her still in the room. "Oh. Merry Christmas."

"Goodbye."

She didn't wait for a response. Head held high, she marched out the door. Once on the other side, she closed her eyes, almost collapsing to the floor as a wave of deep loss hit her.

Ms. Snelling's chair scraped as she stood. "Oh, dear. Are you all right, Ms. Beaumont? You look like you're about to faint."

"I—I'm okay," she stammered. "Thank you...." she added politely.

It was exactly as Cassie had feared. Simon Dodson, professional matchmaker, was an expert at finding love for everyone except himself.

Chapter 16

"Hold the elevator!" Cassie shouted, rushing across the condo foyer on Wednesday afternoon. When she saw that the lone occupant was Mr. Oliver, she automatically slowed her steps. No need to rush; he'd take sadistic delight in letting the doors shut in her face. To her amazement, he thrust out his arm and stopped them from closing.

Cassie hardly knew what to think. "Thank you," she managed as she hurried into the elevator, loaded down with her mail, the newspaper, her purse and a couple of last-minute Christmas purchases.

The newspaper.

She hadn't even realized Mrs. Mullinex hadn't "borrowed" it since their dinner together. That was progress.

"My pleasure," Mr. Oliver said as the elevator doors glided shut. "Can't thank you enough for the great dinner."

It seemed wrong to confess that if it hadn't been for Simon she would never have thought to invite Mr. Oliver.

Try as she might, she couldn't get Simon out of her mind. She'd given it her best shot, told him how she felt and done what she could to convince him that he shared her feelings. But she hadn't expected the strength of his conviction in denying his love for her. Nor could she understand why he fought it so hard.

What bothered her most was his inability to admit to her face that he didn't love her. If he had, she might have believed him. However, for reasons she'd likely never know, he refused to accept her love.

"Nice young man…"

"I'm sorry," Cassie said. "I didn't catch what you said?"

"That Simon of yours. He's a fine young man. You've chosen well."

"I…thank you," she whispered. No need to explain that he wasn't "hers," or that she wouldn't be seeing him again. Cassie had been sincere when she'd told him she wouldn't pine away for the rest of her life. He'd made his decision and she'd made hers.

The elevator stopped, and Mr. Oliver held the door for her to exit first. When they stepped into the hallway, Mrs. Mullinex opened her condo door and, seeing the two of them, waved cheerfully. Cassie noticed that the other woman's eyes immediately went to Harry Oliver.

"Oh, what perfect timing," Phyllis said. Her hair was brushed into soft waves and she looked lovely.

"Good afternoon, Harry," she purred.

"Hello, Phyllis."

Cassie hid a satisfied grin. Apparently there'd been a breakthrough in that relationship. Wonderful!

"I was hoping to see you," she said, smiling shyly at Harry. "I thought I'd invite my dearest friends over for eggnog on Christmas Eve. I do hope you can join me." As if she realized she'd directed the invitation solely to Mr. Oliver, she turned to Cassie. "I'd like it if you could come, too."

"Why…thank you, I'd be honored." Cassie's brother and Angie had invited her to spend Christmas Day with Angie's family. They'd been generous to include her, and Cassie had gratefully accepted.

"I wonder…" Phyllis began. "If you'd like to invite your young man, please do. That Simon is quite the charmer."

She nodded. "I'll mention it if I talk to him between now and Christmas Eve." That was highly improbable, but again she didn't feel it was necessary to go into details.

"Why wouldn't you be talking to him?" Mrs. Mullinex pressed. "'Tis the season and he's your sweetheart."

Cassie glanced away. "Actually, he isn't."

"You don't mean that!"

"They might've had a spat," Harry suggested.

"In that case, dear, I urge you to settle it before Christmas." She looked at Harry and blushed. "Don't let too much time elapse before you set things right."

Harry stepped closer to Phyllis. "I couldn't agree with you more."

Rather than tell them there was nothing to settle, Cassie just thanked them for their advice.

They made an arrangement to meet, and Cassie let herself into her condo. The festive cheer of the season greeted her, and for a moment all she could do was stand and stare at her Christmas tree and the other decorations, at the Christmas cards lined up on her mantel and the pile of wrapped gifts. She struggled to ignore her heavy heart.

As she tossed the mail on the kitchen counter, Simon's bold handwriting, slanted across a business-size envelope, instantly caught her attention. She grabbed it with both hands. Two or three minutes must have passed before she mustered the courage to tear it open.

With her pulse hammering in her ears, she pulled out a refund check for the total amount of his fee. The check was wrapped in a single sheet of white paper. When she unfolded the sheet, she found it blank.

He'd made the check out to her and in the memo line, he'd written one word: *refund*. She had always assumed he'd keep the money. Perhaps this was the only way he had of relieving his conscience. The only way of saying he had regrets, too. Not knowing just what she'd do with it, Cassie propped the check against the base of a blooming poinsettia—the very one he'd given her. She'd need to think about her response.

She could refuse to cash it out of pure stubbornness. That seemed foolish. When she'd paid Simon, she'd explained that the funds had come from a special savings account, which she'd set up to pay for her wedding. Perhaps he was saying he wanted her to have that wedding.

No, she mused, shaking her head. She couldn't second-guess him, couldn't drive herself insane trying to analyze his motives.

The phone rang and, still absorbed in her thoughts, Cassie picked it up. "Hello," she murmured.

"Hello." The male voice was unfamiliar. "My name is John Fitzsimmons and I was given your number by a... mutual friend."

"What can I do for you, John?" she asked, suspicion springing to life.

"Well...I was hoping we could meet for coffee." He sounded nervous.

"What friend?"

"Ah..."

"Is it Simon?" she asked. It hadn't taken her long to catch on. The matchmaker in him was incapable of letting this go. He'd found the man he believed to be her ideal match. Obviously, Simon was hoping to assuage his guilt by making sure she had the opportunity to meet John—an opportunity she'd already declined.

"Simon suggested it might be better if I implied it was someone else, but I'm not much good at prevarication."

"I'm not, either."

John chuckled. "He said you backed out at the last minute."

"I did," she confirmed.

"I know it's none of my business, but would you mind telling me why?"

Cassie bit her lip and debated how wise it would be to reveal the truth, then decided she owed him that. "I apologize because I realize I let you down, but…unfortunately I fell in love with someone else."

"Oh." She heard a world of disappointment in that one word. He didn't say anything for a moment. "Did you tell Simon this?"

"Yes, I was in his office on Monday." Could that have been just forty-eight hours ago? It seemed far longer; it seemed like a lifetime.

John hesitated again. "Then I don't understand why Simon was so insistent that I call you."

Cassie, however, was completely aware of his motivation. "I'm afraid…well, the man I fell in love with is Simon."

"Oh." There was a wealth of meaning in his short response. "I guess it would be safe to say he doesn't return your feelings?"

Cassie believed he did. "Apparently not," she said softly, hoping the pain she felt wasn't obvious.

"I guess that explains why he urged me to contact you."

She disagreed, but didn't voice her opinion.

"I realize you...like Simon, but seeing that he doesn't feel the same way, it might help if we met. Simon spoke highly of you on several occasions and I thought the two of us might have a lot in common."

"What did he say about me?" she asked.

"Well..." He drew out the word. "He said that you're thoughtful and caring of others."

Despite herself, Cassie smiled. Simon had chosen to forget her negative attitude toward her neighbors and how she'd done everything she could to get out of host-ing the pre-Christmas dinner party.

"He said you're wonderful with children."

"He did?" She closed her eyes and remembered the sad little girl who'd come to visit Santa. All that child wanted for Christmas was for her father to come home. Even the hardest heart would've been affected by such a request.

"He also said how generous you are to others."

Cassie wasn't sure that was true.

"And he told me you're one of the most beautiful cli-ents he's ever had the pleasure of working with. He said your beauty is special because it's internal as well as external."

"That was kind of him." Simon would cringe if he heard her say that. He didn't receive compliments gladly.

"Actually, Simon couldn't say enough good things about you. He urged me to ask you out and not to take no for an answer. You will meet me, won't you?"

She probably should but couldn't dredge up any enthusiasm for even a casual meeting. She needed time to deal with her complicated feelings for Simon. Her love was as strong now as when she'd stepped into his office two days earlier, and yet it was useless to believe he'd change his mind.

"I don't know," she said honestly.

"What would it hurt?" John asked. "All I'm suggesting is that the two of us have coffee together."

He had a point, but she hesitated. "It's, uh, nice that you'd still like to meet, especially since you know how I feel about Simon."

"I do. From everything Simon had to say, it sounds as if we're a perfect match. Or—" and she could hear the smile in his voice "—the most suitable one."

That might've been true a few weeks ago, but it wasn't anymore. She loved Simon.

"I think perhaps we should drop it for now," she said.

To her surprise, John laughed. "Simon told me you'd say that, but he also said I should be persistent."

Cassie straightened and a chill went down her spine. "Did he?"

"Yes. In fact, he said I shouldn't listen to any arguments. He went so far as to say he's introduced dozens of couples over the past few years and in all that time he's never met two people who were a better fit for each other than you and me."

Cassie had to restrain a laugh. Simon was doing his utmost to push her into the arms of another man, and his determination only served to confirm that she'd been right all along.

But telling John this would be touchy. "Why do you suppose he praised me so much?" she asked him.

"Well…"

"I suppose you've noticed that Simon isn't really one for flattery."

"Yeah."

"When I first met him, I wasn't sure what to think."

"Me neither," he said.

"He seemed way too dictatorial."

"I hear a lot of people have the same feeling. The friend who told me about Simon and his matchmaking business said I shouldn't take offense at his gruff manner."

"Did his attitude change?" she asked. "Did he start to react to you in a different way?"

"Not really. Why?"

"He did with me."

"Oh. That's the reason you asked why he had so many wonderful things to say about you, isn't it?"

"Yes."

"So you think he's in love with you, too?"

"I do."

John sighed. "Seems funny, doesn't it, that a match-maker would have such a hard time admitting he's in love."

Cassie wasn't exactly laughing. "In any other circumstances, you and I would probably have gotten along famously—and maybe even decided to marry."

"Maybe," he concurred. "Who's to know."

"Thank you for calling, John. I want nothing but the very best for you."

"Thanks." He paused and she could hear Elvis Presley's "Blue Christmas" in the background. "I guess this means you're definitely not going out with me."

"That's true."

"Okay."

"Bye." She started to hang up when John stopped her.

"Yes?" she said.

"Cassie, I was wondering if you'd take my phone number—in case you have a change of heart."

"It's in my phone, John. I have it."

"You won't lose it, will you?"

"No, I won't lose it," she promised. "Merry Christmas, now."

Late the following day, Christmas Eve, Cassie was

grateful for Mrs. Mullinex's invitation. She hated the idea of spending the evening alone.

Although she wasn't Catholic, she thought she might attend midnight mass at the cathedral after that. The beauty of the service and the music would lift her heart and infuse her with holiday spirit.

The small get-together at Mrs. Mullinex's was congenial, with Harry and Phyllis exchanging fond smiles over their fruitcake and eggnog. Love seemed to be blossoming all around her. First Shawn and Angie, and now her two cantankerous neighbors.

She toasted her newfound friends and after a respectable length of time made her excuses. They all hugged and wished each other a Merry Christmas, and she did the same.

As she left she saw a male figure heading toward the elevator. From behind he resembled Simon. He was about to step through the elevator doors when she called his name.

"Simon?"

He turned abruptly, a frown darkening his face.

"What are you doing here?" she asked.

"Why did you turn John Fitzsimmons down?"

"I think you know," she said calmly.

"You're a stubborn woman."

"You mean you've only noticed that now?" She unlocked her door and entered the apartment.

After a moment's hesitation, Simon followed her inside.

Chapter 17

Simon says: The perfect Christmas is the one I spend with you.

Simon strode into Cassie's apartment but couldn't seem to stop moving, from door to window and back again.

Cassie wished she dared to throw her arms around him and halt his frantic pacing.

"Why wouldn't you agree to at least meet John?" The anger seemed to radiate from him.

"Simon, you know why. I'm in love with you."

His eyes slammed shut and he clenched his jaw. "I don't want your love."

"So you said." That didn't change the way she felt, though.

"What harm would it have done to meet John?"

"None, I suppose," she said with a shrug. "But I felt I would've been doing him a disservice."

It was as though he hadn't heard her. "In other words, despite your assurances that you're willing to move on with your life, you refuse to do so," he challenged.

Cassie sat on her sofa while Simon continued pacing. She tracked his movements with her eyes. "Don't worry. I'll date other men—when I'm ready."

He whirled around and glared at her.

Cassie felt it was her turn to pose a few questions. "Why are you fighting this?" she asked, looking up at him. "And...why are you here at all?"

"I had to talk to you about John." Simon shook his head. "Don't you realize marrying *me* would be a disaster?"

"Really?" It didn't escape her notice that he hadn't denied anything—and that he'd brought up marriage. Evidently the subject had been on his mind, which was encouraging. "Why's that?"

Simon abruptly stood still. "I suspect I'm not telling you anything you don't know. I'm not...comfortable with emotions on a personal level. I prefer to analyze and guide other people's emotional lives. I have a hard time admitting this, but I've always steered clear of the intensity, the giving up of control...." He sounded so unlike the confident, self-assured man she'd come to know, and his vulnerability made him even more appealing.

"I hate this confusion," he muttered. "I'm good at helping my clients sort through their feelings, good at writing about them—but not good at experiencing them. It makes me...miserable."

"I've been pretty miserable myself," Cassie said.

"Then we should both find ways of dealing with these emotions because I'm not changing my mind."

"So you've said."

"I mean it, Cassie."

She wasn't going to argue. "Yes, I know."

He stared at her, eyebrows raised. "Don't be so agreeable. I'm not used to it, and I don't know how to react when you're amenable to everything I say."

She nodded.

"See? That's what I mean." He pointed accusingly at her. "Listen. I know what kind of man makes a good husband—and I'm not it."

Cassie had to smile. "That's something I *don't* agree with. You've shown me truths about myself. Let me do the same for you."

Simon shook his head as if that possibility was beyond him.

Cassie wasn't about to let him assume he was incapable of love when she knew otherwise.

She stood and walked purposefully toward him. He was still pacing, so she caught his hand. Her fingers curled around his and he turned back to stare at her. Not giving him a chance to object, she leaned forward and placed her mouth on his.

Simon slipped one hand around the back of her head and kissed her with a hunger that thrilled her.

"We'll start with teaching you to accept my love," she whispered when he broke off the lengthy kiss.

Again he briefly closed his eyes.

"Love is one thing," he muttered. "But you want children. I don't know about children except in theory. I'm not good with them," he said. "They cry and make messes in their diapers and drool."

"That they do."

"I don't understand why people willingly submit themselves to the uncertainty and stress of raising children." He splayed his fingers through his hair.

Even as he spoke she heard the longing in his voice. Despite his claims to the contrary he desired a family, just like most people did. Just like *she* did. Unable to resist a moment longer, she slid her arms around his waist and hugged him close. He resisted at first and attempted to break free.

Cassie held tight. Smiling up at him, she stood on the tips of her toes, rested her hands on his shoulders and pressed her mouth to his. It was only a matter of seconds before he became fully involved in the kiss.

When her legs were about to give way, Simon tore his mouth from hers and stepped back, still holding on to her, which was a good thing. Otherwise Cassie would have collapsed in a heap on the floor.

He wagged a warning finger at her. "No more of that."

"Sorry." She felt she should probably apologize but giggled instead. "I couldn't help myself. Oh, Simon, you're right. I do want children—your children. We'll have very special babies."

His expression was wry. "They won't cry and make messes and—"

"Of course they will," she said, nudging him.

"Like I already said, I have no skills in this area."

"But I don't, either. We'll learn together, the way other parents do."

She wasn't sure if she'd convinced him or not because he continued to stare at her.

Then, as if he'd noticed the Christmas decorations for the first time, he frowned and said, "When you came to me, you talked about a perfect Christmas."

She nodded.

"I'm not big on Christmas."

"I think that's kind of a weak argument," she told him. "Seeing how every assignment you gave me had to do with the holidays."

"Only because there's a surfeit of them at this time of year."

"True, but there are plenty of others and you *chose* the Christmas-related tasks."

"You've found some hidden meaning in that?"

"Yes. It's obvious to me that you enjoy the holidays."

When he started to protest, she held up a hand.

"Let me amend that. You enjoy watching other people enjoy Christmas. You understand why it's important to them, the same way you understand—in theory—why love and marriage and children are important. If you don't like Christmas, it's because you're alone. You don't have anyone to share it with. But, Simon, that's about to change."

"Aren't you making assumptions you have no business making?"

"Is this really so difficult?" she asked.

"Yes," he groaned.

Cassie gently laid her head against his chest and sighed meaningfully.

His sigh echoed hers. "Oh, I give up. You knew I'd fallen in love with you." He drew her toward him and rested his chin on her head.

"I *hoped* so."

"I do love you, Cassie."

"And I love you."

He leaned down and shattered what remained of her composure with a single kiss.

"You seriously want to marry me?" he whispered.

"More than I've wanted anything in my entire life."

"And children. You want children."

She nodded, knowing he wanted them as much as she did. "Two or three, at least."

He closed his eyes.

"You're going to be a wonderful father. And a wonderful husband."

"Our babies are going to inhabit my heart the same way you have. I see it happening already." He gazed down at her with such tenderness it nearly brought tears to her eyes.

"Inhabit your heart," she repeated. "And you've moved into mine."

"I couldn't forget you for even a second," he whispered, holding her close and breathing the words against her hair. "I'm not sure what it is about you that's different from all the other women I've met, the other women who fell in love with me…or thought they did. I just know you were right when you told me I loved you."

His arms tightened around her. "You're right about Christmas, too."

"I figured as much."

"Am I so easy to read?"

"No."

"We're going to have a very good life together," he murmured. "And every Christmas—"

Her phone rang, interrupting him. Cassie was content to let it ring until Simon released her.

Checking call display, she said, "It's my brother."

"You should answer it."

Nodding, she reached for the receiver. "Hello, Shawn."

"Merry Christmas." Shawn's greeting sounded happier than she could remember hearing in a long, long time.

"Merry Christmas," she said in return.

"You seem happy… Any particular reason?"

"Simon's here."

Shawn hooted with laughter. "He couldn't hold out, could he?"

"Thankfully, no. Christmas came early for me."

"Me, too," Shawn said. "Come and join us, both of you."

Half an hour later, the four of them sat in front of a crackling fire in Angie's small rental house in West Seattle. The clock above the mantel chimed midnight.

"It's Christmas," Angie sang out as she leaned against Shawn.

Simon's arm was around Cassie's shoulder. "Christmas," she echoed. Then she spoke softly into his ear. "My *perfect* Christmas, Simon. I have it right here, right now, with you."

The No. 1
New York Times bestseller

Meet Phoebe, Alix, Margaret and – for the first time – a man, Bryan Hutchinson, in Lydia's newest knitting class "Knit to Quit".

Catch up with other Blossom Street regulars, including Anne Marie and her adopted daughter Ellen.

With romance and friendship on the horizon, it's going to be a busy summer on Blossom Street!

www.mirabooks.co.uk

Can you tell from first impressions whether someone could become your closest friend?

Lydia, Jacqueline, Carol and Alix are four very different women, each facing their own problems in life. When they are thrown together by the hands of fate, none of them could ever guess how close they would become or where their friendship would lead them.

Make time for friends.
Make time for Debbie Macomber.

www.mirabooks.co.uk

A time for sharing...

Every Wednesday a group of four women meet, each with her own share of worries and troubles.

As friendships deepen, these women start to confide in each other, but will listening and sharing be enough for them to move forward, leaving their pasts behind?

Make time for friends.
Make time for Debbie Macomber.

www.mirabooks.co.uk

Welcome to Cedar Cove –
a small town with a big heart!

When family court judge Olivia Lockheart causes a scandal by denying a couple's divorce, the whole town starts talking about it.

Meanwhile, her daughter Justine must decide if she should stop waiting for love and accept a marriage of convenience.

And Olivia's best friend, Grace, wonders if her own husband is having an affair.

In Cedar Cove, nothing stays secret for long.

www.mirabooks.co.uk

Welcome to Cedar Cove –
a small town with a big heart!

Grace Sherman's life was happy and untroubled –
until her husband just disappeared.

But life can – and does – go on. Cedar Cove is
abuzz with talk of weddings and babies. Romance
is blossoming between friends, and there
are troubled relationships to solve.

And will Grace ever find out what happened
to her husband?

www.mirabooks.co.uk

Welcome to Cedar Cove – a small town with a big heart!

Recently divorced Rosie and Zach's unusual custody arrangement means that they will be moving between each other's places, not the kids!

Will Judge Olivia stay with Jack, the local newspaper owner, or get back together with her ex-husband?

And who is the mysterious man who died at the local bed-and-breakfast?

In Cedar Cove, it won't be a mystery for long!

www.mirabooks.co.uk